Praise for *Patient Zero*

"Terrifyingly terrific!"   —Sherrilyn Kenyon, #1 *New York Times*
bestselling author of the Dark-Hunter series

"A fast-paced, creepy thriller . . . prickly as a hospital needle . . . This
guy is good."   —Joe R. Lansdale, author of *Lost Echoes*

"Maberry has outdone himself with a deliciously diabolical plot and
bone-chilling scenarios."   —L. A. Banks, *New York Times* bestselling
author of the Vampire Huntress Legends series

"A first-rate thriller with a bioterror angle that is as horrific as it is plausible . . . Joe Ledger rules."
—Douglas Preston, coauthor of *The Wheel of Darkness*
and *The Book of the Dead*

"Jonathan Maberry deserves to take his place among the best suspense
writers of recent years."   —John Connolly, author of
The Reapers and *The Killing Kind*

"His writing is powerful enough to sing with poetry while simultaneously scaring the hell out of you."   —Tess Gerritsen,
author of *The Keepsake* and *The Bone Garden*

"It is almost impossible to find a noir-thriller; the two genres are so dis-
tinct and separate. Until now. Jonathan Maberry has succeeded in merg-
ing the two to such a wondrous extent that we may have to coin
neonoir-thriller just to describe it. This book stole a whole evening and
most of a night from me, and I was glad of the theft! *Patient Zero* intro-
duces a cop who is as compelling as any character I've read in years. If
you took the pace of Grisham, the eerie atmospheric style of Peter
Straub or Tom Piccirilli, the Wambaugh-type cop who has become a
rarity, and the thriller skill of Lee Child, you'd have the best of all
worlds. You'd in fact have Jonathan Maberry's new novel. This is the
new voice of the thriller!"   —Ken Bruen, author of *Cross* and *Priest*

Jonathan Maberry

Patient Zero

St. Martin's Griffin
New York

PATIENT ZERO. Copyright © 2009 by Jonathan Maberry. All rights reserved. Printed in the United States of America. For information, address St. Martin's Press, 175 Fifth Avenue, New York, N.Y. 10010.

www.stmartins.com

Book design by Jonathan Bennett

Library of Congress Cataloging-in-Publication Data

Maberry, Jonathan.
      Patient zero : a Joe Ledger novel / Jonathan Maberry—1st ed.
         p. cm.
      ISBN-13: 978-0-312-38285-8
      ISBN-10: 0-312-38285-5
         1. Detectives—Maryland—Baltimore—Fiction.
   2. Terrorism—Prevention—Fiction.   3. Bioterrorism—Fiction.
   4. Zombies—Fiction.   I. Title.

   PS3613.A19P38   2009
   813'.6—dc22   2008038234

10   9   8   7   6   5

This book is dedicated
to the often unsung
and overlooked heroes
who work in covert operations
and the intelligence communities.

Author's Note

Much of the technical information in this novel is based upon actual science. With very few exceptions, the surveillance equipment, computer systems, and weapons used by the fictional Department of Military Sciences are real, though several of these items are not yet available on the commercial market.

Prion diseases, including fatal familial insomnia, are also real; the parasites and control diseases used by Gen2000, however, are purely fictitious, though inspired by similar pathogens currently present in science.

A great number of people have provided help, advice, and technical information. Any technical errors still remaining are mine. Also, thanks to Michael Sicilia of Homeland Security; the superb team at the Philadelphia Forensic Science Bureau led by Chief Inspector Keith R. Sadler and Captain Daniel Castro; Ken Coluzzi, Chief of Lower Makefield Police Department; Frank Sessa; Dr. Bruno Vincent of the Institut de Pharmacologie Moléculaire et Cellulaire; Kenneth Storey, Ph.D., Carleton University; Pawel P. Liberski, M.D., Department of Molecular Pathology and Neuropathology, Medical University of Lodz; and Peter Lukacs, M.D.

Part One
Walkers

A hero is no braver than an ordinary man,
but he is braver five minutes longer.

—RALPH WALDO EMERSON

Chapter One

WHEN YOU HAVE to kill the same terrorist twice in one week, then there's either something wrong with your skills or something wrong with your world.

And there's nothing wrong with my skills.

Chapter Two

Ocean City, Maryland / Saturday, June 27; 10:22 A.M.

THEY CAME FOR me at the beach. Nice and slick, two in front, one big cover man behind in a three-point close while I was reaching for my car door. Nothing flashy, just three big guys in off-the-rack gray, all of them sweating in the Ocean City heat.

The point man held up his hands in a no-problem gesture. It was a hot Saturday morning and I was in swim trunks and a Hawaiian shirt with mermaids on it over a Tom Petty T-shirt. Flip-flops and Wayfarers. My piece was in a locked toolbox in the trunk, with a trigger guard clamped on it. I was at the beach to look at this year's crop of sunbunnies and I'd been off the clock since the shooting pending a Monday-morning officer-involved discussion with the OIS team. It had been a bad scene at the warehouse and they'd put me on administrative leave to give me time to get my head straight about the shootings. I wasn't expecting trouble, there shouldn't have *been* trouble, and the smooth way these guys boxed me was designed to keep everyone's emotions in neutral. I couldn't have done it better myself.

"Mr. Ledger . . . ?"

"Detective Ledger," I said to be pissy.

No trace of a smile on the point guy's face, only a millimeter of a nod. He had a head like a bucket.

"We'd like you to come with us," he said.

"Badge me or buzz off."

Buckethead gave me *the look*, but he pulled out an FBI identification case and held it up. I stopped reading after the initials.

"What's this about?"

"Would you come with us, please?"

"I'm off the clock, guys, what's this about?"

No answer.

"Are you aware that I'm scheduled to start at Quantico in three weeks?"

No answer.

"You want me to follow you in my car?" Not that I wanted to try and give these fellows the slip, but my cell was in the glove box of the SUV and it would be nice to check in with the lieutenant on this one. It had a weird feel to it. Not exactly threatening, just weird.

"No, sir, we'll bring you back here after."

"After what?"

No answer.

I looked at him and then the guy next to him. I could feel the cover man behind me. They were big, they were nicely set—even with peripheral vision I could see that Buckethead had his weight on the balls of his feet and evenly balanced. The other front man was shifted to his right. He had big knuckles but his hands weren't scarred. Probably boxing rather than martial arts; boxers wear gloves.

They were doing almost everything right except that they were a little too close to me. You should never get that close.

But they looked like the real deal. It's hard to fake the FBI look.

"Okay," I said.

Chapter **Three**

BUCKETHEAD SAT BESIDE me in the back and the other two sat up front, the cover man driving the big government Crown Vic. For all the conversation going on the others might have been mimes. The air conditioner was turned up and the radio was turned off. Exciting.

"I hope we're not going all the way the hell back to Baltimore." That was more than a three-hour ride and I had sand in my shorts.

"No." That was the only word Buckethead said on the ride. I settled back to wait.

I could tell that he was a leftie from the bulge his shoulder rig made. He kept me on his right side, which meant that his coat flap would impede me grabbing his piece and he could use his right hand as a block to fend me off while he drew. It was professional and well thought out. I'd have done almost the same thing. What I wouldn't have done, though, was hold on to the leather handstrap by the door like he was doing. It was the second small mistake he made and I had to wonder if he was testing me or whether there was a little gap between his training and his instincts.

I settled back and tried to understand this pickup. If this had something to do with the action last week on the docks, if I was somehow in trouble for something related to that, then I sure as hell planned to lawyer up when we got wherever we were going. And I wanted a union rep there, too. No way this was SOP. Unless it was some Homeland thing, in which case I'd lawyer up *and* call my congressman. That warehouse thing was righteous and I wasn't going to let anyone say different.

For the last eighteen months I'd been attached to one of those interjurisdictional task forces that have popped up everywhere post 9/11. A few of us from Baltimore PD, some Philly and D.C. guys, and a mixed bag of Feds: FBI, NSA, ATF, and a few letter combinations I hadn't seen before. Nobody really doing much but everyone wanting a finger in the pie in case something juicy happened, and by juicy I mean career beneficial.

I kind of got drafted into it. Ever since I'd gotten my gold shield a few years ago I'd been lucky enough to close a higher-than-average number of cases, including two that had loose ties to suspected terrorist organizations. I also had four years in the army and I know a little bit of Arabic and some Farsi. I know a little bit of a lot of languages. Languages were easy for me, and that made me a first-round draft pick for the surveillance van. Most of the people we wiretapped jumped back and forth between English and a variety of Middle Eastern languages.

The task force seemed like it would be pretty cool but the reality of it was that they put me on wiretap in a van and for most of the last year and a half I drank too much Dunkin' Donuts coffee and felt my ass grow flat.

Supposedly a group of suspected low-level terrorists with tenuous links to fundamentalist Shias were planning on smuggling something in that we were told was a potential bioweapon. No details provided, of course, which makes surveillance a bitch and largely a waste of time. When we (meaning us cops) tried to ask them (meaning the big shots from Homeland) what we were looking for, we were stonewalled. Need-to-know basis. That sort of thing tells you everything about why we're not all that safe. Truth is that if they tell us then we might play too significant a role in the arrest, which means they get less credit. It's what got us into trouble with 9/11, and as far as I can tell it really hasn't gotten much better since.

Then this past Monday I caught a little back and forth from a cell phone we were spooking. One name popped up—a Yemen national named El Mujahid, who was a pretty big fish in the terrorist pond and was on Homeland's must-have list—and the guy talking about him spoke as if El Mujahid was somehow involved in whatever the crew in the warehouse were cooking. El Mujahid's name was on all of the DHS lists and in that van I had nothing to do but read, so I'd read those lists over and over.

Because I rang the bell I got to play when the takedown was scheduled for Tuesday morning. Thirty of us in black BDUs with Kevlar body and limb pads, helmet cams and full SWAT kit. The whole unit was split into four-man teams: two guys with MP5s, a point man with a ballistic shield and a Glock .40, and one guy with a Remington 870 pump. I was the shotgun guy on my team and we hit this portside warehouse hard and fast, coming in every door and window in the place. Flashbangs, snipers on the surrounding buildings, multiple entry points, and a whole lot of yelling. Domestic shock and awe, and the idea is to startle and overpower so that everyone inside would be too dazed and confused to offer violent resistance. Last thing anyone wanted was an O.K. Corral.

My team had the back door, the one that led out to a small boat dock. There was a tidy little Cigarette boat there. Not new, but sweet. While we waited for the go/no-go, the guy next to me—my buddy Jerry Spencer from DCPD—kept looking at the boat. I bent close and hummed the *Miami Vice* theme and he grinned. He was about to retire and that boat probably looked like a ticket to paradise.

The "go" came down and everything suddenly got loud and fast. We blew the steel dead bolt on the back door and went in, yelling for everyone to freeze, to lay down their weapons. I've been on maybe fifteen, eighteen, of these things in my time with Baltimore PD and only twice was anyone stupid enough to draw a gun on us. Cops don't hotdog it and generally neither do the bad guys. It's not about who has the biggest balls, it's about overwhelming force so that no shots are ever fired. I remember when I went through the tac-team training, the commander had a quote from the movie *Silverado* made into a plaque and hung up in the training hall: "I don't want to kill you and you don't want to be dead." I think Danny Glover said that. That's pretty much the motto.

So, usually the bad guys stand around looking freaked out and everyone bleats about how innocent they are, yada yada.

This wasn't one of those times.

Jerry, who was the oldest man on the task force, was point man and I was right behind him with two guys at my back when we kicked the door, hustled down a short corridor lined with framed inspection certificates, and then broke left into a big conference room. Big oak table with at least a dozen laptops on it. Just inside the door was a big blue phone-booth–sized container standing against the wall. Eight guys in business suits seated around the table.

"Freeze!" I yelled. "Put your hands above your heads and—"

That was as far as I got because all eight guys suddenly threw themselves out of their chairs and pulled guns. O.K. Corral, no doubt about it.

When IAD asked me to recollect how many shots I fired and who exactly I fired them at, I laughed. Twelve guys in a room and everyone's shooting. If they're not dressed like your buddies—and you can, to a reasonable degree of certainty, determine that they're not civilian bystanders—you shoot and duck for cover. I fired the Remington dry then dropped it so I could pull my Glock. I know the .40 is standard but I've always found the .45 to be more persuasive.

They say I dropped four hostiles. I don't notch my gun, so I'll take their word for it. I bring it up, though, because one of them was the *thirteenth* man in the room.

Yeah, I know I said that there were eight of them and four of us, but during the firefight I caught movement to my right and saw the door to the big blue case hanging loose, its lock ripped up by gunfire. The door swung open and a man staggered out. He wasn't armed so I didn't fire on him; instead I concentrated on the guy behind him who was tearing up the room with a QBZ-95 Chinese assault rifle, something I'd only ever seen in magazines. Why he had it and where the hell he found ammunition for it I never did find out, but those rounds punched a line of holes right through Jerry's shield and he went down.

"Son of a bitch!" I yelled and put two in the shooter's chest.

Then this other guy, the thirteenth guy, comes crashing right into me. Even with all that was going on I thought, *Drug addict*. He was pale and sweaty, stank like raw sewage, and had a glazed bug-eyed stare. Sick bastard even tried to bite me, but the Kevlar pads on my sleeve saved my gun arm.

"Get off!" I screamed and gave him an overhand left that should have dropped him, but all it did was shake him loose; he blundered past me toward one of the other guys on my team who was blocking the door. I figured he was making for that sweet Cigarette outside, so I pivoted and parked two in his back, quick and easy. Blood sprayed the walls and he hit the deck and skidded five feet before coming to rest in a motionless sprawl against the back door. I spun back into the room and laid down cover fire so I could pull Jerry behind the table. He was still breathing. The rest of my team kept chopping the whole room up with automatic fire.

I heard gunfire coming from a different part of the warehouse and peeled off from the pack to see what was happening, found a trio of hostiles in a nice shooting blind laying down a lot of fire at one of the other teams. I popped a few of them with the last couple of rounds in my mag and dealt with the third hand-to-hand and suddenly the whole thing was over.

In the end, eleven alleged terrorists were shot, six fatally including the cowboy with the Chinese assault rifle and the biter I nailed in the back—who, according to his ID, was named Javad Mustapha. We'd just started going through IDs when a bunch of Federal types in unmarked black fatigues came in and stole the show, kicking everyone else out onto the street. That was okay with me. I wanted to check on Jerry. Turned out that none of our team was killed, though eight of them needed treatment, mostly for broken ribs. Kevlar stops bullets but it can't stop foot-pounds of impact. Jerry had a cracked sternum and was one hurting pup. The EMTs had him on a gurney, but he was awake enough to wave me over before they took him away.

"How you feeling, dude?" I asked, squatting next to him.

"Old and sore. But tell you what . . . steal me that Cigarette boat and I'll be feeling young and spry."

"Sounds like a plan. I'll get right on that, pops."

He ticked his chin toward my arm. "Hey, how's your arm? The EMT said that fruitcake bit you."

"Nah, didn't even break the skin." I showed him. Just a bad bruise.

They took Jerry away and I started answering questions, some of them for the Feds in the unmarked BDUs. Javad hadn't been armed and I'd drilled him in the back so there would be a routine investigation, but my lieutenant told me it was a no-brainer. That was Tuesday morning and this was Saturday morning. So why was I in a car with three Feds?

They weren't talking.

So, I sat back and waited.

Chapter **Four**

Easton, Maryland / Saturday, June 27; 11:58 A.M.

THEY PUT ME in a room that had a table, two chairs, and a big picture window with a drawn curtain. An interrogation room, though the sign outside had read Baylor Records Storage. We were somewhere in Easton off Route 50, more than seventy miles from where they'd picked me up. Buckethead told me to sit.

"Can I have a drink of water?"

He ignored me and left, locking the door.

It was nearly two hours before anyone came in. I didn't kick up a fuss. I knew this routine. Park someone in an empty room and leave them to stew. Doubt and a guilty conscience can do a lot when you're alone. I didn't have a guilty conscience and no doubts at all. I simply lacked information, so after I did a visual on the room I went into my own head and waited, reviewing the number of thong bikinis I'd seen. I was pretty sure the count was twenty-two, and of those at least eighteen had a legal and moral right to wear a thong. It was a good day at the beach.

The guy who finally came in was big, very well dressed, maybe sixty but there was no trace of middle-age soft about him. Not that he looked especially hard, not like a muscle freak or a career DI. No, he just looked capable. You pay attention to guys like him.

He took a seat opposite me. He wore a dark blue suit, red tie, white shirt, and tinted glasses that made it hard to read his eyes. Probably on purpose. He had short hair, big hands, and no expression at all.

Buckethead came in with a cork restaurant tray on which was a pitcher of water, two glasses, two napkins, and a dish of cookies. It was the cookies that weirded me out. You generally don't get cookies in situations like this and it had to be some kind of mind trick.

When Buckethead left, the guy in the suit said, "My name is Mr. Church."

"Okay," I said.

"You are Detective Joseph Edwin Ledger, Baltimore Police, age thirty-two, unmarried."

"You trying to fix me up with your daughter?"

"You served forty-five months with the army, honorably discharged. During your time in service you were involved in no significant military actions or operations."

"Nothing was happening while I was in the service, at least not in my part of the world."

"And yet your commanding officers and particularly your sergeant in basic wrote glowingly of you. Why is that?" He wasn't reading out of a folder. He had no papers with him at all. His shaded eyes were fixed on me as he poured a glass of water for each of us.

"Maybe I suck up nicely."

"No," he said, "you don't. Have a cookie." He nudged the plate my way. "There are also several notes in your file suggesting that you are a world-class smartass."

"Really? You mean I made it through the nationals?"

"And you apparently think you're hilarious."

"You're saying I'm not?"

"Jury's still out on that." He took a cookie—a vanilla wafer—and bit off an edge. "Your father is stepping down as police commissioner to make a run for mayor."

"I sure hope we can count on your vote."

"Your brother is also Baltimore PD and is a detective two with homicide. He's a year younger and he outranks you. He stayed home while you played soldier."

"Why I am here, Mr. Church?"

"You're here because I wanted to meet you face-to-face."

"We could have done that at the precinct on Monday."

"No, we couldn't."

"You could have called me and asked me to meet you somewhere neutral. They have cookies at Starbucks, you know."

"Too big and too soft." He took another bite of the wafer. "Besides, here is more convenient."

"For . . . ?"

Instead of answering he said, "After your discharge you enrolled in the police academy, graduated third in your class. Not first?"

"It was a big class."

"It's my understanding that you could have been first had you wanted to."

I took a cookie—Oreo for me—and screwed off the top.

He said, "You spent several nights of the last few weeks before your finals helping three other officers prepare for the test. As a result two of them did better and you didn't do as well as you should have."

I ate the top. I like it in layers. Cookie, cream, cookie.

"So what?"

"Just noting it. You received early promotion to plainclothes and even earlier promotion to detective. Outstanding letters and commendations."

"Yes, I'm wonderful. Crowds cheer as I go by."

"And there are more notes about your smart mouth."

I grinned with Oreo gunk on my teeth.

"You've been recruited by the FBI and are scheduled to start your training in twenty days."

"Do you know my shoe size?"

He finished his cookie and took another vanilla wafer. I'm not sure I could trust a man who would bypass an Oreo in favor of vanilla wafers. It's a fundamental character flaw, possibly a sign of true evil.

"Your superiors at Baltimore PD say they're sorry to see you go, and the FBI has high hopes."

"Again, whyn't you call me instead of sending the goon squad?"

"To make a point."

"About . . . ?"

Mr. Church considered me for a moment. "On what not to become. What's your opinion of the agents you met today?"

I shrugged. "A bit stiff, no sense of humor. But they braced me pretty well. Good approach, kept the heat down, good manners."

"Could you have escaped?"

"Not easily. They had guns, I didn't."

"Could you have escaped?" He asked it slower this time.

"Maybe."

"Mr. Ledger . . ."

"Okay, yes. I could have escaped had I wanted to."

"How?"

"I don't know, it didn't come to that."

He seemed satisfied with that answer. "The pickup at the beach was intended as something of a window to the future. Agents Simchek, Andrews, and McNeill are top-of-the-line, make no mistake. They are the very best the Bureau has to offer."

"So . . . I'm supposed to be impressed. If I didn't think the FBI was a good next step I wouldn't have taken your offer."

"Not my offer, Mr. Ledger. I'm not with the Bureau."

"Let me guess . . . the 'Company'?"

He showed his teeth. It might have been a smile. "Try again."

"Homeland?"

"Right league, wrong team."

"No point in me guessing then. Is this one of those 'we're so secret we don't have a name' things?"

Church sighed. "We do have a name, but it's functional and boring."

"Can you tell me?"

"What would you say if I said 'but then I'd have to kill you'?"

"I'd say drive me back to my car." When he didn't move, I added, "Look, I was army for four and Baltimore PD for eight, the last eighteen months of which I've been a gopher for the CT task force. I know that there are levels upon levels of need-to-know. Well, guess what, Sparky: I *don't* need to know. If you have a point then get to it, otherwise kiss my ass."

"DMS," he said.

I waited.

"Department of Military Sciences."

I swallowed the last of my cookie. "Never heard of it."

"Of course not." Matter-of-fact, no mockery.

"So . . . is this going to turn out to be some kind of cornball Men in Black thing? Thin ties, black suits, and a little flashy thing that'll make me forget all this shit?"

He almost smiled. "No MIB, nothing retroengineered from crashed UFOs, no rayguns. The name, as I said, is functional. Department of Military Sciences."

"A bunch of science geeks playing in the same league as Homeland?"

"More or less."

"No aliens?"

"No aliens."

"I'm no longer *in* the military, Mr. Church."

"Mm-hm."

"And I'm not a scientist."

"I know."

"So why am I here?"

Church looked at me for almost a minute. "For someone who is supposed to have rage issues you don't anger very easily, Mr. Ledger. Most people would be yelling by this point in an interview of this kind."

"Would yelling get me back to the beach any sooner?"

"It might. You also haven't asked for us to call your father. You haven't threatened me with his juice as commissioner."

I ate another cookie. He watched me dismantle it and go through the entire time-honored Oreo ritual. When I was done he slid my glass of water closer to me.

"Mr. Ledger, the reason I wanted you to meet the FBI agents today was because I need to know if that's what you want to be?"

"Meaning?"

"When you look inside your own head, when you look at your own future, do you see yourself in a humorless grind of following bank accounts and sorting through computer records in hopes of bagging one bad guy every four months?"

"Pays better than the cops."

"You could open up a karate school and make three times more money."

"Jujutsu."

He smiled as if somehow he'd scored a point and I realized that he'd tricked me into correcting him out of pride. Sneaky bastard.

"So, tell me honestly, is that the kind of agent you want to be?"

"If this is leading up to some kind of alternative suggestion, stop jerking me off and get to it."

"Fair enough, Mr. Ledger." He sipped his water. "The DMS is considering offering you a job."

"Um . . . hello? Not military? Not a scientist?"

"Doesn't matter. We have plenty of scientists. The military connection is merely for convenience. No, this would be something along the lines of what you do well. Investigation, apprehension, and some field work like at the warehouse."

"You're a Fed, so are we talking counterterrorism?"

He sat back and folded his big hands in his lap. " 'Terrorism' is an interesting word. Terror . . ." He tasted the word. "Mr. Ledger, we are very much in the business of stopping terror. There are threats against this country greater than anything that has so far made the papers."

" 'So far.' "

"We—and when I say 'we' I embrace my colleagues in the more clandestine agencies—have stopped fifty times as many threats as you would believe, ranging from suitcase nukes to radical bioweapon technologies."

"Yay for the home team."

"We've also worked to refine our definition of terrorism. Religious fundamentalism and political idealism actually play a far less important role, in a big-picture sense, than most people—including heads of state, friendly and not—would have the general public believe." He looked at me for a moment. "What would you say is the most significant underlying motive for all world strife—terrorism, war, intolerance . . . the works?"

I shrugged. "Ask any cop and he'll tell you that," I said. "In the end it's always about the money."

He said nothing but I could sense a shift in his attitude toward me. There was the faintest whisper of a smile on his mouth.

I said, "All of this seems to be a long way from Baltimore. Why'd you bring me here? What's so special about me?"

"Oh, don't flatter yourself, Mr. Ledger, there have been other interviews like this."

"So, where are those guys? You let them go back to the beach?"

"No, Mr. Ledger, not as such. They didn't pass the audition."

"I'm not sure I like how you phrased that."

"It wasn't meant to be a comforting comment."

"And I suppose you want me to 'audition' next?"

"Yes."

"How does that play out? Bunch of mind games and psych tests?"

"No, we know enough about you from your current medical records and fifteen years of psych evaluations. We know that in the last couple of years you've suffered severe losses. First your mother died of cancer and then your ex-girlfriend committed suicide. We know that when you and she were teenagers you were attacked, and that some older teens beat you nearly to death and then held you down and made you watch as they raped her. We know about that. We know you went through a brief dissociative phase as a result, and that you've had some intermittent rage issues, which is one of the reasons you regularly see a therapist. It's fair to say you understand and can recognize the face of terror when you see it."

It would have felt pretty good to demonstrate the whole rage concept to him right then, but I guessed that's what he would be looking for. Instead I made my face look bored. "This is where I should get offended that you've invaded my privacy, et cetera?"

"It's a new world, Mr. Ledger. We do what we must. And yes, I know how that sounds." Nothing in his tone of voice sounded like an apology.

"So, what do I have to do?"'

"It's quite simple, really." He got up and walked around the table to the curtain that hung in front of the big picture window. With no attempt at drama he pulled back the curtain to reveal a similar room. One table, one chair, one occupant. A man sitting hunched forward, his back to the window, possibly asleep. "All you need to do is go in there, then cuff and restrain that prisoner."

"You kidding me?"

"Not in the least. Go in there, subdue the suspect, put him in cuffs, and attach the cuffs to the D-ring mounted on the table."

"What's the catch? That's one guy. Your goon squad could have—"

"I am aware what overwhelming force could do, Mr. Ledger. That's not the point of this exercise." He reached into his jacket pocket and produced a pair of handcuffs. "I want *you* to do it."

Chapter **Five**

Easton, Maryland / Saturday, June 27; 2:08 P.M.

THE FIRST THING I noticed when I opened the door to the interrogation room was the stink. Smelled like a treatment plant. The guy didn't stir. He was slim, probably shorter than me, dark-skinned—Hispanic or Middle Eastern. Black hair that was sweat-soaked and lank. He wore a standard orange prison jumpsuit and he seemed completely out of it, his head hanging almost down to his knees.

I stepped into the room, conscious of the big mirror on my left. Mr. Church would be watching me, probably eating another vanilla wafer. The door closed behind me and I turned to see Buckethead staring at me through the glass. For a second I thought he was smiling, and then his expression registered. It was more like a wince, a flinching twist of his face as if he expected a scorpion to jump out at him. Even behind a steel door the agent was spooked by this guy. Swell. I held my cuffs in my right hand and extended my left in a calm, assertive gesture, palm outward. It looks placating but it's right there in case you need to block, grab, or hit.

"Okay, pardner," I said calmly. "I need you to cooperate with me here." A beat. "Can you hear me, sir?"

The man didn't move.

I angled around the table, coming up on his left. "Sir? I need you to stand up with your hands on your head. Sir . . . *Sir!*"

Nothing.

I moved closer. "Sir, I need you to stand up—"

And he did. All at once his head snapped up and his eyes popped open as he shot to his feet and spun toward me. My heart skipped. I *recognized* the guy. The pale, sweaty face, the glazed pop-eyed stare. It was Javad—the terrorist I'd shot and killed back in Baltimore. He hissed like a cat and threw himself at me. He was maybe one-fifty, five seven, but he hit me in the chest like a cannonball, driving us both across the room so hard that my back crunched against the rear wall. I hit my head and sparks burst in my eyes. I jammed my forearm under his chin as Javad snapped at me like an animal, lunging forward over my arm, his teeth banging together with a weird porcelain clack. He grabbed my shirt with both hands, trying to pull us closer together.

The DVD player in my head kept running and rerunning the scene back at the warehouse where I'd shot him in the back. Granted, I wasn't the one who checked his vitals afterward, but I'd put two .45 slugs in him from fifteen feet. Pretty much does the trick. If it doesn't then your only logical ammunition upgrade is Kryptonite. But for a guy who should be dead, he was pretty damn spry.

Even though this was all happening too fast I still had time to register the look in his eyes. Despite the twisted, ferociously hungry snarl of his face and the snapping of his teeth, his eyes were totally empty. No flicker of awareness, no trace of self-knowledge, not even the fire of hate. This wasn't the deadeye stare of a shark, nothing like that. This was freak-show stuff because there was nothing there; it was like looking into an empty room.

I think that terrified me more than the teeth that were biting the air an inch from my windpipe. Right then I knew why the other applicants had failed this audition. They'd probably been big men like me, strong men like me, and maybe they'd been able to hold him off this long—just long enough to look into those soulless eyes. I think that's when they failed. I don't know if Javad tore their throats out. I don't know if this was the point where they started screaming for help and Church sent Buckethead and his goon squad in with Tasers and riot sticks. What I did know was that looking into those eyes nearly took the soul out of me. I could actually feel my throat closing up, could feel an icy wire sending electricity down through my bowels.

I saw terror and hopelessness there. I saw death.

But here's the thing, you see, I'd seen those things before. I may not have been on any of the world's battlefields, but Church was right when he'd said that I've seen the face of terror. It went a lot deeper than that, though. It isn't just terror that I understood . . . I knew the face of death. I'd been bedside when cervical cancer took my mom. I was the last thing she saw before she slipped into the big black nothing, and I saw the light and life go out of her; I saw her eyes change from living eyes to those of a dead person. You can never forget that; the image is burned onto the front of your brain. I was also the one who found Helen after she'd swallowed half a bottle of drain cleaner. She'd left a goodbye message on my voice mail and was already gone when I kicked in the door. I saw her dead eyes, too.

I've also looked into the dead eyes of men I've killed on the job. Two men in eight years, not counting the four at the warehouse.

So, I'd looked into dead eyes before, I know what I saw there. I saw death and terror and hopelessness. Not my mom's, not Helen's, not the criminals I've killed—no, the deadness I see is my own, reflected in eyes that have nothing of their own to show. You can't fake that dead look. A lot of warriors have that look because they are in harmony with death. Church probably knew all this. He knew everything else about me. He knew my psych file. That bastard knew.

Javad lunged forward again, his fingers tearing my shirt, his stink that of a carrion bird. No . . . that wasn't right, that wasn't it. Javad's smell was that *of* carrion. He smelled like the dead. Because he *was* dead. This whole train of thought shot through my brain in a microsecond, its speed and clarity amplified by terror.

Terror's a funny thing, though. It can take your heart from you and bare your throat to the wolves; it can make you go all hot and crazy, which almost always gets you killed . . . or it can make you go cold. That's what happens to warriors—real ones, the kind who are defined by conflict. Like me.

So I went cold. Time slammed to a halt and the whole room seemed to go quiet except for the muffled hammering of my own heart. I stopped trying to get away from something I couldn't escape—I was jammed into a corner and Church wasn't sending the damned cavalry— so I did what Javad was doing. I attacked.

I swung my right hand around in a palm shot that turned his head so hard to the right that I heard his neck bones grind. It would have stopped anyone; it didn't stop him any more than the two slugs had stopped him. But it gave me a few seconds' escape from those teeth, and even as Javad started wrenching his face back toward me I hooked my leg around his and chopped at the back of his knee. Maybe he couldn't feel pain but a bent knee is a bent knee—it's a gravity thing. He canted to one side and

I used his sagging weight to spin and drive him into the wall. I caught him by the back of the hair and slammed him face forward into the wall once, twice, again and again. His jaw disintegrated; but I grabbed what was left of his chin and twisted my fingers into his hair and then I pivoted my hips as hard and as fast as I could, taking his head with me. My body turned faster and farther than his neck could.

There was a huge wet *snap!*

And then Javad was gone. His body switched off like someone had kicked the plug out and he simply dropped. I stepped back and let him fall.

I could barely breathe; sweat poured down my face, stung my eyes. I heard a sound behind me—I wheeled around and Church was leaning against the frame of the open doorway.

"Welcome to the new face of global terrorism," he said.

Chapter Six

Easton, Maryland / Saturday, June 27; 2:36 P.M.

"WHAT *WAS* HE?"

We were back at the table. They'd let me clean up in a bathroom. I showered and dressed in borrowed gym clothes. The shakes had started in the shower. Adrenaline accounted for a lot of it, but it was more than that. After thirty minutes my hands were still trembling and I didn't care if Church saw it.

He shrugged. "We're still working on a name for his condition."

"*Condition?* That son of a bitch was *dead!*"

"From now on," Church said, "we may have to consider 'dead' a relative term."

I had to sit with that for a while. Church waited me out.

"That is the same guy I shot at the warehouse, right? I mean, I put him down hard. I saw blood and bone on the walls . . ."

"Javad Mustapha, an Iraqi national," Church agreed, nodding. "Your shots were mortal but not immediately so; he was still alive when he was transported to the hospital where he was pronounced DOA. He 'revived' shortly after arrival." He spread his hands. "We controlled that incident and you won't find specific mention of it in the papers or in any official report."

"Holy Christ . . . are we talking zombies here?"

Church smiled faintly. "We're calling him a 'walker.' Short for 'Dead Man Walking.' The head of my science team has too much of a pop culture sensibility. And before you ask, it's not anything super-natural."

"How did this happen? Some kind of toxic spill . . . a plague . . . ?"

"We don't know. A prion disease, perhaps, or a parasite; maybe both, but certainly something that causes hyperactivity of the stem cells. True to the nature of parasites, the infected have a totality of pur-pose built around procreation. Not sexually, of course, but through a bite that is apparently one hundred percent infectious. We've only be-gun to research it."

"Is it only his bite that's infectious?" I asked. It felt like ice-cold army ants were marching around in my gut.

"We've done a number of tests on sweat and other body fluids but the strongest concentration of the disease is in the saliva. The bite transmits the infection."

I looked at the bruise on my arm. "I'm not wearing Kevlar. If I'd been bitten in there . . ."

He looked at me.

Anger was a white-hot furnace in my chest. "You're a total rat bas-tard, you know that?"

"As I said, Mr. Ledger, this is the new face of terrorism. A fierce, terrible bioweapon we don't yet understand. It may take us months to even construct a viable research protocol, which means that time is completely against us. We think that your friend Javad in there was the bioterrorist approximation of a suicide bomber, that he was the 'patient zero' for an intended plague directed at the U.S. The blue case recovered at the scene was some kind of climate-controlled containment system, quite possibly to protect the other cell members from their own weapon. None of the others at the warehouse showed any signs of infection." He paused. "We *think* we stopped them."

"You . . . 'think'?" I heard how he leaned on the word.

"Yes, Mr. Ledger, but we don't know. And we have to know, just as we have to be ready in case this happens again. If Javad is the only plague vector then we'll scratch one up for our side and start looking for their next trick, or try to be ready for whenever they try this trick again. If, on the other hand, there are other teams out there ready to launch others like Javad . . . well, that's part of the reason the DMS was formed."

"Then you'd sure as hell better check with the task force commander because two panel trucks pulled out of that warehouse the night before we hit it. We tracked one and lost one . . ."

"Yes. Losing one was sloppy."

I fought the urge to flip him the bird. "Who's behind this? Is this an Al Qaeda thing, because the task force was never able to pin that down?"

"That's still uncertain, though we have some suspicions. The other members of the cell were a mixed bunch. Al Qaeda, Shia extremists, two Sunni extremists, and even one from the Egyptian Islamic Jihad."

"Shia and Sunni working together?"

"Interesting, isn't it?" Church said dryly. "The name you picked up in your wiretap—El Mujahid—lends a little weight to the idea of collaboration. He's been known to work with several of the more extreme splinter groups."

"I assume you interrogated the surviving cell members?"

He said nothing.

"Well . . . ?"

"They're all dead. Suicide."

"How? Didn't you search them for cyanide pills in their teeth and all that shit?"

Church shook his head. "Something a bit cleverer than that. Each of them had been infected with a pathogen of a type as yet unidentified; they needed to take a drug every eight hours to keep the disease dormant. Without the drug the disease becomes active with incredible speed and immediately begins to erode vascular tissue. We didn't know this until they started bleeding internally, and even then we barely got enough information out of the last one to understand the shape of it. The control substance was hidden in ordinary aspirin tablets. We would never have known to look."

"Is this the same disease that my dancing partner in there had?"

"No. And as far as we can tell it's noncommunicable. I have some of the top scientists in the world working with the DMS, and so far they've been scratching their heads. Some of them are actually impressed."

"So am I. This is some pretty sophisticated stuff we're talking about."

"And yet simple; you wouldn't even need much in the way of guards and threats. One person with the pill bottle to control them all is all they'd need. Very easy to manage. This level of sophistication raises our opinion of this cell and makes their potential that much greater."

I said, "What happened to the other guys? The ones who auditioned before me? Did they get bitten?"

"One did, I'm sorry to say. Two others did not."

"Jesus Christ!"

It was an effort not to leap across the table and tear his throat out. I watched Church's face, saw the shift of his body language as the anger in my voice registered. If I'd gone across that table he'd have been ready for me. "What about the other two? You go rescue them?"

"No. They both managed to cuff the suspect."

"Then I don't understand."

"It isn't only the physical component of the test that matters, Mr. Ledger. Each of them faced the moment of truth, as you yourself are doing now, and each of them reacted . . ." He paused, pursing his lips. "Inadequately."

"In what way?"

"In ways that identified them as unsuitable candidates." He waved his hand, dismissing that line of discussion.

"Why am I here?"

"Ah, the golden question. You're here, Mr. Ledger, because we are scouting for candidates to flesh out our DMS team. We're a new agency. We have lots of funding and we have a nicely vague set of parameters. Our intelligence division is hard at work to infiltrate and report on cells such as the one your team took down in Baltimore. We're surveilling the location where the first panel truck went, and we have high hopes of discovering the destination of the other."

"And you want me to sign up?"

He showed his teeth again. Kind of a smile. "No, Mr. Ledger, I want you to go to the FBI academy as planned."

"I don't—"

"Only now you'll have a clearer focus on which parts of that training to pay more attention to. Medical and management courses would be worthwhile. You can probably imagine which others would be of use."

We sat for a while with that comment hanging in the air.

"And when I'm done?"

Church spread his hands. "If the threat is over—truly over—you may never hear from me again. If you look for proof of my existence, or of the existence of this organization, you'll find nothing of any use; and I don't advise trying. You will of course say nothing about what happened here. I make no threats, Mr. Ledger; I believe I can trust both your intelligence and common sense in this matter."

"What if there are more of these things, these . . . *walkers?*"

"In that eventuality I will very probably be in touch."

"You have to know that this isn't over. It can't be. Nothing's that simple."

"I appreciate your cooperation today, Mr. Ledger."

With that he stood and offered me his hand. I looked at it and then at him for maybe ten full seconds during which neither his hand nor his eyes wavered. Then I stood and shook his hand. As he left Buckethead and the others came for me and drove me back to my car. They didn't say a word, though on the drive back each of them cut me wary glances every now and then.

As they drove off I memorized the license number. Then I got into my SUV and sat for maybe twenty minutes, staring through the window at the beach and the happy people playing in the sun. A second wave of the shakes hit me and I had to clamp my jaws shut to keep my teeth from chattering. It was like the way I felt after 9/11. The world had changed again. Just as "terror" had become a far more common word to us all then, terror was a much scarier word to me now.

What would I do if Church called me back?

Chapter **Seven**

Sebastian Gault / Helmand Province, Afghanistan / Six days ago

HIS NAME WAS El Mujahid, and it meant "fighter of the way of Allah." Farm life had made him strong; his devotion to the Koran had given him focus. His love for the woman Amirah had given him purpose and very probably driven him mad, though from the profiles he'd paid to have done on this man, Sebastian Gault thought that the Fighter was already a bit twitchy before Amirah screwed his brains out.

That made Gault smile. More kingdoms have risen and collapsed, more causes fought and died for over sex—or its teasing promise—than for all the political ideologies and religious hatred that ever existed. And as far as Amirah went, Gault could certainly sympathize with the brutish El Mujahid. Amirah was a ball-twisting vixen of truly historic dimensions, a true Guinevere—she could inspire great heroics, could stand by and support the rise of well-intentioned kingdoms, but at the same time she drove kings and champions to mad deeds.

Gault poured himself a glass of water and settled into his chair. It was a battered plastic folding chair by a rust-eaten card table set inside a canvas tent that smelled of camel dung, gasoline, and gunpowder.

Add the coppery stink of blood and you'd have the perfume of fanaticism, which Gault had smelled in a hundred places over the last twenty-five years. In the end it always smelled like money to him. And money, he knew, was the only force in the universe more powerful than sex.

Gault leaned back and sipped his water and observed El Mujahid through the open tent flap. The Fighter stood right outside and was growling orders to his men. Even those who were bigger and more physically powerful than the Fighter seemed shrunken in his presence, their wattage dialed down as his shone like the sun. Once he sent them out to do whatever bit of nastiness he assigned them, they would swell like giants and through them El Mujahid's fist would reach out and strike with godlike force across borders and around the world.

Gault thought the man was very well named; a name that could have been a code, a disguise, but wasn't. It was as if the man's peasant parents—a couple of nearly illiterate dust farmers from some godforsaken corner of Yemen—had known that their only child was destined to become a warrior. Not merely a soldier for Allah, but a general. It was a powerful name for a child, and as the boy grew into a man he had embraced the potential of his name. Unlike so many of his peers he was not recruited by groups of militant fundamentalists—*he* sought *them* out.

By the time El Mujahid was thirty he was on the wanted lists of over forty nations, and on the top ten most wanted list of the United States. He had ties to Al Qaeda and a dozen other extremist groups. He was single-minded, relentless, smart—though not particularly wise—and when he spoke, others listened. That made him terribly feared, but feared in the way a guided missile was feared.

Amirah . . . ah, thought Gault, now she was something entirely different. If the Fighter was the missile, then the Princess—for that was what her name meant—was the hand at the controls. Well . . . she shared those controls with Gault. By his estimation it was the most effective, harmonious, and potentially lucrative collaboration since Hannibal met an elephant handler. Probably more so.

The tent flap whipped open and the Fighter strode inside. He never simply walked anywhere—he had the same swagger as Fidel Castro, moving through space as if he wanted to bruise the air molecules and teach them their place. It always reminded Gault of the character of the Roman general Miles Gloriosus from the old Broadway musical *A Funny Thing Happened on the Way to the Forum*. Gloriosus's opening line, bellowed from offstage, was: "Stand aside everyone . . . I take *large* steps." Sometimes Gault had to dig his fingernails into his palms to keep from smiling when El Mujahid strode into the room.

The Fighter snatched up the water bottle and poured himself a glass, sloshing half of it on the table, and threw it back. Gault wondered at what point affectation had given way to true personality trait.

"The teams are leaving now," the Fighter said as he dragged over a chair and threw himself into it. The cheap seat creaked under his bulk, but he ignored it. He was a handsome man with unusual looks for someone of Yemen birth. His eyes were a pale brown, almost gold, and his skin, though tanned by the blistering sun, was not as dark as many of his countrymen. Over the last eighteen months Gault had arranged for highly skilled cosmetic surgeons to do some touch-up work on the Fighter, including resizing his ears, a comprehensive dye job on his hair—head to feet—tonal changes to his vocal chords, and some bone smoothing on his brow and chin. They were all small operations but the total effect was that El Mujahid looked even more like a European. Like a Brit. Give him a modern haircut, lose the fierce mustache, and put him in an Armani suit, Gault considered, and he could pass for northern Italian or even Welsh. The anomaly of the Fighter's complexion, and his ability to speak an uninflected English with a hint of a British accent, factored heavily in Gault's plans for the man, and Gault had paid good money to make sure that under the right circumstances the Fighter would make a believable non-Arab. He'd even provided a series of audiotapes to allow the Fighter to practice speaking with an American accent.

Gault looked at his watch—a Tourneau Presidio Arabesque 36 that he'd taken from a former colleague who had no further need for checking the time of day. "As always, my friend, you are precise to the minute."

"The Koran says that—" But that was all Gault heard. El Mujahid loved his long-winded scripture quotations and as soon as the big man was in gear Gault tuned him out. He sometimes forced himself to mentally say "yada yada yada" to drown out the doctrine. That worked well, and he had himself trained to start paying attention again when the Fighter wrapped it up with his trademark closer: "Allah is the only God and I am his wrath on Earth!"

Grandiose, but catchy. Gault liked the "wrath" part. Wrath was useful.

"Very apt," he said of the unheard scripture. "Your men should be praised for their devotion to the cause and to the will of Allah."

Gault was a lapsed Presbyterian. Not completely atheist—he believed some kind of god existed somewhere; he just didn't think the human race had the Divine All on speed dial . . . and whatever calls they did make were certainly not being returned. To Gault religion was something to be factored in to any equation. Only a fool dismissed its power or ignored its useful potential; and only a suicidal fool allowed even a hint of disingenuousness to flavor his words. Financial backer or not, Gault would find himself lying in parts all over this corner of Afghanistan if El Mujahid thought that he was mocking his faith. The Fighter's swagger might have started as affect, but his faith had never been anything but absolute.

The Fighter nodded his thanks for the comment.

"Will you stay for dinner?" Gault asked. "I had some chickens flown in with me. And fresh vegetables."

"No," the Fighter said, shaking his head with obvious regret. "I'm crossing over into Iraq tomorrow. One of my lieutenants has stolen a British half-track. I will oversee the placement of antipersonnel mines and then we need to put it somewhere that the British or Americans can find it. We'll stage it well . . . the front end will have been damaged by a land mine and there will be one or two British wounded in the cab.

Very badly wounded, unable to speak, but clearly alive. This has worked many times for us. They care more about their wounded than they do about their cause, which should convince even the stupidest of men that they do not have God in their hearts or holy purpose to guide their hands."

Gault bowed in acknowledgment of the point. And he admired El Mujahid's tactics, largely because the Fighter understood Allied thinking—they always favored rescue over common sense; which made sabotage so effective for men like El Mujahid, and which made profit so deliciously easy for Gault. Since long before the American body count had hit quadruple digits three of Gault's subsidiary companies had landed contracts for improved plastics and alloys, both for wheeled vehicles and human assets. Now half the soldiers in the field wore antishrapnel polymer undershirts and shorts. Quite a few lives had even been saved, not that this mattered in anything except price negotiations during contract meetings; but it was there. So, the more damage El Mujahid could do with his clever booby traps the more defensive products would be purchased. And even though plastics, petrochemicals, and alloys were only eleven percent of his business, it still brought in six hundred and thirty million per year, so it was all a win-win situation.

"Ah, I understand, my friend," he said, putting authentic-sounding regret into his voice. "You go in safety and may Allah bless your journey."

He saw the effect the words had on the big man. El Mujahid actually looked touched. How delicious.

Amirah had long ago coached Gault in what to say when it came to matters of the faith, and Gault was as good a student as he was an actor. After his second meeting with the Fighter—and after Gault had privately noticed the subtle signs indicating how thoroughly his luggage was being searched every time he came here—he'd started packing a worn copy of a French edition of *Introduction to Islam: Understand the Pathway to the True Faith,* a book written by a European who had gone on to become a significant and very outspoken voice in Islamic politics. Gault and Amirah spent hours with the book, underlining key passages, making sure important pages were dog-eared, and ensuring that the bookmark was never in the same place twice. El Mujahid had never openly spoken of what he believed to be Gault's process of conversion, but each time they met the big man was warmer to him, treating him like family now, where once he had kept him at arm's length.

"I'll be finished in time for the next phase of the program," the Fighter said. "I hope you have no worries about that."

"Not at all. If I can't trust you who can I trust?" They both smiled at that. "All of the transportation steps are locked down," Gault added. "You'll be in America by the second of July . . . the third at the very latest."

"That cuts it close."

Gault shook his head. "The timetable leaves less time for random events to interfere. Trust me on this, my friend. This is something I do very well."

El Mujahid considered for a moment, then nodded. "Well . . . I have to go. A sword rusts in its sheath."

"And an unfired arrow becomes brittle with disuse," Gault said, completing the ancient aphorism.

They stood and embraced, and Gault suffered through the big man's enthusiastic hugs and backslapping. The man was a foul-smelling oaf and as strong as a bear.

They swapped a few pleasantries and the Fighter strode out of the tent. Gault waited until he heard the growl of El Mujahid's truck. He got up and stood in the tent's opening and watched the Fighter and the last of his team disappear in swirls of brown dust and diesel exhaust as they crested a hill and dropped down the other side.

Now he could concentrate on his real work. Not plastics or polymers, not body armor for Yanks about whom he didn't give a moment's real thought. No, now he would meet with Amirah and visit her lab to see what his gorgeous little Dr. Frankenstein had on the slab.

His satellite phone vibrated in his pocket and he checked the screen display, smiled, and thumbed the button. "Is everything coded?"

"Of course," said Toys, which is what he always said. Toys would forget to breathe before he'd forget to engage his phone scrambler.

"Good afternoon, Toys."

"Good afternoon, sir. I hope you are well."

"I'm visiting our friends. In fact, your favorite person just left."

"And how is El Musclehead? I'm so sorry to have missed him," Toys said with enough acid to burn through tank armor. Toys—born Alexander Chismer in Purfleet—never bothered to hide his contempt of El Mujahid. The Fighter was gruff, dirty, and politically expansive; Toys was none of those things. Toys was a slim and elegant young man, naturally fastidious, and, as far as Gault could tell, absolutely unburdened by any weight of morality. Toys had two loyalties—money and Gault. His love for the former bordered on the erotic; his love for the latter was in no way romantic. Toys was sexually omnivorous but his tastes ran to expensive fashion models of both sexes and of the kind once known as heroin chic. Besides, Toys was the ultimate business professional and he had steel walls between his personal affairs and his responsibilities as Gault's personal assistant.

He was also the only person on earth Gault truly trusted.

"He sends his love," Gault said; Toys gave a wicked laugh. "How are the travel arrangements coming along?"

"It's all done, sir. Our sweaty friend will have a wonderful world tour without incident."

Gault grinned. "You're a marvel, Toys."

"Yes," Toys purred. "I am. And, by the way . . . have you seen *her* yet?" His voice dripped with cold venom.

"She'll be here in a few minutes."

"Mm, well, give her a big wet kiss from me."

"I'm sure she'd be thrilled to hear that. Any news or are you just calling to chitchat?"

"Actually, the bloody Yank has been calling day and night."

Gault's smile flickered. "Oh? What's the urgency?"

"He wouldn't tell me, but I gather it has something to do with our friends abroad."

"I'd better call him."

"Probably best," agreed Toys, and then added, "Sir? I'm not entirely confident that the Yank is, how should I put it? A reliable asset."

"He's usefully placed."

"So is a rectum."

Gault laughed. "Be nice. We need him for now."

Toys said, "You need better friends."

"He's not a friend. He's a tool."

"Too right he is."

"I'll sort him out. In the meantime get your ass on a plane and meet me in Baghdad."

"Where do you think I'm calling you from?" Toys asked dryly.

"Are you reading my mind now?" Gault said.

"I believe that's in my job description."

"I believe it is."

Gault smiled as he disconnected the call. He punched in a new number and waited while it rang through.

"Department of Homeland Security," said the voice at the other end.

Chapter **Eight**

U.S. Route 50 in Maryland / Saturday, June 27; 4:25 P.M.

THE DRIVE BACK to Baltimore gave me time to think, and the thoughts I had weren't nice ones. I wanted to kick Church's ass for busting a big wet hole in my peace of mind. He had made me fight a dead guy.

A. Dead. Guy.

I think I logged forty miles of my trip with that thought playing over and over like a skipping record. It's kind of a hard thought to get past. Me. Dead guy. In a room. Dead guy wants a piece of me. Find a comfortable chair for that to sit in.

Javad was not alive when he attacked me. I may not be a scientist but one of those bottom-line factoids everyone—Eastern, Western, alternative health, all of them—will agree on is that dead guys don't try to bite you. In movies, yeah okay. Not in Baltimore. But Javad was dead, so there was that. Another twenty miles blurred by.

What was it Church had said? Prions. I had to look that up when I got home. What little I knew was Discovery Channel stuff. Something related to Mad Cow maybe?

So, okay, Joe . . . if it's real then make some sense of it. Mad Cow and dead terrorists. Bioweapons of some kind. With dead guys. DMS. Department of Military Sciences, sister org to Homeland. What kind of math does that make? I put the new White Stripes CD in the deck and tried to not think about it. Worked for nearly four seconds.

I pulled off the road, went into a Starbucks, ordered a Venti and a chocolate chunk cookie—screw Church, what does he know about cookies? I paid the tab, left my stuff on the counter, went into the bathroom, splashed water on my face, and then threw my guts up in the toilet.

I could feel the shakes starting to come back, so I washed my face, rinsed my mouth out with handfuls of tap water, pasted on my best I-didn't-just-kill-a-zombie expression, and left with my coffee.

Chapter Nine

Sebastian Gault / Helmand Province, Afghanistan / Six days ago

INTO HIS PHONE Sebastian Gault said, "Line?"

"Clear," the voice responded, indicating that both ends of the call were on active scramble.

"I hear you've been trying to call me. What's the crisis this time?"

"I've been calling you for days." The voice at the other end was male, American with a Southern accent. "It's about the dockside warehouse."

"I figured. Have they hit it yet?"

"Yes, just like you said they would. Full hit, total loss." The American told Gault about the task force hit. He quoted directly from the official reports filed with Homeland and the NSA. He referred to Homeland as Big G.

Gault smiled, but he made his voice sound deeply worried. "Are you sure the entire cell is terminated? All of them?"

"The task force report said that some were killed during the raid and the rest died from what they're calling 'suicide drugs.' They've got nobody to question. No one's going to disappear to Guantánamo Bay for any friendly chats."

"And the *subject*? What about him?"

"KIA at the site."

"Killed?" Gault asked, giving the word the kind of dubious inflection it now deserved. It wasn't lost on the American, who hesitated before continuing with his report.

"One of the Baltimore cops took him down. He was taken to a local hospital as a DOA and I'm told that he's on ice somewhere."

Gault considered this. If the subject was in a morgue storage drawer then the plan was going off the rails. He had been infected with Generation Three of the *Seif al Din*, the Sword of the Faithful. He should not have been lying idly about. However, Gault seriously doubted that this was the case. "Find out for sure."

"I've put a top guy on it and should be able to lock it down soonest."

"What about the other two shipments?"

"They left by truck the day before the place was hit."

"Did everything go as planned?"

"Sure. They successfully tailed the one we wanted and lost the other. It all went fine. Right now they're surveilling the big plant and doing satellite flybys and thermal scans with helos. But no one has gone in because of a general sit-and-wait order."

"Issued by whom?"

The American cleared his throat. "The Geek Squad."

"Geek Squad" was their personal code for the DMS.

"Perfect."

"Glad you think so," said the American, "but I think you're playing with goddamn fire here."

"Have a little faith," chided Gault.

"Faith, my ass. How are we going to evacuate the plant, that's my question? The Geeks may only be watching now but a go order can come down any second, and I don't think I can stop them from—"

Gault cut him off. "I'm not asking you to. Just sit tight and keep your eyes and ears open. I'll be reachable for the next three or four days. In the meantime, download everything including the official warehouse assault report to my PDA." He parted the tent flaps and looked out at the rocks and sand, at the sparse bunchgrass and withered scrub date palms. This part of Afghanistan always looked like a wasteland. Then a flash of movement caught his eye and he saw three people coming toward him from the mouth of a small cave halfway up the valley—a woman with two heavily armed guards flanking her. Amirah, coming to take him to the lab. He let out the held breath that had started to burn stale in his chest.

"But it's too late to evacuate the staff . . ." the American said.

"Are you that concerned for their well-being?"

The American laughed. "Yeah, right. I'm thinking of what the Geek Squad could do with what they find in there."

"They'll do exactly what we want them to do." He meant to say "what *I* want them to do," but decided to throw the American a bone. "Keep me posted. If you can't reach me then make sure my assistant has regular updates."

The American made a rude noise. There was no love lost between him and Toys.

"You sure this bullshit is going to work?"

"Work?" Gault echoed softly as he watched Amirah walk toward him and saw that her step was lively, filled with excitement. He knew what kinds of things excited this woman. "It already *has* worked."

He closed the phone and put it in his pocket.

Chapter Ten

"DR. SANCHEZ'S OFFICE."

"Kittie? It's Joe. Rudy free?"

"Oh, he's gone for the day. I think he went to the gym—"

"Thanks." I cleared the call and then thumb-dialed the number for Gold's on Pratt Street. They got Rudy to the phone.

"Joe," he said. Rudy sounds like Raul Julia from *The Addams Family* years. "I thought you were in Ocean City. Something about a tan, an endless stream of bikinis, and a sixer of Corona. Wasn't that the great master plan?"

"Plans change. Look, you free?"

"When?"

"Now."

A slight pause as he shifted gears. "Are you okay?"

"Not entirely."

Another shift, this time from concern to caution. "Is this about what happened at the warehouse?"

"In a way."

"Are you feeling depressed or—"

"Cut the shit, Rudy, this is off the clock." He got that. Since long before Helen's first suicide attempt Rudy had been my shrink some of the time and my friend all of the time. Now I needed my friend, but I wanted his brain, too. "Get dressed and come outside. I'll be there in five."

I MET RUDY Sanchez ten years ago during his residency at Sinai. He'd worked with Helen since the first time she'd been checked in after the spiders started coming out of the walls. Now we were both dealing with Helen's suicide in different ways. I needed him for my part of it, and he needed me for his. None of Rudy's patients had ever killed themselves before, and he took it pretty hard. There's professional detachment and then there's basic humanity. Rudy's a great shrink. He was born for the profession, I think. He listens with every molecule of his body and he has insight.

He came out of Gold's wearing electric-blue bike shorts and a black tank top, carrying an Under-Armour gym bag.

"You have a bike?" I asked, looking around.

"No, I drove."

"What's with the shorts?"

"There's a new fitness trainer. Jamaican gal . . . tall, gorgeous."

"And . . . ?"

"Bike shorts show off my package."

"Jesus Christ."

"Jealousy is an ugly thing, Joe."

"Get in the fucking car."

We drove to Bellevue State Park, bought some bottled water, and walked off into the forest. I hadn't said much of anything in the car and Rudy let it be, waiting for me to open up, but after we'd been walking for five minutes he cleared his throat. "This is getting pretty remote for a therapy session, cowboy."

"Not what it is."

"Then what? Does the FBI want you to get your forestry merit badge?"

"Need privacy."

"Your car won't do it?"

"Not sure about that."

He smiled. "You ought to consider seeing a therapist about that paranoia."

I ignored him. The park trail brought us into a small clearing by a brook. I led the way down to the scattering of rocks. For a small brook it had a nice steady burble. Useful. Not that I really expected long-range mics, but safe is better than careless.

"Okay, don't take this the wrong way, Rudy, but I'm going to take off all my clothes. You can turn around. I wouldn't want you to lose confidence in your package."

He sat down on a rock and picked up some small stones to toss. I stripped down to the skin and first examined every inch of my boxers, checking the seams and label. Nothing, so I put them back on.

"Thank God," Rudy said.

I shot him the finger and went through the process with the borrowed clothes.

"What are you looking for?"

"Bugs."

"Bugs as in creepy crawlies or bugs as in I'm being ape-shit paranoid and my psychiatrist friend had better keep the Thorazine handy?"

"That one," I said as I put the sweats on and sat on a rock five feet away.

"What's going on, Joe?"

"That's the thing, Rude . . . I don't know."

His dark eyes searched my face. "Okay," he said, "tell me."

And I did. When I was finished Rudy sat on his rock and stared for a long time at a praying mantis that was sunning herself on a leaf. The sun was a ruby-red ball behind the distant trees and the late afternoon heat was giving way to a breezy coolness as twilight began to gather.

"Joe? Look me in the eye and tell me that everything you've said is true."

I told him.

He watched my pupils, the muscles around my eyes, looking for any shifts in focus. Looking for a tell. "There's no chance this Mr. Church was playing some kind of game on you? There's no chance this Javad was in on it?"

"A few days ago I shot him twice in the back. Today I smashed the guy's face to jelly and then snapped his neck."

"That would be a no, then." His color was starting to look bad as all of this sank in.

"Could a prion do that?"

"Before today I would have said no unreservedly. And I still don't think so."

"What the hell are prions anyway? I can't remember what I remember about them."

"Well, there's a lot of mystery attached to them. Prions are small proteinaceous infectious particles that resist inactivation by ordinary procedures that modify nucleic acids. Does that make sense?"

"Not even a little."

"Sadly it doesn't get much simpler. Prions are cutting-edge science and we are quite sure that there is more we don't know than we do know. Prion diseases are often called spongiform encephalopathies because of the postmortem appearance of the brain with large vacuoles in the cortex and cerebellum; makes the brain look like Swiss cheese. The diseases are characterized by loss of motor control, dementia, paralysis, wasting, and eventually death, typically following pneumonia. Mad cow disease is a type of spongiform encephalopathy. Coming back from the dead, however, is definitely *not* a known symptom."

"So . . . prions couldn't turn a terrorist into one of these monsters?"

"I don't see how. You said Church was only guessing. It's been what . . . five days since you shot Javad? That's not a lot of time to do that kind of medical research. Church may be completely wrong as to the cause."

"Doesn't change the fact that Javad was dead, though."

"Dios mio."

"Rudy . . . you do believe me, right?"

He stared at the mantis some more. "Yes, cowboy. I believe you. I just don't want to."

I had nothing to say to that.

MR. CHURCH SAT in the interrogation room and waited. There was a discreet tap on the door and a woman entered. She was medium height, slender, and had looks that Church had once heard referred to as "disturbingly pretty." She wore a tailored gray suit and skirt, low-heeled pumps and coral blouse. Short dark hair, brown eyes with gold flecks. No rings, no jewelry. She looked like a Hollywood accountant or an executive at one of the snootier ad agencies.

"You saw?" Church asked.

She closed the door and glanced at the laptop Church had on the table before him, the screen lowered to hide its contents. "Yes. And I'm not happy with losing the walker." Her voice was low and throaty with a London accent. "I know we have other subjects, but—"

Church dismissed that with a little movement of his head. "Grace, give me an assessment of his capabilities based on what just happened."

She sat. "On the plus side he's tough, resourceful, and vicious, but we already knew that from the warehouse videos. He's tougher than any of the other candidates."

"What's on the minus side?"

"Sloppy police work. Two lorries left the warehouse the night before his task force raided it, one was tracked, one wasn't. Ledger was involved."

"I think that when we acquire all of the records from the task force things might look different where Ledger's involvement is concerned."

Grace looked dubious.

"What else is in the minus column?" Church asked.

"I don't think he's emotionally stable."

"Have you read his psych profile?"

"Yes."

"Then you already knew that."

She pursed her lips. "He's no yes man. He'd be hard to control."

"As a team player, sure; but what if he was a team leader?"

Grace snorted. "He was a sergeant in the army with no combat experience. He was the lowest-ranking member of the joint task force. I hardly think . . ." Grace stopped, sat back in her chair and cocked an eyebrow. "You like this bloke, don't you?"

"Liking him is irrelevant, Grace."

"You really see him as management material?"

"Still to be determined."

"But you're impressed?"

"Aren't you?"

Grace turned and looked at the window to the other room. Two agents in hazmat suits were strapping Javad's corpse to a gurney. She turned back to Church. "What would you have done if he'd been bitten?"

"Put him in Room Twelve with the others."

"Just like that?"

"Just like that."

She turned away for a moment, not wanting Church to see the contempt and horror in her eyes. Her face reflected the horror, shock, and grief she—and so many others in the DMS—felt. It had been a dreadful week. The worst of Grace's life.

"Your assessment," he prompted.

"I don't know. I think I'd need to see him in a few other situations before I would want to see him wearing officer's rank. After what happened at the hospital we can't afford to have anything less than first chair when it comes to team leadership."

"If it was your choice to make, would you invite him into the unit?"

She drummed her fingers on the table. "Maybe."

He pushed the plate toward her. "Have a cookie."

She saw that the plate held Oreos and vanilla wafers. She declined with a polite shake of her head.

Church raised the screen of the laptop and turned it so they could both see it. "Watch," he said and pressed the play button. A high-resolution image appeared of a group of men in black combat fatigues moving rap-idly through an office hallway.

"The warehouse?" she asked. "I've seen this already."

"You haven't seen this part." On the screen Joe Ledger stepped into shot about twenty yards ahead of the agent whose camera had provided the footage. Ledger spotted two task force officers taking fire from three hostiles who were shooting from a secure position behind a stack of heavy crates. Bullets tore chunks from the paltry cover behind which the agents crouched. Ledger came up on their seven o'clock, well out of their line of sight; he had his pistol in his hand but to open fire from that distance would have been suicide. He might get one or two but the other would turn and chop him up. There was no cover at all between Ledger and the hostiles, but he hugged the wall, running on cat feet, making no noise that could have been heard above the din of the gunfire.

When Ledger was ten feet out he opened fire. His first shot caught one of the hostiles in the back of the neck and the impact slammed him into the crates. As the other two turned Ledger closed to zero distance and fired one more shot and the second hostile staggered back, but then the slide on Ledger's gun locked open. There was no time to change magazines. The third hostile instantly lunged at him, swinging his rifle barrel to bear. Ledger parried it with his pistol and then everything turned into a blur. All three hostiles were down.

Grace frowned but declined to comment as the file repeated in slow motion, leaning forward at the point where the slide locked back on Ledger's gun. The slow-mo even caught the elegance of the ejected brass arching through the air. Ledger had the pistol held out in front of him so it was obvious that he recognized the predicament of the empty magazine but he did not visibly react to it. His hands separated and while he was still in full stride he used the empty gun to check the swing of the hostile's rifle while simultaneously jabbing forward with his left hand, fingers folded in half and stiffened so that the secondary line of knuckles drove into the attacker's windpipe. As this was hap-pening Joe's left foot changed from a regular running step into a longer lunge and the tip of his combat boot crunched into the cartilage under the hostile's kneecap; and a fraction of a second later Ledger's gun hand came up and jabbed the exposed barrel of the pistol into the hostile's left eye socket.

The attacker flew backward as if he'd been hit by a shotgun blast. Ledger completed his step and was smoothly reaching to his belt for a fresh magazine when the footage ended.

"Bloody hell!" Grace gasped. It came out before she could stop the words.

"Elapsed time from the slide locking back to completed kill is 0.031 seconds," said Church. "Tell me why I want him for the DMS."

She hated when he did this to her. It was like being in school, but she kept her annoyance off her face. "He showed absolutely no hesitation. He didn't even flinch when his gun locked open, he simply went into a different form of attack. It's so smooth, like he'd practiced that one set of moves for years."

"In light of that video and your assessment would you consider him a likely candidate for us?"

"I don't know. His psych evals read like a horror novel."

"Past tense. His dissociative behavior was directly related to a specific traumatic event that happened when he was a teenager. His service record since then doesn't show an unstable personality."

She shook her head. "That trauma happened during a crucial phase of his life. It informed the rest of his development. It's why he began studying martial arts. It's why he joined the army, and it's why he became a policeman. He keeps looking for ways to channel his rage."

"It seems to me that he's found ways to channel it. Very useful ways, Grace. If he was lost in rage then his pathology would be different. A rageaholic would have taken up something confrontational; instead he's refined his abilities through an art known for its lack of flamboyance."

"Which could be interpreted as someone desperate to maintain control."

"That's one view. Another is that he's found control, and it's saved him."

Grace drummed her fingers on the table. "I still don't like those old psych evaluations. I think there's a ticking bomb there."

"You should read your own, Grace. The recent ones," Church said mildly, and she shot him a withering look. "Tell me, Grace—if he'd been with Bravo or Charlie teams at St. Michael's do you think things would have gone differently?"

Grace's jaw tightened. "That's impossible to say."

"No it isn't. You know why things went south at the hospital, and you saw this tape. My question stands."

"I don't know. I think we would need to observe him a lot more."

"Okay," he said. "Then go and observe him."

With that he got up and left the room.

Chapter **Twelve**
Baltimore, Maryland / Saturday, June 27; 6:54 P.M.

RUDY GOT QUIET as we walked back to my SUV. I undid the locks but he lingered outside, touching the door handle. "This *cabrón* Church . . . what's your take on him?"

"Car could be bugged, Rude."

"Fuck it. Answer the question. Do you think Church is a good guy or a bad guy?"

"Hard to say. I certainly don't think he's a *nice* guy."

"Given what he has to do, how nice should he be?"

"Good point," I said. I reached in and keyed the ignition, then turned the radio up loud. If the car was bugged that might help, though I suspected it no longer mattered.

"He's asking you to take a lot on faith. Secret government organizations, zombies . . . do you feel that he was trying to trick you in some way?"

"No," I said, "I don't think he was lying about that. Even so . . . I can't seem to wrap my head around all this. It's impossible. It doesn't fit, it's all too . . ." I couldn't put it into words, so I stared at the day around us. Birds sang in the trees, crickets chirped, kids laughed on the swings.

Rudy followed my gaze. "You find it hard to believe in those things when you can stand here and see this?"

I nodded. "I mean . . . I know it was real because I was there, but even so I don't *want* it to be real." He said nothing and after a moment I hit him with another bomb. "Church said he'd read my psych evaluations."

Rudy looked like I'd slapped him. "He didn't get them from me."

"How do you know? If he's on the same level as Homeland you could be bugged and monitored out the wazoo."

"If I get so much as a whiff of violation—"

"You'll what? Raise a stink? File a lawsuit? Most people never do. Not since 9/11. Homeland counts on it."

"Patriot Act," he said the way people say "hemorrhoids."

"Terrorism's a tough thing to fight without elbow room."

He gave me an evil glare. "Are you defending an intrusion into civil liberties?"

"Not as such, but look at it from the law enforcement perspective. Terrorists are fully aware of constitutional protections, and they use that to hide. No, don't give me that look. I'm just saying."

"Saying what?"

"That everyone thinks this is an either/or situation and it's more complicated than that."

"Patient records are sacred, amigo." He only ever calls me that when he's pissed.

"Hey, don't jump on me. I'm on *your* side. But maybe you should consider the other side's point of view."

"The other side can kiss my—"

"Careful, bro, this whole car could be bugged."

Rudy leaned close to the car and said, loudly and distinctly, "Mr.

Church can kiss my ass." He repeated it slowly in Spanish. *"¡Besa mi culo!"*

"Fine, fine, but if you get disappeared don't blame me."

He leaned back and gave me a considering look. "I'm going to do three things today. First, I'm going to go over every square inch of my office and if I find *anything* out of place, any hint of violation, I'm going to call the police, my lawyer, and my congressmen."

"Good luck with that." I climbed in and pulled the door shut.

"The second thing I'm going to do is see what I can find out about prions, something that indicates whether they can somehow reactivate the central nervous system. Maybe there have been some studies, some papers."

"What's the third thing?"

He opened the door. "I'm going to go to evening mass and light a candle."

"For Helen?"

"For you, cowboy, and for me . . . and for the whole damn human race." He got in and closed the door.

We didn't speak at all on the drive back.

Chapter **Thirteen**
Gault and Amirah / The Bunker / Six days ago

WITH EL MUJAHID and his soldiers gone that left only six people in the camp besides Gault. Four guards, a servant, and Amirah, who was both the wife of El Mujahid and the head of Gault's covert research division here in the Middle East. She was a gorgeous woman and a freakishly brilliant scientist whose insight into disease pathogens bordered on the mystical.

While he waited for her he switched on his PDA and accessed the files the American had sent, most of which were official reports on the task force raid. Most of it had gone exactly as arranged—although the American did not know that. There were a lot of things Gault chose not to share with the nervous Yank. He did wonder, however, why the crab processing plant had not yet been raided. He made a note to ask Toys to look into that.

The tent flaps opened. He turned to see *her* standing there, and for a moment all thoughts of raids and schemes evaporated from his head.

Amirah was slim, average height, dressed in the black *chadri* that showed only her eyes, and she might have gone unnoticed in a bazaar or on a crowded street. Unless, of course, any sane man made eye contact with her, then the anonymity would disintegrate like a sand sculpture in the face of a zephyr. This woman could stop traffic with her eyes. Gault had seen her do it. Conversations always faltered when she entered a room, men actually walked into walls. It was the strangest of reactions because it was so contrary to Muslim tradition. To catch a woman's eye once is okay, to do so twice was *haram*, a social and religious gaffe of serious consequence, especially in the traditional circles in which this woman and El Mujahid traveled. And yet no one—not one man Gault had seen—had ever looked into her eyes and not been affected.

It wasn't sex, either, because all a man could see of Amirah were her eyes, and in the Middle East there were millions of women with beautiful eyes. No, this went deeper than sex, deeper even than religious law. This was power. Real, palpable, earthshaking power; and it was there in Amirah's eyes, as if her eyes were a window into the heart of a nuclear furnace.

The first time Gault had seen her was two months before the Americans invaded Iraq. They were two among thousands at an anti-Coalition rally in Tikrit. He had been there, quietly recruiting and waiting for contact that, his sources had told him, could bring him to El Mujahid. Gault had felt something touch him, almost like hot fingers scraping the skin of the back of his neck, and he'd turned to see this woman standing fifteen feet away, staring at him. He'd been at a loss for words for the first time in his life, totally riveted by the impact of those eyes and of the fierce, vast intelligence behind them. She had walked up to him, affecting the modest gait of a good Muslim woman, and while the crowd was entirely focused on Saddam, who was giving a rousing speech in which he promised to rebuff any U.S. attempt to set foot on Iraqi soil, the woman bent close and said: "I am Amirah. I can take you to paradise."

In any other circumstances that line would have been cheap, a prostitute's come-on; but to Gault it was the code phrase he'd been waiting to hear for many weeks. He was so taken aback, so startled that this was the messenger he'd come to Tikrit to find, that he almost flubbed the countersign, but after two or three stammering attempts he managed to say: "And what will I see there?"

She had said three magical words that filled Gault with great joy. Leaning a few inches closer Amirah had whispered, *"Seif al Din."*

What will I see there?

Seif al Din. The Sword of the Faithful.

That moment flashed through Gault's mind as Amirah stepped into the tent. He got to his feet, smiling, wanting to take her in his arms, to tear away that ridiculous black rag she wore. He saw his need mirrored in her eyes and she smiled. All he could see of her smile was the soft crow's feet at the corners of those lustrous brown eyes; and he knew that her smile was as much a promise as it was an acknowledgment. They could do nothing, share nothing while they were here in El Mujahid's tent. Two guards stood behind her, both giving him hard stares.

"Mr. Gault," she said in a docile voice. "My husband has instructed me to share with you the results of our experiments. Will you please accompany me to the bunker?"

"I need to get going. I have to be in Baghdad by—"

"Please, Mr. Gault. This is my husband's wish." She put just enough juice in the word "wish" to make it clear that it meant "order." *Jolly well done,* he thought as he saw the guards behind her stiffen and harden their stares. It was all drama, nicely staged for effect.

"Oh, very well," Gault said with an affect of bad grace and stood up with a sigh.

Amirah backed out of the tent and the two guards took position so that one was between her and Gault and the other between Gault and any chance of flight. El Mujahid was a careful individual, and that worked well for Gault, too. He followed Amirah to another tent that was set very close to a rock wall. Inside the tent were ornate wall hangings, and a third guard stood with his back to one of these, an AK-47 at port arms, his face as hard as a fist. At a word from Amirah, he stepped back and allowed her to push the heavy brocade aside. Behind it was the mouth of a shallow cave. Amirah, Gault, and two of the guards entered it, walked ten feet, and then turned with the cave's natural bend. Around the corner, out of sight of the entrance, was a blank wall of rough gray-brown rock hung with desiccated moss. The guards told Gault to turn around and face the mouth of the cave, but Gault knew what was happening behind him. Amirah would reach into the moss and pull a slender piece of wire—something that would never be caught in any but the most scrupulous search of the cave—and there were a lot of caves in Afghanistan. She would pull the wire twice, wait four seconds and then pull it three more times. At that point a piece of the uneven wall would fold down to reveal a computer keypad. Amirah would then tap in a code, a randomly selected set of numbers and letters that changed daily, and once the code was accepted she would place her hand on the geography scanner. As far as El Mujahid knew only two people on earth knew that code—he and his wife; but Gault also knew it. Gault knew everything about the cave, the keypad, and the bunker that lay behind this wall. He had paid for it and had built dozens of computer trapdoors into the system.

He also knew how to destroy that bunker and its contents so that not one piece of useful data could be recovered. Granted, a large portion of Afghanistan would be sterilized as well, but those—as the Americans were so fond of saying—were the breaks. All he had to do was enter a code on his laptop. And if that didn't work, Gault always had a backup plan ready; and if he disappeared his assistant, Toys, could initiate one of several retributive plans.

Gault heard the hiss of hydraulics and the guard grunted at him, indicating that he was allowed to turn. The whole back end of the cave had swung out to reveal an airlock as sophisticated as anything NASA had ever used.

"Please," Amirah said, gesturing that he enter. One of the two guards remained in the cave while the other stepped into the airlock with Gault and the Princess. The massive door hissed shut and there was a series of complex sounds as various locks and safeguards engaged. A red light flicked on above the door and they turned to face the exit door as a green light came on above it. Amirah went through another code procedure, but this time the guard did not order Gault to look away. Now the guard grinned at Gault, who gave him a wink.

"How are the kids, Khalid?"

"Very well, sir. Little Mohammad is walking now. He is all over the place."

"Ah, they grow up so fast. Give them a kiss for me."

"Thank you, Mr. Gault."

The second door opened and a wash of refrigerated air filled the chamber. "Ready?" Amirah asked.

"Say, Khalid . . . why don't you go into the office and watch some videos. Give us a couple of hours."

"Happy to, sir."

They stepped out of the airlock and into the bunker that was as different from the camp outside as a diamond was from a lump of coal. There was a big central room packed with state-of-the-art research equipment and intelligence-processing hardware including satellite downlinks, high-speed Internet cable hard lines, plasma display screens on nearly every surface, and a dozen computer terminals. Surrounding the central lab were glassed offices, the supercooled chamber for the bank of Blue Gene/L supercomputers, and the five clean rooms with their isolated air and biohazard control systems. Down one corridor was the staff wing, with bedrooms for the eighty technicians and the twenty support staff.

The setup had cost a fortune. Fifty-eight million pounds, all routed through convoluted banking threads that would require an army of forensic accountants to follow. Nothing could be tied directly to him or to Gen2000. It was Gault's belief that this was not only the most sophisticated private research facility in the world, but also the most productive and diverse. Genetics, pharmacology, molecular biology, bacteriology, virology, parasitology, pathology, and over a dozen other related sciences merged into one compact but incredibly productive factory floor that had paid for itself four times over with patents filed under the names of over seventy doctors who were on his payroll through one university or another, not the least of which was the first reliable drug for treating the rare blood cancers, new-onset sarcoidosis, and asbestos-related diseases that have cropped up in survivors of the World Trade Center collapse. The irony of that made Gault want to laugh out loud considering he'd advised bin Laden about the likely and potentially useful postcollapse health hazards before the Al Qaeda operatives had even enrolled in flight school.

Amirah led the way past the rows of technicians, still playing her role as the dutiful wife of the great leader even though these people were *hers*, every last one of them. Only Abdul, her husband's lieutenant, and a small squad of his personal guard were currently beyond her control, and they were outside. And even that sense of loyalty would change in time. Everything was going to change.

She led Gault into the conference room, then closed the door and engaged the lock, an action that turned on a red security light outside. The room had no windows. Just a big table and a lot of chairs.

Amirah turned away from the door, tore away her *chadri*, and attacked Gault.

She was fast, savage, *hungry*.

She pushed him back, forcing him down on the table, tearing at his clothes, biting at each bit of exposed flesh; and he grabbed her and clawed her skirts up over her legs. He knew that she would be naked underneath. They had planned this moment, *needed* it. He was as ready as she was and as he used his heels to slide farther onto the table she climbed over him, swung a leg across his hips, and as he pulled her toward him she thrust down onto him. It was hot and hard, painful and sloppy, but it was so intense. Their bodies ground into one another. Love was lost in the avalanche of need, buried beneath the immediacy of their hungers.

El Mujahid was sometimes as brutal and intense, but he was always quick, and Amirah could endure and outlast any man. Almost any man. With Gault it was different. Instead of a gallop to the precipice and then that quick plunge into unsatisfactory disappointment, they raced on and on, their bodies running with sweat, their hearts hammering like primitive drums, their breath burning into each other's mouths.

When they came, they both screamed. The conference room was soundproof. He'd made sure of that.

Chapter **Fourteen**
Baltimore, Maryland / Saturday, June 27; 7:46 P.M.

I DROPPED RUDY at his office. As he got out of the car he said, "Joe . . . I know how obsessive you can get about things."

"Me? Really."

"I'm serious. Church is on some creepy level of government and he told you to leave it alone. I think you should take him at his word."

"Yeah, let me get right on that."

"What's your alternative? Poke at it with a stick until all the hornets come out of the nest? Think about it . . . Church didn't approach you through channels, that means he wants this kept off the record. That frightens me, cowboy, and it should frighten you."

"I'm too wired to be scared. God . . . I think I need to get totally shitfaced tonight."

He closed the door and leaned in through the window. "Listen to me, Joe . . . go easy on the booze. No screwing around. You've experienced two major traumas in only a few days. No matter how much of a macho façade you put on I know that killing those men at the warehouse had to do you some damage."

"They dealt the play."

"Like that matters? Just because they were doing something immoral doesn't take away your emotional connection to it. This isn't to say that you were in any way wrong. God knows I hope I would have the physical and moral courage to do what you did in there. You're a white hat, Joe, but that comes with a price tag. You have a heart and a mind and pretty soon you're going to have to open up those doors and take a close look at what kind of damage is there as a result of this."

I said nothing.

"I'm saying this as your friend as well as your therapist."

I still said nothing.

"Don't think I'm kidding, Joe. This isn't something you can shrug off. You're required to have sessions with me about this, and you can't go back on the job until I file my report. As of yet I don't have anything to file. You've blown off two scheduled sessions so far. You need to talk about it."

I stared out the window for a minute. "Okay."

In a softer tone he added, "Look, cowboy, I know how tough you are . . . but believe me when I tell you that nobody is *that* tough. A complete separation from your feelings is not proof of manly strength . . . it's a big glaring neon warning sign. I know you think you called me today to ask my opinion as a pal and as a medical doctor, but I have to believe that you're reaching out for support for what you've been through. As far as this thing with Javad and Mr. Church goes . . . well, if you were capable of simply shrugging that off with no traumatic effects then I would either be afraid of you or afraid for you."

"I'm feeling it," I assured him.

Rudy studied my face. "I have a two o'clock open on Tuesday."

I sighed. "Yeah, okay. Tuesday at two."

He nodded, pleased. "Bring Starbucks."

"Sure, what do you want?"

"My usual. Iced half-caf ristretto quad grande two pump raspberry two percent no whip light ice with caramel drizzle three-and-a-half-pump white mocha."

"Is any of that actually coffee?"

"More or less."

"And you think I'm damaged."

He stepped back and I drove off. I could see in the rearview that he watched me all the way out of the parking lot.

Chapter **Fifteen**
Baltimore, Maryland / Saturday, June 27; 7:53 P.M.

I HEADED HOME and as soon as I was in the door I went straight to the bathroom, stripped and stuffed everything, even my boxers, into the trash and then stood under the hottest spray I could stand and tried to boil the day off my skin.

My cat, Cobbler—a marmalade and white tabby—hopped up on the toilet tank and watched me with his big yellow eyes.

I knotted a towel around my waist and thought about the beers in the fridge, but even though the adrenaline was out of my bloodstream the shakes were still right there beneath the surface. I passed on the beer and put a frozen pizza in the oven, and turned on the TV. Normally I'd surf over to one of the horror or SF channels and see who was eating whom, but right now I wanted no part of that. All I needed now was to stumble on a rerun of *Dawn of the Dead* and I'd probably lose it. So I put on the news. The top story was a follow-up on the fire at St. Michael's Hospital that had occurred the same night as the warehouse raid. Over two hundred dead and half the hospital burned to the ground. They were calling it the worst hospital fire in modern U.S. history.

More depression I didn't need, so I surfed over to a different news channel and watched a few minutes of the preevent press hype over the big Fourth of July event in Philly. They were rededicating the Liberty Bell and also installing a brand-new one—the Freedom Bell—that had been built according to the specs of the original. Something the First Lady and the wife of the Vice President had cooked up as part of their Patriotic American Women organization. Lots of rah-rah stuff to build morale for the troops in the field and raise domestic support for our overseas action. The whole event was going to center around the ringing of the Freedom Bell, which would be symbolic of American democracy and freedom ringing out around the world. Must have sounded good to Congress because they approved it and hired some woman to make the new bell, and she was supposed to be a descendant of the British metalsmith who'd cast the original Liberty Bell. My task force team was one of over a dozen similar groups that were supposed to be on site during the festivities, though overall security was naturally a Secret Service gig. We were basically thugs in suits for the day, just in case bin Laden showed up with a hundred pounds of C4 strapped to his chest. Life in post-9/11 America. Happy holidays, bring the whole family.

I switched off the set and closed my eyes. What was it Church had said? *Mr. Ledger, we are very much in the business of stopping terror. There are threats against this country greater than anything that has so far made the papers.*

"No kidding," I said aloud.

So how did I work this? I'm self-aware enough to know that I have a somewhat fractured personality. Not exactly multiple personality disorder, but clearly there were different drivers at the wheel depending on my mood, and depending on my needs. Over the years I'd been able to identify and make peace with the three dominant personalities: the Modern Man, the Warrior, and the Cop. At the moment all three of them were trying to grab the wheel.

The Modern Man, the civilized part of me, was in full-blown denial mode. He didn't want to believe in monsters and he wasn't all that comfortable with secret government departments and all that James Bond crap. The Warrior was okay with the cloak-and-dagger stuff because it partly defined him, it allowed him the chance to be who and what he was: a killer. He was useful in a firefight, but I seldom let him out to play.

He was lousy at tea parties. Then there was the Cop. That part of me had become dominant over the last few years, and he also upheld the nobler parts of the Warrior's personality—the codes of ethics, the rules.

With my eyes closed I settled back into meditative breathing and let the parts of me sort it all out. It was almost always the Cop who got the others to shut the hell up. The Cop was the thinker. I dismantled this thing bit by bit and laid everything on the table so the Cop could take a good long look.

There were parts that didn't fit. The most obvious was the fact that the terrorists we took down at the warehouse had been such a mixed bag. These guys aren't known for tolerance and team spirit.

The suicide plan was also weird. Each of hostiles at the warehouse had been infected by a disease and had to take regular doses of an antidote to stay alive. That was impressive, but it also seemed like overkill. It was too sophisticated for its own purposes, considering that the mere threat of it should have been enough. It also spoke of a degree of technological sophistication that was, as far as I could judge, beyond the reach of your average extremist cell. If this was all real, and if it turned out that the plague that created these walkers was developed by the same mind, or minds, that created the control disease, then the DMS might be facing an actual real-world mad scientist. In another mood, or perhaps on another day, that might actually be funny. Right now it scared the hell out of me.

Then there was Javad. Was he really dead and somehow reanimated? Impossible? You bet; and yet I know what I saw.

From now on, Church had said, *we may have to consider "dead" a relative term.*

I found it hard to believe that Javad was the only infected person. There hadn't been a lab at the warehouse. Church had to know that, too; and I should have remarked on it. The oven timer dinged and I opened my eyes. I took the pizza with me into the little nook off the kitchen where I had my computer. I ate a slice while it loaded. Then I got to work. The Cop in me was in gear now. Church had said that if I looked I wouldn't find anything about him or the DMS. I wanted to put that to the test, so I stayed up all night searching the Internet.

I did a search on the warehouse Church had been using. Baylor Records Storage. To dig deep I had to log on through the department Web site, and there was a serious risk in that. Everything is logged, everything is tracked.

"Screw it," I said, and kept going. But Baylor Records turned out to be a dead end. Previous owner was dead and there were no direct heirs, so the government had snapped it up for back taxes. Easy enough for someone like Church to commandeer. I searched all night to see if there was any connection between Baylor Records and the old container company warehouse where we'd taken down the terrorist cell; but if a connection existed I couldn't find it.

Early Sunday morning Rudy called to say he'd spent all of last night and this morning researching prions.

"What happened to 'leave it alone, Joe'?"

"What can I tell you," he said tiredly. "So we both need therapy."

"You find anything interesting?"

"Lots, but none of it germane to what you mean. The whole prion thing seems less and less likely, though. As dangerous as they are the infection rate is extremely slow. It can take months or years for it to manifest. I'll keep looking, though. And don't forget about our session on Tuesday."

"Yes, mother."

"Don't start with me, cowboy," he warned, and hung up.

The rest of Sunday went like that. I logged hour after hour on the Net, and Rudy and I shared URLs via e-mail and IM, but we didn't seem to be getting any closer to an explanation for what Javad was or how he came to be like that. Around midnight I finally shut off the machine, took a shower, and shambled off to bed. I was hitting brick walls everywhere I went, and I guess another person would have thrown in the towel, but that's not my sort of thing. I just needed to rest and then attack this again with a fresher set of wits.

Chapter Sixteen

THEY LAY EXHAUSTED on the table, their clothes tangled around her waist and his ankles, his body purple and red with claw marks and bites. He never left a mark on her, not even the smallest of love bites. That would be suicide.

They never spoke of love afterward. Never told each other how much this meant, or how much they meant to each other. They already knew what the other would say. It had all been said in that first moment of eye contact. Pillow talk would limit the feeling, it would define what did not need to be defined and therefore cheapen it all to some kind of clandestine Romeo and Juliet pap. This was much bigger and, Gault hoped, likely to end with less personal tragedy.

She spoke first, saying simply, "I've had some vague reports. Baltimore?"

"Mm, yes," he drawled. "Seems our warehouse is a total loss."

"What about Javad?"

He paused, staring at the speckled surface of the acoustic ceiling tiles, deciding which version of the truth to tell her. He loved Amirah but there were levels of privacy that even she didn't get to enter; which would make it easier if he had to kill her one of these days. He liked to keep his options open. "Uncertain."

"He hasn't gotten out. I've been tracking the news feeds . . ."

"I know, which means that we still have to move forward with the next few steps of the operation."

"What about the other two locations? If the Americans know about the warehouse . . ."

"Don't worry," Gault said. "They know about one of them—the big one; but not about the other one. Right now they're holding off, probably hoping to find where the other lorry went."

She nodded, the motion massaging his bicep, which was starting to fall asleep. "When will you evacuate the plant?"

"Why bother? We don't really need it anymore and I'm rather hoping they raid it."

Amirah turned her head sharply. "Why?"

"How, why, and when they raid that plant will tell us a great deal about their intelligence gathering, and their wits."

"Shouldn't those details be handled by your American friend?"

"He's too close to it to risk any direct involvement. Besides," Gault said, "there's something else I need him to focus on. There are some indications that there is another player in the game, possibly a new counterterrorism organization or department. Right now this is just guesswork, but it bears looking into."

Amirah sat up and her black robes fell down to cover her with an unintentional display of rumpled modesty. She pushed a strand of glossy black hair away from her face. Without the *chadri* her face was incredibly beautiful. Full lips, high cheekbones, a broad clear brow, and those eyes. Gault loved those eyes. Like a falcon or some creature out of myth.

"Is it the Brits? You think Barrier is—"

He shook his head. "No, not Barrier. Something the Yanks have cooked up, but as I said—I'm not sure who yet. I have feelers out through Homeland, the FBI, a few other agencies. If I'm right then they'll show their hands soon enough."

"You should put your pet monkey on it. He's tenacious."

Gault smiled. "His name is Toys . . . and yes, he is tenacious." *In fact*, Gault thought, *he'd love to cook you over a slow fire.*

"So . . . what are you going to do about the plant?"

"I rather think I'm going to let them raid it. I can't think of a better way of inspiring useful fear than letting me break in and see what's going on in that place. It'll do us worlds of good."

"But what about El Mujahid? He's the master of creating fear, and his mission is already in the works. If you allow the raid on the warehouse does that mean you'll use that instead of what my husband is—"

"Hardly," Gault assured her. "I'm relying on the Fighter to deliver the master stroke; but a raid on the plant will surely set the atmosphere . . . after which everything will go exactly as we want."

She frowned at him, chewing a lip as she considered this. He knew that she was sorting through the possible outcomes based on what she knew—what he'd *allowed* her to know. She would come to very logical conclusions, and on the whole they would be right; but they would be incomplete. Which was fine.

"Don't worry, my princess," Gault said, and turned onto his side so he could stroke her hair and brush the back of his hand against her cheek. "This is going very, very well for us. We need the Yanks to think they're containing the situation. If they have a new special operations group, then it will help focus attention in the right direction for us. The best manipulations are always those in which the mark thinks he is in charge."

Amirah kissed him. "You have the mind of a scorpion, my love."

"Now, what do you have to show me?"

Her eyes lit up. "If creating great fear is what you want, then you'll be very happy with what we've done since the last time you were here."

"As good as Javad?"

"Oh no . . . this is much, much better."

He almost said "I love you." Instead he kissed her deeply and passionately and then whispered in her ear: "Show me."

Chapter **Seventeen**
Baltimore, Maryland / Monday, June 29; 6:03 A.M.

NEXT MORNING I called a friend who worked early shift at DMV records and asked her to run Buckethead's plates, but that went nowhere. No such plates existed. Big surprise.

I logged back onto the department server to reread the task force report on the warehouse; it was gone. Completely gone. No file name, no incident folders, nothing.

"You bastard," I said aloud. Church had impressed me before, but now he was beginning to scare me. He threw enough weight to be able to locate and remove the official records of Homeland Security's Inter-jurisdictional Counterterrorism Task Force. That meant accessing local, state, and federal computer mainframes. Holy shit.

There was a hard copy of the report in my desk at the squad room, but I had doubts that it would still be there if I went in to get it. This wasn't helping my feelings of paranoia. I turned and looked around my apartment. How aggressive would these guys be? Surely they wouldn't . . .

One second later I was searching my apartment from top to bottom looking for microphones, phone bugs, fiber-optic surveillance threads. I looked hard and I looked everywhere. I found nothing. That didn't mean there was nothing to find, though; Homeland and that whole crew had a lot of very sneaky toys that were designed not to be found. All the search resulted in was a two-degree drop in my paranoia and an itchy spot between my shoulder blades like someone had a laser sight on me.

Cursing under my breath I headed into the bedroom to put on a suit in preparation for the OIS hearing, but as I was picking out a tie the phone rang. I snatched it up thinking it was Rudy.

"Detective Ledger? This is Keisha Johnson."

I recognized her voice. She was the lieutenant overseeing the Officer Involved Shooting investigation for the Task force raid. I thought about the searches and calls I'd made despite Church's warning to stay away from this and had a brief panic attack.

"Yes . . . ?" I said cautiously, heart in my throat.

"In your absence we reviewed all of the videotapes from the raid last Tuesday, and after several discussions with your commanding officer and the supervisors for the task force, we've concluded that your shooting was in keeping with the best policies and practices of the Baltimore Police Department and no further hearings or actions will be required at this time."

I said something clever like: "Um . . . what?"

"Thank you for your willingness to cooperate, and good luck at

Quantico. We'll be sorry to lose such a fine officer." And with that she hung up.

I stared at the phone in total shock. There was no way that an OIS hearing would be handled like this. Not ever, not even if everyone involved agreed that the shooting was completely righteous. Department policy mandated a hearing, token or not. This was weird and I didn't like it one damn bit. The paranoia was back stronger than ever. But the logic was all twisted. If I'd somehow rattled Church's cage by trying to find some answers, why would he smooth the way for me by canceling the hearing? I couldn't see the advantage to him in it.

I sat back down at my computer and pulled up the list of URLs Rudy had sent on prion diseases. Maybe that would give me a direction to follow, and I spent hours buried in science that was beyond me, but not so far beyond that it couldn't scare me. I learned that prion diseases are still very rare, about one case out of a million people worldwide, and only about three hundred cases here in the States. It was rare but seriously dangerous, and the mysteries surrounding the little buggers often led to panic reactions. The whole mad cow thing was prion disease at its worst, and the haste with which tens of thousands of cattle were slaughtered showed the degree of fear associated with the threat. Not that any of this helped. I'm pretty darn sure Javad didn't get the way he was from eating a bad McBurger. Then I clicked on another of Rudy's URLs which took me to an article on a prion-based disease called "fatal familial insomnia" in which a small group of patients worldwide suffered increasing insomnia resulting in panic attacks, the development of odd phobias, hallucinations, and other dissociative symptoms. The whole process takes months and the victim generally dies as a result of total sleep deprivation, exhaustion, and stress. I searched all around the topic and though there was no connection at all to a state resembling living death the concept stuck in my head. Unending wakefulness. No sleep. No rest. No dreams.

"Jesus . . ." It was a horrifying thought, and what a terrible way to die.

Could Church have been wrong? Was Javad actually suffering from a disease whose symptoms led the doctors to believe he was dead when maybe he was really in a coma? His coming back from the dead could have been nothing more sinister than waking up from a cataleptic coma. Some part of that felt right to me, but as I read on I hit another speed bump. Several of the sites said that the victims could not be put to sleep, not even through artificial means. They didn't lapse into a terminal coma at the end of their suffering. They died, and apparently stayed dead. Besides, even if Javad had been in some kind of walking catatonia it didn't explain how he'd shrugged off the two .45s I'd put in his back. Clearly there was too much of the picture that I couldn't see, and it was maddening.

Chapter Eighteen
Grace, Maryland / Monday, June 29; 8:39 A.M.

GRACE COURTLAND SAT in her comfortable leather swivel chair and sipped a Diet Coke and watched the eight color monitors that showed the inside of Joe Ledger's car, each room of his apartment, and the consulting room in Dr. Rudy Sanchez's office. She'd been amused when they'd each searched for bugs. None of them had found anything, of course. If they had someone on her staff would lose his job. For what the DMS paid for holographic relay technology it had better *not* show up on a sweep or be visible to the naked eye. The DMS had deep pockets and Mr. Church liked having toys that no one else in the schoolyard had.

Her desk was stacked with reports on Ledger. Bank account records, tax returns, school transcripts, his complete military record, and copies of everything filed about him since he joined the Baltimore Police. She'd read it all, but Joe Ledger was still a puzzle. There were so many things about him that made him excellent material for the DMS, and Grace was finding it harder and harder to hold to her position that Ledger was a screwup. If it wasn't for that damning evidence on the task force duty log . . .

That morning she'd read through Ledger's military service file. He had scored high marks in every area of training and had excelled in close-quarters combat, surveillance and countersurveillance, land warfare, and all immediate action drills. There were several letters recommending Ledger for OCS, but each included notes saying that Ledger had declined the offer. One handwritten note, from Colonel Aaron Greenberg, base commander at Fort Bragg, read: "Staff Sergeant Ledger has indicated that his goal is to use his army training to better prepare him for a career as a law enforcement officer in his hometown of Baltimore, MD. I expressed to him that this was a gain for Baltimore PD but a real loss for the army."

It was a pretty remarkable letter, but she chose to interpret it as a lack of ambition. What really caught her attention, though, was the transcript of a deposition of Ledger's company commander, Captain Michael S. Costas. Following the warehouse raid Church had sent agents to depose Costas under oath and after signing a secrecy agreement. Costas spoke freely and glowingly about Ledger, but one exchange in particular must have struck Church—it was the only section highlighted in yellow:

DMS: Captain Costas, in your professional opinion do you believe Joe Ledger to be reliable?

COSTAS: Reliable? That's a funny question. Reliable in what way?

DMS: If he were to become part of a special branch of the military?

COSTAS: You mean like Homeland? Something like that?

DMS: Something like that, yes.

COSTAS: Let me put it this way. I've been in the army since I was eighteen, and a Ranger since I was twenty. I've been in combat in the Mog and in Desert Storm. I've also served in training schools for Rangers and I've learned to trust my judgment on which men are going to become very good and which are likely to be only passable.

DMS: And it's your belief that . . . what? That Ledger was one of those who would become very good?

COSTAS: Hell, I knew that about him before he went to Ranger school. No, what I saw in Joe during his time in my company is that he was going to be great. Not good . . . but truly great. You don't see his kind very often, not unless you've been in a lot of war zones. I *have* been in a lot of war zones and I can tell you right now that Joe Ledger is a hero waiting to happen.

DMS: A hero?

COSTAS: Trust me, if you can inspire him, if you can tap into the core of that man, into what he *believes* . . . then by God he'll show you things you'll never see in another soldier. I guarantee it.

"Hero indeed," Grace muttered, turning up her nose at Costas's effusiveness; but as she immersed herself in Ledger's life something shifted inside of her. She reread it, then slapped the report cover shut. "Bollocks."

Ledger was a good fighter, that much was certain, but with all the DMS had to face could they risk having someone like him aboard? The soldier in her wanted to have nothing to do with him. And yet, the woman in her wasn't so sure. On the screen Ledger hammering away at his computer keyboard, his face intent, his blue eyes bright and—

"Stop it, you stupid cow," she said aloud, and turned away from the screen for a moment. This was counterproductive bullshit. This was a side effect of being alone in a lonely job in a foreign country. This was hormones and biology and that was all.

But when she turned back to the screen Joe's eyes were still as blue.

She punched a button that brought up an Internet display screen that mimicked whatever Ledger was looking at, and Grace forced herself to concentrate on the prion information he was reading. The dry complexity of the medical information was a relief and she could feel the small flare of emotionality subside within her. Grace sipped her Diet Coke and slammed the can down on her desk. There was no way she was going to approve him coming on board. No way in hell.

Chapter **Nineteen**

MR. CHURCH SAT back in a heavy leather chair, taking occasional sips from a bottle of spring water. The wall in front of him was covered, floor to ceiling, with video monitors. One screen showed Dr. Rudy Sanchez taking notes in his private office while a patrol sergeant broke into tears as he confessed an ongoing love affair with a precinct secretary that his wife had now started to suspect. Church paid no attention to the cop, but he studied Sanchez very closely. He selected a vanilla wafer from a dish and bit off a piece.

Another screen showed Joe Ledger bent over his computer and as he typed the keystrokes were displayed in a digital text bar below the screen.

But what interested him most was the screen on the upper-left side of his display board. On that one Grace Courtland was sipping a Diet Coke and staring with great apparent fascination at Joe Ledger. The camera he had installed in her office was something not even she would find. It was two or three generations above the equipment she used, and her stuff was cutting edge. Church had better sources.

He watched her face, the shape of her mouth, the shift of her eyes as she watched Joe Ledger. Church chewed his cookie. Even if anyone had been there his face would have given away none of his thoughts.

Chapter **Twenty**

I DECIDED TO come at this from a different route, so I called Jerry Spencer, my friend from DCPD who'd gotten his sternum cracked at the warehouse. Jerry was thirty years on the job and was the best forensics man I ever met. If anyone had caught a whiff of this DMS thing it'd be him.

He answered on the fifth ring.

"Jerry. Hey, man, how's the chest?"

"Joe," he said. No inflection.

"How are you? You still out on medical or—"

He cut me off. "What do you need, Joe?"

His tone was matter-of-fact, so I decided to be straight with him. "Jerry, have you ever heard of a federal agency called the DMS?"

There was a long silence on the line, and then Jerry said, "No, I haven't, Joe . . . and neither have you."

Before I could work out a response to that he hung up.

"Uh-oh," I murmured, and for the next ten minutes all I did was sit there and stare at the phone. Jerry had been gotten to; a blind man could see that. It strained my head to imagine how much force it would take to spook a guy like Jerry enough to have him blow me off like that.

Cobbler jumped into my lap and I stroked his silky fur while I chewed on the problem.

Until now I'd hesitated doing a direct search on the DMS for fear of that acronym, or the words "Department of Military Sciences," setting off some kind of alarms. For a while now the government has used different software packages to locate certain combinations of words in e-mail or Net searches. Type in something like "bomb" and "school" and it's supposed to raise a red flag. Doing this kind of search could land my ass in a sling. On the other hand how could I just leave this be? How could Church expect me to forget it? Even if Church was right and the whole Javad/prion/walking dead thing was over—a one-shot fluke that we lucked into and solved before it got out of the box—that still didn't alter the fact that the incident changed my whole world. Now I know how those folks feel who see a UFO or Bigfoot—not the nutcases, but the ones who are absolutely sure they've seen something outside of normal reality, and have nowhere to go with it.

What would happen if I did that search? I mean . . . what would Church really do as a result? I met the man, and even though I could see him feeding a busload of orphans and nuns to hungry wolves if it furthered his aims, I didn't take him for petty vindictiveness.

So, what would he do if I did a search on "Department of Military Sciences"?

"Kiss my ass, Church," I said, and hit the enter key.

I got a few hits for college ROTC programs under that name, but in terms of national security or secret agencies, absolutely nothing came up on the search. A waste of time? Maybe. Or maybe I had lobbed a serve into Church's court.

Chapter Twenty-One

Gault and Amirah / The Bunker / Six days ago

THE LEVEL-A PVC hazmat suit was air-cooled and very comfortable, but Gault still felt like a big marshmallow. He stood close to the airlock. In one hand he held a wireless remote that would trigger the emergency release on the lock in case he had to make a run for it; in the other he held a Snellig 46, an electric wire-dart pistol. Amirah stood behind a Plexiglas wall and her fingers hovered over a computer keyboard.

"What stage is it in?" Gault asked. Their suits were soundproof and the intercoms were of the best quality.

"Advanced stage one."

Gault cocked an eyebrow. "It's still alive?"

The creature standing there certainly didn't look alive. The brown skin had faded to a sickly bruise-yellow; its mouth was slack, lips gray and rubbery. It was only when Gault shifted a few feet to one side in order to see the thing's eyes that he could detect any trace of intelligence; but even then it was rudimentary.

"I resequenced the hormonal discharge to make the blood chemistry more hospitable for the parasites. They spread the prions at a much more accelerated rate now. The nonessential functions shut down more quickly," Amirah said brightly. "Higher brain functions deteriorate at a faster rate now."

"How much faster?"

Amirah paused and turned and flashed him a triumphant smile. "Eight times."

He frowned. "This is Generation Three?"

She laughed. "Oh no, Sebastian . . . we've passed that phase a long time ago. What you're seeing is Generation Seven of the *Seif al Din* pathogen. We've broken through almost all of the symptomatic barriers."

Gault's head whipped around and he stared at the subject then up at the big wall clock. "*Seven* . . . Christ! When was infection begun?"

"Right before I came to meet you."

Gault licked his lips. "That's . . . what, an hour?"

She shook her head. "Less. Forty-seven minutes, and I think we can get that down even more. That rate is based on injection only; we added a new parasite to the salivary glands so infection from bites is much faster, a matter of minutes. By Generation Eight we should have it down to seconds."

The creature shook its head like an animal shaking off a biting fly. The hazmat suits prevented the subject from hearing or smelling them, which were the two most significant response triggers; however, the sight of them was causing it to become agitated. Without human scent or sound that hadn't happened with earlier generations. Gault moved his hand experimentally, wanting to see if the creature would track him.

Suddenly it lunged.

Without warning or hesitation it threw itself at Gault, springing across the cold metal floor of the display area, hooked fingers clawing the air as it tried to grab him. Gault cried out and staggered back, but he brought up the Snellig and fired the weapon's twin flachettes into the monster's naked chest. He pressed his thumb down on the activator and sent 70,000 volts into the infected predator.

The subject let out a scream like a cougar—high and full of hate—but it dropped down into a fetal ball, twitching as the current burned through it.

"That's enough," he heard Amirah shout, and Gault sagged back, releasing the button. His chest was heaving and his heart hammering.

Amirah laughed as she came out from behind the Plexi screen. "The new parasite has enhanced predatory aggression by at least half, and it begins far sooner. Even from a nonfatal bite the infection will take hold within minutes and begin reducing cognitive function. In cases of a more serious bite, or in the presence of other traumatic injuries, the infection will spread exponentially faster."

"He could have killed me!" Gault snapped, rounding on her and pointing the Snellig at her chest. For a white-hot moment he almost pulled the trigger.

But she was still laughing, shaking her head. "Oh, don't be such an old woman." She used the toe of one booted foot to pull back the creature's upper lip. Gault saw that the pale gums were smooth. Amirah said, "I had its teeth pulled in preparation for the demonstration. I'm not an idiot, Sebastian."

Gault said nothing for a moment, his jaw locked, lips curled back from his teeth in as savage a snarl as he'd seen on the face of the subject. Then, by slow degrees, he forced himself to let go of the moment. He made his face relax first and gradually straightened his body from the defensive crouch. "You could have effing well warned me!"

"That would have been less fun."

"God, you're a wicked bitch," he said, but now he was smiling, too. It was completely artificial but he made it look convincing, thinking, *You are so going to pay for that, my dear.*

Amirah either couldn't tell how upset he truly was, or didn't care—and the hazmat suit hid most of his face—but she looked at the wall clock and then walked back to her control console, pulling off her hood. "The new hormone sequence has one more really marvelous effect," she said as she punched some keys. There was a heavy metallic *chunk* as steel panels slid back on the floor. She hit another button and four curved sections of inch-thick reinforced glass rose from the floor. Their sides fit together with only a faintness of the seam visible. The glass walls hissed upward until they reached a large circular track in the ceiling. As the upper edges slid into the tracks there was another chunking sound and the walls stopped moving. Amirah watched the wall clock all the while. The subject lay in the center of a big glass and steel jar.

"Wait for it," she murmured as the digital counters ticked away the seconds. "Should be right about now. Generation Seven is so wonderfully quick."

The creature suddenly opened its eyes and peeled back its lips to issue a hiss of animal hatred. No sound escaped the barrier, but Gault still flinched. Then he blinked and looked from the subject to the clock and back again.

"Wait . . ." he said, "that doesn't . . ."

Amirah's gorgeous dark eyes sparkled with delight. "Reanimation time is now under ninety seconds."

He tore off his hood and threw it onto a nearby console. "God," he gasped, staring at the monster.

"If you were worried that the Americans might harvest one of our subjects for research it doesn't matter now. They can have all of the subjects we've already sent . . . but any preventive measure they design will be built on the wrong generation of the disease."

She walked over and placed her palm on the glass and even when the subject lunged at her and slammed its face against the inner wall on the other side she didn't flinch. There was an adoring look on her face as she stared at the subject.

Gault came to stand next to her. The subject kept banging against the glass, its infected brain unable to process the concept of transparency. Even without scent it knew that its prey was there. That was the only thought it could hold on to.

In an awed voice, Amirah whispered, "Once we release these new subjects into the population the infection will spread beyond control. They won't be able to keep ahead of it."

Gault nodded slowly but his mind was working at computer speed, putting everything he'd seen and everything Amirah had said into context. It was an effort to keep his feelings about all of this off his face.

"This is unstoppable," Amirah said with a predatory hiss in her voice. "We can kill them all."

"Now, now," he said, wrapping his arm around her, "let's not lose focus here. We don't want to kill them all, darling. What would be the point in that? We simply want to make them all very, very sick."

He stroked her breast through the hazmat material.

She said nothing but he saw her turn away as if to look at some gauges and he was certain she was trying to hide her expression. "You told me to continue with the research, to improve the model. What do you expect me to do with everything I've developed? Just destroy it?"

"Yes, I bloody well do," he said, but then he stopped, lips pursed, considering; then something occurred to him. "Actually . . . hold on a bit."

She turned back to him, her face showing hurt and suspicion. "What?"

"I have a wonderful idea," he purred. "I think I figured out how to use your new monster. Oh yes, this is both juicy and delicious."

Still frowning, she said, "Tell me!"

"Before I do you have to promise me that you'll use it only as I suggest. We can't really let this generation of the pathogen out. Not ever. You do understand that, don't you?"

She said nothing.

"Do you understand?" He said it again, slowly, reinforcing each syllable.

"Yes, yes, I understand. You really are such an old woman at times, Sebastian."

"Dear heart . . . we want to buy the world, not bury it."

Amirah gave him a slow three-count and then nodded. "Of course," she said. "I just wanted you to see what we could accomplish. We've created a new kind of life, an entirely new state of existence. *Unlife.*"

He stepped back from her and stared, the devious smile still frozen onto his mouth.

Unlife.

God Almighty, he thought.

"Now . . . tell me your idea," she said, breaking through the shell of his shocked and fragile thoughts. "How can you use my new pathogen to help us in our cause?"

And suddenly Gault was snapped out of his reverie and out of his shock and was completely present in his mind. She had said "cause," not program. Not scheme, or plan. Cause. *That is a very interesting choice of a word, my love*, he thought.

So he told her and he watched her face as she listened; and he paid special attention to the muscles around her eyes and the dilation of her pupils. What he saw told him a lot. Perhaps too much, and it both elated him and hurt him. By the time he was done her beautiful face was suffused with a terrible light.

Amirah pulled him close and wrapped her arms around him. They held tightly together, ignoring the absurdity of the PVC suits.

"I love you," she said.

"I love you, too," he said, and meant it.

And when this is done I may have to feed you to one of your pets, he thought. And he meant that, too.

Chapter Twenty-Two
Balkh, Afghanistan / Five days ago

1.

THE TOWN OF Balkh in northern Afghanistan was once one of the great cities of the ancient world. Now, even with a population of over one hundred thousand the town is largely in ruins. The Iranian prophet Zoroaster was born there and for centuries it was the center of the Zoroastrian religion. Now, like much of Afghanistan it varies between poverty and desperation, with some rare spots of music, color, and the laughter of children too young to grasp the realities of the life that awaits them.

South and a little east of the city is the small town of Bitar, a village caught like an eagle's nest in the spiky crags of a mountain pass. Only one serpentine road led up into it and a worse one wound down. Camels manage it because they're stubborn, but even they slip once in a while. There are eighty-six people living in Bitar, most of them childless parents whose sons have died fighting either for the Taliban or against them; or who have gone off to work the poppy fields and never returned. A few of the youngest children walk seven miles to go to school. There are only thirty camels in the whole town. The chickens are all skinny. Only the goats look hardy, but they are a hardy breed used to very little. For plumbing the people have well water that smells of animal urine and old salt.

Eqbal was sixteen and his parents had not yet lost him to the poppy fields or the wars. Eqbal was destined to service Allah through service to his family. It was his *qawn* identity, he was sure, to be a farmer and in that way both preserve old ways and yet provide for the future. Despite war and strife, Eqbal believed in the future and to him it was bright with promise. Wars pass, but Afghanistan, graced by the love of Allah, endures.

Every morning Eqbal would rise with the day, clean himself, and then dress in loose robes and place a *kufi* cap on his head so that he would be ready to say his first prayers of the day, following the precise requirements of *salat*. First standing and then kneeling and finally prostrate in humility before the grace and majesty of God.

Though a young man of uncomplicated faith and one who had dedicated himself to the simple rigors of the farm life there in the dusty desert, Eqbal was not a simple-headed youth. As he tended his flocks or did chores around the farm he was often deep in complex thought, sometimes wrestling meanings out of the passages in the Qur'an; sometimes working to understand the complexities of delivering a breeched goat without losing either mother or kid. He did not think fast, but he always thought deep, and when he came to a conclusion he was generally correct.

Had he lived Eqbal would have very likely become the headman of the village, and certainly a man to be counted. But Eqbal did not live.

Eqbal would not live to see his seventeenth birthday, which was eight days away.

"Eqbal!" called his father, who was laid up with a broken ankle. "How is that goat coming along?"

The young man crouched over the gravid goat, who was crying out in pain as Eqbal worked his hands inside the birth canal to try and turn the kid. The other goats picked up her nervousness and the air was a constant barrage of snorts and baas. Eqbal's hands were red with blood and mucus and sweat shone brightly on his face as he worked, brow knitted, his clever fingers feeling along the tiny legs of the unborn goat.

"I think I have it, Father!" he called as his fingertips encountered the soft ropy length of the umbilical cord. "The cord is twisted around the hind legs."

He heard the scrape of a crutch as his father shuffled toward the open window. "Be gentle now, boy. Nature does not want you to hurry."

"Yes, Father," Eqbal said. It was one of his father's favorite sayings, and it matched the slow process of thought and action that made Eqbal his father's son. Patience was as valuable to a farmer as seeds and water.

He curled one finger around the cord and gently—very gently—pulled it down and over the kid's legs, then felt inside to make sure that there was no other obstruction. With great care he pushed on the kid to turn it inside the mother, who continued to bleat and cry.

"It's clear, Father."

"Then step back and let her do her own work," his father advised, and Eqbal glanced up to see his father's face in the window. He, too, was slick with sweat. The pain of his broken leg—shattered in a terrible fall on the cliffside—was etched into the lines on his face. His color was bad, but he was smiling at his son as Eqbal slowly withdrew his hand from the goat and sat back to watch.

The bleating of the goat changed in pitch as the baby began to slide along the birth canal. It was still painful, but now the goat did not sound desperate, merely tired and sore.

Within two minutes the wet, slime-slick little body slid out of her and flopped onto the straw-covered ground. Immediately the mother struggled to her feet and began licking at it, sponging clear her baby's nose and mouth and eyes.

"A female, Father," said Eqbal, turning again to look at his father. He froze, confused at the expression on his father's face. Instead of relief or joy, his face stared at him with a an expression that was a twisted mask of shock and horror.

"Father . . . ?"

Then Eqbal saw that his father was not looking at him . . . but behind him.

Eqbal whirled, thinking that it was one of the men from the Taliban group in the caves to the south; or a collector from the poppy farms come to take someone else off to work in the fields. Eqbal's hand was straying toward his shepherd's crook when he froze in place; and he could feel his own face contorting into lines of dread.

A man stood behind him.

No . . . not a man. A *thing*. It was dressed like a man but in strange clothes—light blue pants and a V-necked short-sleeved shirt. Eqbal had seen TV, he had been to the clinic in Balkh, he knew what hospital scrubs were; but he had never seen them out here. This man wore them now, and they were dirty and torn and stained to a dark shining purple wetness by blood. Blood was everywhere. On the man's clothes, his hands, his face. His mouth. His teeth . . .

Eqbal heard his father scream and then his whole world was torn in red madness and pain.

2.

EL MUJAHID SAT comfortably in the saddle of his four-wheeled ATV, leaning back against the thick cushions, heavy arms folded across his chest. Three hundred yards up the slope the screams were already starting to fade as the last of the villagers died. He did not smile, but he felt a strange joy at so much death. It had all worked so well, and so quickly. Far more quickly than the last time. Four subjects, eighty-six villagers. He checked his watch. Eighteen minutes.

His walkie-talkie crackled and he thumbed the switch and held it to his mouth.

"It is done," said his lieutenant, Abdul.

"Are you tracking all four subjects?"

"Yes, sir."

"And the villagers."

"Five have already revived," said Abdul, and the Fighter thought he detected a slight tremble in the man's voice. "Soon they will all be up."

The Fighter nodded to himself, content in the knowledge that *Seif al Din*, the holy Sword of the Faithful, was in motion now, and nothing could deny the will of God.

In the village the rattle of gunfire seasoned the air like music.

Chapter Twenty-Three
Baltimore, Maryland / Tuesday, June 30; 9:11 A.M.

I MADE IT through the rest of the night and all through the morning without federal agents appearing to kick down my door. Days of searching for the DMS, Javad, the two trucks, and Mr. Church had gone exactly nowhere. I now knew way too much useful information about spongiform encephalitis, including mad cow disease and fatal familial insomnia, but I had nowhere to go with it. Hoorah for me.

I took a hot shower, dressed in khakis and a Hawaiian shirt that was big enough to hide the .45 clipped to my belt; and then headed out to my appointment with Rudy. But first I had to stop at Starbucks and pick up his silly-ass drink.

"I'M SORRY, JOE," said Kittie, the receptionist, when I arrived at Rudy's office, "but Dr. Sanchez didn't come back from lunch. I called his cell and his home number but they go straight to his answering machine. He's not at the hospital, either."

"Okay, Kittie, tell you what . . . I'm going to go swing by his place and see what's what. I'll give you a call if I find anything. You call me if he gets in touch."

"Okay, Joe." She chewed her lip. "He's okay, though, isn't he?"

I gave her a smile. "Oh, sure . . . could be any number of things. He'll be fine."

Out in the hallway my smile evaporated. Sure, any number of things could explain this.

Like what?

On the elevator down I began to feel a little sick. Now was not a good time for Rudy to suddenly go missing. I thought about the message I'd probably sent to Church via my Internet searches and began to get a big, bad feeling in the pit of my stomach.

I stepped out of his building and looked around the parking lot. His car wasn't there, not that I'd expected it to be. So I walked over to mine, clicked the locks and opened the door.

And stopped dead.

I had my gun out before I even fully registered what I was seeing. I spun around and scanned the entire lot, pistol down by my leg. My heart was a jackhammer. There were over fifty cars and half a dozen people going toward them or walking toward the building. Everyone and everything looked normal. I turned back to the front seat. There, on the driver's side, was a package of Oreo cookies. The plastic had been neatly sliced and one cookie was missing. In its place was one of Rudy's business cards.

I holstered my gun, picked up the card and turned it over. On the back was a note. Nothing complicated, no threats. Just an address that I knew very well and one other word.

The address was the dockside warehouse where I'd killed Javad the first time.

The single word was: "Now."

Part Two
Heroes

Unhappy the land that is in need of heroes.

—BERTOLT BRECHT

Chapter Twenty-Four

IT TOOK TWENTY minutes to drive back to the docks and I had murder in my heart.

When I pulled up to the parking lot entrance I slowed to a stop and stared. The place had changed a hell of a lot in the last few days. There was a brand-new heavy-duty front gate that hadn't been there when we'd raided the place, and a chain-link fence topped with coils of razor wire. There was a second inner fence that looked innocuous except for the metal signs every forty feet that read: DANGER—HIGH VOLTAGE. I saw four armed security guards, all of them dressed alike in distinctly nonmilitary uniforms. Some kind of generic guard-for-hire rig, but that didn't fool me. They all had the trained military look. There are certain levels of training you can't disguise with polyester sports coats and khaki slacks.

I have to admit that I debated going in quick and dirty, knocking these guys on their asses and coming up on Church out of a shadow . . . but I didn't. It was a cute thought but not a good one and it probably wouldn't do Rudy or me any good. So I drove right up to the gate and let them take a good look at my face.

"May I see some identification, sir?"

I didn't make a fuss, just flashed them my badge and picture ID. The guard barely looked at it. He already knew who I was. He waved me through and told me to park by the staff entrance on the far side. I did as instructed, aware that they were watching me; and in my sideview mirror I caught a glimpse of a guard walking the perimeter of the roof. I strolled over to the door, taking only enough time to see other new features, like the tidy little security camera above the door and keycard lock. I didn't need a key, though, because the door opened before I could knock. Inside the entrance was one of the most striking women I'd ever seen. She had gold-flecked brown eyes, and an athletic figure that looked hard in the right places and soft in the right places. Her hair was cut short and she wore black fatigue pants and a gray T-shirt with no markings. Nothing like "DMS" stenciled on the front. No sign of rank, either, but her bearing was officer level. You could tell that right off. She had a Sig Sauer .9 in a shoulder rig and the grips looked worn from hard use.

"Thanks for coming, Detective Ledger," she said in a London accent. Her face showed signs of sleep deprivation and strain, and her eyes were red-rimmed as if she'd been crying. It could have been allergies, but under the circumstances I didn't think so. I wondered what had happened to upset her; was it the same thing that had caused Church to send his invitation? Whatever it was it didn't take a genius to get the idea that it wasn't good.

The woman didn't offer her name, give me a salute, or want to shake hands. She also didn't ask me to surrender my piece.

So I said, "Church."

"He's waiting for you."

She led the way down a series of short hallways to the conference room where my tac team had run into the trigger-happy terrorists. The same room where Javad had first attacked me during the raid. The big blue case was gone and the bullet-riddled conference table had been replaced with some generic government desks and computer workstations. A flat-panel TV screen filled a good portion of one wall. Décor change notwithstanding, the room gave me a serious case of the creeps. I could still feel the bruise on my forearm where Javad had bitten me— and there but for the grace of Kevlar.

The woman nodded toward a wheeled office chair in one corner. "Please have a seat. Mr. Church will be with you in—"

"Who are you?" I interrupted.

She gave me a three-count before she said, "Major Grace Courtland."

"Major?" I asked. "SAS?"

That got the tiniest flicker, a microsecond's widening of her eyes, but she recovered fast. "Make yourself comfortable, Detective Ledger," she said and left.

I turned in a slow circle and took in the room, looked for and found the three microcameras. They looked expensive and of a kind I hadn't seen before. I'd bet a year's pay that Church was sitting in another room watching me. I was tempted to scratch my balls. This whole thing was bringing out the screw-you fifteen-year-old in me, and I had to watch that. Give in to any kind of pettiness and you lose your edge real damn fast.

So instead I strolled the room and learned what I could, even with Cookie Monster watching. There was a second and much heavier door at the far end of the room that looked brand-new—I remembered it being a regular office door before—and when I inspected it I could see the recent carpentry and smell the fresh paint. I tapped it. Wood veneer over steel, and it was dollars to doughnuts that the wall had been reinforced, too.

I heard the door behind me open and I turned as Mr. Church entered with the British woman behind him. He was dressed in a charcoal suit, polished shoes, and the same tinted glasses. He made no comment about my investigation of the room, he just pulled up a chair and sat. Major Courtland remained standing, her face a study in disapproval.

I took a step toward him. "Where the fuck is Dr. Sanchez?"

He brushed lint from his tie. If he was threatened by me in any way he did a workmanlike job of not showing it. Courtland shifted to a flanking position with her hands folded across her stomach, perfectly positioned to make a fast grab for her pistol.

"Do you know why you're here, Mr. Ledger?"

"I can make a few guesses," I said, "but you can go stick them up your ass. Where is Rudy Sanchez?"

Church's mouth twitched in what I think was an attempt not to smile. He said, "Grace?"

Courtland walked over to the wall with the TV screen and hit a button. A picture popped on at once and it showed an office with a desk and a chair. A man sat on the chair with his hands cuffed behind him and a blindfold around his eyes. Rudy. A second man stood behind him. He held a pistol barrel against the back of my friend's head.

Rage was a howling thing in my head and my heart was throbbing in my throat like it was trying to escape. It took everything I had to stand there and hold my tongue.

After a moment Church said, "Tell me why I shouldn't have the sergeant put two in the back of Dr. Sanchez's head."

I forced myself to turn away from the screen. "He dies you die," I said.

"Yawn," he said. "Try again."

"What good would it do you or your organization to kill him? He's an innocent, he's a civilian."

"He stopped being a civilian when you told him about the DMS and about our patient zero. You put that gun to his head, Mr. Ledger."

"That's a crock of shit and you know it. Nine-eleven may have wrinkled the Constitution but it didn't run it through a shredder."

Church spread his hands. "I repeat my question. Tell me why I shouldn't have Sergeant Dietrich shoot Dr. Sanchez. We're a secret organization and we're playing for the highest possible stakes. Nothing, not even the Bill of Rights, matters more than what we're doing and that is in no way an exaggeration."

I said nothing.

"Mr. Ledger, if terrorists had a truck filled with suitcase nukes and one of them went off in each of twenty cities around the country it would do less damage to America as a whole, and to its people, than if another carrier like Javad got out into the population. If a plague of this kind starts we could not stop it. The infection rate and aggression factor would make it uncontrollable within minutes." He chewed his gum for a minute and then repeated that. "Minutes."

I held my tongue.

"If we cannot count on your complete loyalty and complete cooperation, you are worthless to us. You would be useless to *me*." Even behind his tinted glasses I could feel the impact of his stare.

"What is it you want?"

"Time is very short, so this is the deal, Mr. Ledger: we have a need to put a new tactical team into operation asap. Ordinary military and even our standard special forces units are not appropriate for this, for reasons we can discuss later. Major Courtland already has one team at operational readiness; our other team is on the West Coast involved in something of nearly equal importance. One local team isn't enough. I need a third team. I need it to be tight and I need it yesterday. I also need someone to lead that team into the field. I've narrowed the list of possibles down to six candidates. Five others and you."

"Hooray for me. What does this have to do with Rudy Sanchez?"

"I want you to give me your word that you will join us and become *one* of us. Not some reckless outsider. You are either DMS or you're not."

"Or what, you'll kill Rudy?"

Church jerked his head toward Courtland. She punched a button on the wall. "Gus? Uncuff Dr. Sanchez. Bring him a sandwich and keep him company." She turned off the monitor.

I turned back to Church. "Why all the frigging drama?"

"To make a point. If I'd had more time to be dramatic I'd have had your father, your brother and his wife, your nephew, and even your cat in here."

"I'm a short step away from popping a cap in you," I said.

He leaned close. "I don't *care*. Dr. Sanchez is here because you made a breach of security. How we'll handle that is another matter. Right now we need to stop playing ping-pong here and get to the point."

"Then damn well *get* to it."

"I told you what I need."

"A team leader?"

He nodded. "I need to start training the new team today because if we're really lucky, Mr. Ledger, that team may have to go into the field within days, maybe within hours. I don't have time to coax you or stroke your ego or appeal to your patriotism."

"So . . . what? You wanted to make me afraid?"

"An apocalypse is an abstract and unreal concept. The sudden loss of everyone you love and care about is not. Time is not our friend."

"You're saying that there are more of these walker things, aren't you?"

"Yes." Even though I expected that answer it was like a punch in the mouth. He said, "We haven't stopped this thing yet, Mr. Ledger. At best we slowed it down by a few days."

"You should have figured that out before. It's the logical—"

"We did figure it out, but we had nowhere to go with the supposition. Our code breakers have been working round the clock to determine the location of any cells connected to the one you took down. We know where one is because of the truck the task force tailed. We have not risked hitting that site because there may be more sites and we don't want to panic these people. Play it wrong and they could go dark and we'd lose the trail, or they could release the plague right away. We've recovered enough information to make us reasonably sure they are sticking to a prearranged deadline, so we don't want to hurry that along. Because we did not intercept that truck, and did not raid the place to which it went, we're trying to make them believe they've given us the slip. The raid, after all, was half a day after the truck left."

"Trucks," I corrected. "There were two. We tailed one and lost one."

"Too bloody right you did," muttered Courtland, and I gave her a hard look to which she merely cocked a challenging eyebrow.

"So why the urgency to train a hit team if you're not about to make a hit?"

"I didn't say that. It's my intention to have a team covertly infiltrate the one facility we have under surveillance."

"Infiltrate to what end? To locate other cells or to find more walkers?"

"Either will do."

I swallowed a dry throat. "What makes you think that the other hypothetical cells will still be in place? Once this cell here at this warehouse went dark the others would probably have followed a protocol of some kind—"

"Very likely," Major Courtland cut in, "but we have to go forward with what leads we have. On the upside, however, the other facility shows no sign of activity, no rats fleeing, so maybe they think they're clear. In the absence of more intelligence a quiet infiltration is our safest option."

I frowned. "And with all the military special ops and guys like SWAT and HRT you want to form a new team? There are guys out there with years more experience than me. Does the name 'Delta Force' ring any bells with you people?"

"It's more complicated than that," Church said. He gestured toward the far door, the one with the heavy scanner. "The other potential team leaders are in the adjoining room. Each of them is tough, experienced, and aware of the threat. All of them are active military—two Rangers, one Navy, one Marine Force Recon, and yes, even one from Delta Force. All of them have more combat and tactical experience than you do, though admittedly you bring other qualities to the game. You're all unique in one way or another but we don't have time to discuss that at the moment. I need to get the team leader status sorted out right now."

"What do you want us to do? Play rock-paper-scissors to see who gets the job?"

"Grace?" he said, and she went over to the heavy-duty door and unlocked it.

"If you'll come this way, Detective."

I stood up slowly. "This is a lot of James Bond bullshit to decide a human resources issue isn't it?"

Church remained seated. He nodded his head toward the doorway, so I walked over and peered inside. Five guys in civilian clothes: three sitting and two standing. All of them looked tough and all of them looked either confused or pissed off. They seemed frozen in an agitated tableau as if the door opening had interrupted them in the middle of a heated debate.

I turned back to Church. "You still haven't told me how you want us to sort this out."

He made that face again that might have been a smile. I've seen the big hunting cats make that same kind of face. "Think outside the box, Mr. Ledger."

"Okay," I said, "but you have to pick up the tab afterward."

He gave me a single short nod.

I stepped into the room. All of the men were looking me up and down, a couple of them giving me evil stares that would have scared the paint off a tank. Courtland left and pulled the door closed behind her. I heard the heavy lock engage.

Chapter Twenty-Five
Gault / The Hotel Ishtar, Baghdad / Five days ago

GAULT WAS ON the road, moving in a roundabout way from Amirah's bunker in the Helmand Province of Afghanistan across the border to Iran, where he changed identities three times in fourteen hours and then entered a safe house run by a client of a client, where he ate, made some calls, and then changed identities again—back to Sebastian Gault. Gault was welcome in Iran and most other countries because his company was one of the world's top suppliers of pharmaceuticals for humanitarian aid. He traveled with three kindhearted but clueless members of the World Health Organization as they visited remote villages in western Iran where a TB outbreak had been reported. Gault did a few stand-ups for a Swiss news service about the need for swift action in stemming the spread of the new strain of TB, and then thanked the Iranian government for allowing free passage for the WHO doctors. When he crossed the border into Iraq he was met by a military escort of British soldiers who got him safely all the way to Baghdad.

Toys met him in the lobby and they shook hands.

"I trust you had a comfortable trip," said his personal assistant, taking Gault's bag and leading him to the elevator. As they crossed the lobby they were both aware that everyone was looking at them. Toys was a not tall man but he had tall energy. He was slender, fit, and had impeccable posture; and he always managed to look cool and well groomed no matter where they were. Gault had seen him ankle deep in the mosquito swamps of Kenya looking as collected as if he were at a cocktail party at Cannes. But to anyone watching it was immediately clear which of them was the alpha. Gault was taller, more physically imposing, with swept-back hair and piercing dark eyes. He was ruggedly handsome, where Toys was delicately so. By himself Toys could command almost any room, but his light dimmed considerably in Gault's presence. Gault knew this; and so did Toys. They were both comfortable with the arrangement.

They chitchatted on the lift, talking of relatively unimportant Gen2000 matters. Once they were in the suite of rooms they shared at the Hotel Ishtar Toys swept the place with the newest generation of Interceptor surveillance sensors and everything came up clean. Even so, they avoided any sensitive topics for an hour, at which point Toys swept it again, knowing that surveillance teams often deactivate active listening in the first few minutes after someone checks in to a hotel knowing that a smart spy would sweep the room. They typically reactivate their bugs in forty minutes, so he gave it a full hour. It still came up clean.

Toys busied himself with unpacking while Gault took a hot bath. Later, with Gault snugged into a bathrobe and ensconced in a cushy armchair, a tall gin and tonic quietly melting on a nearby table, Toys settled down onto a more decorative faux Louis XIV chair, legs crossed, rolling a neat whiskey between his palms.

"You got a text message while you were in the bath," Toys said primly. "Just one word: 'Clean.' That's from El Musclehead?"

Gault smiled and nodded. "His team field-tested an entirely new generation of the *Seif al Din* today. That was the code to let me know the operation was successful." He gave Toys the details.

"That's disgusting," Toys said, but if he had any real emotional re-action to the slaughter not one drop of it registered on his face.

"It's a solid step forward," Gault reminded him.

With a waspish sniff Toys said, "So, tell me about the happy couple."

Gault told him everything, including his observations of the telltale clues in Amirah's voice and facial expression. Toys listened without in-terruption, but when Gault was done he shook his head. "I think she's been stuck too long in that bunker with all her toys, making monsters. She's probably halfway to being a monster herself by now. Are you sure she shares your goals?"

Gault shrugged. There was a time, early in their affair, when he thought that he and Amirah would become some kind of king and queen of the economic world. His plan would clearly work, was working al-ready, and he estimated that at the very least his various companies would net something like twenty to thirty billion. Best-case scenario hovered deliciously around the one hundred billion mark. He could conceivably become the richest man on earth. But so much of that hinged on Amirah staying within the confines of the operation.

When it was clear Gault was not going to answer Toys tossed back the rest of his drink and got up to make a fresh one. The phone rang and Toys answered.

"I've been trying to reach your boss all day," snapped the American. "Is the line clear?"

"What do you think?" Toys asked. "Hold on . . . he's right here." He handed the phone across to Gault.

"What can I do for you?" Gault said. Toys leaned in close to eaves-drop.

"This morning the heads of all of the special operations divisions were given a briefing by the head of this new Geek Squad."

"Ah! So . . . who's running it?"

"That's the weird part. We received certain documents, ostensibly from the head of this new branch, but on several of them the name of the person in charge was different. Some identified him as Mr. Elder, Mr. St. John, Mr. Deacon, and Mr. Church. Now, whether these refer to the same man or for section heads is unknown, but I got the impression they were code names for one guy—the one who was giving us our briefing. He was introduced to us as Mr. Pope. I have some careful feelers out there and I should be able to lock it down."

"That fits with what Toys has been able to dig up," Gault said. "What interests me is whether you've been able to get a man inside, as I asked."

"Yeah," said the American. "I have."

Chapter Twenty-Six
Baltimore, Maryland / Tuesday, June 30; 2:42 P.M.

I STOOD BY the door and looked them over. My nerves were still jangling from seeing that gun against Rudy's head and I don't know whether I believed Church would have killed him or not. I felt like there was this gigantic Big Ben–sized clock ticking right over my head.

The room was mostly bare except for a few folding chairs and a card table on which was an open case of bottled water, a tray of sandwich meats and cheeses, and an opened loaf of white bread. Apparently the DMS budget didn't extend to decent catering.

The guy closest to me, standing to my left, was maybe six feet but he must have been two-forty and all of it was in his chest and shoulders; his face had a vaguely simian cast to it. Next to Apeman was a taller, leaner guy with a beaky nose and a long scar that ran from his hairline through his right eyebrow and halfway down his cheek. Opposite Scarface was a black guy who looked like every army top sergeant you ever saw: buzz cut, a boxer's broken nose, and a lantern jaw. Behind Sergeant Rock was a red-haired kid in his early twenties who had a jovial face. In fact he was the only guy smiling in the room. To the Joker's right was a real moose of a guy, easily six six, with ropy muscles and heavily scarred hands. Jolly Green Giant was the first to speak.

"Looks like we got another candidate."

I walked into the center of the group.

Scarface grunted. "Make yourself comfortable. We've been in here for almost three hours trying to sort out which one of us should head this team."

"Really," I said and kicked him in the balls.

He let out a thin whistling shriek of pain that I ignored as I grabbed the shoulder of his windbreaker and jerked him hard and fast so that he collided with Apeman and they both went down.

I spun off that and stomped down on the Joker's foot and then pivoted to bring the same foot up again, heel first into his nuts. He didn't scream, but he hissed real loud; and I nailed Sergeant Rock with a palm-shot to the chest that sent him sprawling onto the food table, which collapsed under him.

That left Jolly Green Giant standing and he gaped at me in shock for maybe a half second before he started to swing; but that was a half second too long, and I darted forward and drove the extended secondary index-finger knuckle of my right hand into his left sinus, right next to his nose, giving it a fast counterclockwise twist on impact. He went back like he'd taken a .45 round in the face.

I pivoted again to see Apeman pushing his way out from under Scarface but he was only halfway to his feet and I swept his supporting leg out from under him and he fell hard on his tailbone, almost—but not quite—catching himself by planting his hand flat on the ground. I stamped on his outstretched fingers and then chop-kicked him in the chest before spinning off to face Sergeant Rock—who had come up off the collapsed card table with an impressive display of rubbery agility.

The other four guys were down and it was just him and me.

He held his hands up and I knew that I wouldn't be able to sucker him again, but then he smiled and turned his karate guard into a palms-out. Not a surrender so much as an acknowledgment of set and match.

I gave him a nod and stepped back, and edged away from the other four. Two of them were down for the count. Jolly Green Giant was sitting in the corner holding his face; if he had any kind of sinus issues that punch I gave him would likely become a migraine. Scarface was lying on the floor in a fetal position, hands cupped around his balls, groaning. The Joker was getting to his feet, but he had no fight left in him. Apeman was sitting against a wall trying to suck in a breath.

I heard the door click open and I stepped to one side as I turned, outside of everyone's reach. Church and Courtland came in. He was smiling, she wasn't.

"Gentlemen," he said quietly, "I want you to meet Joe Ledger, the DMS's new team leader. Any questions?"

Chapter **Twenty-Seven**
Baltimore, Maryland / Tuesday, June 30; 2:43 P.M.

"HOW LONG DID this take, Grace?" Church asked.

"Four-point-six seconds." It sounded like the words were pulled out of her with pliers. "Or eight-point-seven if you count from close of door."

The other candidates stared at Church and at me and one of them—Apeman—looked like he was going to say something, but he caught some look from Church and held his tongue and glared. There was not a whole lot of love in the room.

"Get up," Church said to them. His voice wasn't bitter or harsh, merely quiet. Sometimes quiet is worse, and I watched the faces of each man as they climbed to their feet. Jolly Green Giant and Sergeant Rock showed no trace of animosity on their faces, and the latter even looked amused. Joker's face was cautious, guarded. Scarface looked equal parts deeply embarrassed and angry. Apeman stared hot death at me as he stood up; he rubbed his chest and gave me a sniper's squint.

My hands were shaking, but adrenaline will do that. Plus the image of Rudy with a gun to his head wouldn't leave my mind.

"I want to see Rudy," I said. "Now."

Church shook his head "No. There are other things you need to do first."

"He'd better be okay—"

He smiled. "Dr. Sanchez is currently eating his way through an entire catering platter and probably psychoanalyzing Sergeant Dietrich's rather complicated childhood. He's fine and he can wait."

No one said anything. "Okay," I said, surprised at how calm my voice sounded. "So now what do we do?"

"Major Courtland will bring you up to speed. The entire staff will meet in the main hall in thirty minutes." He paused and then held out his hand. "Welcome aboard, Mr. Ledger."

"I don't mean to offend you two," I said, taking his hand, "but you're both total assholes." I gave his hand my best squeeze and damn if the son of a bitch didn't match me pound for pound.

"I'll cry about that later," Church said.

We let go of each other and I folded my arms. "If I'm going to be team leader, where's the actual team?"

"You just kicked the effing hell out of them," Courtland said.

I turned and looked at the five men. *Oh crap.*

I've worked with street thugs, murderers, and the worst kind of lowlifes for years and have knocked in their heads, shot them, Tasered them, and sent them to prison for life, but none of them ever gave me the kinds of looks I was getting from my "team." If they'd had a tree limb and a rope I'd be swinging in the wind.

I thought I heard Church give a quiet chuckle as he turned and left.

Maybe this was the moment where I was supposed to make some kind of speech, but before I could say anything Courtland beat me to it.

"Get cleaned up," she snapped. "Ledger . . . come with me." She started for the door.

I started to follow her but sensed movement and turned to see Apeman coming toward me. His face was purple with rage, hands balled into white-knuckled fists.

"You suckered me, asshole, and first chance I get I'm going to wipe the floor up with you."

"No," I said, "you're not." And I punched him in the throat.

I stepped out of the way as he fell.

The room was dead silent and I deliberately turned my back on the other four as I said to Courtland, "I hope to hell you have a medic here, 'cause he's going to need one."

Chapter **Twenty-Eight**
Sebastian Gault / The Hotel Ishtar, Baghdad / Five days ago

"LINE?"

"Clear," said the Fighter.

"What have you to report, my friend?" Gault was chin deep in a tub of soapy water, the Goldberg Variations playing quietly on the CD player. The young woman in the other room was asleep—knowing this call was coming in, Toys had slipped something into her drink before escorting her to Gault's room. She'd sleep for four more hours and wake up without feeling any adverse effects. It was useful being a chemist and having an assistant without a conscience.

El Mujahid said, "Everything in place."

"Jolly good. Once you complete the first stage my lads in the Red Cross will make sure the correct transfers take place. With any luck you should be on a hospital ship heading out of the Gulf by midnight."

"Sebastian . . . ?" said El Mujahid.

"Yes?"

"I'm putting a lot of trust in you. I expect you to hold up your end of things."

"My hand to Allah," Gault said as he used his toes to turn on the hot water tap, "you can certainly trust me. Everything will go smoothly."

There was a short silence at the other end of the line, and then the Fighter said, "Tell my wife I love her."

Gault smiled up at the ceiling. "Of course I will, my old friend. Go with God."

He clicked off and tossed the phone onto the closed lid of the toilet. He was laughing when he did it.

Chapter Twenty-Nine

AFTER MAJOR COURTLAND called in the medical team she joined me in the hallway and I could tell she was reevaluating me. Her eyes roved over my face like a scanner and I could almost hear the relays click in her head. Across the hall was a men's room and I started toward it but she stopped me with a touch on my arm.

"Ledger . . . what made you think Mr. Church wanted you to do that?"

I shrugged. "He said time was short."

"That's not the same thing as telling you to go in there and start kicking everyone's ass."

"You have a problem with it?"

She smiled again, a nice smile. It transformed her from a cobra to something a hell of a lot more appealing: an actual human being. "Not at all. As much as I hate to say it I'm rather impressed."

" 'Hate to say it'?" I echoed.

"You are a very hard person to like, Mr. Ledger."

"Call me Joe. And no, I'm not. Lots of people like me."

She didn't comment on that. "Let me put it another way . . . you're a very hard man to trust. Especially in an operation of this kind."

"Grace—may I call you Grace?"

"You may call me Major Courtland."

"Okay, Major Courtland," I said, "it isn't my goal in life to get you to trust me. You jokers pulled me into this. I didn't submit a résumé. I'm *not* military. So if you have issues about trust or anything else up to and including *liking* me, then, seriously, please go and screw yourself. Major."

She blinked once.

"I did not and *do not* want my life tied up in cloak-and-dagger bullshit, dead guys, or pissing contests with either the testosterone crowd in there or some prissy-assed Earl Grey–drinking, scone-munching *major* who isn't even my freaking boss. I don't know you and I don't give a rat's ass if you trust me."

"Mr. Ledger—"

"I have to take a piss." I headed down the hall to the bathroom.

I USED THE toilet and then washed my face first with hot water and then cold, dabbed it dry with a fistful of paper towels, and then leaned on the edge of the sink, staring at my face in the mirror. My skin was flushed and my eyes had the jumpy look you usually see in junkies. My hair stuck out in all directions.

"Well," I said to my reflection, "aren't you a picture?"

I didn't have a comb so I used wet fingers to plaster down my hair, and as I stood there the full weight and enormity of what was going on hit me like a freight train. I bowed over the sink, tasting bile, ready to throw up . . . but my trembling stomach held. I raised my head again and looked into my eyes and saw fear in there, the naked realization of what all this meant.

There were more of *them* out there. More walkers. And I was being asked to step up and be . . . what? Some kind of Captain Heroism who would lead the boys in the Red, White, and Blue to victory? What was I getting myself into? This wasn't task force duty, this wasn't even SWAT-team level. I'd never even smelled anything this big before and now I was expected to train and lead a black ops team? How frigging insane was this? Why were they asking me? I'm just a cop. Where are the guys who actually *do* this for a living? How come none of them were here? Where's James Bond and Jack Bauer? Why me, of all people?

My reflection stared back, looking dazed and a little stupid.

Working the task force had not prepared me for this. After eighteen months of that—and the years since the World Trade Center—I'd come to share the more or less common view that the terrorists had fired their worst shots and were now hiding in caves and reevaluating the wisdom of having overplayed their hand. Now Church tells me that they hold the key to a global pandemic.

By raising the actual dead?

God Almighty. Flying planes into buildings is bad enough. Chemical weapons, anthrax, nerve gas, suicide bombers . . . that stuff has collectively been the definition of terrorism to the global consciousness for years, and that's been *more* than bad enough. This was so much worse I didn't know if I could put it into any reasonable perspective. If they were trying to spread Ebola it wouldn't be this bad because Ebola doesn't chase and try to bite you. Whoever was behind this was one sick son of a bitch. Smart, sure, but sick. This went beyond religious fundamentalism or political extremism. Right at that moment I was sure we were looking at something born out of a mind that was truly and genuinely evil.

I don't think I clearly understood Church until that moment. If I were in his place, looking into that same future, how would I handle it? How ruthless would I be? How ruthless *could* I be?

"I think you already answered that question, boyo," I murmured, thinking about the five men in that room.

Church may act like a Vulcan but he had to be feeling all this stuff, too. If so, then the strain of holding back all of his emotions, all of his humanity, must be terrible. If I were going to work for him, then I'd have to look for signs of that pressure, look for cracks. Not only in me, but in him, too. On the other hand Church could be a monster himself . . . just one on our side. There were guys like that. Hell, after World War II our own government hired a bunch of Nazi scientists. Better the devil you know. More to the point, there was the comment

FDR supposedly made about Somoza. Something like, "He's a son of a bitch, but he's *our* son of a bitch."

Great. I'm going to work for a monster in order to fight other monsters. So what did that make me?

The bathroom floor seemed to tilt a bit as I headed for the door.

Chapter **Thirty**

El Mujahid / Near Najaf, Iraq / Five days ago

"THEY'RE COMING," SAID Abdul, El Mujahid's lieutenant. "Two British Apache attack helicopters. Four minutes."

"Excellent," the Fighter murmured. He took one last look around and then handed a bundle of clothes to Abdul. "There is nothing of value here. Burn them."

The half-track sat askew in the middle of an intersection of two lonely roads, thirty-six kilometers from Najaf. Smoke still curled up from beneath the chassis. Additional smoke rose from a dozen corpses. There was blood everywhere, muted by sand to the color of dusty roses. Two cars were in flames—an old Ford Falcon and a Chinese Ben Ben—both with registration numbers that would tie them to Jihadist sympathizers. The entire picture was perfect: a battle fought to a tragic victory. A half-track crippled by a roadside bomb; a few British soldiers, outnumbered by insurgents, taking heavy casualties as they bravely fought through an ambush. All of the hostiles dead. Of the seven Brits in the truck, four were dead—badly mangled and burned—and three clung to life.

"Go, go, go," whispered El Mujahid, and his lieutenant melted away and slipped down into a rat hole hidden by a spring trapdoor covered with coarse dry bushes. In the stillness nothing moved, and the only sound apart from the *whup-whup-whup* of the helo rotors were the piteous moans of the wounded.

"Allah akbar!" said El Mujahid, and then used his thumb to test the edge of the piece of jagged metal debris he had selected. He laced the tip of the metal against his forehead, right at the hairline; he drew a breath, held it, and then exhaled sharply as he ripped the metal through his skin, tearing down from upper left to lower right, through his eyebrow, across the bridge of his nose, along his cheek all the way to his jawline. Pain exploded in his face and blood surged from the cut. He could feel tears in his eyes and he had to bite down against the whitehot agony of the wound. It was worse—far worse—than he expected and it nearly tore the cry from his throat.

The helicopters were nearly overhead. With a gasp he flung the metal from him and slumped back into the wreckage, deliberately snorting blood out of his nose and mouth, making sure that the droplets touched everything. By the time the first helicopter landed he was perfectly placed, his torn face transformed into a mask of bright blood, his clothing soaked. His heart raced and he could feel blood flow from the wound with each pulse beat.

He closed his eyes and as he heard the first footfalls as the soldiers leaped from the helicopter he raised one gory hand and reached toward them, and now he let out the scream. It was a wet gargling cry, inarticulate and savagely hurt.

"Here!" he heard a voice yell, and then the half-track rocked as men clambered inside. There were hands on him, touching him, probing him, feeling for his pulse.

"This one's alive. Get the medics!"

Fingers scrabbled around his throat, feeling for the little dogtag chain, pulling it free. "Sergeant Henderson," a voice said, reading the name. "One hundred third armored."

"Clear the way, let me get to him," said a different voice; and then there was a compress against his face as the medics worked to save the lives of the British wounded.

It took every ounce of strength that the Fighter possessed not to smile.

Chapter **Thirty-One**

WE WERE IN Courtland's office, just the two of us. Everything was still not unpacked and I had to sit on a plastic folding chair. We were both drinking bottled spring water. One wall of the office was a big picture window that looked out onto the harbor. The afternoon sunshine made everything look peaceful, but the lie buried within the illusion was appalling. I turned away from the window and looked at Courtland.

"I'd prefer to have given you the complete version of this, but as Mr. Church pointed out, we don't have the time, so the learning curve will be more of a straight line." She sat back and crossed her legs. Even in the fatigue pants I could tell she had nice legs. Except for her personality, which so far was somewhere between a cranky alligator and a defensive moray eel, most things about her were nice. I even liked her husky voice and thick British accent. I just didn't particularly like *her*.

"Fire away," I said.

"After 9/11 your government formed Homeland Security and Great Britain created a similar and rather more secret organization, code name of Barrier. You won't have heard of it. MI5 and MI6 get most of the press, which is as it should be. Barrier was given a lot of power and freedom of action and was therefore able to stop several major threats against my country that would have been, to us, as devastating as the World Trade Center attack was on you. As I was involved in some of those operations I was loaned out to your government when the DMS was formed."

"Did you help create the DMS?"

"No," she said, "that was Mr. Church's doing, but there were some similarities in both structure and agenda between the DMS and Barrier, and the lines of communication, at least where antiterrorism is concerned, are wide open between the White House and Whitehall. As you probably know there are many such task forces around the country, and all of their intel passes in one way or another through DMS hands. Church is wired in everywhere. When your wiretap flagged the name El Mujahid it rang a bell at the DMS and Church ordered an immediate infiltration of the task force. By the time the team was formed we had three agents in place."

"Really? Then you *do* have a working field team?"

"Did," she said as a shadow passed across her face. "But we'll get to that. First I need to tell you about the cell your task force took down. After the raid our computer specialists were able to salvage several laptops and we've been systematically decrypting their coded records. We haven't learned as much as we'd like but we are making some headway. So far we've decoded what amounts to shipping manifests for weapons, medical supplies, research equipment, and even human cargo."

"You mean agents they've smuggled in?"

She shook her head. "No . . . actual human cargo. Like Javad. Brought into this country in temperature-controlled containers like the one you found here."

"How many others?"

"We've only found references to three, including Javad."

"Shit," I said.

"The import records indicate that the other walkers were brought into the country less than twenty-four hours before your task force raided the place. The other two must have been shipped out late the previous day; and there's a high probability they were in those two lorries."

"That's why you took all of the files from the task force, isn't it? You wanted the surveillance logs for traffic in and out of this place and you want all of it off the record."

Again she gave me that appraising look, as if her idiot nephew had learned to tie his own shoelaces. "Yes," she admitted.

"So where did the other containers go?"

It took her a few seconds to decide whether to tell me.

"Look, Major," I said, "either you level with me on everything or we're done here. I don't know why you have a bug up your ass about me, and I frankly don't care, but you are wasting my time hemming and hawing." I started to get to my feet but she waved me back down.

"All right, all right," she snapped, "sit down, dammit." She opened a folder, removed a sheet of paper and slapped it down on the desk. "This is the log for the night before the raid. Two lorries left the warehouse lot. One eight minutes after midnight, the other at oh-three-thirty. Task force agents were assigned to follow both and report their destinations. One was tracked to a crab-processing plant near Crisfield, Maryland. The other was 'lost' in traffic." She stabbed an entry with a forefinger. "You were tailing the one that got lost in traffic."

I plucked the paper off the desk, glanced at it, and then tossed it down. "Good God, Major, if this is any indication of the precision of your intel then I'm going to grab my loved ones and make a run for the hills."

"You're denying that you were assigned to the tail?"

"No, I was definitely assigned to tail the truck, Major, but I didn't *do* that tail. Four blocks into the follow I was pulled and replaced by another officer. My lieutenant called on the task force's secure channel and had me report back to the surveillance van because there was more cell phone chatter and I was the only guy on shift who understands Farsi. I spent twenty minutes listening to one of the hostiles talk to an Iraqi woman living in Philadelphia. Mostly they talked about blow jobs and how much he wished she'd give him one. Really cutting-edge espionage stuff. You can believe me when I tell you, sister, that when I tail someone I don't lose them."

She leaned back in her chair and we stared at each other like a pair of gunslingers for maybe ten, fifteen seconds. There were a lot of ways she could have handled her response, and what she said would probably set the tone for whatever professional relationship we were going to have. "Bloody hell," she said with a sigh. "Will you accept my apology?"

"Will you stop trying to frighten me to death with your icy glare?"

Her smile was tentative at first, still caught on some of the thorns of her earlier misconceptions, but then it blossomed full and radiant. She stood up and reached across the desk. "Truce," she said.

I stood and took her hand, which was small, warm, and strong. "We have enough enemies, Major, it's better if we're at each other's backs rather than each other's throats."

She gave my hand a little squeeze, then let it go and sat back down. "That's very gracious of you." She cleared her throat. "Since we, um, lost that one lorry we have an investigative operation going to locate it. That's a major priority."

I said, "What do we know of the cell itself?"

"Bits and pieces. We know that they're using a higher level of technology than we've seen before from the terrorist community; and it's just this sort of thing that justifies the existence of the DMS. Understand, the DMS was proposed at the same time as Homeland but was rejected as being too expensive and unnecessary; the belief at that time being that terrorists may be capable of hijacking planes but were incapable of constructing advanced bioweapons." She sounded disgusted. "It's racist thinking, of course. To a very great degree the moguls in London and Washington still think that everyone in the Middle East is undereducated and out of touch with the twenty-first century."

"Which is bullshit," I said.

"Which is bullshit," she agreed. "What changed their thinking was something called MindReader, which is a piece of software that Mr. Church either procured or invented. I don't know which and he won't tell me. Point is that MindReader is a cascading analysis package that no other agency has, not even Barrier or Homeland. It looks for patterns through covert links to all intelligence-gathering databases. The tricky part is taking into account different operating systems, different languages—both computer and human—different cultures, time zones, currency rates, units of measure, routes of transport, and so on. MindReader cuts through all of that. It's also what we're using to try and decrypt the damaged files."

"Nice toy."

"Indeed. We began to see indications of the acquisition of materials, equipment, and personnel suggesting the creation of a bioweapons laboratory of considerable sophistication. A lab capable of both creating and weaponizing a biological agent."

"I thought those materials were monitored? How'd they swing all that?"

She gave me a calculating look. "How would you have done it?"

"What country are we talking?"

"Terrorism is an ideology not a nationality. Let's say you're a small group living under cover in a Middle Eastern country, not necessarily with the blessing of your resident state. Your group is composed of separatists from a number of the more extreme factions."

I thought about it. "Okay . . . first I'd have to know that most of what I would need for a conventional bioweapon would be on that list of monitored items. I can't go to the corner drugstore and buy a vial of anthrax; I'd need to buy my materials in small quantities through several layers of middlemen so that no red flags go up. That takes time and it's expensive. Secrecy has to be bought. I'd buy some stuff in one country, other stuff elsewhere, spreading it around. I'd buy used stuff if I could, or buy parts piecemeal and assemble them—especially hardware. I'd have them shipped to different ports, places where the watchdogs aren't as alert, and then go through some dummy corporations to reship them and reship them again. So, this would take both time and money."

She gave me an approving smile. "Keep going."

"I'd need lab space, testing facilities, a production floor . . . preferably someplace where I could dig in. Stuff like this isn't pick up and carry, so I don't want to work on the run. I need a nest. Once I'm set and I've spent whatever time it takes to make my weapon I'd have to sort out the problem of getting my weapon from my lab to the intended target. And if we're doing advanced medical stuff like plagues and new kinds of parasites, like the crap we're dealing with here, then that's harder because you need access to supercomputers, ultrasterile lab conditions, and a lot of medical equipment."

"Spot on," Courtland said. "Mr. Church would probably give you a biscuit for that assessment. MindReader caught a whiff of biological research equipment being bought, as you say, piecemeal. Very carefully, you understand, and in small quantities to avoid ringing the kinds of alarms that have in fact been rung. It took a while for any of this to be noticed because it wasn't precisely the sort of thing we were expecting to find, and without MindReader we would never have spotted it at all. These materials were being ordered by firms located within nations that had been hit by crop blight, livestock disease, or similar natural calamity. Anyone who didn't have a suspicious mind would think that these countries were scrambling to find cures for the diseases that were creating famine and starvation affecting their own people."

"Like mad cow disease," I suggested.

"Top marks. Except for India and a handful of others, virtually every nation on earth depends on beef production and that disease was responsible for millions of cattle deaths and billions of pounds of economic loss. It would be natural for such countries to do anything they could to find a cure."

"Seems to me that you guys should have hit that plant already." I saw her eyes shift away for a moment. "If the DMS has a combat team then they should have been deployed. You keep dodging my questions about what happened to the rest of your team, Major."

"They died, Mr. Ledger." It was Church's voice and damn if I didn't hear him approach. Few people can sneak up on me. I turned quickly to see Church standing in the doorway, his face dour. He came into the room and leaned against the wall by the window.

"Died how?"

Courtland looked at Church, but he was looking at me. He said, "Javad."

"I killed Javad—"

"Twice, yes; but the first time you encountered him he was still technically alive. Infected, sure; dying, to be certain . . . but alive. He was being transported to a hospital for a postmortem."

"Yeah, and—?"

"He woke up on the way to the morgue."

"God . . ."

Courtland said, "The bite of a walker is one hundred percent infectious . . ."

"So you both said."

"If a person receives a fatal bite then shortly after clinical death the disease reactivates the central nervous system and, to a limited degree, some organ functions, and the victim rises as a new carrier. If a person receives even a mild bite the infection will kill them in about seventy hours, which at best gives us three days to locate any victims and contain them."

"I'm not sure I like the word 'contain,' " I said.

"No one will like that word if it comes to that," Church said.

"Bite victims begin to lose cognitive functions quickly," Courtland continued, "and even before clinical death they become dissociative, delusional, and uncontrollably aggressive. In both the predeath and postreanimation phase the carriers have a cannibalistic compulsion."

Church said, "This is all information we learned after the fact."

I looked at them. "What the hell happened?"

Church's face was as ice. "We didn't know what Javad was at first. How could we? The learning process for us was very . . . awkward."

"What does that mean?"

"You read about the fire at St. Michael's Hospital? The night of the task force hit?"

I sat there, not wanting to hear this. Grace looked away but Church stared back at me with a dreadful intensity.

"Javad woke up hungry, Mr. Ledger. Only two DMS agents accompanied the body to the morgue. We lost contact with them shortly after arrival. Major Courtland and I were actually at the hospital but were conducting an interview in another wing. When the alert came in we called in all available teams, but by the time they arrived on the scene the infection had spread to an entire wing of the hospital. Major Courtland's

Alpha Team had perimeter duty and Bravo and Charlie teams entered the hospital to try and contain the situation."

"We thought there had been an attempt by other terrorists to recover the bodies of their fallen comrades," Courtland said. "But it was only Javad. By the time the teams were inside the infection was completely out of control. Javad had gotten all the way down to the lobby and was attacking people in the waiting area. Mr. Church was able to subdue him—and before you ask, no, we didn't know what Javad was at that point. He was a suspected terrorist, albeit one we *thought* had been killed. Our agents were confused because the attackers appeared to be patients, doctors, nurses. Our men . . . hesitated. They were overwhelmed."

"How many of them did you lose?"

"All of them, Mr. Ledger," Church said. "Two teams; twenty-two men and women. Plus the two agents who had been in the ambulance. Some of the finest and most capable tactical field operatives in the world. Torn to pieces by old women, children, ordinary civilians . . . and ultimately by each other."

"What . . . did you do?"

"You read the newspapers. The situation needed to be contained."

I leaped to my feet. "*Jesus Christ!* Are you telling me that you deliberately burned down the entire fucking hospital . . . ? What kind of sick son of a bitch are you?"

Without turning he said, "Earlier, when I told you that if this plague gets out, there will be no way to stop it, I was not exaggerating. Everyone would die, Mr. Ledger. Everyone. We are talking the actual apocalypse here. Counting Javad, our patient zero, we have a loss of life totaling one hundred and eighty-eight civilians and twenty-four DMS operatives. Two hundred and ten deaths as a result of one carrier. Friends of mine are dead. People I knew and trusted—and all of this spread from a single source that was, more or less, contained. We lucked out in that the attack was inside a building that had reinforced windows and heavy-duty doors we could lock. And, to a small degree we were on the alert, though not for something like this. If no security had accompanied his body to the hospital . . . well, it's doubtful we'd be here having this conversation. Same goes if the terrorist cell had followed through with its plan. Had Javad been turned loose, say, in Times Square on New Year's Eve, or South Central L.A. on a Saturday afternoon, or at the rededication of the Liberty Bell in Philadelphia this coming weekend, we would never have been able to contain it. Never. Now we are reasonably sure that there are more strike cells, each one likely to have one or more walkers. We know where one is and we have that under heavy surveillance. If there are others we need to find and neutralize them. We have to do everything we can to locate and destroy these other carriers. If we don't then we will have failed all of humanity. We may already be too late." He turned toward me, and his face was filled with a terrible and savage sadness. "To stop this thing . . . I'd burn down heaven itself."

I stood there, stunned and sick. "Why the hell did you drag me into this shit?"

"I brought you here because you have qualities I need. You are an experienced investigator with an understanding of politics. You can speak several useful languages. You have extensive martial arts training. You are tough and you are ruthless when it comes down to it. You've demonstrated that you lack hesitation in a crisis. Hesitation got our other teams killed. You're here because I can use you. I want you to lead my new team because my existing agents are being slaughtered and I need it to damn well stop!"

"But why now? Why didn't you tell me this the other day when I *auditioned* for you?"

"Things have gotten worse," said Courtland. "The other day we thought we had this under control, that we really had gotten the jump on it. We were wrong. We programmed MindReader to search all available databases for anything that might be related. One of the things we programmed it to find were cases of attacks involving biting."

"Oh crap . . ."

Church said, "So far there have been three cases. All isolated, all in the Middle East. Two in very remote spots in Afghanistan and one in northern Iraq."

"When you say 'isolated' . . ." I began.

"All three were identical: small villages in remote areas that have natural barriers—mountains in two cases, a river and a cliff wall in the other. Each village was totally wiped out. Every single man, woman, and child was killed. Every body showed signs of human bites."

"And, what, the villagers were all walkers now?"

"No," said Courtland. "Every person in each village had been shot repeatedly in the head. No other bodies were found."

"What does that tell you?" Church asked.

"God Almighty," I breathed. "The isolation, the cleanup afterward . . . it sounds like someone's been taking the walkers out for test-drives."

"The most recent one was five days ago," Courtland said.

"Okay," I said softly. "Okay."

"This time they left a calling card," Church said, "a video of the slaughter and a message from a hooded man. We're running voice recognition on it but my guess is that it will be El Mujahid or one of his lieutenants."

"The attack took place in a small mountain village called Bitar in northern Afghanistan," said Courtland quietly. "Military authorities were tipped off to the attack but arrived hours after it was over. They found a tape that had been left for them on one of the bodies of the dead. Barrier intercepted it and was only fortunate enough to keep it from being generally released. We're lucky it wasn't posted on YouTube."

"If you're in," Church said, "then as soon as possible I want you to lead Echo Team in a quiet infiltration of the crab plant in Crisfield. That will put you and the members of your team in terrible danger. I make no apologies about it . . . I brought you here because I need a weapon. A thinking weapon. Something I can launch against the kind of people who would use something like Javad against the American people." He paused for a moment. "The only people who have ever faced a walker and lived are in this room. So let me ask you, Mr. Ledger," he said softly, "are you in or not?"

I wanted to kill him. Courtland, too. I could feel my lips curling back and past the stricture in my throat. With a hiss in my voice I said, "I'm in."

Church closed his eyes and sighed. He stood with his head bowed for a moment. When he opened his eyes he looked ten years older but far, far more dangerous.

"Then let's get to work."

Chapter **Thirty-Two**
British Army Field Hospital at Camp Bastion / Helmand Province, Afghanistan / Five days ago

OF ALL OF the British forces in Iraq the Sixteenth Air Assault Brigade had suffered the worst casualties. Their turnover of troops was steady, with fresh battalions moving into the field to replace those units that had suffered losses or had suffered too many days under the unforgiving Iraqi sun which daily beat down at above 120 degrees. Wounded soldiers—British, American, and a mixed bag of other Allied troops— were brought in with disheartening regularity. The triage process had taken on an assembly-line pace. Get them in, stabilize the most serious wounds, check their IDs, and then airlift the worst cases out to hospital ships in the Gulf. Less seriously wounded were transported by helicopter or armored medical bus to bases scattered around the country, where they would remain on the chance that they might be rotated back to their units. Great Britain had diminished its presence in Iraq since 2007 and it was more politically useful to keep the same experienced troops in the country than to send in fresh ones.

The serious cases would eventually be transported home to the Royal Centre for Defence Medicine at Selly Oak Hospital in Birmingham. Too many of them would ultimately fall under the care of the British Limbless Ex-Servicemen's Association who would try—and sometimes fail—to secure proper disability benefits for them and see them through rehab as they worked to find a new version of their civilian lives.

Captain Gwyneth Dunne lived with these facts day after day. Running the British Army Field Hospital at Camp Bastion was like working a busy ER in one of the outer rings of Hell, or at least that's how she described it to her husband, who was stationed with the 1st Royal Anglian regiment in Tikrit. She was a registered nurse whose training was in pediatrics, but the wizards at Division had decided that this qualified her to triage battle-wounded soldiers. It was a total ongoing cockup.

She was at her desk in a Quonset hut that had two overhead fans that did nothing but push around stale hot air, reading through the computer printouts on the three wounded soldiers from the ambush near Najaf. Lieutenant Nigel Griffith, twenty-three; Sergeant Gareth Henderson, thirty; and Corporal Ian Potts, twenty. She didn't know any of them; probably never would.

The door opened and in walked Dr. Roger Colson, the senior triage surgeon.

"What's the butcher's bill, Rog?" Dunne asked, waving him to a chair.

He sank down with a sigh, rubbed his eyes, and gave her a bleary look. "It's not promising. The officer, Griffith, has a chest wound that's going to need more surgical attention than we can give here. The good news is that there's a pretty good Swedish chest cutter on HMS *Hecla*. I'm having him prepped for airlift."

"Does he have a chance?"

Dr. Colson lifted one hand and waggled it back and forth. "Shrapnel in the chest wall. We managed to reinflate the left lung, but he has some fragments near the heart. It'll take a deft hand to sort him out."

"What about the others?"

Colson shrugged. "They should both go out with Griffith. Corporal Potts is probably going to lose his left leg below the knee. Maybe the hand as well. We don't have a microsurgeon here and they don't have one on the hospital ship, either, so even if he keeps the hand he'll lose most of its function, poor bastard." He rubbed his eyes again, which were red and puffy from too many hours staring at wounds that he didn't have the staff or materials to properly treat. "The best of the lot is Sergeant Henderson. Very bad facial laceration. He'll be disfigured but the eyes were spared, so there's that."

"I never met Henderson. He's a new lad, transferred from the Suffolk regiment."

"Mm," Colson said, indifferent to that part of it. "Should have stayed in Suffolk and raised sheep."

"You want him transported out?" Dunne asked.

"I should think so. Injury like that will take a long time to heal and he looks like he might have been a handsome bloke. Injury of this kind will have traumatic personal effects."

Dunne looked down at the three printouts of the survivors spread out on her desk. She picked up Henderson's and examined the face of the thirty-year-old sergeant from the farmlands. "He was a handsome lad."

She shook her head and turned the page over to show the doctor.

"Ah well," Colson said sadly, "he doesn't look like that anymore. Pity, the poor blighter."

Chapter Thirty-Three
Baltimore, Maryland / Tuesday, June 30; 3:12 P.M.

AS CHURCH AND Courtland led me through a series of hallways I said, "I'm going to take a flyer here and assume that you know that there is no way this prion thing is simply the weapon *du jour* of a group of religious fundamentalists."

"No kidding," Church said.

The warehouse was very large, with suites of offices, workrooms of all kinds, and several big storage rooms. There were scores of jump-suited workmen shifting crates, running wires, and swinging hammers. Guards patrolled the hallway and every one of them looked like he'd had his sense of humor surgically removed. Not a lot of smiling in that place, and I could certainly understand why. I wondered how many of the people in the halls had lost friends at St. Michael's.

"So the real reason you didn't hit the crab plant is because of what happened at St. Michael's," I said. "You're thinking that if the DMS's cream of the crop would fall prey to fatal hesitation then anyone else would, too. Even special ops."

"You'd make a bloody good terrorist," Grace said with an approving smile.

"I'm hoping he'll make a *great* terrorist," Church corrected and pushed through the door.

Grace Courtland gave me a wink as she followed. I wondered why her team was not being offered the job. Maybe they were still too shocked and too hot after what happened to their friends at St. Michael's. More likely they were too valuable to throw away on what clearly could be a suicide mission or a trap. I didn't for a moment think that Church wouldn't be aware that I would think that, but it did give me a bit of a measure between what Church needed to get done and what he could spare compassion on. Big gap, probably getting wider every minute.

Chapter Thirty-Four

Baltimore, Maryland / Tuesday, June 30; 3:16 P.M.

WE ENTERED THE main warehouse floor, which was big enough to be an airplane hanger. Back in the shadows I could see a number of vehicles, mostly civilian with a few military Hummers and transport trucks sprinkled throughout. There were two big storage bins lining one wall, one marked EQUIPMENT and the other ARMS. A soldier with an M-16 stood outside the arms locker, eyes slowly scanning the room, his finger laid straight along the outside of the trigger guard. One corner of the room had been turned into a makeshift training area with several hundred square feet of blue gym mats.

The other candidates I'd tussled with—minus the clown I'd punched in the throat—were seated in the front row of an otherwise empty section of folding chairs. I could feel their eyes on me, and two of them gave me cautious nods: Sergeant Rock and the Jolly Green Giant. The latter held an ice pack to his face.

Across from them was a second row of chairs and these were filled with a dozen hard-looking men and women in fatigue pants and black T-shirts. No one wore any patch or insignia indicating branch of service or rank, but at least half of them had military tattoos of one kind or another.

Church stepped onto the mats and gave each group a long, considering stare. Even in that vast room he gave the impression of size and substance. All conversation ceased immediately and every eye was on him. I've seldom encountered a more commanding presence and though he was surely aware of the effect he had on everyone there wasn't the slightest sign that he was jazzed by it. It was a fact of life to him, or, more probably, a tool.

Grace and I stood at the edge of the training floor, she on the side with the dozen—her team, I presumed—and me closer to the four men I was supposed to lead.

"Time is short," Church began, "so let's cut right to it. With the loss of Bravo and Charlie teams at the hospital we are critically shorthanded. Over the next three months we will recruit and train at least a dozen additional teams, but that doesn't help us right now." He paused and looked at Grace's team. "Echo Team needs to build, train, and get to combat readiness asap. I expect each member of Alpha Team to assist in any way possible."

Grins began to form on the faces of some of the Alpha Team bucks, but Church said, "Understand me here. If anyone, any single person, no matter what rank or MOS, does anything to interfere with the training process—whether by a harmless stunt or some kind of hazing nonsense—I will take it as a personal insult. It will be better for you to wake up in a room full of walkers, let me assure you."

That wiped the smile off everyone's face. We all knew he meant it, and I was starting to get a pretty good idea that he was a total whack job.

But he was our whack job.

He turned to Echo Team. "Lieutenant Colonel Hanley has chosen to spend the rest of the day in intensive care. Apparently his larynx got in the way of his good judgment. Pity about that." He looked real broken up about it, too. Church pointed to me. "Captain Ledger is now your team leader, effective immediately. You will all offer him your very best support." He didn't add a cheesy "or else" but everyone heard it.

He waited for questions. Perhaps "dared" is another word, and then beckoned me over. When I was within range for a quiet comment I murmured, " 'Captain' Ledger? I was only an E6 in the army."

"If 'captain' doesn't suit you, we can discuss it later."

"Look . . . what's my brief here? Is this a hand-to-hand session? Do you have a curriculum you want me to follow?"

"No, but in short I need you to know their capabilities and their flaws so that you know who to trust and at what moment."

"With Alpha Team watching?"

"Yes."

I shook my head. "Not going to happen. If my guys are going to have to go in alone, then we train alone. Show them some respect."

I was aware of having said "my guys," and Church was aware of it, too. He smiled. "Fine then." He signaled to Grace. "Captain Ledger will be using the gym floor. Take your team to the small arms range."

She hesitated and then nodded, called to her team and led them away.

Church walked over to a chair on which was a stack of thick folders. He handed the top four folders to me. "These are the records for your team. These are the men who have the best overall qualifications and whom we could get on site in time to meet you. I have a few others on their way here from the field, but the earliest ETA from that group would be thirty hours. These other folders are possibles. I'm having them all brought in and if you have time I want you to review the candidates and make your selections."

"Who do I have to clear them with?"

He shook his head. "No red tape in the DMS, Captain. Your team, your call."

Jesus Christ, I thought. *No pressure there.* I said, "Listen, Church, since you yanked me out of my life and stuck me with this job, and since you seem to want to give me a lot of personal freedom of action and authority, I hope you're as good as your word when I want to do things my way."

"Meaning?"

"Meaning, as of this moment there's the police department way, the federal law enforcement way, the military way . . . and my way. If you want me to function at my best then you're going to have to accept that I'm going to have to make up some of my own rules. I don't know enough about your playbook and, quite frankly, I don't like the way you operate. If I'm not a cop anymore then I'm something else, something new. Okay, then from here on out I'll decide what that is; and that includes building, shaping, and leading my team. My team, my rules."

We stood there like a couple of mountain gorillas, eyeing each other to see if this was going to be a fight or a collaborative hunt. He smiled. "If you're looking for an argument, Captain, you're wasting your breath and you're wasting your own training time."

"Do I have to salute you?" I asked, keeping the smile off my face.

"I would prefer not."

"What about my job? I'm supposed to report back to work tomorrow and I have to let someone know at the precinct. And my—"

He cut me off. "If time allows, you and I can sit down and go over whatever details need seeing to. I'll even have someone go and feed your cat. All of that is beside the point. Right now, I need you to step up and be the team leader."

"I want to see Rudy."

"Dr. Sanchez and I will have a talk first. You can see him later."

"Can you tell me one thing at least?"

"Make it quick."

"Who the hell *are* you?" When he didn't respond I said, "Will you at least tell me your first name?"

"As far as you're concerned, it's 'Mister.' " Blindsiding this guy was never going to be easy. "Have fun getting to know your men, Captain Ledger," he said. "I'm sure they're all dying to get to know you better."

With that he turned and left.

"Son of a bitch," I said softly and turned to face my team.

Chapter Thirty-Five

HMS *HECLA* / Royal Navy Hospital Ship / Four days ago

THE MEDIVAC CHOPPER airlifted the wounded British soldiers from the field hospital at Bastion, across Pakistani airspace into the Gulf of Oman where it touched down on the helipad at the stern of the HMS *Hecla*, a hospital ship, and an hour later the ship headed out of the Gulf into the Arabian Sea and steered west toward the Gulf of Aden and then turned northwest into the Red Sea.

Within forty minutes of the transfer of wounded from the helicopter to the *Hecla*, Lieutenant Nigel Griffith was in surgery. Griffith survived the operation but coded in recovery. The ICU team brought him back once, then again, and finally Griffith's heart simply failed.

Corporal Ian Potts was treated and made comfortable, but the doctors were already planning the amputations of his hand and leg.

Of the third man from the ambush, Sergeant Gareth Henderson, it was later reported that he died as a result of head trauma. His death was observed and recorded by Nurse Rachel Anders and Dr. Michael O'Malley, both of whom were temporary medical staff from the Red Cross, coming off a six-month volunteer stint aboard and expecting to transfer off the *Hecla* to join an international infectious disease medical research team stationed in the Great Bitter Lake region of Egypt. His body was wrapped in a body bag and transferred to the cold room in the ship's hold, along with forty-one other corpses from the meat grinders in Iraq and Afghanistan.

At 2:55 that morning a second helicopter landed on the stern of the *Hecla*, and Nurse Anders and Dr. O'Malley boarded the chopper along with four very large wheeled metal equipment cases. Drugs and medical supplies for the research team. The helo lifted off and flew east toward the lake. When it landed, Anders, O'Malley, and the two others were greeted warmly by the research team, all of whom were strangers but each of whom were happy to have their team strengthened.

O'Malley oversaw the unloading of the metal cases personally while Anders loitered outside the tent, smoking a cigarette, ostensibly relaxing after a harrowing tour. Two men approached: a tall sandy-haired man in a lightweight white suit and a slightly shorter dark-haired man in dun-colored trousers and a Polo shirt. The tall man bent and kissed her on both cheeks. "It's good to see you, Rachel. I trust the flight was without incident."

"Everything went well," she said, exhaling as she spoke.

"Jolly good." The man gave her a wink and then slipped in through the tent flaps. The shorter man lingered for a moment to survey the surroundings before following his companion inside. In the tent the doctor looked up suddenly from behind one of the cases, but his face changed from alarm to pleasure instantly.

"You gentlemen are up and about early," O'Malley said, rising and extending his hand.

"Early bird and all that," the tall man said. He nodded to the case behind which the doctor stood. "Still snug in there?"

"I was just about to open it."

"Oooh, I just can't wait," murmured the shorter man with asperity.

The doctor undid the locks and lifted the lid, then swung open the side doors so that the contents were revealed. Inside the case a large man lay in a fetal curl, his head swathed in white bandages. He turned his face toward the newcomer and opened his eyes, which were red-rimmed with fatigue and pain.

"Sebastian," he whispered.

Gault smiled down at him and then extended his hands; together he and Dr. O'Malley helped El Mujahid to his feet while Toys hung back by the tent entrance and watched; he wore a smile but it did not reach as far as his cold cat-green eyes. The Fighter was a little unsteady and his bandages were stained with blood seepage, but for all that he still exuded an aura of great animal strength. They helped him into a chair and O'Malley set to work removing the soiled wrappings. The gash was ugly and it disfigured the Fighter's face. Gault privately thought that El Mujahid might have done too thorough a job because his lip had a sneering curl, proof that nerves and muscles had been damaged. All that had really been required was a disfiguring wound; but, he reflected, never tell a tradesman how to do his own job, and El Mujahid's job was mayhem and slaughter. He flicked a glance at Toys, who appeared to be mildly disgusted, but whether it was from the ugly wound or the man whose features it distorted was not clear. Gault figured it was both.

O'Malley gave him a shot for the pain, though El Mujahid appeared not to need it; and he gave him vitamins, antibiotics, and a stimulant. When he had applied a fresh dressing Gault thanked him and suggested the doctor join Nurse Anders outside for a smoke. Toys went with him.

When they were alone, Gault pulled over a folding chair and sat down, bending close to the Fighter. "You did yourself quite a nasty, my friend. Are you sure you can complete the mission? It will be a lot of travel. Another helicopter, a ship, trucks, and all of it in a few quick days. That's enough to tire the average bloke, but with that injury . . ."

The Fighter grunted. "Pain is a tool; it is a whetstone to sharpen resolve."

Gault wasn't sure if that was a quote from scripture, but it sounded good.

"The trigger device is already in the States," Gault said, "in a safe in the hotel room we've booked for you. The combination is Amirah's birthday."

Gault looked for the flash of anger in El Mujahid's eyes, saw it, and mentally nodded to himself. *Yes,* he thought, *he knows about us.* It was something Gault had begun to suspect, but he didn't yet understand why El Mujahid was leaving the matter off the table.

Aloud he said, "I suggest you leave it in the safe until the very last minute. We wouldn't want an accident, would we?"

"No," said the Fighter in a soft voice, "we wouldn't want that."

TOYS STOOD JUST beyond the campfire light, lost in the deep black shadows cast by a stand of date palms. He was staring at the entrance to the tent where Gault and El Mujahid were deep in conversation. As soon as he had left the tent his smile had vanished as surely as if some hand had reached into his mind and flicked off a switch. His features changed in the absence of observation. He became a different kind of creature.

"Amirah," he murmured aloud, his lips curling into a feral sneer at the taste of the name. Before Gault had met her, before he'd allowed himself to fall in love with that woman, his friend and employer had been perfect. Brilliant, wonderfully ruthless, efficient and inflexible. In short—beautiful. Now Gault was getting sloppy and he was getting far too confident. Overconfident. Against Toys's frequent cautions Gault was taking unnecessary risks, spinning plans within plans, and all of it because of that mad witch.

"Amirah," he said again.

God, how he would love to see her bleed.

Chapter **Thirty-Six**
Baltimore, Maryland / Tuesday, June 30; 3:25 P.M.

THE FOUR OF them stared at me. Half an hour ago we were strangers and I was beating the crap out of them; now I was supposed to lead them on an urban infiltration mission against unknown odds and, very likely, plague-carrying walking corpses. How could I open a dialogue with these men with all of that hanging in the air?

Okay, I thought, *if you're going to do this, Buddy boy, then you'd better get it right the first time.*

"Attennnn-*hun*!"

They shot to their feet and snapped to attention with all the speed and precision of career military. I walked up to stand in front of them and gave them all a hard, steady look. "I don't make threats and I don't like speeches, so this one will be short. If you're here then you know what's going on. Maybe some of you know more about this than I do. Whatever. You four are supposed to be the best of a good lot, all active military. Until this afternoon I was a Baltimore police detective. Church says that I'm a captain, but I haven't seen any bars on my collar or a paycheck with 'Captain' Ledger on it, so it might still sound hypothetical to some of you. But from this point on I'm in charge of Echo Team. Anyone who doesn't like it, or doesn't think they can work with me can leave right now without prejudice. Otherwise hold your line. You have one second to decide."

Nobody moved a muscle.

"That's settled then. Stand at ease." I gave them a quick rundown of my military and law enforcement career, and then told them about my martial arts background. I wrapped it up by saying, "I don't do martial arts for trophies or for fun. I'm a fighter, and I train to win any fight I'm in. I don't believe in rules and I don't believe in fair fights. You want a fair fight, join a boxing club. I also don't believe in dying for my country. I have a kind of General Patton take on that: I think the other guy should die for his. Any of you have problems with that?"

"Hooah," murmured Sergeant Rock, which was more or less Ranger slang for "fucking-A."

"We may actually be doing a field op as early as tomorrow. We don't have time for male bonding and long nights around a campfire telling tales and listening to a harmonica. They brought us on board to be field ops. First-liners and shooters. We're going to try a quiet infiltration, but if we get a kill order then scared or not we're going to put hair on the walls. When we lock and load, gentlemen, then those living dead motherfuckers had better start being scared of us because, by God, sooner or later we are going to wipe them out. Not hurt 'em, not slow 'em down . . . we are going to kill them all. End of speech."

I shifted to stand in front of Sergeant Rock. His dark brown skin was crisscrossed with scars, old and new. "Name and rank."

"First Sergeant Bradley Sims, U.S. Army Rangers, sir."

Sir. That would take some getting used to. "Okay, Top, why are you here?"

"To serve my country, sir." He had that noncom knack of looking straight through an officer without actually making real eye contact.

"Don't kiss my ass. Why are you here?"

Now he looked at me, right into me, and there were all kinds of fires burning in his dark brown eyes. "Few years ago I stepped back from active duty to take a training post at Camp Merrill. While I was there my son Henry was killed in Iraq on the third day of the war. Six days before his nineteenth birthday." He paused. "My daughter Monique lost both her legs in Baghdad last Christmas when a mine blew up under her Bradley. I got no more kids to throw at this thing. I need to tear off a piece of this myself."

"For revenge?"

"I got a nephew in junior year of high school. He wants to join the army. His choice if he enlists or not, but maybe I can do something about the number of threats he might have to face."

I nodded and stepped to the next man. Scarface. "Name and rank."

"Second Lieutenant Oliver Brown, Army, sir."

"Duty?"

"Two tours in Iraq, one in Afghanistan."

"Action?"

"I was at Debecka Pass."

That was one of the most significant battles of the second Iraq War.

I'd heard a general on CNN call it a "hero maker," and yet the mainstream news barely mentioned it. "Special Forces?"

He nodded. He did it the right way, just an acknowledgment without puffing up with pride. I liked that. "That where you picked up the scar?"

"No, sir, my daddy gave me that when I was sixteen." That was the only time he didn't meet my eyes.

I moved on. Joker. "Read it out," I said.

"CPO Samuel Tyler. U.S. Navy. Friends call me Skip, sir."

"Why?"

He blinked. "Nickname from when I was a kid, sir."

"Let me guess. Your dad was a captain and they called you 'Little Skipper.' "

He flushed bright red. Hole in one.

"SEALS?"

"No, sir. I washed out during Hell Week."

"Why?"

"They said I was too tall and heavy to be a SEAL."

"You are." Then I threw him a bone. "But I don't think we're going to be doing much long-distance swimming. I need sonsabitches that can hit hard, hit fast, and hit *last*. Can you do that?"

"You damn right," he said, and then added, "Sir."

I looked at the last guy. Jolly Green Giant. He towered several inches over me and had to go two-sixty, all chest and shoulders, tiny waist. Yet for all the mass he looked quick rather than bulky. Not like Apeman. One side of his face was still red and swollen from where I'd hit him.

"Give it to me."

"Bunny Rabbit, Force Recon, sir."

I shot him a look. "You think you're fucking funny?"

"No, sir. My last name is Rabbit. Everyone calls me Bunny."

He paused.

"It gets worse, sir. My first name's Harvey."

The other guys tried to hold it together, I have to give them that—but they all cracked up.

"Son," said Top Sims, "did your parents *hate* you?"

"Yeah, Top, I think they did."

And then I lost it, too.

Chapter **Thirty-Seven**
Sebastian Gault / The Hotel Ishtar, Baghdad / Four days ago

SO MANY PARTS of Gault's plan were in motion now, and it was all going beautifully. Gault and Toys, together and separately, had been on-site to oversee the most critical phases, and it had been like taking a stroll in a summer garden. No one they knew could move around the Middle East with the freedom Gault enjoyed; certainly no one in the military. Even ambassadors had five times the restrictions that were imposed on him. He, however, was unique. Sebastian Gault was the single biggest contributor—in terms of financial aid and materials—to the Red Cross, the World Health Organization, and half a dozen other humanitarian organizations. He had poured tens of millions into each organization, and he could say, with no fear of contradiction or qualification, that he had helped to ease more suffering and save more lives than any other single person in this hemisphere. Without benefit of a government behind him, with no armies, no overt political agendas, Gault, through Gen2000 and his other companies, had helped eradicate eighteen disease pathogens, including a new form of river blindness, a mutated strain of cholera, and two separate strains of TB. His comment at the World Health Summit in Oslo had first been a beauty of a sound byte and had later more or less become the credo of independent health organizations worldwide: "Humanity comes first. Always. Politics and religion, valuable as they are, are always of second importance. If we do not work together to preserve life, to treasure it and keep it safe, then nothing we fight for is worth having."

In truth, the wisest statement Gault had ever heard—and he heard it from his own father—was that "everyone has a price." Good ol' dad had added two bits of his personal wisdom as codicils to that. The first was: "If someone tells you that they can't be bought it's a matter of you having not offered the right amount." And the second was, "If you can't find their price, then find their vice . . . and own that."

Sebastian Gault loved his father. Damn shame the man had smoked like a furnace, otherwise he might be here to share in the billions rather than lying dead in a Bishops Gate cemetery. Cancer had taken him in less than sixteen months. Gault had been eighteen the day before the funeral, and had stepped right in as owner-manager of the chain. He sold it immediately, finished college, and invested every dime in pharmaceutical industry stock, taking some risks, acting as his own broker so that he saved his fees for reinvestment, buying smart, and constantly looking toward the horizon for the next trend. Unlike his peers he never bothered looking for the Golden Fleece pharma stock—the elusive wonder drug that will actually cure something. Instead he focused on new treatment areas for diseases that might never be cured. It wasn't until well after he made his first billion that he even paid attention to cures; and even then it was cures for diseases that nobody cared about, things that affected tribes in third-world shit holes. If it hadn't been for Internet news he might never have even gone in that direction, but then he had a revelation. A major one. Cure something in the third world, take a visible financial loss on the effort to do so, and then let the Internet news junkies turn you into a saint.

He tried it, and it worked. It was easier than he expected. Most of the third world diseases were easy to cure; they exist largely because no major pharmaceutical company gives a tinker's damn about starving people in some African nation whose name changes every other week. When Gault's first company, PharmaSolutions, found a cure for swamp blight, a rare disease in Somalia, he borrowed money to mass-produce and distribute the drug through the World Health Organization. The WHO—the most well-intentioned and earnest people in the world, but easily duped because of their desperate need for support—told every-one in the world press about how this fledging company nearly bank-rupted itself to cure a tragic disease. The story hit the Internet on a Tuesday morning; by Wednesday evening it was on CNN and by Thurs-day midday it was picked up by wire services everywhere. By close of business on Friday PharmaSolutions stock had doubled; by the close of business the following week the stock price had gone vertical. That was the first time Gault, then twenty-two years old, made it onto the cover of *Newsweek*.

By the time Gault was twenty-six he was a billionaire several times over. He openly pumped millions into research and scored one cure af-ter another. When he launched Gen2000 he stepped into the global pharmaceutical arena for real, but by then he owned billions in stock in other pharma companies. The fact that at least half of the diseases for which he ultimately found a cure were pathogens cooked up in his lab never made it into the press. It wasn't even a rumor in the wind. Enough money saw to that; and so far his father—bless his soul—had been right. Everyone had a price or a vice.

Toys was reading the London *Times*. "Mmm," he murmured, "there's speculation—again—about your being given a knighthood; and another rumor about a Nobel Prize." He folded down the paper and looked at Gault. "Which would you prefer?"

Gault shrugged, not terribly interested. The papers dredged that much up every few weeks. "The Nobel win would drive up the stock prices."

"Sure, but the knighthood would get you laid a lot more often."

"I get laid quite enough, thank you."

Toys sniffed. "I've seen some of the cows you bring home."

Gault sipped his drink. "So how would a knighthood change that?"

"Well," Toys drawled, " 'Sir Sebastian' would at very least get some well-bred ass. As it is now you seem to rate your playmates by cup size."

"Better than the half-starved creatures you find so thrilling."

"You can never be too thin or too rich," Toys said, quoting sagely.

They were interrupted by the chirp of Toys's cell phone. Toys looked at it and handed it over without answering. "The Yank."

Gault flipped it open and heard the American's familiar Texas drawl. "Line?"

"Clear. Good to hear from you." As usual Toys bent close to listen in.

"Yeah, well, the shit's hit the fan round here and we've all been scrambling. I've been in continuous meetings for the last couple of days. There's the matter of a tape from Afghanistan. An attack on a village. You follow me?"

"Of course."

"You should warn me about shit like that, dammit. That's set a lot of brushfires and Big G has been trying to take over the whole show. There's been a lot of pressure to crowd the new team out."

"The DMS?"

He could almost hear the American flinch at the use of an uncoded word. "Yeah. The President wants them in, and everyone else wants them out, and I mean out: closed down."

"Any chance of that?"

"None, far as I can see. For whatever reason the President seems to be defending this group against all comers. I actually witnessed him read the riot act to the National Security advisor in front of a couple of generals. It's getting ugly in D.C.

"I'm working on planting one of my guys in this group."

"How sure are you that you can?"

The American paused. "Pretty sure."

Toys raised his eyebrows and mimed applause. Gault said, "Keep me posted."

He closed the phone and set it aside. Toys walked back to his chair and settled into it and the two of them considered the implications of the call.

Toys said, "Perhaps I've been underestimating that bloke."

Chapter **Thirty-Eight**

"OKAY," I SAID, "so we danced a bit earlier. Is anyone too damaged to train? More to the point, is anyone too banged up to go into combat today or tomorrow if it comes to it?"

"Well . . . my nuts still hurt," Ollie said, then added, "sir. But I can pull a trigger."

"I'm good," Bunny said. He tossed the ice pack onto the floor beside the mats.

Skip winced. "Nuts for me, too, sir. I think they're up in my chest cavity somewhere."

"They'll drop when you hit puberty," Bunny said under his breath. He looked at me. "Sir."

"Skip the 'sir' shit unless we're not alone. It's already getting old."

"I can fight," Skip said.

I nodded to First Sergeant Sims. "What about you, Top? Any damage?"

"Just to my pride. Never been blindsided before."

"Okay." I nodded. "Church wants Echo Team to be operationally ready to carry out an urban infiltration sometime in the next day or two. The last two combat teams were KIA by these walkers. I haven't seen the tapes yet, but they tell me those guys were at full complement and fully trained, but because of the unknown nature of the enemy at the time they became confused, and that caused hesitation, which proved disastrous. The five of us are supposed to be the new bulldogs in the junkyard. Sounds great, sounds very heroic—but on a practical level I've never led a team before."

"As pep talks go, coach," Bunny said, "this one kinda blows."

I ignored him. "But what I *have* done is train fighters. That I know I can do. So, because I'm the big dog I get to teach you four to fight the Joe Ledger way."

So far the Joe Ledger way had involved them getting their asses handed to them, so they weren't all that eager to rush in. Not a "rah team" moment.

"How exactly are we supposed to kill these walker things?" Skip asked. "They, er, being dead and all."

"Try not to get bitten, son," Bunny said. "That's a start."

"In the absence of further info from the medical team we'll proceed on the assumption that the spine and/or brain stem is the key: damage that and you pull the plug on these things. I kicked the living shit out of the first one—Javad—and I might as well have been shaking his hand; but then I broke his neck and he went right down. Seems reasonable that there's activity in the brain stem area, so for us the new sweet spot is the spine."

"Let me ask something," Skip said. "The way you dropped Colonel Hanley . . . don't you think that was a little harsh?"

"Church said something that had me scared and pissed off." I told them about Rudy sitting there with a gun to his head.

"She-e-e-it," Top said, stretching it out to about six syllables.

"That's not right," Skip said.

"Maybe not," I admitted, "but it put me in a zero-bullshit frame of mind. I don't play well with others when they get between me and what I want."

"Yeah," said Bunny, "I feel you."

"Even so," Skip said, "it reduced our operational efficiency by one man."

Top answered that before I could. "No it didn't. Hanley was a loud-mouth and a showboat. He got mad and focused his anger on the cap'n as if he was the problem at hand. A man thinking with his heart 'stead of his head has stepped out of training. He'd get us all killed."

"Yeah," Bunny agreed, "the mission always comes first. Don't they teach you that in the navy?"

Skip shot him the finger, but he was grinning.

THE FOUR OF them went to change out of civvies into the nondescript black BDUs that one of Church's people supplied—correct sizes, too, even for Bunny. I was about to head off to the bathroom to swap out of my clothes when I saw Rudy standing by the row of chairs, an armed guard by his side. I walked over to Rudy and we shook hands, then gave each other a tight hug. I looked at the guard. "Step off."

He moved exactly six feet away and stared a hole through the middle distance.

I punched Rudy lightly on the shoulder. "You okay, man?"

"Little scared, Joe, but okay." He glanced covertly at the guard and lowered his voice. "I've spent the last few minutes talking to your Mr. Church. He's . . ." He fished for an adjective that probably didn't exist.

"Yeah, he is."

"So, you're *Captain* Ledger now. Impressive."

"Ridiculous, too."

He lowered his voice another notch. "Church took me on a quick tour. This is not some fly-by-night operation. This is millions of taxpayer dollars here."

"Mm. I still don't know anything about how it runs. I've only seen two commanding officers—Church and this woman, Major Grace Courtland. Have you met her?"

Rudy brightened. "Oh yes. She's very interesting."

"Is that the shrink talking or the wolf in shrink's clothing?"

"A little of both. If I was crass I'd make a joke about wanting to get her on my couch."

"But of course you're not crass."

"Of course not." He looked around the room. "How do you feel about all this?"

"Borderline freaked. You?"

"Oh, I'm well over the border into total freakout. Luckily I have years of practice at a professional appearance of calm tranquility. Inside I'm a mess."

"Really?"

"Really." His smile looked frozen into place. "Church told me about St. Michael's and about that village in Afghanistan."

I nodded, and for a moment I had this weird feeling that we were standing there surrounded by ghosts.

"And now you're working for them," Rudy said.

"Working for them maybe isn't the right way to say it. It's more like we're both working against the same enemy."

"The enemy of my enemy is my friend?"

"Something like that."

"Church said that you might be leading a small team against these terrorists. Why not send the entire army, navy, and marine corps all at once?"

I shook my head. "The more feet on the ground the bigger the risk of uncontrollable contamination. A small team wouldn't get in each other's way; there would be fewer instances where a soldier would be faced with the choice of whether to shoot an infected comrade. It simplifies things. And . . . if worse comes to worst and the infection has to be contained like it was at St. Michael's then there are fewer overall losses of assets."

"'Assets'?" Rudy echoed.

"People."

"*Dios mio.* How do you *know* all this?"

"It's just common sense," I said.

"No," he said, "it's not. I wouldn't have thought of that. Most people wouldn't."

"A fighter would."

"You mean a warrior," said Rudy.

I nodded.

Rudy gave me a strange look. Behind him my four team members came filing in dressed in black BDUs. Rudy turned and watched as they walked over to the training area. "They look like tough men."

"They are."

He turned back to me. "I hope they're not so tough that they're hardened, Joe. We're not just fighting against something . . . we're fighting *for* something, and it would be a shame to destroy the very thing you're fighting to preserve."

"I know."

"I hope you do." He looked at his watch. "I'd better go. Mr. Church is going to introduce me to the research teams. I think he's trying to recruit me, too."

"Ha! That'll be the day."

But Rudy gave me a funny look before he turned and headed back into the offices with the guard a half step behind him, rifle at port arms. I watched them until they passed through the far doorway.

"Shit," I murmured. I walked over to the team and had just opened my mouth to explain the first drill I wanted them to do, but I never got the chance as behind us a door banged open and Sergeant Gus Dietrich came pelting into the room.

"Captain Ledger! Mr. Church wants you immediately."

"For what?" I asked as Dietrich skidded to a halt.

Dietrich hesitated for a fraction of a second, the new chain of command probably still uncertain in his head. He made his decision quickly, though. "Surveillance teams found the missing truck. We think we found the third cell."

"Where?"

"Delaware. He wants you to hit it."

"When?"

"Now," said a voice, and I wheeled to see Church and Major Courtland striding across the floor. "Training time's over," he said. "Echo Team is wheels up in thirty."

Chapter **Forty**

FOUR HOURS AGO I was buying coffee for Rudy at a Starbucks near the Baltimore aquarium and now I was ankle deep in shit and sewer water in a tunnel under Claymont, Delaware. Life just gets better and better. I was even wearing my street shoes, too. Once we'd gotten the go order there was no time to find boots my size or change into fatigue pants.

We all wore Kevlar chest protectors, limb pads, gun belts, and tactical helmets and night-vision goggles. We had enough weapons to start a small war, which was pretty much the plan.

We'd taken a chopper from Baltimore and offloaded in the parking lot of an abandoned elementary school near Route 13 near Bellevue State Park. Not a lot of foot traffic out that way. From there we'd piled into the back of a fake UPS van borrowed from the local vice squad's surveillance team and they drove us around behind a liquor warehouse up the street from Selby's Fine Meats. We used the warehouse's cellar to access the storm drains and from there into the main sewer line that was supposed to have a vent in the meatpacking plant. My handheld GPS tracker pointed the way.

Ollie Brown was on point and I liked the smooth way he moved, making very little noise despite the water; he checked his corners and kept his eyes pointing in the same direction as his gun sights. The big guy, Bunny, was our cover man, tailing us with a M1014 combat shotgun that looked like a toy in his hands, and in the bad light he looked like a hulking cave troll as he walked bent over, filling the tunnel. I was second in the string, with Top Sims and Skip Tyler behind me. I didn't have a silencer for my .45 so Sergeant Dietrich had loaned me a Beretta M9 with a Trinity sound suppressor and four extra magazines. I didn't have a long gun, though everyone else did; handguns were always my thing.

We moved like ghosts, no chatter, just a line of men moving through shadows to face monsters. It was unreal, I felt like I was in a video game. Shame real life doesn't have a reset button.

In the chopper we'd sketched out what plans we could. "Here's the skinny," I said as we nodded our heads together over a map in the narrow confines of the chopper's cabin. "Church has a en route to give us a thermal scan of the place, but that's about as much intel as we have. He's also arranging to have phone lines cut and Major Courtland said that they'll get a presidential order allowing them to disrupt all cell reception in the area. We don't want one of the hostiles texting his buds on his *LG Chocolate*."

"LOL," Bunny murmured.

"We'll come up through the sewers. We pulled up the schematics for the storm drains and there's a big line that goes right under the plant, very nicely placed for a quiet walk-in once the lights are off. Questions?"

"Mission priorities?" asked Top.

"Mr. Church wants prisoners for interrogations. We'd all like more intel before we kick the doors on that crab plant. From all indications that's going to be the big enchilada. The computer geeks think this meatpacking place is a storage depot for our hostiles, not a main action center."

"Does that mean taking a bullet to give him his prisoner?" Ollie asked, his eyes hard, challenging.

"No, but don't let it fall that way. Shoot to wound, try to disable whenever possible, but don't get killed."

"High on my to-do list, boss," observed Bunny, and Skip nodded.

"What about those zombie motherfuckers?" asked Top.

"If we're lucky the walkers will be in their containers, locked up and on ice."

"And if we're not lucky?"

"If it doesn't have a pulse, Top, you have my permission to blow it all the way back to hell."

They all nodded. It was the only part of the plan that they liked. I could see their point. In the annals of warfare there was a long history of men getting killed because they lacked clear intelligence. We had jack shit.

Before we boarded the chopper I said, "Look, we don't know each other and we haven't even had the chance to train as a team. Church is asking us to hit the ground running. Let's do just that. None of us are green at this sort of thing, so let's act and function like professionals. Chain of command is me, then Top. Everyone else is equal. We all watch each other's backs as well as our own. Five of us go in, five of us come out. We all clear on that?"

"Hooah," Top said.

"Hoo-fricking-ah," agreed Skip.

That was half an hour ago; now we were in the sewers and as we walked I had to fight to keep my whole attention on the matter at hand. If there was ever a better definition of too much too soon I don't want to hear it. I wondered how unsettled the others were, and how that would affect them once things got hot.

Ollie stopped, one fist raised, and we froze in place. He pointed to our ten o'clock and I saw the rusty iron ladder bolted to the wall. It was covered in moss and rat shit and it ran up into a black hole in the ceiling. Thick frigid white mist snaked down through a grille set into the concrete.

"Scope," I whispered to Skip and he produced a fiberscope camera that was attached to the display screen of a miniature tactical video system. We clustered around and studied the screen display. It showed an empty room lined with stained metal tables. No movement except for the mist.

"Must be cold as hell up there," Top said. He glanced at me. "Them walkers need to be kept on ice, right?"

"Let's hope so; but even if it's cold up there let's not take anything for granted."

"Skip," I said, "up the ladder. Look for trips and traps."

But after he was up there for a minute he quietly called down, "Clear. No electronics. Just a padlock. I need the bolt cutters."

Bunny pulled them from his pack and handed them up. There was a sharp metallic snap and then Skip was handing down the chain in sections. That was good news as far as it went, but it still spooked me. Any time something is too easy, it isn't.

"Go, go, go," I hissed as one by one Echo Team climbed the ladder and took defensive positions inside the room. I went up next to last and gave the room a quick eyeball, but it really was empty, just an old meat-cutting room with roller tables and hooks on chains so that sides of beef or pork could be swung in on ceiling-mounted rails from the killing rooms, then once cut they would be rolled along the metal tables into an adjoining room for cleaning and packaging. Waste and blood was flushed down the floor gutters to the sewers. The function of the room was obvious and I don't think any of Echo Team missed the irony of being in a room made for butchery.

The mist was ankle deep and clung to the floor, obscuring our feet. It stank of raw sewage and decay. The ambient temperature had to be right above freezing although the air was oppressively humid. There were doors on either end of the room. One led to the disused packaging shed, which was empty except for old heaps of dirty Styrofoam meat trays and rolls of plastic wrap; the other door was locked.

"I got it," Ollie said, and as he knelt in front of it he pulled a very sweet set of professional lockpicks from his thigh pocket. It was as good a set as I'd ever seen and he handled them with practiced ease. It wasn't the sort of thing soldiers carry; I'd have to ask him about it later.

There was a soft buzz in my ear and I held up my hand for silence. There was some static on the line but Grace Courtland's voice was clear and strong. "Thermal scans show multiple tangos." "Tango," or "T," was field code for "terrorist."

"Count how many?"

"Clustered. Maybe twenty, maybe forty."

"Say again."

She repeated it and asked me to confirm reception.

"Echo One copy."

"Alpha on deck," she said, "local law on standby."

"Copy that. Orders?"

"Proceed with caution."

"Copy. Echo One out."

I called the men over and we crouched down, heads together. "Thermal scans say that we have upward of twenty warm bodies in the building. No way to know how many walkers—their heat signatures are too low."

I saw the news register on each man's face. Skip looked scared, Bunny looked mad. Top's eyes narrowed and Ollie's face turned to stone.

"Five men in, five men out," I reminded them.

They nodded, but I added, "This isn't the O.K. Corral. We don't know for sure that everyone in here is a hostile. Check your targets, no accidents, and I don't want to hear about 'friendly fire.'"

"Hooah," they said, but without much enthusiasm.

"Now . . . let's go kick some undead ass."

Chapter Forty-One
Claymont, Delaware / Tuesday, June 30; 6:23 P.M.

OLLIE FINISHED PICKING the lock and Bunny teased the door open, wary for trip wires and alarms, but no bells rang and nothing blew up as the door swung inward on rusty hinges. There was no other sound except the distant hum of motors.

I took point this time. My soaked sneakers wanted to squelch so I placed my feet carefully, taking my time to stay silent. The hall was empty and long, filled with gray shadows and the ever-present mist. We hugged one wall and moved forward in line, staying low, watching front and back, checking every door we passed. When the corridor ended at an L-junction I paused and peered carefully around the edge, keeping my head well below the normal light of sight. I made a "follow me" sign and we turned left to follow the hall. We found one locked door, which Ollie opened without effort, but it was just a storeroom.

I lingered for a moment in the doorway trying to estimate the probable enemy numbers based on the amount of stored goods. I noticed Top nearby doing the same thing. He gave me a raised eyebrows look. Either there were twenty really hungry terrorists in this place or the count was closer to forty, maybe twice that.

We backed out and closed the door.

The hall took on a curve and we followed it for another twenty yards until we reached a set of those big vinyl double doors of the kind that flap open when you push a cart through them. We flanked the doors, staying low, and listened.

It took a second to settle into the vibrational rhythm of the place, mentally filtering out the sounds of compressors and other ambient noises that you might expect in a dilapidated old building. Then we heard it.

A low, inhuman moan.

It suggested a dreadful hunger and it was on the other side of the door.

Skip shot a nervous glance at Top, who gave him a wink that was supposed to look casual and light, and didn't. I saw the looks on everyone's faces and I made them meet my eyes. It would reinforce the orders I'd given them. Prisoners—if possible.

Then there was a sound to our right farther along the curving corridor and as we looked there was a dark movement and then the weak overhead lights threw a shadow on the wall. A silhouette of a guard with a slung assault rifle. A guard, not a walker.

Ollie was closest so I gave him the nod and he went down onto the floor like a snake and eased into a low shooting position. I saw the guard's booted foot round the corner first and then his whole body, and then there was a *phfft-phfft* sound as Ollie squeezed off two silenced shots. The man's head snapped back and he sagged against the wall; Bunny ran past me and reached the guard before he had a chance to collapse onto the floor. Between Ollie's shot and Bunny's quick feet the whole thing looked choreographed, practiced. In human terms it was terrible, but in the way of warriors it was beautiful, a demonstration of the soldier's art taken to its most polished level.

The cop part of my mind noted that Ollie's handgun of choice was a silenced .22. An assassin's weapon. The low weight of the bullet made a dot of an entry wound but didn't have the mass to exit the skull, so the bullet just bounced around and snaped off all the switches. Ollie had taken him in the head with both shots. Most shooters, even the very good ones, are not good enough to confidently try two in the head without a double-tap to the body to stall movement; and he'd taken the shots from thirty feet. Ollie had brought his A-game with him.

Back at the vinyl door we set ourselves for our entry. Foggy mist curled out from under the door like the tentacles of some albino octopus. The smell was worse here. The sewers had been bad but the stench here was of meat rotting on the living bone, a vital corruption I'd only smelled once before—when I killed Javad. The second time.

We flanked the door and Top pulled out a little handheld dentist's mirror and angled it under the door, slowly turning it left and right. Inside there was a whole row of big blue cases. Not a surprise but it didn't exactly make me want to do the Snoopy dance. From what I remembered of the building schematics this had to be the main production floor, but the row of cases blocked all but a narrow strip; and in the center of the row stood a guard. He had his back to us and he was craning to look through a slender gap between two of the cases. We heard more of the moaning and now we could orient sound with location. Something was happening on the far side of the cases, on the big production floor. The guard was eager to see it. So was I.

I holstered my pistol and drew my knife. I held a finger to my lips then touched my chest. The others nodded. Bunny and Top curled their fingers under the flaps of the door. At my nod they pulled the flaps open as quickly as silence would allow, and I moved into the room fast and hard. I reached around and clamped my left palm over the guard's mouth and used my thumb and the edge of my index finger to pinch his nose shut; at the same time I kicked him in the back of the knee with one foot and as he suddenly fell back against me I cut his throat from ear to ear, taking the carotids, the jugular, and the windpipe in one deep sweep. I pulled him back and pushed him into a forward crouch so that his nodding head would prevent the spray of arterial blood. He was dead before he knew he was in threat and it hadn't made a sound. Bunny and Skip took the body and eased it down as I straightened. I wiped the blade and sheathed it, drew my pistol and thumbed off the safety.

There were four cases in the row and they completely blocked the door and hid us from whoever else was in the room. I took the dentist's mirror from Top and checked around both ends of the row. On our right I could see down a corridor formed by a second row of cases that were lined up at a right angle to the first set and a row of laboratory tables cluttered with equipment. There was one guard standing in the gap between the two sets of cases, and near him were six men in stained white lab coats. Everyone was looking through the gap into the center of the main room.

I faded back and used the mirror to peer around the left end of our row. Two guards stood shoulder to shoulder about twenty feet away, also looking toward the center of the room, but this time I could see what they were looking at. What I saw froze the blood in my veins to black ice.

The room was large, as big as a school auditorium, with a high ceiling set with grime-covered louvered windows. Against the far wall was a third row of blue cases, and against the left wall were more lab tables. Scattered throughout the room were at least a dozen armed guards, all of them with automatic weapons; and maybe four more men in lab coats. But in the far left corner was a big cage made from industrial-grade chicken wire and steel pipes. Ten of the blue cases stood with their doors wide open, and three guards were using electric cattle prods to drive a snarling, staggering line of walkers toward the cage.

The cage was packed, wall to wall, with children.

Chapter **Forty-Two**

THE CHILDREN WERE huddled into a pack inside the cage, their eyes wide, their mouths trembling. I could see some of them weeping but they made no sound, though whether it was terror of the walkers or threats from the guards that stilled their tongues I couldn't tell.

I pulled back and handed the mirror to the others, making them each take a fast look.

I mouthed the words "we need prisoners," but I don't know if any of them were able to process the thought. Top, the only man among us who had kids of his own, had the most murderous expression I'd ever seen on a human face.

I held up three fingers and everyone got set, Ollie and Skip on the left flank, Bunny and Top with me. I counted down fast.

"Go!" I snarled, and we rushed into the room.

Chapter **Forty-Three**

BUNNY OPENED UP with the shotgun on the two closest guards, blasting them into red tangles of flailing limbs; Top shot two of the lab techs and then turned his fire on the cluster of guards. I could hear shots and screams as Ollie and Skip tore into the guards on the far side. I raced straight forward, gun up and out, and shot the guard standing by the door to the cage. It was a long shot; bad aim could kill one of the kids, but I had no choice. The walkers were yards away. My shot took the guard in the mouth and he rebounded off the chicken wire and fell, his fingers still curled around the latch. As he fell the door swung open.

The guards with the cattle prods turned toward us. Two of them tossed down their prods and fumbled for their guns. I shot one twice in the chest but even as I was swinging my barrel toward the other the nearest walker leaped at him and buried its teeth in his throat. They fell together in a thrashing heap. I shot the remaining guard who was caught in a moment of bad choice: drop the prod and grab his gun or fend off the walkers. My bullet knocked him into the arms of a walker. The creature, a middle-aged Asian man in a track suit, bore him down and began savaging him. I shot the walker in the back of the head.

A man rushed at me from my right and I turned to see that there had been at least eight more guards on the other side of the first row of blue cases. They opened up with AK-47s and I had to dive for cover behind one of the lab tables. I dropped, rolled, and came up by the far corner and emptied my magazine into them, dropping two. As I ejected the mag and slapped another in, Top Sims caught them from an oblique angle, chopping down three of them with bursts from his MP5. Skip Tyler opened up from the other side and the guards tried to fight their way out of a crossfire.

Behind me there was a huge shriek of noise and I spun to see the children surge through the open door of the cage. Three walkers lunged at them and that fast I was up and running, shooting above the heads of the children, trying to make head shots while dodging incoming fire. The children were hysterical and in their panic they flooded across the entire production floor. The gunfire from Echo Team faltered as the children surged around the lab techs and guards, trying to flee the walkers, looking for any way out and finding only guns and teeth and terror.

One of the lab techs whipped back one flap of his white shirt-jacket and pulled a Sig Sauer and shot a ten-year-old girl in the chest.

"Fuck prisoners!" I heard someone snarl and the tech died in a hail of bullets. The voice I'd heard had been my own, the bullets mine and Top's.

A guard brought an Uzi up and tried to shoot me even though there was a line of children between us. I shot him through the eye.

"Run!" I yelled to the kids. "Go that way!" I pointed toward the door, even tried to shove some of the kids that way, but their terror was too deep, too complete.

"Behind you!" I heard Bunny roar, and I crouched and spun to see a walker—a hulking brute in a football jersey—lunge at me, his mouth already smeared with blood. He was coming so fast that I knew that a head shot wouldn't stop him, so I drove into him with a sliding side kick to the thigh that jerked him to a stop, and as I pivoted off the kick I brought the gun up under his chin and blew off the top of his head. As he fell backward another walker leaped over him. This one was a young woman in what had once been a very expensive tailored suit. I shot her in the throat but the bullet tore only flesh and the slide locked back on my gun. There was no time to reload as she slammed into me; so I pivoted to let her mass whip around and past me. Her fingers never managed to grab me and she flew off and slid ten feet along the floor. With a human being the shock and impact of the fall would have given me a few seconds to reload; but the walker came right off the floor and dove at my legs, trying to bury her teeth in my flesh. With my left hand I drew my knife and drove the blade down as hard as I could in the back of her skull, right above the collar. The furious tension was instantly gone and she dropped to the ground, a piece of my pant leg caught between her teeth.

Top Sims came from my left and stood cover while I reloaded, dropping a lab tech and a walker by the time I had the new mag in and the slide released.

There was a bull roar and we pivoted to see Bunny being rushed by three walkers. There were a half dozen kids huddled behind him and his shotgun was empty. He slammed the folding stock of the shotgun across the face of one walker and I could tell that he was unnerved when the monster just shook it off. Years of training condition us to fight even the most aggressive person, but none of us had trained to fight the dead, to fight things that could not be hurt, that could barely be stopped.

I started in his direction, but Top waved me off. "I got it!"

Bullets burned the air around me and I turned to see a pair of guards using an overturned table as a shooting blind. Dumbasses. The table was aluminum. I put four rounds through the thin metal, two sets of two, and both men fell back with sucking chest wounds.

A blur of movement made me turn again and a little boy of about seven wrapped his arms around my left thigh and clung to me, screaming, his face streaked with tears. A walker came loping across the floor, red teeth bared in a hungry grimace. I shot him in the chest and head and then shot a guard. The clinging child let go and I turned to see him falling to the floor. One side of his face was streaked with blood from a terrible bite. The walker had gotten him before he'd run to me for help. The child's body twitched and thrashed, and lay still.

God Almighty.

Across the room I saw Skip and Ollie moving along the fringes of the room with a line of children between them, killing every adult they encountered.

A guard nearly clipped me with a short burst from his AK-47, but I saw the movement of the barrel and beat him to the trigger pull. Behind him I saw that there were still some children in the cage. The door was closed but unlocked and the children had fingers hooked through the chicken wire trying to hold the door closed as six walkers fought to pull it open. Only the walkers' lack of coordination had kept the children safe this long, but inch by inch the door was opening. I tore across the room.

Gunfire made me dodge to the left and a line of bullets chased me along a lab table, shattering glass and filling the air with a spray of jagged shards. I dodged around a lab tech so that he was chopped apart by the gunfire. A guard was at the end of the table drawing a bead on Skip. There were too many children around, so I bashed down on his wrist with my gun barrel and chopped him across the throat with my left hand. He pitched back out of my way. I brought the gun up and shot three of the walkers, using two shots for each, concentrating on the ones farthest away from the children. They collapsed down and then I plowed into the remaining three undead. I used my last two bullets to kill one of them point-blank, and as his body sagged I front-kicked his corpse into the zombie next to him. The two of them crashed down and I spun to take the last creature standing, a man in jeans and a Hellboy T-shirt. I slammed into his chest with my forearms so that his weight crashed the cage door shut. He lunged his head over my arm and caught the strap of my Kevlar vest in his teeth. I tried boxing his ears with cupped palms, but that did no good, so I grabbed him by the hair and the back of the belt and rammed him headfirst into the wall. His skull collapsed on the first impact; the bones in his neck splintered on the third. I dropped him as the zombie who'd fallen under the one I'd kicked came crawling out from under, scuttling toward me on hands and knees. I axe-kicked the back of his neck and he dropped, twitching for a moment, and then lay still.

I put my back to the cage as I switched magazines. My last one. The room was still in turmoil, but now each of my men had set up defensive stations. Top and Bunny had at least ten kids behind them and they were standing shoulder to shoulder, taking careful aim to bring down walkers, techs, and guards. Across the room, Skip Tyler had six kids tucked into a niche made from a collapsed table and a line of blue cases. There were bodies heaped in front of him. Ollie was by the entrance, and as the last few guards tried to race past him to escape he coldly shot them down.

In the center of the room there were still half a dozen walkers, a few guards, and some kids. Everyone was covered with blood and I could see why none of my guys had gone to rescue those children. It was impossible to tell if they were infected or not.

I had twelve rounds left and there were still six kids out there. I had to try.

I rushed in, firing as I ran, dropping guards and walkers alike. One of the kids ran toward me and I knelt down, waving him on even as I aimed past him, but when he was ten feet away I saw that his eyes were empty and his mouth was open, teeth bared. It was the little kid who had clung to me for safety.

"God," I whispered through a throat filled with hot ash. I shot the child.

For one moment there was a lull in the gunfire as the child pitched backward from the point of impact and slid to a stop on the floor. I could feel every set of eyes in the room on me, burning me with their stares. The children huddled behind my men cringed and cried out in renewed terror.

Then one of the other children in the center of the room snarled with unnatural hunger and rushed at Skip's group.

The gunfire began again.

When it stopped nothing moved in the center of the room except a pall of gun smoke and white fog that was now polluted with red.

I stood on the fringes of the carnage, my pistol held out in front of me, one bullet left. The thunder I heard in my ears may have been the echo of the gunfire, or it may have been my own heart pounding out like the drums of damnation.

Slowly, filled with fear and horror at what we had all just done, I lowered my gun.

Chapter Forty-Four
Claymont, Delaware / Tuesday, June 30; 6:35 P.M.

I CALLED IT in.

There was an overturned table behind me and I leaned against it while I surveyed the room. A pall of acrid gun smoke hung like a blue veil in the humid air, and the kids kept crying. Each of my men looked stricken. Except for Ollie Brown, whose face showed nothing at all. He could give Church a run for his money. Skip looked sick; Bunny's and Top's faces were rigid with fury.

I wondered what expression was on my face. Maybe shock, probably fear; but if my features truly reflected what I felt then my expression would be mingled horror at what had been about to happen to these poor kids and a dead sickness for what I had just done. That I'd been forced to do it made no difference to me at all. I felt unclean.

Five minutes ago there had been dozens of people in this room.

Now most of them were dead. I'd killed at least a quarter of them myself. I'd killed so many people that I'd lost count. The realization hit my brain like a fist. I'd killed before, but this was worse. Ten times worse than the task force raid. And part of the guilt I felt was a secret shame because deep inside my soul the warrior part of me was beating his chest and yelling in exultant triumph even while the more civilized parts of me cringed.

I took a step toward Top's group but the children behind him shrieked and pulled back, terrified of me. They'd seen me gun down at least two other children. They were too young to understand about the infection. They couldn't know I wasn't a monster, too. Top gathered a few of them in his arms, shushing them, murmuring quiet words as Bunny stood by, awkward and helpless. I stayed where I was.

There was a noise and I looked up to see Alpha Team flooding into the room, weapons up and out. Major Courtland was in front with her pistol in her hands, Gus Dietrich was on her flank. They skidded to a stop and stared at the scene of total carnage.

"Bloody hell . . ." gasped Courtland, and her words could not have been more aptly chosen.

Dietrich stared openmouthed, and the agents of Alpha Team looked from the heaps of corpses to the crowds of weeping children to the bloodied members of Echo Team.

Courtland recovered first. She keyed her radio. "Alpha One to base. We need full medical teams double-quick. We have multiple civilian victims requiring immediate medical attention and evac." She paused as she did a quick head count. "Civilians are all children. Repeat, civilians are children times seventeen. Send all available medical units."

I pushed off from the table and walked over to her, my eyes stinging from the smoke.

She opened her mouth to say something, then caught herself, paused, and finally said, "Are you all right, Captain?"

I very nearly bit her head off. It was such a stupid and clumsy question, but I buried that reaction. What else could she say?

"I'll live," I said. "Tell your people . . . there are zero infected among the children. All of the bite victims are . . ." I couldn't finish it.

She swallowed and relayed the info, then clicked off her mike. "Your men?"

"No casualties."

Courtland nodded, and for a moment we shared a look. Soldier to soldier, or warrior to warrior. The ugly truth was that there were going to be casualties among my men. This event would scar every single one of them.

She looked around as the first wave of EMTs spread out through the room. The children shrieked and wept. Some of them ran toward the men and women in uniforms and the EMTs gathered them up in their arms, some of the medics and soldiers weeping as they held the kids. Other children shrank back, all trust in adults having been torn out of them. A few sat in unmoving silence, speaking of damage that went all the way down to the cellar of their souls.

"Was this how it was at St. Michael's?" I asked.

She shook her head. "No. Everyone there died. My team was outside the whole time."

I nodded. "This morning I was just a cop," I said.

"I know."

There was more to say but it didn't need to be said aloud. We both understood.

"We got a live one!" Dietrich called, and we turned to see a wounded lab tech trying to crawl out from under a dead walker. In his nearly mindless state of pain he reached out to the nearest person in a soundless plea for help. Ollie Brown stood over him, a sneer of contempt on his face. He drew his pistol and racked the slide.

"Stand down!" I bellowed, starting forward, but Brown was already bringing the barrel down toward the tech. Suddenly Gus Dietrich stepped forward, grabbed Ollie's wrist and swung it violently upward. The pistol blast was shockingly loud, even to my wounded ears, but the bullet just buried itself in the wooden roof timbers thirty feet above.

I got up in Ollie's face. "Stand down right now, Lieutenant."

His face was ugly with fury, but after a long moment the tension bled out of his limbs. Top Sims stepped between him and the lab tech, his hand on his holstered pistol.

"Let him go, Sergeant," I said, and Dietrich carefully released Ollie's wrist and took a short step to one side, his eyes hard. To Ollie I said, "Secure your weapon."

Ollie's eyes bored into mine and then past me to the tech, and for a second I thought he was going to try for the shot, but then he eased the hammer down, flicked on the safety, and holstered his piece. EMTs immediately stepped up to triage the wounded man.

"What the hell's wrong with you?" I snapped. "What part of the mission orders sounded like 'shoot unarmed prisoners'?"

"He's a piece of shit." Ollie sneered.

"He's the only person we have left to interrogate."

Ollie said nothing, so I grabbed him by the elbow and pulled him a few yards away. I wasn't nice about it and when he tried to pull his arm away I dug into a nerve. Even with his stone face the pain showed through. I eased the pressure and he jerked his arm free.

"Okay, Ollie, let's sort this out right here, right now."

"There's nothing to sort out," he said, then added a sarcastic, "sir."

"You're one more smartass remark away from getting bounced off this team." He blinked at that and snapped his mouth shut on whatever he was about to say next. I leaned close. "You're a top-notch fighter, Ollie, and I'd rather keep you than lose you, but if you can't follow orders then you are no good to me or anyone. Now I'm going to ask you only once and that's it. Are you on my team or not?"

Ollie met my stare for a long ten-count and then he inhaled sharply through his nose and exhaled slowly. "Fuck it," he said.

I waited.

"I'm in."

"My rules, my way?"

He nodded and closed his eyes for a few seconds. "Yes, sir." No sarcasm this time.

"Look at me," I said. He opened his eyes. "Say it again."

"Yes, sir. Your rules, your way."

I nodded and stepped back. "Then we won't discuss this again." I turned and walked away, passing Dietrich and Courtland without comment, and rejoined Echo Team. After a moment Ollie followed.

To the team I said, "I guess they'll debrief us once we're back in Baltimore. They'll need to know everything." I paused. "I have a friend, Dr. Rudy Sanchez. He's a police psychiatrist, and he's a good man."

"A shrink?" Skip asked.

"Yeah. He's at the DMS, and I want each of you—each of *us*—to take a few minutes and sit down with him."

"Why?" asked Skip.

Top turned to him. "Tell me something, kid; when you woke up this morning did you think that by suppertime you'd be killing zombies and gunning down little kids?"

Skip dropped his eyes and looked dejectedly down at the floor.

Top laid a big hand on his shoulder, gave it a squeeze. "Believe me, Skip, you don't want to go to sleep tonight with this in your head and no one to talk to."

Ollie just stood there with his eyes glistening and his fists balled into knots.

Bunny said, "I ain't ever gonna sleep again."

Chapter **Forty-Five**
The DMS Warehouse, Baltimore / Tuesday, June 30; 8:51 P.M.

A CHOPPER TOOK us back to the warehouse in Baltimore. On the way Grace told us that quarters had been set aside for each of us. "It's not much," she said over the whine of the rotor, "we had small offices converted into bedrooms. Mr. Church has asked that you and your men go to your quarters and wait until called for. He doesn't want any of you talking to other DMS personnel until he's had a chance to meet with you himself. Don't worry, you're not under suspicion, it's just that a lot of the DMS staff are new and some have not been informed about the nature of this crisis. Security is paramount."

We didn't like it but we all understood and we flew the rest of the way in silence. I noticed that Top was pretending to sleep but was actually studying Ollie, who had turned stiffly away from Courtland and me and was staring out the window. When Top noticed me watching him, he smiled and closed his eyes. After that he really did look like he was sleeping, but I didn't believe it.

IT WAS NEARLY dark when we landed. A guard met me as I debarked and took me to Church's office. His face showed little emotion, and he sure as hell didn't rush up to embrace me, but I could see his eyes behind the tinted lenses of his glasses as he gave me a thorough up-and-down appraisal. He waved me to a chair and then sat down behind his desk; and the guard poured me a cup of coffee before he left.

"Grace said that there were no injuries sustained by Echo Team."

I almost said, "Nothing that will show," but it was trite. He seemed to guess my thought, though, and nodded.

"And you managed to secure a prisoner."

I said nothing. If he knew about Ollie—and I'm sure he did—he left it off the table.

"What's going to happen with those kids?"

"I don't know. They've all been admitted to the hospital with FBI protection. The Bureau's taken over the problem of identifying them. Some of the children are too traumatized to even give their names. None of them remember how they were taken. A few had recent burns on their skin consistent with liquid Tasers, so we can assume they were taken unawares, perhaps randomly."

"Experimenting on kids puts a whole new spin on this thing."

"Yes," he said, "it does, and I want to hear your full report on what happened today, Captain, but first I want your assessment of the crab plant. When is the absolute soonest you can hit it?"

"There's maybe a slim chance that the hostiles in the other plant won't know about the hit we just did. The cell lines were jammed, right? And you cut the landlines, right? It's late in the day," I said. "Communication between the cells would necessarily be at a minimum anyway. I think we have to hit it by noon tomorrow."

"Why not right now? We have sufficient firepower to do a hard entry."

I shook my head. "There are three reasons why that's not going to happen tonight. First, you need to interrogate your prisoner. Second, the meat plant was full of kids. Who the hell knows how many civilians are in the crab plant. If you go in all John Wayne then you could get a lot of innocent people killed."

"And the third reason?"

"Because that plant belongs to Echo Team and I don't want anyone else jumping our action. Look, you hired us on to be your first team. Well, you got what you paid for. I know you had to be here watching the feeds from the helmet cams. So you know what we went through in there, and you know how tight my guys are. Alpha Team may be DMS elite or some shit but they were a half-step off getting to first base. They should have been in there faster. I shouldn't have had to call them once things got hot."

"Grace Courtland and Gus Dietrich are superb agents. As good as anyone on Echo Team," Church said. "At one point all of them were, but . . . since St. Michael's they've been showing signs of stress disorder. In the last two days their team drills are down by fourteen percent and their live ammunition drills show hesitation. None of that was there before St. Michael's."

Now I understood. I put my cup down and leaned my elbows on his desk. "So we understand each other here?"

"If what you saw in Delaware has taught us anything it's that we are losing ground on this thing. I want the crab plant hit tonight. Now."

"No way. My team needs to rest. You talk about reduction in combat efficiency, well, you put a top team into a critical situation without time to rest then you don't *have* a top team anymore. You have tired men who will be off their game. Going right back out would get them killed. Twelve hours to sleep and plan the hit."

"Two hours' sleep and they debrief in the helo."

After a minute, I said, "I see the science team. Then we go in three hours. That's not negotiable. I won't lead my team to a slaughter. I'll go in alone before I do that."

For a moment it looked like he was considering that as a suggestion. Then he nodded.

"Okay." He took a vanilla wafer and gestured to the plate. "Have one."

I had an Oreo. "Do you want reconnaissance or scorched-earth?"

"My science division needs data. Computers, lab equipment, pathogen samples . . . we need to leave the place intact."

"What kind of backup can we expect?"

"The works. Alpha Team will be on deck and they'll be first in if you need them; F-18s in the air, helo support for extraction if it gets hot. Special Forces strike teams can be inside in ten minutes; and the National Guard is on standby. If it turns into a firefight we have the edge. If the perimeter is breached we'll take a closer look at the scorched-earth option."

He didn't have to explain that if there was a containment breach and my team was inside then we'd be flash-fried along with the hostiles. And even though that's what I would order myself it didn't make me feel any better about it.

"What's going on with the prisoner? I thought you'd be interrogating him by now."

"That would be nice," he agreed, "but he has two bullets in his chest cavity. He's in surgery. They'll page me the moment he's stabilized enough to answer questions."

"And what if the control disease kicks in before then?"

"Then there will be that much more pressure on you to bring me another prisoner when you hit the crab plant."

"Swell." I finished my coffee. "Okay, take me to your mad scientists."

Chapter **Forty-Six**
The DMS Warehouse, Baltimore / Tuesday, June 30; 9:20 P.M.

AS HE LED me to the labs, Church said. "Dr. Sanchez has agreed, conditionally, to help us through the current crisis."

"What are his conditions?"

"He'll be here as long as you are. Apparently he thinks you need a minder." He appeared amused. "Major Courtland is bringing him up to speed on everything."

"Rudy's not a fighter."

"We all serve according to our nature, Captain. Besides, your friend may be tougher than you know."

"I didn't say he wasn't tough. I just don't want to see you put a gun in his hand."

"Noted."

We entered a huge loading dock that had been newly enclosed by cinderblock, and the smell of limestone and concrete hung thick in the damp air. There was a row of oversized trailer homes of the kind used as temporary offices on construction sites. As we passed each, Church threw out a single identifying word. Cryptography. Surveillance. Operations. Computers.

We passed one whose door was marked with a TWELVE in black block letters, and Church made no comment about this one. There were four armed guards outside, two facing out, two facing the unit's only door, and a tripod-mounted .50 stood behind a half-circle of sandbags, its wicked black mouth pointing at the trailer door. I slowed for a moment, frowning, feeling the tension that was screaming in the air, and I felt a chill like an icy hand close around the back of my neck.

"Damn," I breathed. "You have more of them in there?"

"Among other things, yes," he said softly. "It's also our surgical suite, and that's where our prisoner is. But to answer your question, we have a total of six."

"Like Javad?"

Church's face seemed to harden as he said, "The six walkers were all from St. Michael's. One doctor, three civilians, two DMS agents."

"My . . . God!"

"This evening I'm having three of them sent to our Brooklyn facility for study. The others will remain here."

"For study? But . . . you're talking about your own people."

"They're dead, Captain."

"Church, I—"

"They're dead."

Chapter Forty-Seven
Hotel Ishtar, Baghdad / June 30

"WHO WAS ON the phone?" Gault asked as he came out of the bathroom, a plush crimson robe cinched around him. "Was it Amirah?"

Toys handed him a cup of coffee on a china saucer. "No, it was the Yank again."

"What did he want? No—let me guess. The Americans finally raided the crab plant? Bloody well time, too—"

"No," said Toys. "It seems they've raided the other facility. The one in Delaware. The meatpacking plant." He overpronounced the word "meatpacking," enjoying the implications of each syllable.

Gault gave a bemused grunt and sipped his coffee. "That's unfortunate." He sat and chewed his lip for a few seconds. "What about the other plant? They were supposed to locate and infiltrate that first."

Toys sniffed. "Leave it to the U.S. government to always do the right thing at the wrong time. What's that phrase you like so much?"

" 'Bass ackwards.' "

Toys giggled. He loved to make Gault say it.

Gault finished his coffee and held his cup out for more. Toys refilled it and they sat down; Gault in the overstuffed chair by the French windows, Toys perched on the edge of the couch with his saucer on his knees. An iPod in a Bose speaker dock played Andy Williams singing Steve Allen, with Alvy West on alto sax. *Meet Me Where They Play the Blues.* Toys had been converting all of Gault's vast collection of historic big-band music to the iPod. Gault wondered where he found the time.

When the song ended, Toys said, "This alteration in the timetable . . . is that going to change things? With El Musclehead, I mean."

"I've been working that through in my head. The timing is tricky. It really would have been better if they hit the crab plant first, and I can't understand why they didn't."

"Could they have decrypted the files from the warehouse? You said it was only a matter of time."

"A matter of very precise time. I paid good money to make sure that those files would not be cracked this quickly. The flashdrive was deliberately and very precisely damaged and the programs corrupted just enough to have given us at least forty hours more, even if they used the best equipment." He shook his head in frustration. "Dr. Renson and that other computer geek assured me that no technology exists to do it faster."

"What about MindReader?"

Gault waved that away. "MindReader's a myth. It's Internet folklore cooked up in some hacker's fantasies. They've been mythologizing about it since the nineties."

Toys was insistent. "What if it's real?"

Gault shrugged. "If it's real and the DMS has it, then, yes, they could scramble the timetable. But so what? At this point nothing they do can stop the program."

"You're the boss," Toys said in a wounded tone of voice that he knew needled Gault. "But it doesn't answer the question of what to do about the crab plant . . . and whether this will spoil the whole operation."

"No," Gault said after some consideration, "no, it won't spoil the plan. Too many things are in motion now. But as far as the plant goes, it won't be a total disaster."

Toys studied his face and began to grin. "You're making that face. I *know* that face, What have you got cooking over there?"

Gault gave him an enigmatic smile. "Expect another call from the Yank sometime soon."

"Hm," purred Toys, "I'll be waiting with bated breath."

Chapter Forty-Eight

The DMS Warehouse, Baltimore / Tuesday, June 30; 9:24 P.M.

THE INTERIOR OF the lab was somewhere between a scientist's wet dream and a god-awful mess, with heaps of books and spilled stacks of computer printouts, coffee cups everywhere and tables laden with every manner of diagnostic and forensics equipment. Gas chromatographs, portable DNA sequencers, and a lot of stuff I'd never seen before even at the State Crime Lab. Sci-fi stuff. Machines pinged and beeped and blipped and a dozen technicians in white lab coats pushed buttons and made notes on clipboards and exchanged grim looks. In the middle of all of this was one desk, bigger than all the others, that was a shrine to pop culture geekiness, and though I pride myself on seldom showing surprise I went a little slack-jawed at what I saw. In an astonishing display of either the blackest humor on record or spectacular bad taste, there were horror magazines, bobble-heads of zombies from half a dozen movies, at least fifty zombie novels with dog-eared pages, and the entire collection of resin action figures of Marvel superheroes as decaying zombies. Seated like a happy school kid in the middle of this oasis of poor taste was a sloppy thirty-something Chinese guy with a bad haircut and a Hawaiian shirt under his lab coat. Church stood beside the desk—but not too close—and his immaculate suit and air of command seemed like a statement by comparison.

"Captain," Church said, "let me introduce Doctor Hu."

I stared. "Doctor Who? Are you shitting me? This some kind of goofy code name or something?"

"H-U," Church said, spelling it.

"Oh."

Without rising Hu offered his hand and I shook it. I expected something slack and moist but he broke the stereotype and gave me a hard, dry shake. What he said, though, was, "You're the hotshot zombie killer. Man, I just saw the footage from Delaware. Wow! Freaking awesome! You can *kick* zombie ass"

He smelled like old baked bread, which is not as good as it sounds. "I thought you guys called them walkers."

"Yeah, sometimes." He shrugged. "It's more PC, I guess. Doesn't stress the troops."

I gave his toys a significant nod. "And you wouldn't want to appear insensitive."

Hu grinned. "Denial is stupid. We're fighting the living dead. Would you prefer we call them 'undead citizens'? I mean, I originally wanted to call them ALFs."

I looked from him to Church. "Alien lifeless forms," Church said with a wooden face.

"Get it?" Hu said, "Because they're illegal aliens."

I said, "How do people not shoot you?"

He spread his hands. "I'm useful."

And I swear to God I saw Church's mouth silently form the words "Only just." Aloud he said, "Dr. Hu enjoys his jokes more than does his audience."

"You said as much about me the first time we met."

"Mm." Church turned to the scientist. "Please answer any questions Captain Ledger has."

"What's his clearance level?"

Church was looking at me as he said, "Open door. He's in the family now." With that he walked over to a nearby workstation, pulled out the chair, sat, crossed his legs, and appeared to totally tune us out.

Hu looked me up and down for a moment, nodding to himself, then he beamed a great smile. "You have any background in science?"

"Forensics on the job," I said, "a few related night courses, and a subscription to *Popular Science*."

"I'll use smallish words," he said, trying not to sound as condescending as he was. "We're dealing with a weaponized disease of immense complexity. This didn't evolve, this isn't Mother Nature getting cranky and throwing out a mutation. This isn't even a disease pathogen that *could* have evolved. We're into the bizarro zone here. Somebody brewed this up in a lab, and whoever made this is smart."

"Joe Obvious speaks," I said.

"No," he said, "I mean scary smart. Whoever did this should have a shelf full of Nobel Prizes and a whole alphabet soup behind his name. *I* don't have the stuff to make this and Mr. Church buys me lots of nice toys. This would take a major research facility, electron mikes, clean rooms, and a lot of shit you never heard of maybe. Maybe stuff no one's ever heard of. This is radical technology, Captain."

"Call me Joe."

"Joe?" He snapped his fingers. "Hey . . . your name's Joe Ledger."

"Yeah, I thought we'd pretty well established that."

"You into comic books. Y'know . . . Dr. Spectrum?" He had an expectant look on his face. "Dr. Spectrum, the superhero from Marvel Comics? His secret identity is 'Joe Ledger.' That's pretty cool, don't you think?"

"All things considered," I said, "no, not very much."

"Doctor . . ." Church said with a note of soft warning in his voice.

"Okay, okay, whatever. We're talking about the disease," he said, and for a moment I saw the scientist behind the geek façade. "Look, science is only occasionally cool and a soul-crushing bore the other ninety-nine percent of the time. Aside from the fact that the empirical process requires endless repetition on each and every freaking step, there's also the reality of state and federal regulations on what we can and cannot do. A lot of research opportunities are limited and some are blocked. Biological weapons, that sort of thing."

"Even with the military?"

"Yes."

"Even supersecret military?" I said, half smiling.

He hesitated. "Well, okay, that starts getting to be a bit more fun, but even then you can't publish half the time, which means you don't get prizes and you don't write bestsellers."

"No groupies?"

"You joke, but there *are* women attracted to brains. We don't all die virgins."

"Okay. And this relates to zombies how?"

"I think we have ourselves a genuine mad scientist. A supervillain." He seemed really happy about the idea. I kind of wanted to punch him.

I glanced at Church, who raised his eyebrows in a "you're the one who wanted to talk to him" kind of look.

Hu said, "I'm serious. We have someone with deep intellect and vast resources. I mean that: *vast*. Bear in mind that lots of terrorists come from oil-producing nations. It would take that kind of money for our Dr. Evil to do this sort of thing."

"Got it. So has your supervillain actually managed to raise the dead?"

"No, look . . . these walkers are not actually dead . . . but they're not alive, either."

"I thought those were pretty much the only two choices."

"Times change. You know that movie, *Night of the Living Dead*? Well, I think 'living dead' is a pretty good name for what we got here." He took a Slinky off his desk and let it flow back and forth between his palms. "Here's the thing, the body is designed by evolution to have natural redundancies, without which we'd never survive injury or illness. For example, you only really need about ten percent function of the liver, twenty percent function of one kidney, part of one lung. You can live with both arms and legs removed. There are millions of pages of research and case evaluation of patients who have continued to *live* well past the point where their bodies should have shut down. In some cases we can discover why, in some cases we're still in the dark. With me so far?"

"Sure."

"Now look at the walkers. If they were truly and completely dead then we wouldn't be having this conversation. I'd still be in Brooklyn and you'd be doing whatever you were doing before Mr. Church shanghaied you. Why? Because the dead are dead. They have zero brain function, they don't get up and chase people."

"Javad Mustapha was dead," I pointed out. "I killed him. Twice."

Hu shook his head. "No, you killed him once, and that was during your second encounter with him. Mind you, when you shot him during that raid you gave him what should have been mortal wounds, and he would have died had it not been for the presence of this pathogen; but this little bastard of a disease did not *allow* Javad to die. You see, this disease shuts down any part of the body that is not directly related to the purpose of its existence."

"Which is?"

"To spread the disease. These things are designed to be vectors. Very aggressive vectors. The disease simply shut off the areas damaged by your bullets. Don't look at me like that; I know how *weird* this sounds, but someone cooked up something that nearly kills its victims but at the same time prevents them from dying as we previously understood death. Plus, they added a little of this and a little of that so that the host body—the walker—aggressively spreads the pathogen. It's marvelous but it's bizarre, because the disease is constantly trying to kill the host while working like a bastard to keep parts of it alive."

"That doesn't make sense."

"Sure it does, but not in the way you think; and to a degree that *does* fit with nature . . . sort of. When you have an infection the fever you get is the immune system's attempt to burn it out of the bloodstream. Sometimes the fever does more harm than the disease. Psoriasis, rheumatoid arthritis . . . they're a couple of examples of the immune system doing harm because it's trying to fix the wrong problem, or trying too hard to fix a minor problem. In nature there are plenty of examples," he said, "but what we have here is someone who has taken that concept into a totally new direction. We have a fatal disease, several parasites, gene therapy, plus some other shit we haven't sorted out yet, all present in a molecular cluster unlike anything on record. If these guys weren't trying to destroy America they could make billions off the patents alone."

"Does this have anything to do with fatal familial insomnia?"

He raised his eyebrows. "Bonus points for even knowing that name. The answer to that is . . . yes and no. That's the prion disease they used as a starter kit, but they've tricked it out with the other stuff. Even now it has some of the characteristics of a typical TSE."

" 'TSE'?"

"Prions are neurodegenerative diseases called 'transmissible spongiform encephalopathies,' or TSEs," he explained. "We still know very little about prion transmission and their pathogenesis. We do know that prions are proteins that have become folded and in that form act differently from normal proteins. These are strange little bastards . . . they have no DNA and yet they're capable of self-replication. Usually sporadic cases strike about one person per million, and at the moment these account for, say, about eighty-five percent of all TSE cases. Then you have familial cases, which account for ten percent of TSEs, and which are passed down through bloodlines in ways not yet understood, since inherited traits are genetic and, like I said, prions have no DNA. The remaining five percent are *iatrogenic* cases, which result from the accidental transmission of the causative agent via contaminated surgical equipment, or sometimes you see it occurring as a result of cornea or dura mater transplants, or in the administration of human-derived pituitary growth hormones. Still with me?"

"Clinging on by my fingernails. How come these prions are making monsters instead of just killing people?"

"It's a design requirement of this new disease cluster. Prions produce a lethal decline of cognitive and motor function, and that allows the parasite-driven aggression to cruise past conscious control. Somebody took the prion and attached it to these parasites. Don't even ask how because we don't know yet. It'll be a new process, something they invented. They essentially turned a TSE into a fast-acting serum transfer pathogen, but with all sorts of extras, most notably aggression. The victim's aggression is amped up in such a way as to closely imitate the rage response some PCP and meth addicts have on the downside of a strong high. Ever see the movie *28 Days Later*? No? You should. The sequel rocks, too. Anyway, that movie dealt with a virus that stimulated the rage centers in the brain to the point that it was so dominant that all other brain functions were blocked out. The victims existed in total, unending, and ultimately unthinking rage. Very close to what we have here."

"What, you think a terrorist with a Ph.D. in chemistry watched a sci-fi flick and thought 'Hey, that's a good way to kill Americans'?"

Hu shrugged. "After all the stuff I've seen in the last week, I wouldn't be surprised. Now, there may be some higher brain functions but if so it would be far lower than the most advanced Alzheimer's patient."

"An Alzheimer's patient is still going to feel pain, and I beat the shit out of Javad and he didn't so much as blink."

"Yeah, well, we're getting into one of our many gray areas. Remember that we're not dealing with a natural mutation, so a lot of what we know will be based on field observation and clinical testing."

"So . . . if we're talking disease why are we also talking *living dead*? How does that work?"

"That's something we're working on with the walkers we harvested from St. Michael's," Hu said, and for the moment there was no fanboy smirk on his face. "This disease cluster reduces so much of the body's functions that it goes into a kind of hibernative state. That's what we've been calling 'death' for these cases, but we're wrong. When you shot Javad his body was already ravaged by the disease and the injuries hastened the process. He slipped into a hibernative coma that was so deep that the EMTs who checked his vitals got nothing. Consider this," he said, shifting in his chair, "animals can hibernate and to a very, very limited degree so can humans. Not easily, but it sometimes happens. You see it once in a while in hypothermia cases. But when a ground squirrel hibernates its metabolism drops down to like one percent of normal. Unless you had sophisticated equipment you'd think it was dead. Even its heart beats so infrequently that a cut wouldn't bleed much because the blood pressure is too low."

"Can't some yogis do the same thing?"

"Not even close. Even in the deepest yogic trance their metabolism is maybe ninety-nine or at most ninety-eight percent of normal. These walkers, on the other hand, are going into hibernative states as deep as a ground squirrel's. Much deeper than a hibernating bear. Almost anyone who checked their vitals would declare them dead. We had to use machines to establish this and even then we almost missed it. What we have here is someone who has managed to either splice ground squirrel DNA to that of humans—and before you ask, no, they are *not* compatible according to what we know of modern transgenics—or they've found a way to alter the chemistry of the body to cause artificial hibernation. Either way, we can see the effect but we're nowhere close to understanding it." He set down the Slinky and leaned forward. "Once the victim is in hibernation this disease cluster reorganizes the functioning matrix of the body. It somehow uses the fatal familial insomnia protein to wake the victim up again and keep them awake; but during the hibernation the parasite has closed off those areas of the body that have been severely injured—as with the gunshot wounds. Our walker gets up because the parasite has kept the motor cortex going as well as some of the cranial nerves—the ones governing balance, chewing, swallowing, and so on. However, most of the organs are in shutdown and the reduced blood and oxygen flow has caused irreparable brain damage to the higher functions such as cognition. The heart pumps only a little blood, and the lungs operate at an almost negligible level. Circulation is so significantly reduced that necrosis begins to occur in disused parts of the body. So, we have nearly a classic brain-dead, flesh-hungry, rotting zombie. It's beautiful, man, absolutely freaking beautiful."

The urge to hit him was getting tougher to control.

"Can they think at all? Are they problem-solving?"

He shrugged. "If the walker is capable of conscious thought, we haven't seen evidence of it. But really, we don't know what they can't do, or what variations might emerge in a larger cross section of the population. Maybe that's why they had the kids today—trying the pathogen on a new test group. Body chemistry is different in kids. But overall, these are brain-dead meat machines. They walk, growl, bite, and that's it."

I blew out my cheeks. "Can they feel pain?"

"Unknown. Certainly they don't react to it. There's not even a flinch mechanism that we've seen. Though at St. Michael's we learned that they'll recoil from fire. They appear to be oblivious to, or are capable of disregarding, other forms of pain and the threat of pain."

"They die, though," I said. "Brain and brain stem injuries seem to do the trick."

"Right, and if I were you I'd stick with that. But whether they can be otherwise injured in the classic sense . . . that's complicated. Our walkers have a hyperactive wound-healing capacity. Not on the scale of Wolverine from *X-Men* who regenerates back to complete health, but more on the lines of car tires when they're filled with a can of that sealant stuff. Wounds do seal, as we know, otherwise we'd bleed out from a paper cut. Proteins called fibrins and high-molecular-weight glycoprotein-containing fibronectins bond together to form a plug that traps proteins and particles and prevents further blood loss; and this plug establishes a structural support to seal the wound until collagen is deposited. Then some 'migratory cells' use this plug to stretch across the wound, during which platelets stick to this seal until it's replaced with granulation tissue and then later with collagen. In the walkers this whole process is running at superspeed. Shoot one and the wound closes right away. If this were a natural mutation we'd consider it an evolutionary response to a highly dangerous environment; fast healing in the presence of the potential for frequent cuts. But this is designer stuff; and again, our Dr. Evil has a gold mine of a patent in his hands because that process alone might be a potential cure or treatment for hemophilia and other bleeding disorders. And the battlefield uses would be worth billions." He leaned close. "And if you and your Rambo squad can take out the geniuses behind this then *I'm* going to swipe this shit and file the patents, and then I'll buy Tahiti and retire."

"I'll see what I can do." I sighed. "What about treatment, something to kill these prions? Can we give people something to amp up their immune systems?"

He shook his head. "The body's immune system doesn't react to prion diseases the way it does to other diseases; it doesn't kick in and the disease spreads too rapidly with nothing to slow it down. Once it takes hold there is no treatment."

"Terrific."

"And killing a prion is incredibly difficult. In labs, where growth hormones are cultivated from extracted pituitary glands, solvents of various kinds have been used to purify the tissue; these solvents kill everything . . . except the damn prions. Even formaldehyde won't kill them, which really boggles me. Radiation treatment and bombardment with ultraviolet light doesn't kill them. We—and by that I mean my fellow wizards in the scientific community as a whole—have tried virtually everything to kill TSEs including treating diseased brain tissues with all manner of chemicals including industrial detergent—and the prions simply won't die. They don't even die with the host organism. Bury a corpse with a prion disease and dig up the bones a century later . . . and the prions are still there. They are, after all, simply proteins."

"Is that all of it?" I asked.

"I could go on and on about the science—"

"I mean, are those all of the highlights? Is there anything else I *have* to know if I'm going to lead my team into that crab plant?"

Again Hu looked at Church and now the distant look was gone from Church's eyes. He nodded to the doctor. "Well," Hu said, "there's the issue of infection."

"Right, it's transmitted through a bite. I saw enough of that first-hand about three hours ago. I saw those bastards biting kids."

I looked to see how that hit Hu but there wasn't a flicker of compassion on his face. He was too caught up in how cool he thought this all was. I wondered how he'd feel if he was in a locked room with a walker.

Hu gave me a devious grin. "It's a bit worse than that. A whole lot worse, actually."

Chapter **Forty-Nine**
The DMS Warehouse, Baltimore / Tuesday, June 30; 9:39 P.M.

"WHAT'S WORSE?"

We turned to see Grace Courtland entering the lab with Rudy right behind her. Rudy looked terrible. His face was the color of old milk, except for dark smudges under his eyes; his lips were a little wet and rubbery, and his eyes had the glassy and violated look of a victim of some dreadful crime.

"Jeez, Rude, are you okay—?" I said quietly as I moved to intercept him.

"Later, Joe. It's been a hard day for everyone, but let's talk later."

Church got to his feet and joined the group. "Captain, your friend Dr. Sanchez has already been entertained by Dr. Hu. And I believe Major Courtland has shown him the St. Michael's tapes."

Rudy looked at the floor for a moment, then he took a deep breath and tried to master himself. I hadn't yet seen those tapes, so having gotten my own tour of hell I could pretty well imagine what horrors were banging around in his head. It made me feel like a total shit for having gotten him dragged into this.

"You're about to tell him about the rate of infection, Doctor?" Rudy asked in a voice that was steadier than I expected.

"Yep, but he's your friend . . . why don't you break the news to him."

Rudy nodded. He cleared his throat. "Joe . . . I'm not sure which I think would be worse, a real case of supernatural zombies like out of the movies or what we have here."

"Definitely what we have here," Hu said. Courtland agreed, and even Church nodded.

"This is a lousy way to start a conversation," I said. "I would have thought that zombies would pretty much be your worst-case scenario."

Rudy grimaced and shook his head. "You understand what prions are, right? Okay, with any disease there is an incubation period, and for prion pathologies it's typically very long, anywhere from several months to thirty years in humans."

"I told him about the parasites," Hu said.

Rudy nodded. "Prions, though extremely dangerous, are far from being short-term weapons and could at best represent a time-bomb effect. Whoever made this disease pioneered some new way to speed up the process of infection. Now it happens in minutes."

"Seconds," I corrected. "Like I said . . . I *saw* it."

Hu said, "We're seeing all kinds of variations in terms of infection, time of death, and speed of reanimation. We're only just beginning to build models to study it but we're nowhere near understanding it. The pattern's funky, and I'll bet you my whole set of Evil Dead action figures that we've either got mutations or more than one strain. In either case we are seriously screwed."

Rudy said, "I think we can safely say that when the carrier and victim are in an agitated state, as we had in the hospital and in Delaware today, then the process happens very fast. Adrenaline and ambient temperature both accelerate the process."

"This is why this is such a major threat," Church interrupted quietly. "There has always been a lag factor with diseases, even weaponized diseases, and we don't have that here."

"Okay. Message understood. If any infected people get out we're screwed."

"And when in doubt, Captain," said Church, "shoot to kill."

"Dios mio," Rudy murmured, but I met Church's stare and gave him a microscopic nod.

"What about inoculation? Can you juice my team in case we get bit?"

"No way," Hu said. "Remember, the core of this thing is a prion and a prion is simply a misfolded normal protein. Any vaccine that would destroy the prion would destroy all forms of that protein. Once we identify all the parasites we might be able to kill that, and maybe that'll do some good. No, I think that your team has to consider prophylactic measures instead."

"Is this thing airborne? I mean, if all we have to do is protect against a bite, then we can suit up with Dragon Skin or Interceptor, or some other kind of body armor. There's plenty of stuff on the market."

"I don't think it's airborne," Hu said dubiously, "but it might be vapor borne, which means spit or sweat might carry it. In a tight room at high temperatures . . . you might want a hazmat suit of some kind."

"Hard to fight in a hazmat," I pointed out.

Church held up a finger. "I can make a call and have Saratoga Hammer Suits here by morning." I guess all of us looked blank, so he added, "Permeable chemical warfare protective overgarments for domestic preparedness. It's a composite filter fabric based on highly activated and hard carbon spheres fixed onto textile carrier fabrics. It's tough, but light enough to permit agile movement as well as unarmed and armed combat. It's been out for a bit, but I can get the latest generation. I have a friend in the industry."

"You always have a friend in the industry," Hu said under his breath, which got a flicker of a smile from Grace. A DMS in-joke apparently.

Church stepped away and opened his cell phone. When he came back he said, "A helo will meet us at the staging area for the crab plant raid by six A.M. with fifty suits."

"I guess you do have a friend in the industry," Rudy said.

"And the big man scores," Hu said, and held up his hand for a high five but Church stared at him with calm, dark eyes. Hu coughed, lowered his hand, and turned to me. "If you go in with body armor and those suit thingees you should be okay. Unless . . ."

"Unless what?"

"Unless there are a lot of them."

"Let's hope not."

"And unless there's more to this disease than we think."

"What are the chances of that, Doctor?"

He didn't answer, which was answer enough.

"Damn," I said.

Chapter **Fifty**
Amirah / The Bunker / Tuesday, June 30

THE PHONE WOKE her and for a moment Amirah did not know where she was. A fragment of a dream flitted past the corner of her eye and though she could not quite define its shape or grasp its content, she had an impression of a man's face—maybe Gault, maybe El Mujahid—sweating, flushed with blood, eyes intense as he raised himself above her on two stiffened arms and grunted and thrust his hips forward. It was not a lovemaking dream. It had more of the vicious indifference of a rape, even in the fleeting half-remembrance of it. The most lasting part of the dream was not the image of the man—whichever man it had been—but from a deep and terrible coldness that entered her with each thrust, as if the man atop her was dead, without heat.

Amirah shook herself and stared at the phone on her desk that continued to ring. She glanced around her office—it was empty, though she could see workers in the lab on the other side of the one-way glass wall. She cleared her throat, picked up the phone, and said, "Yes?"

"Line?"

"It's clear." She said it automatically, but then pressed the button on the scrambler. "It's clear now," she corrected.

"He's on his way." Gault's voice was soft and in those four words Amirah could hear the subtle layers of meaning that she always suspected filtered everything he said.

"How is he?"

"No longer pretty."

Amirah laughed. "He was never pretty."

"He's no longer handsome, then," Gault corrected.

"Is . . . he in much pain?"

"Nothing he can't handle. He's very stoic, your husband. I think if he had a bullet in his chest he would shrug it off as inconsequential. Few men have his level of physical toughness."

"He's a brute," Amirah said, flavoring her voice with disgust.

There was a pause at the other end as if Gault was assessing her words, or perhaps her tone. *Did he suspect?* she wondered, and not for the first time.

"He'll have some time to rest while he travels. He needs to regain his strength. We provided him with plenty of drugs to keep the pain under control; and let's face it, stoicism only really works when people are watching. We don't want him to fall into despair while he's all alone in his cabin."

Amirah said nothing. She probably should have, she knew, but the image of the mighty El Mujahid sitting alone and in pain in a tiny interior cabin on some rusty old freighter was compelling.

Into the silence, and as if reading her mind, Gault said, "Don't fret, my love; I own the ship's surgeon as well as the captain."

"I'm not fretting, Sebastian. My concern is that his wounds not become infected. We need him to be in the best possible shape for the mission." She was careful to use the word "mission" now, having slipped once before when she called it the "cause." She wasn't sure Gault had noted the error, but he probably had. He was like that.

"Of course, of course," he said soothingly. "Everything is taken care of. He'll be fine and the plan will go off as we planned. Everything is perfect. Trust me."

"I do," she said, and she softened her voice. "I trust you completely."

"Do you love me?" he asked, a laugh in his voice.

"You know I do."

"And I," he said, "will always love you." With that he disconnected the call.

Amirah leaned back in her chair and stared thoughtfully at the phone, her lips compressed, the muscles at the sides of her jaw bunched tight. She waited five minutes, thinking things through, and then she opened the bottom drawer of her desk and removed the satellite phone. It was compact, expensive, and new. A gift from Gault. It had tremendous range and there were signal relays built into the ceiling of the laboratory bunker so that her call would reach up into space and would from there be bounced anywhere on the planet. Even as far as a helicopter flying across the ocean to catch a freighter that was far out to sea.

Chapter **Fifty-One**
The DMS Warehouse, Baltimore / Tuesday, June 30; 9:58 P.M.

RUDY AND I walked down the corridor together. Church had lingered to speak with Hu. I looked at my watch. "Hard to believe this is the same day, you know?"

But he didn't want to talk about it out in the corridor. I asked a guard where our rooms were and he led us to a pair of former offices across the hall from each other. My room was about the size of a decent hotel bedroom, though it had clearly been repurposed from an office or storeroom. No windows. Functional gray carpet. But the bed in the corner of the room was my own from my apartment. The computer workstation was mine, as was the big-screen TV and La-Z-Boy recliner. Three packed suitcases stood in a neat row by the closet. And on top of my bed, head laid on his paws, was Cobbler. He opened one eye, found me less interesting than whatever he was dreaming about, and went back to his meditations. We went inside and Rudy sat down on the recliner and put his face in his hands. I poked inside the small half-fridge they'd provided and took out a couple of bottles of water, and tapped him on the shoulder with one. He looked at it and then set it down on the floor between his shoes. I opened my water, drank some, and sat on the floor with my back against one wall.

Rudy finally turned to me and I could see the hours of stress stamped into his face and the unnatural brightness of his eyes. "What the hell have we gotten ourselves into here, cowboy?"

"I'm sorry you got dragged into this, Rude."

He shook his head to cut me off. "It's not that. Well, it's not *all* that. It's the whole . . ."—he fished for the word—"*reality* of this. It's the fact that something like the DMS exists. That it *has* to. It isn't that we learned about some supersecret organization. Hell, Joe, there are probably dozens of those. Hundreds. I'm enough of a realist to accept that governments need secrets. They need spies and black ops and all of that. I'm a grown-up, so I can deal with it. I can even accept, however unwillingly, that we live in post-9/11 times, and that to some degree terrorism is a part of our daily lives. I mean, find me a stand-up comic who doesn't make jokes about it. It's become ordinary to us."

I sipped more water, letting him work through it.

"But today I've seen things and heard things that I know . . . I *know* . . . will forever alter my world. On 9/11 I said, as so many people did, that nothing would ever be the same again. No matter how much we all settled back into a day-to-day routine, no matter how indifferent we become to what color today's terror alert is, it's still true. That was a day like no other in my life. Today is hitting me as hard as 9/11. Maybe harder. You know what I did? I spent ten minutes in a toilet stall crying my eyes out."

"Hey, you're human," I began, and again he cut me off.

"It's not that and you know it, Joe, so don't coddle me. You want to know why I cried? It wasn't cultural angst any more than it was grief for all those people who died at the hospital the other day or in Delaware this afternoon. Eight times as many people died in the earthquake in

Malaysia last month. I didn't cry over that. Millions of people die every year. I can have sympathy but any grief—any genuine personal grief—would be borrowed. It is no more a true life-changing expression than the heightened sense of concern a community feels for a kid who falls down a well. Two months later no one can remember the kid's name. Your life doesn't pivot on that moment. It can't, because otherwise the process of making each human death personal would kill us all. But this . . . this is truly a life-changing moment. That's not even a question. I've been marked by it. As you have. As everyone here at the DMS has. I don't know how many of these people you've met but I had the whole tour and I see it in everyone's eyes. Church and Major Courtland hide it better; but the others . . . what I see in their eyes is going to be in my eyes when I look in the mirror. Not just for a while, but from now on. We're all marked."

"Yeah, I know, Rude, but it's not like we're talking the Mark of Cain here."

He gave me such a long withering look that I wanted to squirm. "No? Look, I'm not pointing a finger at any country, any faith, any political party. This is a failing in the whole species. *We,* the human race, have committed a terrible and unforgivable sin; and before you embarrass us both by asking—no, I'm not having a Catholic moment. This is far more fundamental than church or state. This is ours to own because we know better. As a species, we *know* better. We really do understand right and wrong, same as we really do grasp all the subtle shades of gray. We have had thousands of years of religious leaders, philosophers, free thinkers, and political scientists explaining the cause and effect of destructive behavior. You'd think by now, at the point where we are this technologically advanced and where communication between all races is not only possible but globally instantaneous, that we'd have learned something, that we'd have benefited from all those previous mistakes. You'd think we'd have become more forward-thinking and farsighted. But we're not. With computer modeling we can virtually look into the future and see how things will go if we follow these courses, and yet we don't do a thing to change direction. Maybe the true human flaw is our inability to act as if the next generation matters. We never have. Individually maybe, but not as a nation, not as a species."

Rudy rubbed his eyes.

"Today," he said slowly, "I watched video proof of the criminal indifference of the human race. People who are certainly intelligent enough to know better have created a weapon so destructive that it could destroy the entire human race, and why? To further a religious or political view. If this was the act of a single person I'd say that we're dealing with psychosis, a fractured mind . . . but this is a deliberate and careful plan. The people involved have had sufficient time to think it through, to grasp the implications. And yet they continue with the program. Today you saw them experimenting with children. *Children*." He sighed. "They know better and they still don't care. If there's a better description of the Mark of Cain I haven't heard it."

"That's them, Rudy. Not us."

"No, no," he conceded tiredly. "I know that. It's just that I don't trust that our government is any wiser. Or any government. We did, after all, invent the bomb; and we've experimented with bioweapons and germ warfare. No, cowboy, we all bear some trace of Cain's mark. All of us, whether we're directly involved at the policy level or not."

"Some of us are trying to do something about this shit, Rudy. Let's not paint everyone with the same brush."

He sighed. "I'm tired, Joe . . . and I'm not attacking you. I'm feeling my way through this." He looked at me for a long time. "But, you're marked, too. Not with guilt, but with the awareness of the beast that lives in all of us, in every human heart. The awareness is in your eyes. I've played poker with you; I know that you can hide it better than me, better than most. Better than Grace Courtland. Not as well as Church. Point is that you carry the same mark as everyone else here. As I do." He made a grimace that was his best attempt at a smile. "It's a bonding experience. We'll always be linked by this shared knowledge. All of us linked by the human race's most recent demonstration of its absolute bloody-minded determination to commit suicide."

"Like I said, not everyone's part of the problem, Rude. Some of us are trying our damnedest to be part of the solution."

He gave me a bleak and weary smile. "I hope that's not bravado, cowboy. I sincerely hope you believe that."

"I do. I have to."

He closed his eyes and sat there for a long minute saying nothing, but every few seconds he let out another long sigh. "I haven't had near enough time to process this yet. If I'm going to be of any use I'm going to have to get my own ducks in a row. I mean . . . I've been kidnapped, had a gun to my head, found out that terrorists have an actual dooms-day weapon . . . you'd be surprised how much of that we don't cover in medical school."

"Not even in shrink school?"

"Not even in shrink school."

We sat with that for a bit. "Church told me that you've signed on to the DMS. Why'd you go and do *that*?"

Rudy gave me a wan smile. "Because Church asked me to. Because of what happened at St. Michael's. Because of you. And because I *know*. Not only the secrets, Joe . . . I know the truth of all of this. I'm marked. That makes me a part of this from now on. If I don't do some-thing to contribute to the solution I think I'd go mad."

"Yeah," I said. "I hear you. But how do you feel about being on the 'team'?"

"That's too complex a question for a simple answer. On the surface I guess I appreciate the opportunity to do some good for the people who are in turn trying to save the world."

"And below the surface?"

"I know where your morals are, Joe. You're too reasonable to have a red state/blue state agenda. You're much more of a right and wrong personality, and that works for me. I think Church may be built along some of the same lines. So, I guess that one of the strongest rays of hope I see in this whole thing is the fact that what we have standing between us and a destroyed future are three people—Church, you, and Grace Courtland—who actually see the way the trend is going and are in the position to do something about it."

"That's a lot to put on our shoulders, brother."

"Yes," he said, "it is." He rubbed his eyes. "We all have so much to do. You have to be a hero. I have to get my act together so I can help everybody else keep *their* acts together. And Church and Courtland have to do whatever it is that they do." Rudy got up and patted me on the shoulder. He looked a little bit more like his old self, but I knew that there was a lot of road still to travel. "I'm going to try and get at least an hour's sleep. You should, too."

I said that I would but knew that I wouldn't. There was too much to do and the clock was ticking. I stood in my doorway and watched him shamble off to bed. I felt impossibly tired and was just turning to go back inside when a door banged open at the end of the hall and a white-faced Dr. Hu yelled two words that sent a chill of terror through me: "Room Twelve!"

Behind him I could hear the sudden staccato of automatic weapons fire.

Chapter Fifty-Two

The DMS Warehouse, Baltimore / Tuesday, June 30; 10:21 P.M.

I TORE DOWN the hallway toward the open door. Gus Dietrich was coming out of his room dressed in boxer shorts and a beater. He saw me running and opened his mouth to say something but then I grabbed Hu and shoved him out of my way. Hu hit Dietrich and they fell together through Dietrich's open doorway. I ran into the hall and cut left. My quarters were pretty close to the loading bay and I got to the bay door before any of the armed guards. There was a knot of confused techs and staff milling around at the bay doorway and I bellowed at them to clear a path.

"Got your back," I heard Bunny say as he skidded into the bay right behind me. Top Sims was right behind him.

I turned to the crowd. "Everyone out—*now*! Close the door and kill that fucking alarm!"

They backed out of the room as the three of us hurried past rows of trailers. When we reached Room 12 what we saw stopped us in our tracks. The machine gun emplacement was deserted, the big gun still smoking, the floor littered with shell casings. I could only see one of the four guards—or, what was left of him. His body was bent backward over the low wall of sandbags surrounding the gun, his throat completely torn away. There were small pools of blood everywhere and spatters from what looked like arterial sprays. Whatever had happened here had happened fast and mean.

We moved up quick and quiet. Bunny scooped up an MP5.

"This is getting to be a long damn day," he muttered as he checked the magazine. "It's out." He patted down the dead guard and found a fresh magazine.

"On my six!" I whispered and I could feel him come up behind me. Top flanked us. He'd picked up the dead guard's handgun and was fanning it to cover all the corners. Someone in the crowd must have had some authority because the alarm died, leaving its banshee echo bouncing off the walls.

"Check your targets," I said softly. "We don't know who is infected or how many hostiles we have."

We paused in a tight knot and listened. There were scuffling sounds from two directions: behind the trailer and inside.

"I'll take the inside," I whispered. "You two around the sides."

"This is messed up," said Bunny.

"No shit, farmboy," snarled Top. "Let's go." They faded off to my left, heading down the length of the trailer as I moved onto the bottom step of the double-wide. The door to Room 12 was open and I could see figures moving inside. I saw another weapon on the deck, a Glock nine, but the slide was locked back, so I ignored it as I leaped up onto the top step. I was in a hurry but the cop in me was always watching and I flicked a glance at the door. No visible signs of a forced entry or forced exit. Even though I had no time to worry about that it still bothered the hell out of me.

I braced myself and stepped into the trailer. Inside it was a charnel house. Two lab-coated doctors lay in broken twists of limbs; beyond them three people dressed in hospital gowns were sprawled in pools of red. The prisoner we'd taken at the meatpacking plant had been in a surgical bay that was in a screened-off section of the trailer, but the screens had been torn down and the prisoner's throat had been completely torn away. The doctors who had been working to save his life were dead. The air smelled of cordite and the coppery stink of blood. Each of the corpses had been shot repeatedly in the head. In the very back of the trailer was a fourth patient and he had one of the soldiers down and was tearing at him with broken teeth. The soldier was screaming and flailing his arms to fend off the attack and I couldn't yet see if he'd been bitten, or if so how badly.

I went straight for the walker.

There wasn't time to shout orders or to fall back and wait for reinforcements. Maybe more help was coming, but I didn't know, and I had to trust that they'd handle things outside. I concentrated on the walker who was trying to kill this terrified young man.

The trailer was seventy feet long and I cleared the entire length in a couple of heartbeats. Gunfire erupted from outside and the walker froze in place, lifting its head, dead eyes casting around for the noise. While I was still twenty feet back I scooped up a heavy metal clipboard from a table and hurled it side-armed like a Frisbee. It was weighted with a thick sheaf of papers but I put a lot of shoulder into it. It whistled through the air and caught the walker on the side of the head, knocking him against the wall. He lost his grip on the soldier, who slumped down into a whimpering heap. The blow did no harm, though, and the creature instantly whipped its head around, lips peeling back from its teeth, dead eyes blazing. It lunged at me, but I was in full stride now, matching momentum and force with its angle of attack. As it reached for me I used my hands to slap both arms down and then grabbed its throat with my left and used my right to hit it with a palm shot to the temple. I knew I couldn't hurt it, but my rushing mass slammed it back against the wall and I leaned into the throat grab, feeling the hyoid bone crunch. A normal man would have died right there, trying to suck wind through a throatful of broken junk; but this thing kept snarling. I hit it again, knocking its mouth away from me, and then slammed the side of its head a third time but this time I kept the heel of my palm pressed hard against its temple so that the walker was effectively pinned to the wall with that bloody mouth facing away from me. I wormed my fingers up the side of its head and knotted them in its lank and filthy hair.

I felt it tense all of its muscles to surge back against me, the way an animal will lunge to try and break free of another predator, but that's what I wanted it to do. As the walker lunged off the wall I dropped back a step and pulled with all my strength. The effect was that the walker flew forward toward me far faster than it intended, and I immediately pivoted my hips so that its mass was accelerated even faster. The creature hit the center point of my turn and then flew past me as if repelled by a force field. My grip on throat and hair created torque and my pivot—plus my full body turn—propelled the walker's body mass over and past me; but I still held on. There was a crucial point at which its flying mass sailed faster and farther than my grip on its head allowed, and at that precise moment I snapped down like a housewife shaking out a bed sheet. The zombie's neck snapped with a loud wet crack.

I let go and let it crash down onto an examination table then it toppled lifelessly to the floor.

Outside I heard another crackle of gunfire.

There was a moan behind me and I spun around to see the soldier getting to his knees, one hand clamped to his bleeding cheek. The bite wasn't big, but it was still a bite. Poor bastard. I saw the moment when the realization blossomed in his eyes. He knew he was a dead man and we both knew that there was nothing I could do.

I pointed at him and put steel in my voice. "Stay here, soldier!" He nodded, but his eyes were bright with tears. I turned and ran to the door of the lab, jumped left, and sprinted to the end of the trailer. Two soldiers, both transformed into walkers, were down, sawed in half by Bunny's MP5. A second pair of walkers, both of whom looked like medical personnel, were slumped in the shadows by the wall, their heads showing wounds from small-arms fire. Top had his pistol in a two-hand grip as he moved past them.

"Watch!" Bunny yelled as a bloody-faced figure rose up from behind a stack of boxes and drove at me; but I'd already heard it. I turned into the rush and as it barreled toward me I suddenly shifted to one side and chopped him across the throat with a stiff forearm. His head and shoulders stopped right there but his feet ran all the way up into the air the way a tight end will after he's been clotheslined by a defensive tackle. The walker crashed down onto the concrete and I pivoted to hit it again when Bunny shoved me aside, stamped down on its chest to hold it in place, and put two rounds into its skull.

We both turned to see Top sidestep another walker and chop it down with a vicious side kick to the knee, and by the time its kneecaps cracked to the ground he had the barrel jammed against its temple and fired. The slide locked back after the shot, but the walker fell away into a rag-doll sprawl.

There was a sudden, harsh silence broken only by the fading echoes of the gunfire.

"Top?"

"Clear."

"Bunny?"

"Clear, boss," he said almost in my ear. "We got them all."

I turned and looked up at Bunny, whose face had transformed from its usual boyish humor into something harder and far more dangerous.

He closed his eyes, took a breath, and then nodded to agree with his own assessment. "I'm good, boss," he said after a moment.

Top was looking from corner to corner, checking every shadow, with eyes as cold as a rattlesnake's. He met my glance and gave me a short nod.

Behind us I could hear the wounded soldier sobbing.

Chapter **Fifty-Three**
The DMS Warehouse, Baltimore / Tuesday, June 30; 10:29 P.M.

THE DOOR BURST open and Sergeant Dietrich came in at a dead run, still in his skivvies but with a combat shotgun in his hands, with Grace Courtland at his heels. All of Alpha Team piled in behind them, and I saw Ollie and Skip, both of them looking scared and worried. Ollie had a bath towel wrapped around his hips and his hair was frothy with un-rinsed shampoo; Skip had a fire axe in his hands. They both looked ter-rified of what they might find. Dr. Hu trailed the pack, followed by a few lab coats with frightened faces and wide eyes. The doctors and techs faded over to the wall and stood there looking shocked.

"Stand down!" I yelled as the soldiers raced up. "All hostiles are down."

Dietrich slowed to a stop. "Those idiots locked the bay door," he said, clearly angry that he wasn't able to help.

I pointed at Dr. Hu, who was standing against a wall, tears in his eyes. "Doc, we have an injured man in here. See what you can do for him."

Hu didn't move. "Was he . . . was he . . . ?"

"Yes." I cut a glance at the people clustered in the doorway and low-ered my voice. "He was bitten."

Hu pressed himself back against the wall. "We can't do anything for him!"

"You're a doctor, for Christ's sake . . . he needs help."

He flicked a terrified glance at the trailer and shook his head, unwill-ing to move.

I walked over and took a fistful of the front of his Hawaiian shirt and lifted him onto his toes. "Listen to me, asshole, that boy in there is hurt and he's scared and he's one of us, not some action figure. This is real stuff happening to real people. I want you to do whatever you can for him, and do it right now, or so help me God I'll lock you in there with him."

With a little push I let him go and Hu staggered back and then froze in place, legs bent as if deciding whether to run. He blinked a few times then he gave me a quick nod and went into the trailer, twisting by me so as not to make any contact.

I felt a light touch on my arm and turned sharply to see Grace standing right there. Her eyes searched my face and my body. "Are you hurt?"

"No," I snarled, then bit down on my rage and tried it again. "No, Major, my men and I are fine. But the soldiers detailed here and all the lab techs are dead. So is the prisoner that we nearly died getting for Mr. Church and the docs who were working on him. And all the walkers, too; but one of your soldiers, a young kid . . . he's been bitten."

"Christ," Dietrich growled. He had murder in his eyes.

Grace was appalled. "How did this happen? I don't—?" She stopped, aware of the people around us, and gave me a significant look.

There had to be a hundred people in the bay now, some in fatigues, some in civilian clothes, all of them looking horrified and confused. We saw Church moving through the crowd toward us, with Rudy beside him looking frightened and out of place, so I went to meet them. I got right up in Church's face. "Your security sucks!"

He looked at me for a long moment, and for the first time I saw real emotion bubbling beneath the surface of his professional calm. It was a seething, ice-cold rage. His lip curled back for a moment and then I saw him slam his control back in place, one steel plate at a time.

"First things first," he said, and his voice was nearly calm. He took out his cell and hit a number. "This is Church. Security code Deacon One. Full lockdown." Instantly a different set of alarms rang and revolving red lights mounted high on the walls began flashing. He disconnected and hit a second number. "Lock the surveillance office. Good, now I want all security logs and video feeds from the last twelve hours routed to my laptop immediately. The same goes for traffic cams in a twenty-block radius all directions. Code them eyes only. Stay in lockdown until you hear from me personally. And tell Colonel Hastings that I want two gunships in the air right now to monitor the grounds."

He turned to Dietrich. "Gus, clear this room. Pick six men you trust and hand-lock everyone into their rooms. No electronics. Do it now."

Dietrich pivoted and yelled at the crowd in a leather-throated roar. The throng of agents, soldiers, scientists, and support staff melted back and pushed through the doorways. Ollie and Skip backed out as well, flicking glances at the bodies, at me, and at Church. Bunny and Top stayed put.

"You okay, cowboy?" Rudy's eyes were jumpy with shock.

"Ask me later."

Again Grace caught my eye. I could feel something move between us, some subliminal telepathy, but I couldn't translate it. Not then, not at that moment. With an effort I broke the eye contact and walked over to my guys. "Top, get the team together in one place and text me on my cell to let me know where." I gave him my number.

Top murmured, "This don't smell right, Cap'n."

"No, it doesn't. There's no damage to that door. Someone *let* those things out, and that means someone just murdered four soldiers and all those doctors. I figure Church is going to start a witch hunt. That's fine with me, but I'm going to start one of my own. You with me?"

Top's lip curled back. "I didn't sign on to get ass-raped, Cap'n."

"Damn skippy," agreed Bunny. Muscles bunched and flexed in his jaw. "What do you want us to do?"

"For now, circle up the wagons and sit tight. Keep your eyes open and your mouths shut. You catch wind of anything—I don't care how small—I get to hear it before you take the next breath. Are we clear on this?"

"Sir," they both said tersely. Their faces had to be a mirror of my own: horror, fury, and something else, some dangerous and predatory light that should not shine through the eyes of good people. I couldn't define it any more than I could interpret what Grace had tried to convey, but I understood the sense of it, and I felt it burning in my own eyes.

I took a half-step closer and they leaned forward so that we were almost touching head to head. "Be best if you boys found some black coffee and had a couple of cups."

"Christ, boss," said Bunny, "I'm already so wired I'll never get to sleep as it is . . ." His voice trailed off as he got what I meant.

"I'll make sure everybody's wide awake, Cap'n," murmured Top. "You won't find nobody sleeping on this watch."

"Hooah," I said.

Top punched Bunny lightly on the shoulder and they left, both of them throwing angry looks around the room as if what had happened had been a personal attack made against them. I watched them go, reading their body language. I've been wrong a few times in my judgment of people but not often, and I found it hard to believe that they would have come running unarmed into the bay if either of them had bypassed the security and unlocked Room 12. Even so, I was going to be keeping both eyes open every second of the day and night. As of that moment I didn't trust anyone in the DMS—except Rudy, and he wouldn't even know how to bypass a security system let alone one as sophisticated as this.

Rejoining Church and Grace, I said, "So far, Mr. Church, I'm not entirely sold on your supersecret organization."

He didn't reply.

Dietrich came over. "Room's clear, sir. Building is in full lockdown. Gates are sealed and I deployed the entire security force in pairs. No one goes out of sight of his partner. We're locking people into their rooms." He paused for a moment, looking worriedly at the lab. "Sir, I checked on this guard team myself thirty minutes ago. I know those boys." Dietrich paused, and then with sadness in his voice corrected that comment. "I knew them all pretty well."

"Somebody opened that door," I said, pointing. "Do you see any signs of forced entry?"

Church said, "Let's not make decisions in the absence of information. The security video logs are being fed to my laptop. Let's meet in the conference room and take a look at them. Until then no one speaks to anyone."

The others headed toward the door, but I lingered with Church. "The DMS finally gets a prisoner to interrogate and then this happens. Funny timing, don't you think?"

"Yes, hilarious."

He left and I followed.

Chapter Fifty-Four
Amirah / The Bunker / Tuesday, June 30

ABDUL, THE FIGHTER'S lieutenant, was a grim-faced man with humorless eyes and pocked skin that made him look like a smallpox survivor. He had first bonded with El Mujahid during a series of raids financed by one of the Iranian ayatollahs and together they'd blown up three police stations in Iraq, assassinated two members of the new government and planted bombs that killed or crippled over a dozen American and British troops—all of it in the days following the "liberation" of Baghdad. In the years since then they had cut a bloody path through five countries and the price on Abdul's head was nearly as large as that offered for El Mujahid.

Now that El Mujahid was out of the country it was up to Abdul to ensure that no one knew about the Fighter's absence. He made a series of small raids, including two more attacks on remote villages using the new and ferocious Generation Seven strain of the *Seif al Din* pathogen, and in each case he left behind a CD-ROM or videocassette on which were prerecorded messages from El Mujahid. As the Fighter mentioned specific incidents in the attacks it was that Abdul stage-manage those raids so that they precisely matched all references in the messages.

On the morning following El Mujahid's "rescue" by British troops, Abdul returned briefly to the Bunker to consult with Amirah after first making sure that Sebastian Gault had left. Now they sat in her study, he in a deep leather chair, she perched on the edge of a love seat. The second half of the love seat was piled high with medical test results and autopsy reports.

Abdul sipped from a bottle of spring water and nodded at the reports. "Is that information on the new strain?"

"Test results, yes," she said, nodding. She looked very tired and her eyes were red-rimmed.

"Has he said anything more about it?" Abdul never mentioned Gault's name. He hated the man and thought that even saying his name aloud was an affront to God, not to mention to El Mujahid. Gault and that man-loving scorpion of an assistant of his, Toys. When he thought of what Amirah did and was willing to do with Gault it was very difficult for Abdul to keep a sneer off his face as he confronted this woman. This *whore*. How could she sleep with that man? Even if it furthered the cause and even if El Mujahid had ordered it, it was so . . . *vile* a thing to do. He wanted to spit on the rug between them.

If Amirah was aware of his contempt she hid it very well. She picked up one folder and weighed it in her hand. "This is a detailed schematic of the release device Sebastian has provided for my husband. It is waiting for El Mujahid in a hotel safe." She smiled, stood, and walked them over to him; Abdul was careful not to touch her hand as he accepted them.

When he finished reading he looked up in alarm. "I'm not sure I understand this. This device is booby-trapped. It's set to release the plague according to a preset clock instead of an active trigger."

"Yes."

"Where did you get this? *How* did you get this? It must belong to . . ." He waved a hand, still unwilling to say Gault's name.

"I downloaded it from his laptop," she said. "Or, rather, I arranged to have it downloaded while the laptop was out of his possession."

"He's never without it," Abdul said.

Amirah smiled. "He was distracted." She let it hang there in the air between them and Abdul turned his face away, not wanting this whore to see him blush. When he finally turned back to face her he saw that she was smiling a knowing smile. *Witch!*

"And you're sure that he does not know that this material was taken?"

"He doesn't know any more than he knows I disabled the program that would allow him to blow up this bunker. My computer experts are as good as any in the world. After all, Sebastian paid for the very best."

Abdul almost smiled at the irony of that. He offered her a grunt of a half laugh, though he was truly very impressed. But he was also troubled. "Does the Fighter know about this?"

Amirah chuckled. "You of all people should have more faith in El Mujahid than that. I sent him the schematic which will allow him to rewire the trigger so that it actually works as it was supposed to work." She paused, then with a sneer added, "As Gault promised it would work." His sneer softened to a sly smile. "And I have my own contribution to make to our cause."

When she told him what it was Abdul felt some of his dislike for this woman crumble away. He was almost smiling when she ushered him to the door.

Chapter Fifty-Five

The DMS Warehouse, Baltimore / Tuesday, June 30; 11:01 P.M.

AFTER THE CLEANUP we met in the conference room. Church, Grace, Hu, Dietrich, Rudy, and me. No one was going to be getting any sleep tonight, so we're all drinking strong coffee, but despite everything there was a fresh plate of cookies on the table—vanilla wafers, Oreos, and what looked like, God help me, Barnum's Animal Crackers.

Grace said, "Before we become totally paranoid, are we sure this is a security breach and not an error in protocol? If the door wasn't forced then one of science team might have inadvertently opened it."

"Perhaps one of the walkers got loose and the lab staff panicked," Rudy suggested.

"I don't think so." He had his laptop open on the table and turned it around so we could all watch. He hit a button and an image appeared of the loading bay and the trailer designated as Room 12. "This is a continuous feed. Watch." The image suddenly flickered and then disintegrated into static snow.

"Camera malfunction?" Dietrich asked.

"Unknown. If so then all of the cameras in that part of the building went down at the same time." He held up a hand. "Before you ask . . . they've since come back online."

Grace leaned forward, looking intense. "Sounds like electronic jamming."

"I don't understand," said Rudy.

"All surveillance devices are electronic and are therefore subject to signal overload or signal blocking," Grace told him. "The technology isn't new and these days there are portable jammers small enough to fit in your pocket."

"So this is sabotage?" Rudy rubbed his eyes. "This has been too long a day."

Church ended the video feed. "Considering the timing and location of the signal failure and the subsequent breach of Room Twelve we'll proceed on the assumption that we have been infiltrated by person or persons unknown. We have to find this person and neutralize him."

"Or her," Grace suggested.

"Or *them*," I said. "You've been doing some heavy-duty recruiting lately. We can't assume you've only scooped up one bad apple."

"Agreed. We have to evaluate the incident, learn what we can learn from it, both strategically and in terms of our security. We also have to consider the effect this incident will have on morale."

"Seems pretty damn clear to me," barked Gus Dietrich, "that these assholes wanted the plague released."

"Maybe," said Grace, "or they could have been on a scouting mission and opened the wrong door."

"You like that theory?" I asked her.

"Not much, no, but it's worth keeping on the table. Though I think it's more likely that they wanted the prisoner silenced."

I downed half my coffee. "Church, you said that there was a way to get that access code. How?"

"There are only three practical possibilities, two of which are highly improbable," he said. "First, they got it directly from Grace, Gus, Hu, or from me." He paused for comment, got none. "Second, one of us was careless and left a code scrambler lying about."

Hu was shaking his head before Church finished. He fished his scrambler out and set it on the table. "No way. Not after the speech you gave me when you gave me this thing. It's on the side of the tub when I take a shower and it's in my pajama pocket when I go to bed. Twenty-four/seven I know where this is."

Grace and Dietrich similarly produced theirs. Church didn't bother. The point was made.

"What's the third choice?" I asked.

"That someone else has a scrambler or some compatible device, though that's a bit hard to accept. These scramblers aren't on the market yet. I obtained them directly from the designer. He made five of them and I acquired all five."

"Who has the other one?"

"Aunt Sallie."

"Who?"

Grace smiled. "Aunt Sallie is the DMS's chief of operations. She runs the Hangar—our Brooklyn facility."

"And you call her 'Aunt Sallie'? Kind of conjures an image of a blue-haired maiden aunt with too many cats. Should I assume that you believe this Aunt Sallie person is trustworthy and hasn't left her scrambler lying in her knitting basket?"

Dietrich smiled. "If you're lucky, Captain, no one'll ever tell her you said that."

Grace's smile broadened and it youthened her, stripping away several layers of tension. Even Church looked amused, though with him it was harder to tell. "I think those of us who know her can safely vouch for Aunt Sallie's integrity."

"What about force? Could someone have taken the scrambler from her?"

"I would truly love to see someone try," said Church. Across from him Dietrich was laughing quietly and nodding to himself, apparently visualizing the scenario.

The laughter and smiles, however, died away. I glanced at Rudy, who was quietly observing everyone. I imagine that he, like I, realized that the laughter was a pressure valve. The enormity of what had happened in Room 12 loomed over us.

Church's phone rang and when he looked at the displayed number he held up a finger and took the call, speaking quietly for a couple of minutes. "Thanks for getting back to me so quickly," he said. "Please keep me informed." He clicked the phone off and laid it on the table and any trace of humor that had been on his face was completely gone now. "That was a contact of mine at the Atlanta office of the Bureau. Henry Cerescu, the engineer who designed the code scrambler, is dead. His body was found in his apartment this morning and he'd been dead for about thirty hours. Cleaning lady found him and called the police. No suspects, but the report says that Cerescu's apartment, which doubles as his workshop, was trashed. A complete report will be faxed to us."

"Damn," I said. "Sorry about your friend, Church, but I bet I can tell you what'll be in that report. Most likely it'll look like an ordinary break-in by a junkie. TV and DVD player will be gone, there'll be lots of random damage, a big mess. The smartest way to hide a small crime is to make it look like a bigger one. I'll bet Cerescu probably had the design schematics of his scrambler somewhere, maybe hard copy or on his computer. The hard drive will be gone, too, and most of his papers."

"Very likely," Church said. He took another cookie and pushed the plate toward me. I poked through them and took an elephant and a monkey.

"So where does that leave us?" Grace asked.

"With the certain knowledge that we've been infiltrated by someone with an understanding of what the DMS is," Church said. "And someone who knows me well enough to know how I obtain equipment."

"That can't be a long list," Rudy suggested.

"It isn't," Church agreed, "and I'll be taking a look at that list once this meeting is concluded."

"It still leaves one or more persons inside the DMS," I said. "Inside this building."

"Excuse me," Rudy said, "but am I to presume that if we are here in this room then we are not on the list of potential suspects?"

Church leaned back in his chair and studied Rudy for a few moments, one index finger tracing a slow circle on the tabletop. "Dr. Sanchez, there are very few people I trust implicitly, and in each case that trust is based on many years of experience, opportunity, and evaluation. As for most of the people gathered here, my trust is based on more recent knowledge. You and Captain Ledger were in the science lab with me and were then escorted to your quarters. Major Courtland was with me and Sergeant Dietrich had just completed his rounds with two other officers. One of them walked him to his quarters."

"Okay, but doesn't that indicate that we were not directly involved in opening the door? What makes you sure we're not accomplices?"

Church bit an edge off a cookie, munched it. "I haven't said that I have cleared you of all suspicion, Dr. Sanchez, but as you already said, you can presume that if you're in this room then you are not high on the list of suspects."

That seemed to satisfy Rudy, at least in part, because he gave a curt nod and lapsed back into observant silence.

"We've brought a lot of people on board in the last couple of days," Dietrich said. "The movers, more than half the security team, the decorators, some new lab techs." He paused and looked directly at me. "And all of Echo Team."

"How good was the screening for all of these people?" I asked.

Grace said, "We have three FBI agents on loan to us working as screeners. You've met them, Joe. Agents Simchek, Andrews, and McNeill—the agents who picked you up in Ocean City."

Buckethead and his cronies, I thought. "Okay, but who screens the screeners?"

"I do," Grace admitted, and I could see a troubled look in her eyes. She knew that I had to be thinking about her oversight with the task force logs regarding me and the second panel truck. She'd been under tremendous stress since the massacre at St. Michael's. Stress isn't conducive to a calm and meticulous approach. I kept that to myself for now and I think I caught a flicker of a grateful nod from her.

"I've been supervising the actual screens, though," added Dietrich. "If this is someone who slipped through because of sloppy work then it's on me." I liked that he made no attempt to weasel out of anything. Dietrich was Church's pet bulldog and he seemed blunt and honest. I liked him, and he was low on my personal list of suspects.

"Another question," I said. "Where are we recruiting from? You gave me files on the Echo Team guys, along with a big stack of other possible candidates. Some of those are generic folders—off the shelf from Staples—but some were FBI, a few were military, a couple were even marked "top secret." Am I right in assuming that you're recruiting from all of the military and federal agencies?"

"And law enforcement," Dietrich added with a nod in my direction.

"How? I thought you guys were secret."

"Secrecy is conditional, Captain," Church said. "We all have to answer to someone, and the DMS answers directly to the President." He paused, then added, "A few days ago I met with the Joint Chiefs and the heads of the FBI, CIA, ATF, NSA, and several other branches. I was asked by the President to give a brief description of the DMS and its mission, and to then make requests that each department or branch of service provide me with a list of candidates for inclusion in the DMS. The files were sent to us, and Agent Simchek and his team of screeners did evaluations and ran each candidate through Mind-Reader. Anyone with even a twitch in his or her records was discounted. I will admit, however, that there was a bias toward individuals with skill sets that are appropriate to the current crisis, and that may be our hole. Simchek and his team may have somehow erred on the side of immediate need. That . . . or the traitor has a spotless record and rang no alarms."

"If he was black ops or Delta Force," Grace offered, "then his records might have been altered or sealed. Field agents' names are often deleted from records of actions, especially when the agent is active military and the action technically illegal. Assassinations and infiltrations over enemy lines. It's all plausible deniability, which means this bugger could hide even from MindReader."

"What kind of person are we looking for?" Rudy asked. "A rogue government agent, a terrorist sympathizer . . . ?"

"Unknown," Grace said. "All we know is that this person, or persons, unlocked Room Twelve for reasons unknown."

Church nodded. "This impacts you most of all, Captain. We don't know how, or even if, this relates to the planned raid on the crab plant. Before the meeting Major Courtland advised me to push it back;

Sergeant Dietrich wants to hit it with all the troops and go for a clean sweep. The mission is yours to call, however."

"Jesus Christ," Rudy said, "he just came out of a combat situation. *Two* combat situations—"

I touched his arm to stop him. "No, Rudy. You can get me on the couch later, but right now I can hear the clock ticking big time. If what happened in Room Twelve is not directly related to the crab plant then I'll eat Sergeant Dietrich's gym socks."

"I'll cook them for you," said Dietrich.

"Church," I said. "About hitting the crab plant at dawn?"

"Yes?"

"Fuck that. I want to hit it right now."

Rudy gasped, but Church nodded. "I figured you would. Choppers are on deck and my computer team is getting your communications gear ready."

I grinned at him.

"Joe," said Grace, "are you sure about this?"

"Sure? No. I'd rather hit that place with a five-hundred-pound bomb and scratch them off the to-do list; but now more than ever we need to go soft and see about nabbing some prisoners. I think we should plan immediate interrogations, though."

"Okay," Grace said. "My team will be ready to rush the door at the first sign of trouble. But if you want everyone else to remain back at an unobtrusive distance then it still leaves us with a five-to-ten-minute lag for a full-on attack."

"Joe . . . that's suicide!" Rudy barked. "There's no way that you could—"

"It's my call," I said firmly. "And I can't think of a better plan that we could put into action right now. The longer we wait the more time there is for the spy to get a message out."

"No messages are going out right now," Church said. "We have jammers running everywhere in the building. However, we still have to consider the possibility that messages and intelligence may have been sent out before the lockdown."

I sat back and looked from face to face. "Okay, but we're going to need a diversion. Here's what I have in mind . . ."

Part Three
Beasts

Until the day of his death, no man can be sure of his courage.

—JEAN ANOUILH

Chapter **Fifty-Six**

ECHO TEAM CAME jogging into the big room at the warehouse look-ing very much awake. Wired, scared, and thoroughly pissed-off, but awake. I told them to gear up and they followed Gus Dietrich over to the arms locker. Alpha Team was already there.

Rudy turned to Church. "This is killing you, isn't it?"

Church looked at him.

Rudy said, "I don't know you, Mr. Church. We've only had some weird little talks." He waved a hand. "Zombies and all that. But since what happened in Room Twelve I've been thinking about this situation, about this organization you've constructed. I know only enough about the military to know that this isn't the way things are done; and I do know enough about governments to know that the DMS operates on its own schedule. It's virtually red-tape free. Lots of authority, and it's shared." He chewed his lip for a moment. "Your background has to include some training or practical experience either in psychology, therapy, or psycho-logical manipulation. Maybe all three. You know how to set a mood and cultivate trust; you apparently care about the well-being of your staff. You like toys, and you pride yourself on having the best toys in the schoolyard. The labs here are bizarrely overdone. You have equipment I've never heard of let alone seen in actual use. Everyone I've met here has an above-average IQ. A lot of individuals, not a lot of team players."

"Your point being?" Church asked, though if he was impatient or unnerved it didn't show.

"What Joe and I are seeing is probably DMS lite. I'll bet your Brooklyn hangar is ay-jay squared away. The tightest security, checks, and double checks; a lot of security redundancies. But down here you've had to put this facility together in days. Mind you, what you've accomplished in those days is incredible, and I frankly would never have thought it was possible to do. You're a remarkable man, Mr. Church."

"I don't need an ego-stroke, Doctor."

"Nor am I in the mood to give you one," Rudy said with a touch of asperity in his voice. "My point is that out of necessity you've had to put this whole thing together too fast and under too much pressure. The Brooklyn model is probably a good one but for it to be as tight as you want it would require time. More time than you have. You've probably had to call in markers, ask for favors from other agencies; you've probably had to go through channels in ways you normally wouldn't, and as a result the local reality of the DMS station here at the warehouse has holes in it. And as a result of that . . . people have died."

"Hey Rude, c'mon, man," I said softly.

He ignored me. "I'm not saying any of this to blame you, Mr. Church. Not at all. My point is that you are up against the wall, and all of the practiced cool in the world can't change the effect that has on you as a physical being. Brain chemistry is only ever partially under our control. You are under tremendous physical and psychological strain . . . and right now you are probably tearing yourself up inside because of what happened in Room Twelve."

"I don't think we really have time for this," Church said, but his eyes never left Rudy's face. I don't think he even blinked.

"We don't have time for us to get into it as deeply as we need to," Rudy said, "but we have to address it, in part, right now. My friend's life is being put on the line. For the third time today. My own life is potentially in jeopardy as long as I'm in this facility and as long as there is a traitor here."

"We're all at risk—"

"No. That's not what I mean, and I think you know that. I'm not asking you to open up to me, Church, not here and not ever unless you choose to; but what I am saying is you have to acknowledge that these events and the presence of the traitor are connected to actions you've taken." He held up a finger to keep Church from interrupting him. "Actions you have *had* to take. If we could wind this back and start over again I don't know if there is anything that could have been done differently. This may be an inevitable occurrence given the circumstances. Therefore you need to bear in mind that today's events may have been beyond your control. Yes, you need to tighten security in any way you can. Hindsight advises that. Yes, you need to conduct your search for the traitor, leaving no stone unturned. Yes, you need to triple-check the backgrounds of every single person in the DMS, especially recent hires. But—and this is the real point—you have to keep focused, eyes on the prize, and not let guilt or anger deflect you from the primary purpose here, which is to stop the terrorists from launching this dreadful weapon. If today's tragedy throws you off your game, then we could all die. My advice to you, Mr. Church, is to take your guilt and anger and put them on a shelf, at least until Joe and his team are back from the crab plant. Stay focused and stay in charge."

Church said nothing for maybe five seconds. "Do you think I'm unaware of these things, Doctor?"

"I don't know what you're aware of, Mr. Church. You keep your emotions under check better than anyone I've ever met. But no matter how tough you are, and I imagine you are one very tough hombre, you are still human. Inside you might be seething with rage, and if God is kind I hope he never puts me in your path when you're enraged. You and Joe are a lot alike in that. Controlled most of the time, but there is a point where control goes all to hell and what is left is pure, lethal rage. That's all well and good if you find yourself—God forbid—in a room full of walkers; but I would not like to think that the man directing the subtleties of an operation of this kind is going on rage and looking for payback. The problem is that with you I can't tell how close to a loss of control you are. You aren't a robot, so you have to be suppressing your emotions. Just remember that suppressing emotions is not the same thing as actually removing emotions from your physiological makeup. If you're as smart a man as I think you are then you'll consider what I've said. You have to recognize distracting emotions and make very, very sure that they don't affect the decisions you make, and the time frame in which those decisions are made."

Rudy took a small half-step back. It was as if he diminished in size from a giant to an ordinary man in that subtle move. He switched off his perceptual X-ray, withdrew his own energy from the moment, and left a gap for Church to fill. How Church filled that gap would make all the difference, and I wished I could be inside Rudy's head to see how he was measuring the moment.

Church was silent for maybe fifteen seconds. I held my breath. Then Church gave one of his fractional smiles and a short nod. "I'll take it under advisement."

Rudy studied him and he must have found something in the stone mask that was Church's face, because he nodded in return. "Fair enough."

"Hey, guys," I said, "I hate to break up this Dr. Phil moment but I kind have to go fight some zombies."

Rudy said something very foul in Spanish and Church turned away to assess the teams, though I think he really did it to hide a smile.

Chapter Fifty-Seven

The DMS Warehouse, Baltimore / Tuesday, July 1; 1:16 A.M.

WE PILED INTO the helicopter, a SH-60 Seahawk fitted out with every kind of gunpod and missile launcher in the catalog. Once we were in and the door closed, we huddled down and switched to helmet mikes so everyone could hear above the rotor noise. Church joined us. He put an open pack of small high-protein cereal bars on one corner of the map. *Combat version of cookies*, I thought. *Guy was a freak.*

When we'd boarded I pushed Rudy into a corner. "Sit tight, watch and listen," I said. He nodded, looking scared. He was going only as far as the staging area, but I wanted him next to Church throughout.

The Seahawk's big T700-GE-701C engines roared and the bird lifted off and headed southeast at one hundred and fifty knots, with three other helos—two of them bearing Alpha Team and the other with support staff—in close formation.

"Here's the bottom line," I began once everyone was settled down around the map. "Someone bypassed the security and opened the door to Room Twelve. As a result we have ten casualties: six medical staff, our prisoner, and three soldiers, plus one other soldier who has been bitten and infected by the walkers. That means that pretty soon he'll be dead, too."

Bunny and Top said nothing; they'd been there. Ollie ran a shaking hand through his hair. Skip looked ten years old and terrified.

"Who did it?" Skip asked.

"Unknown at this time."

"This was an accident, right?" Ollie said.

I let silence answer that.

"Oh man," he said. He looked down at the stock of his MP5.

Skip was a half-step slower. "Wait . . . you mean this wasn't an accident? Someone *did* this on purpose?"

"Are we talking a spy here," Ollie asked, "or a terrorist infiltrator?"

"We have to look at both options," Church said, and when Ollie started to say something he added, "And until further notice this discussion is over."

My guys all looked at me, and despite what Church just said I wanted to put my own stamp on things. "Right now we don't know who did this or how many infiltrators we have, so until further notice everyone—and I do mean everyone—is a suspect. You don't like it, too bad. I'm not asking for comments right now, but hear me on this: I will find out who did this and when I do that person is going to live forever in a world of hurt. If anyone knows or learns anything connected with this I want to hear about it. Come to me in private, talk to me one to one. I'm offering a white flag for contact but it expires in twenty-four hours, after which I'm going to be witch-hunting under a black flag. I want to know that you hear and understand."

"Hooah," growled Top.

Bunny nodded. "Loud and clear, boss."

"Yes, sir," said Skip.

Ollie bared his teeth. "We find whoever tried to rat-fuck us, you hold him and I'll cut his balls off."

The tension in the air was thick as quicksand. I handed out intelligence briefs. "Read through the materials. You have fifteen minutes."

"Questions?" I asked when they all put the intel reports down.

Bunny cleared his throat. "Boss, not to be a pain in the ass, but all I've been reading here is 'we don't know this' and 'we don't know that.' I mean . . . what *do* we know?"

"What do you want to know?"

"Well," Bunny said to Church, "for a start who are the hostiles? Saying 'terrorist' kinda tells me dick. Sir."

"I'll tell you what I told Captain Ledger," Church said. "The cell taken down by the task force represents a broad range of terrorist and extremist groups." He turned and looked at Bunny, who was making a face. "Go on, Sergeant," he encouraged, "ask it."

"How does that make sense? I mean, sure we all call it the 'international terrorist community' but it's not like they all get together for bowling night. It's not a club, right? But we're supposed to believe that these guys are, what, a terrorist coffee klatch?"

There were some chuckles and even Church managed a small smile. Probably fake, but still there.

"You find that to be unlikely? You're an NCO with eight years in and you think Homeland is wrong in the way it interpreted the task force intelligence?"

He stared at Bunny and Bunny gave it right back to him. "Yes, sir, I think it's bullshit."

Church gave that smile again. "Of course you do, Sergeant, otherwise you wouldn't be here." He let that sink in for a moment. "And if any of you ever accept info without thinking it through and raising reasonable questions you'll be out of here so fast you'll get motion sick."

"Then . . ." Bunny hadn't expected that kind of comeback and it derailed him for a moment.

"Tell me what we should infer, Sergeant," Church prompted. "Because the intel, as far as details go, *is* correct. Those men were from different groups. We've verified that. Homeland thinks this means the terrorist *community* is uniting to form a front against America. What do you think of that?"

Bunny cut a look at me, and I nodded. I liked that Bunny was following the same logic I'd explored with Church. "Well," he said, grabbing on to a leather strap as the chopper banked into a climbing turn, "we got a lot of ears and eyes out there. CIA got spooks out the yingyang. Every branch of the service has their MI guys wiretapping the shit out of the whole Middle East. If the extremists were forming some kind of 'axis of evil,' " and here he paused for a laugh, and got it, "then there's no way we wouldn't have heard at least *something* about it. All this time and we don't hear a peep? No fucking way."

"Go on." Now Church's smile seemed genuine.

"So . . . has anyone thought that instead of this being the start of the Terrorist Mighty Marching Society, it's more like a kind of whaddya call it? A brain trust?"

"Keep going," I said.

"Maybe someone—maybe the sick fuck who cooked up this prion bullshit—kinda had a great idea but needed an A-team to make it work. Not your run-of-the-mill fanatics but guys with real brain cells. The report from Dr. Hu says that this is—how'd he put it?—'radically advanced' technology. So somehow our bad guy puts the word out that he's recruiting top of the line only."

"I don't buy it," said Ollie.

"Me, neither," agreed Top Sims. "That'd be in the wind, too. We'd have heard something. No, this smart sumbitch has a pipeline into the terrorist community and he's directly recruiting. One to one. It'd be safer that way."

"Sure," Ollie agreed. "Easier to keep it all on the down-low."

"But that brings up another problem," said Bunny, but then he shook his head. "No, maybe a lead. If he's recruiting outside of his own group then you got to figure there's going to be a percentage of times he's going to get turned down. Not everyone's going to want to play that kind of baseball. If this guy is as smart as he seems to be, then he wouldn't let anyone just stroll off who has even a whiff of what he's doing."

Skip snapped his fingers. "Right! We should check international records to see if any terrorists with known skills in high-end weapons or medicine have gone off the board. This guy would probably kill anyone who doesn't sign with his team."

Church turned to me. "Your team seems to be able to read your mind." To the men he said, "Captain Ledger had the same thought and as a result I've initiated just such a database search. At his suggestion we've also begun searching for nonterrorist-affiliated scientists in the appropriate fields who may have disappeared, or whose family members are conspicuously missing."

"Scientists might take all sorts of radical research risks if their wife or daughter were sitting somewhere with a gun to their heads," Top agreed. "My kids were in that kind of danger, there's nothing I wouldn't do." I saw a shadow pass over his face and remembered that he'd buried his son and saw his daughter crippled for life because of this war.

I said, "Okay, tell us why our mystery man is searching so far out of his own group."

Bunny was about to speak but Ollie got there first. " 'Cause even in a large group or small country you're not going to have enough top minds in the right fields who are *also* extremists willing to die for their cause."

"Right," Skip said.

Top nodded. "Yeah, that's too much to ask, and it's too shallow a fishing hole. You need to pick and choose; you need to find the right guys—smart as a motherfucker and willing to die. That's got to be a small club even worldwide."

"What I'm saying," Bunny agreed, nodding. "This stuff is slick. Really slick." He sipped some coffee from a metal travel mug and looked at Church and me over the rim. "No one at Homeland thought of that?"

"Red tape and too many levels of bureaucracy can impede practical thought," Church said.

"Which is a nice way of saying they have their thumbs up their asses," Ollie interpreted.

Church said nothing, but he didn't appear to disagree.

Top narrowed his eyes and looked appraisingly at Church. "Sir . . . I pretty much know why you picked us. And those science geeks you got on our team? I'm gonna guess there's not one of them that ever scored second best in the school science fair."

Church smiled.

"So what we have here," Skip said, "is an all-star squad."

Ollie grinned. "Okay, so they got a geek squad and the DMS has a geek squad. But you also got a crew of first-team shooters. Who do they have?"

I said, "Javad Mustapha—one player on their team—started an outbreak that wiped out two DMS teams and over two hundred civilians. You saw firsthand what the walkers did to those kids and to the guards and lab techs in Delaware; and you know what happened in Room Twelve. We have shooters, they have walkers."

That shut everyone up for a while and we sat there in the belly of the chopper as it tore through the Maryland skies.

"Surprise was a big factor in the loss at the hospital. Same goes for what happened last night," I said. "What are the chances that any of us are going to be surprised if we run into a walker at the crab plant?"

Bunny snorted. "If it moans and moves I'm gonna kill it."

"Hooah." They all said it together.

"And if there are a lot of them?" Church asked.

"I killed me a bunch of walkers in Delaware, sir," said Top, "and I was in a good mood. After Room Twelve I'm a mite pissed off."

"Fucking-A," Skip agreed.

"Fine," Church said, "but here's the thing. Echo Team is going into the plant for a look-no-touch. As you rightly put it, our intel is weak. The mission objective is to get more information because we got virtually nothing of worth from Delaware. If it looks like a pull-back-and-rethink then that's what we'll do. We have the option to upgrade into an assault but there are some operational priorities which include securing undamaged computers and drives, and apprehending suspects. If you have to pull triggers then try—and I mean really try—to bring me back someone with a pulse."

Skip said, "I thought that these clowns die after six, eight hours unless they take a pill. How you going to sweat info out of them with that kind of deadline?"

Mr. Church's face was stone. "My copy of the Geneva Convention got burned up in a fire. I won't need six hours."

They were four very tough men and every one of them was scared silent by the uncompromising tone of his voice. After a moment Ollie cleared his throat. "What do we do if we run into armed resistance?"

"If you draw fire you return fire. This is not a suicide mission, Lieutenant Brown. I've already buried too many of my people in the last week." He paused to make sure everyone was giving him every bit of their attention. "You will try to accomplish the mission objectives in priority order, but you do what you have to do to come back alive."

"Okay," I said, "eyes on the map. The crab processing plant is located on the Chesapeake Bay off Tangier Sound. The southwest side of the building fronts the Pocomoke River eight hundred yards from where the river spills out into the bay. There's a wooden dock where crab boats tie up. The rest of the property is a U-shaped parking lot. Lots of open ground."

Ollie tapped the map. "Almost no cover. If they have cameras with night vision we'd be chopped to pieces. We'll need some kind of diversion or another route in."

"I have something in mind," I said. "The building is one story, flat, and about fifty-five thousand square feet. Before it was used for seafood it was a boat storage warehouse, but has since been converted. We know from the building inspector's report from this past January that the northeast corner is used for offices and bulk storage—empty containers, labels, rolls of plastic wrap, that sort of thing. The rest is the actual plant."

"They still processing crabs in there?" Skip asked.

"Negative. The place is in receivership. The original staff was laid off on February fifteenth."

"So, okay, if this place is closed then why are there, what . . . eight, nine vehicles in the lot?"

"That's one of those things we don't know," I said. "Under ordinary circumstances I would presume that they're there to oversee the company's reorganization; but these three trucks here are all of the same make and model as the one followed to the crab plant by the task force."

"Trucks carrying what?" Bunny asked.

"Cargo unknown, but it could have been one or more of those big blue cases."

Ollic narrowed his eyes as he studied the satellite image. "What kind of traffic in or out since then?"

"Except for a security guard," I said, "none."

Top looked dubious. "We see anyone other than the guard?"

I shook my head. "No. Just the one guard and he works four ten-hour shifts a week, from ten at night to six A.M. Long-range photos have ID'd him as Simon Walford, age fifty-three, a rent-a-cop from a company based in Elkton, though Walford lives right up the road. He's worked the plant for two years and change."

"We know anything about him?" Skip asked.

"Nothing that fits the profile of a terrorist sympathizer. Widowed,

lives alone. No military record, no arrests, no memberships in anything except Netflix and BJ's Wholesale. Cheats on his taxes, but it's
penny-ante stuff to hide income from a side business he has repairing
two-stroke engines. Lawnmowers, weed whackers. Son owns a lawn
care business. His bank records show what you'd expect—virtually no
savings, no portfolio, and maybe two grand in checking. Not living
check to check, but close enough. His e-mail is clean and about the
only thing he uses the Internet for is Classmates.com. His thirty-fifth
high school reunion is in August."

"So he's a nobody," Skip concluded, but Bunny and Top both turned
to him.

"That's not what the man said, boy," Top snapped. "He said that he
has no trail. Doesn't mean the same thing as no involvement."

"Trust no one," said Bunny. "Didn't you ever watch the *X-Files*?"
Skip colored.

"I went over this guy's profile," I said, "and sure, it looks like he's
okay; but he could be anything from a turncoat to a closet mercenary to
a convert to the cause. Or he could be clueless. We don't know until we
get there."

"Just the one guard?" Skip said, eager to correct his mistake. "Four
shifts a week?"

"One we've seen," Church corrected, pleased with the observation.
He leaned over and slid the box of cereal bars toward the young sailor.
Skip hesitated and then took a granola one and looked at it for a full five
seconds without opening it. I wondered if he was going to have it
framed.

"The grounds are not patrolled during the day," I said. "When Walford goes home he locks the gate from the outside. Except for Walford;
no one else has come or gone."

"If I say 'that's weird' I won't get a cookie, will I?" Bunny said, and
Church kind of smiled. Bunny reached out and took a chocolate cereal
bar with a "Mother, May I?" expression on his face. He tore it open and
popped it in his mouth.

There was a burst of squelch and the pilot's voice said, "ETA forty minutes."

"Okay, guys . . . assessment," I said, and everyone's face sharpened.

Skip said, "Nine vehicles . . . so we got nine potential hostiles."

"Truck had two," Ollie said looking at his notes, "so make it ten."

"No," Top said, rustling his copy of the intel report, "look at page four. Trucks are registered to the company. Probably parked there on a regular basis, which means that the two guys who drove it there likely commuted in by car. We have six cars in the lot." He looked up. "Thermal scans?"

"Place packs seafood," Church said. "They got ice machines and refrigeration. Thermal signals are weak. We've picked up a max of four weak human signals at one time. Distortion is too bad to permit any useful guesses as to how many people are in there."

"Whoa, whoa," Bunny said, "if this place has been shut down since the beginning of the year why the hell they running ice machines and fridges?"

I beamed at him. "That's a damn good question, isn't it?"

Church considered him for a moment, then pushed the package of cereal bars all the way over to Bunny. Skip looked crushed.

"Shit," Top muttered. "So we got no idea what the hell we're stepping into. Could be twenty people in there. Could be twenty of those dead-ass zombies in there, too."

"We have to be open to any possibility," I agreed.

Church nodded. "We know this: as of the Presidential Order in my jacket pocket that crab plant is now designated enemy soil. Rules of war apply, the Constitution is suspended. Hostiles are designated as enemy combatants."

"Sucks to be them," Bunny said, munching a cookie.

Chapter Fifty-Eight

WE TOUCHED DOWN behind a volunteer fire station a mile from the plant. A second chopper stood nearby and the lot was crammed with all manner of official vehicles, most of them painted to look nondescript. But I've seen enough of them to tell.

We piled out and hurried in through the station's back door. Gus Dietrich was already there, standing by two wheeled racks of equipment. Each member of the team was issued a communicator that looked like a streamlined Bluetooth. By tapping the earpiece we could change channels. Channel one was secured for team communication, which would be monitored by Church and his command group in a van that was parked a half-mile away from the plant. Other channels were for full-team operations, should it become necessary to bring in the special ops, SWAT, and other specialists on standby. One channel was reserved as my private line to Church.

The Saratoga Hammer Suits had arrived and we all tried them on. They fit like loose coveralls and were surprisingly comfortable and mobile. I did some kicks and punches in the air while wearing my suit, and even with the Kevlar vest and other limb padding it didn't slow me down much at all. Bunny's was a bit tighter and he looked like a stuffed sausage.

We had our choice of weapons. I still didn't have a sound suppressor for my .45, so I kept the Beretta M9, and anyway it was lighter and already loaded with nine-millimeter Parabellum hollow-points. When I looked up I saw Rudy watching me, his eyes showing doubt and concern.

"*Si vis pacem, para bellum,*" I quoted as I holstered the gun.

He squinted as he worked out the translation, " 'If you seek peace, prepare for war.' "

"Hooah," Top murmured from a few feet away.

"That the trademark of the gun manufacturer?" Rudy asked.

"No," I said as I checked the magazine and slapped it back into place. "The ammunition is nine-millimeter Parabellum. The name comes from a quote by the Roman writer Publius Flavius Vegetius Renatus."

"At least formal education wasn't wasted on you," Rudy said. He cleared his throat. "Good luck to all of you. Come back safely." He backed away and sat on the rear bumper of one of the fire trucks, hands in his lap, fingers knotted together in a nervous tangle. He was sweating but I doubt it had anything to do with the heat of this humid July night.

I gave him a wink as I put extra magazines in a Velcro pouch around my waist. Each of my four guys had MP5s fitted with quick-release sound suppressors. I strapped a sturdy fighting knife to my calf—the Ranger combat knife, which is ten and three-quarter inches from pommel to the tip of its black stainless steel blade and is nicely balanced for close fighting or throwing.

Grace Courtland's chopper landed while my men were checking each other's equipment; she led Alpha Team in and they immediately began sorting out their Hammer suits. She walked over to me.

"Enjoying your first day with the DMS?" she said with a wicked grin.

"Yeah. I find it very relaxing."

"Well, maybe tomorrow we can go find some bombs to defuse."

"It'd make a nice change."

She grinned at me, but I could see ghosts behind her smiling eyes. St. Michael's was still as current for her as Delaware and Room 12 were for me. The "mark" was there in her eyes and I knew she could see it in mine. I found the mutual recognition weirdly comforting.

"How's your team?" she asked.

"Ready to do their jobs. Yours?"

"My team will be on deck throughout. You say the word and we'll come running." She paused. "I wish I was going in with you."

"Thanks," I said. "When this is over I would like to get drunk. Care to join me?"

She studied my face for a moment. "That sounds lovely. I'll buy the first round." She offered me her hand. "You're a good man, Joe. Church thought so all along, and he's seldom wrong. Sorry it took so long for me to catch up."

I took her hand. "Water under the bridge."

"Don't get killed," she said, trying to make a joke of it, but her eyes were a little glassy. She turned quickly away and headed over to where her team was loading their gear into the back of a fire truck.

I looked around and saw Church about fifty yards away just closing his cell phone. I signaled to him and went over. "Before we roll I want to set a few things in motion," I said. "I want you to start building me a top-of-the-line forensics team. No second-stringers and nobody I don't know personally."

"Who do you have in mind?"

I pulled a sheet of paper out of my pocket. "This is a list of forensics people I know and trust. Most of all I want Jerry Spencer from D.C. I believe you already know him."

"We offered to bring him on board, but he declined."

"Make a better offer. Jerry is the best crime-scene man I ever met."

"Very well." Church touched my arm. "We have no leads at all on who the spy might be, Captain. That means it could be anyone." He was looking past me to where Echo and Alpha Teams were gearing up. "Watch your back."

He offered his hand, and I took it.

I turned away and yelled out loud. "Echo Team—let's roll!"

Chapter Fifty-Nine

Crisfield, Maryland / Wednesday, July 1; 2:51 A.M.

THE FOURTH OF July was still three days away but there were already fireworks. Not a pretty starfield or fiery chrysanthemums in the night sky—this was a single bloom of intense orange-red that soared upward from the edge of a weather-worn set of wooden steps that led from the choppy waters of the Tangier Sound to the creosote planking of the dock at the Blue Point Crab and Seafood processing plant in Crisfield. The impact followed the roar of heavy marine engines as a blue cigarette boat fishtailed through the black water while an apparently drunk pilot struggled sloppily for control. The boat hit the dock at full throttle and exploded, the full fuel tanks rupturing from the impact and igniting from the laboring engine. There was a deep-throated roar like an angry dragon and flames shot upward to paint the entire sound in shades of Halloween orange and fireplace red.

It was too early in the morning for witnesses, but there dozens of people sleeping aboard their anchored boats and within a few minutes each of them was on a cell phone or ship-to-shore radio. Almost immediately the air was rent with the piercing screams of fire engines and ambulances tearing along the country roads.

Simon Walford was on duty in his guard shack reading a David Morrell novel by lamplight and sipping coffee when the boat hit the dock. He spilled half a cup down the front of his uniform shirt and was sputtering in shock as he keyed the radio handset to try and call the incident in to his supervisor, who did not answer the call. It had been two days since Walford had spoken to anyone in the plant, and two weeks since he had seen a single living soul. The cars were all still in the lot, though. It didn't make sense. He grabbed his walkie-talkie, ran out of his booth, and raced across the parking lot to the dock, but as soon as he saw the flames he knew there would be no hope of finding survivors. The heat from the blaze kept him well back. All he got was a glimpse of a blackened form hunched forward in the pilot's seat, his body wreathed in flames, his limbs as stiff and unmoving as a mannequin.

"Good God!" Walford breathed. He called it into 911, but even before the call went through he could hear sirens in the distance. Had he been a little less shocked by what had happened he might have been surprised at how incredibly fast the local volunteer fire department had been able to respond to the crisis, especially at that time of night. As it was, all he could think of was how helpless he felt. He tried his supervisor's number again, but still got the answering machine, so he left an urgent and almost incoherent message. Shocked and impotent, he trudged back to his station and unlocked the fence to allow the fire trucks to enter.

Chapter Sixty
Crisfield, Maryland / Wednesday, July 1; 2:54 A.M.

WE WATCHED THE boat explosion on Dietrich's laptop.

"Sweet," Skip murmured. We were parked on the side of the road three quarters of a mile from the plant, lights off.

"Christ," complained Bunny, "I'm boiling in this shit."

"Life's hard, ain't it?" said Top, who was sweating as much as the rest of us but didn't seem to care. I'm pretty sure that if Top Sims had an arrow stuck in his kidney he wouldn't let the pain show on his face. Some guys are like that.

"Okay," yelled Gus Dietrich, "the 911 call just went through."

"Light 'er up," I told him, and the driver fired up the engine and punched on the lights and sirens.

So far our hastily formed plan was going well. One of Church's staff engineers had rigged a remote piloting unit to the cigarette boat that had been confiscated when the task force took the warehouse, and they'd gotten two store mannequins from God only knows where and strapped them into the front seats. Dietrich worked the remote controls and made quite a show by zigzagging the boat through the anchored pleasure craft and generally causing a ruckus. If there were any witnesses they would report a drunk driving like a lunatic. The cigarette was loaded to the gunnels with gas cans and small C4 charges which Dietrich radio-detonated as soon as the boat struck the dock. It was way too big an explosion, more like something you see in movies, and it was damned impressive.

Within minutes we were being frantically waved through the open gates by the security guard. Our driver angled left and headed toward the big red-painted emergency standpipe and as we squealed to a halt everyone piled out. The second engine pulled closer to the dock and we had calls in for three more engines to join us. That would put a lot of men and women in identical coats and helmets running around. A few of them would even be actual firefighters. Police cars seemed to appear by the dozen—state and local. I knew that Grace was in one of them, and Alpha Team was peppered throughout the rest. Church was in a command van parked around the bend in the access road, and the special ops teams were in vans behind him. Close, but would they be close enough if we encountered heavy resistance?

As we piled out, Bunny and Top went directly to the standpipe, passing the line of parked cars and trucks that had been spotted by the spy satellite and helo surveillance. Skip and Ollie pulled a hose off the truck and began unlimbering it as they walked backward toward the pipe.

"Camera on my two o'clock," I heard Bunny say in my earpiece. "Slow rotation on a ninety-degree swing."

"Copy that. I'm coming in. Give me some cover." They took their cue and began fitting a hose nozzle to the pipe. I closed on the group, watching the camera out of the corner of my eye. As soon as it swung toward the main part of the lot where all the activity was in full swing I dashed forward and flattened against the wall in what I judged to be the dead spot beneath the box-style camera. When I ran to the wall a firefighter moved from a point of concealment behind the door of the engine and hurried quickly over to take my place. We repeated this process four more times and then Echo Team was all scrunched up against the wall and real firefighters were attaching the hose to the pipe.

"Skip . . . eyes on the camera," I said. Bunny removed a sensor from his pocket and ran it over every square inch of the door and then showed me the readout.

"Standard alarm contact switch," he said. "It'll go off when we open the door."

"Perfect. Ollie, go to work." Ollie had volunteered to tackle the lock, which was a heavy industrial affair. He had to earn his pay, but in less than two minutes he had it unlocked. He kept the door closed, though, because the alarm would ring the second we opened it. If there was no one directly inside then our carnival act was going to pay off, but if even one person was inside then we were screwed as far as stealth went.

"Okay," I said into the mike, "call the cops."

The signal was relayed and a big-shouldered state trooper came loping over. I motioned to him to slow his walk so that the panning camera clearly caught him moving toward the door, and then as soon as it panned away I waved him in and he ran the last few yards. I turned and pounded my fist hard on the door for three seconds and then yanked open the door and we piled inside. Alarms began jangling loudly overhead. As soon as it closed, Ollie turned and reengaged the lock; and the trooper took his cue and continued to beat on the door, shaking it in its frame.

Immediately the five of us fanned out into a half-circle, guns out; but we needn't have bothered—the room in which we stood was big, dirty, and empty. And cold. Like the meatpacking plant had been, maybe thirty-five, forty degrees with damp air and black mold on the walls. The floor was old tile and had a big gutter down its middle, and to our left was a low stone wall beyond which were oversized showers. There was a row of heavy pegs on which were still hung a couple of old oilskin jackets. This was where the crab fishermen must have come in after offloading their catch, to shower the seawater and crab gook off their foul-weather gear before heading into the interior of the plant. There was a line of foul-smelling toilet stalls to our right and the wall in front of us was set with rows of lockers. A corridor broke left past the lockers. All of it was visible in the piss-yellow glow of flickering fluorescent lights.

I signaled Skip to watch the hall while the rest of us shucked our coats and helmets and stowed them out of sight in a shower stall.

Skip signaled us by breaking squelch and then hand-signed that someone was coming. We all faded back. Ollie and Skip went into toilet stalls and crouched on the seats; Top and Bunny hid in shower stalls and I crouched down behind the low concrete wall. I could only see around the edge of it and there were shadows behind me so I was pretty well hidden. I had my silenced Beretta ready in a two-hand grip as I strained to hear the footsteps through the jangling alarm.

Right around the time we heard the running footsteps the alarm stopped. The trooper continued to pound on the door and now he was shouting, too, sounding genuinely outraged that no one had come to check out the fire. Then a man stepped into view with an AK-47 in his hands. He looked nervous and sweaty, his eyes round and white as he stared at the door. He licked his lips and looked around the shower room, but didn't see anything. We'd been careful not to scuff the floor.

After a moment's indecision he backpedaled, opened one of the lockers and put the assault rifle inside, closed it and pulled a small walkie-talkie from his jacket pocket. As he clicked it on he moved into the spill of weak light from one of the few overhead fluorescents that still worked. He was Middle Eastern, with a receding hairline, short beard, and a beaky nose. "I'm at the back door," he said into the walkie-talkie, speaking in Waziri, a dialect from southern Iran. I could just about understand him. "No . . . the door is locked but I think the firemen want to get in. They are banging on the door." He listened for a few moments, but the voice on the other end was too garbled for me to understand. "Okay," he said, and clicked off the radio.

In very good English he yelled: "All right, all right, I'm coming!" He pushed the door open and the big state trooper filled the doorway with his bulk and shone his light right into the man's face.

"Didn't you hear me knocking, sir? Didn't you hear the explosion? How can you not be aware that half the fire companies in the county are in your parking lot?" As ordered, the trooper went immediately into an outraged tirade, which provoked a defensive reaction in the other man, and within seconds the two of them were locked in a screaming match. It was clear the Iranian was regretting opening the door, but he was caught up in his role now, playing the part of a clueless and aggrieved worker who wants no part of something that happened on the docks. He made a lot of noise about being a supervisor for a crew mapping out renovations for a building that had already been sold. He shouted names and phone numbers for the police to call. He also told the cop to get the damn light out of his face; and he had to repeat that three times before the trooper did. Both the Iranian and the trooper could yell like fishwives. I checked my watch. The argument had lasted two minutes. Any second now another trooper would call the big guy away and they'd allow the "supervisor" to go about his business; and sure enough, I heard Gus Dietrich calling the cop away.

"The fire marshal is going to need you to sign a release form," the trooper yelled.

"Sure, sure, fine. Don't harass me. This is bullshit. Here is the card for the lawyer who is handling things. He will be happy to handle whatever needs to be done."

The trooper snatched the card out of the Iranian's fingers and stormed off. It was all very impressive, with exactly the right amount of indignation.

The Iranian pulled the door shut again and double-checked the lock. He keyed his walkie-talkie again and in rapid Waziri relayed what was happening. "Okay," he said at length, "I'm coming back." He pocketed the radio, cast one last look around, retrieved his AK-47 from the locker, and headed back along the hallway. I waited a full minute after the sound of his footfalls vanished before I stood up. The others crept out of hiding to join me.

"Skip, you watch the hall again," I whispered. "You see so much as a cockroach you break squelch twice. Top, Bunny, I want you both to hold this position. Ollie, you're with me. Code names here on out. Small arms only."

They nodded and we began moving. Skip dropped down to a shooter's kneel using one of the rows of lockers as cover. There was enough light to see, but only just; and if it went lights-out we had night vision as backup. Bunny positioned himself behind the low wall so that it would serve as a bunker if we got chased. Top faded to the other side of the big room and vanished into a bank of shadows.

Ollie looked down the shadowy corridor. "Clear," he murmured. We set off into the belly of the beast.

Chapter Sixty-One
Crisfield, Maryland / Wednesday, July 1; 3:15 A.M.

THE BUILDING WAS quiet as a tomb and as cold as a meat locker. I hated that because of what it implied. All I could hear was the faintest hum from the refrigeration compressors on the far side of the warehouse. Our gum-rubber shoes made no sound as Ollie and I crept along, hugging the wall, looking for security cameras, moving from shadow to shadow.

I knew from the schematics that there was a central corridor that ran the length of the building; that much was in the original floor plans, but the hallway in front of us didn't look long enough to go the whole way. We had no plans that showed renovations made since the plant went into receivership. The corridor ran straight for maybe three hundred feet and then vanished in shadows that looked solid enough to be a wall. There were heavy steel doors set about every ten yards and as we moved up to the first one we checked every inch of the floor, walls and ceiling for cameras and saw none.

The first door we came to was set with a simple keycard lock. Nothing that would slow us up for very long if we were in a hurry.

"Bug," I said, and Ollie fished in his pocket and removed two tiny devices. The first was the size of a postage stamp and painted a neutral gray. He handed it to me and I pulled off a clear plastic cover to expose the photosensitive chemicals, and then pressed it to the side of the metal door for three seconds. When I finished counting Mississippi I pulled the strip off and saw that it was now the same color as the door. I turned it over and removed the tape from the other side, exposing a strong adhesive, and then pressed it to the door at about knee level, below where the eye would not naturally fall when opening a door. I examined the results and Ollie and I exchanged a raised-eyebrows look. Unless you knew exactly where to look the thing was invisible, blending in completely with the paint on the door. The little chameleon bugs were supposed to have incredible pickup and could relay info up to a quarter mile.

"Nice," Ollie said as he handed me the second device, a silver disk the size of a nickel. I removed the adhesive backing and placed the device on the underside of the keycard box. The bug would do nothing until someone used a keycard to open the door and then it would record the magnetic code and transmit it immediately to the DMS where it would be processed through MindReader and the code signal would be sent back to us. We each carried master keycards that could be remote-programmed by the DMS techs. Within ninety seconds of someone using a keycard here we'd all have cards with the same code. Our master keycards could store up to six separate card codes. Church really had nice toys, but I hoped it worked as well as promised.

I tapped my earpiece. "First one's in place."

We moved down the hallway and repeated the process at each door. Counting both sides of the hall, there were eleven doors in all; then the hallway ended at a T-juncture, with shorter corridors branching at right angles.

"Split up?" Ollie suggested.

I nodded. "Break squelch once if you find anything, twice if you need me to come running."

"Roger that," he said and melted away.

This part of the building was badly lit, with fluorescent lights hanging from their wires like debris caught in some gigantic spider web. The ceiling was cracked, water dripped from a damaged pipe somewhere in the walls. The floor was wet and the smell back here was awful. I edged forward carefully; debated switching to night vision, but the light was enough so that I could pick my way. My foot touched something and I looked down to see the bloated corpse of a dead rat lying there, its eyes and mouth open, tongue lolling. I stepped over it and moved forward until I reached the first door. It was closed and blocked by a row of dented trash cans filled with all kinds of junk: old coats, bent umbrellas, broken toys, newspapers, soiled diapers. Even with the cold there were flies buzzing everywhere and the stench intensified. I held my breath while I placed the chameleon bug and keycard scanner and was grateful when I could move away.

There was more trash in the hallway. Odd stuff. A deflated football lying on a brand-new left sneaker. An open briefcase whose papers had spilled out and become soaked with rust-colored water. A smashed cell phone. Two Frisbees and a push-up bra. Half a dozen iPods. Dozens of letters—most of them junk mail and bills—still sealed and stamped. The broken body of a headless Barbie doll. An overturned shopping cart filled with aluminum cans.

The sight of the junk scattered in the dark and rusty water gave me the creeps. Bad thoughts were forming in my head and the sane half of my brain was telling me to do an about-face and get the hell out of here. I moved along the hall to bug the last three doors before the hallway ended at another bend. With my pistol in both hands I hugged the near wall and then quick-looked around the corner, dodging my head in and back and then analyzing the flash image. What I saw sent an icy chill rippling down my spine.

Oh man, I thought. *Don't let me be right about this.*

I rounded the corner, still checking for cameras and threats, pistol barrel following my line of vision so that it pointed everywhere I looked. In front of me was a big set of double doors. It wasn't the door or even the stench that made me feel like there wasn't enough air to breathe. The floor was heaped with lots more clothes, more personal items, more human detritus; some of it looked new, undamaged. It looked like stuff that had been taken away from ordinary people. A lot of ordinary people.

The door was sealed with a heavy padlock that was cinched tight through heavy metal rings that had been welded to the steel doorframe.

And the door, the surrounding walls, and the floor were all smeared with some viscous substance that had dried to a chocolaty-brown color. I bent close and saw that hidden by the smeared goo were wires that trailed up the wall and disappeared into small holes that had been drilled through the concrete. I turned and followed the wires down the wall and along the hall for five feet to where they vanished behind a fire extinguisher that was mounted at chest height. Booby trap. Pretty well hidden, too. The question was whether the charge was inside the extinguisher or inside that locked room. Or both.

Screw this. I backed carefully away, then stopped and looked at where the water lapped against the bottom of the door. The rust color was richer and redder by the door as if something inside were feeding pigment to the mix.

Understanding hit me like a punch and I rose quickly and backed away from the door, feeling my heart hammering as an atavistic dread sprang up in my chest. I stared at the stained water and the smears on the walls as the full horror of it sank in. The dark muck smeared on the doors was not mud, and the water wasn't stained with rust.

All of it, every square inch of it, was blood.

Chapter Sixty-Two
Crisfield, Maryland / Wednesday, July 1; 3:23 A.M.

I TOOK A step forward and leaned as close to the door as I could without touching it. Beyond was silence. And yet . . . it was a strange silence, like someone holding their breath on the other end of a phone line. You're sure they're there but you can hear anything. I didn't like this one damn bit and moved back to the bend in the hall. No sign of Ollie and no sounds from his direction. That silence didn't feel good, either, but it wasn't the same as what I'd sensed—or imagined—from beyond that grisly door.

I crouched down behind the trash cans and tapped my earpiece to open a secure channel to the DMS. "Deacon, do you read? This is

Cowboy," I said, using the code names we agreed upon before we saddled up. Rudy had suggested mine. Knowing the military sense of humor, it could have been a lot worse. I knew a guy back in the Rangers who got hung with the code name Cindy-Lou Who.

"Reading Cowboy; this is Deacon." The headsets were so good it was like Church had snuck up behind me again and was whispering in my ear.

I quickly reported what I'd found, including the locked door and the blood.

"Leave it for now. All video went black as soon as you entered the building. We're receiving zero wireless intel. Audio signal is fluctuating but still operational. Assume jamming devices. What's your team status?"

"Scarface is taking a walk down the hall. Joker is on surveillance; rest of team is at door-knock." I decided to give my team the nicknames I'd mentally hung on them when I met them. Joker, Scarface, Sergeant Rock, and Green Giant. "Note this: the ambient temperature whole building is just above freezing. Climate controlled. Confirm understood."

"Understood confirmed." There was a brief pause and I could guess we were both looking at that from the same angle. Church said, "It's your call, Cowboy. Come home, go for a walk, or throw a party."

"Roger that." I paused and considered my options. "Will continue to take a walk. All options open, however. Confirm Amazing is on station." Amazing, shorthand for "Amazing Grace."

"That is affirmative."

"Cowboy out." I tapped the earpiece again to connect to the team channel. "Scarface. What's your twenty?"

There was no answer, not even a squelch click.

"Scarface . . . this is Cowboy. Do you copy?"

Nothing. Shit. I looked down the corridor but it was as empty as before. It told me nothing.

"Green Giant and Sergeant Rock on my six, quick and quiet!"

"Roger that, Cowboy."

I started moving as fast as caution would allow, retracing my steps down the hallway, happy to get away from that terrible door. At the T-junction I paused and looked to see Bunny's hulking form moving quickly toward me with Top Sims two steps behind him.

"Scarface went down there and doesn't answer," I said, and quickly filled them in on the locked and barred room and the detonation wires in the walls.

Bunny frowned. "Trap?"

Top Sims turned to him. "If it looks like a duck and quacks like a duck . . ."

"This is fubar, boss?" Bunny asked, looking up and down the hall. "That little drama at the front door could have been as much a fake-out on their part as ours."

"Probably was," I said, "but until we know for sure we have to try and complete the mission as assigned. Gather intel and get out with a whole skin."

"I dig the 'whole skin' part a lot," said Bunny.

"Hooah," Top agreed, then he gave me a hard look. "Ollie going missing with no shots fired is a little strange, don't you think?"

"A bit."

"We still don't know who the mole is, Cap'n," he pointed out.

"Roger that, First Sergeant, but I'm not going to hang a label on *any* of my men until I know for sure."

Top kept his stare steady for maybe ten whole seconds before he grudgingly said, "Yes, sir."

"Not to piss in the punch bowl here," interrupted Bunny, "but isn't this all a bit beside the point right now? Begging your pardons, I mean, ya'll being senior to a lowly staff sergeant."

"Shove that where the sun don't shine, farmboy," Top said, but he was grinning.

Bunny rubbed his eyes. "Man . . . this is getting to be a long-ass day."

I nodded in the direction of the corridor where Ollie had gone missing. "Primary mission rules still apply. Watch and wait. No shooting except on my say-so, and even then watch your fire and check your targets."

We went right at the T-bend and then left to follow the hall. We were three quarters of the way down the hall when one of the side doors abruptly opened and a man in a white lab coat stepped out, head bent as he frowned over notes on a clipboard, four feet from Top.

There was nowhere to hide, no time to run. The man looked up from his clipboard and his eyes snapped wide. His mouth opened and I could actually see his chest expand as he drew in a sharp breath in order to scream, but Top rose up lightning fast and kicked him hard in the solar plexus with the tip of his steel-reinforced left shoe. It was a savage kick and the man's whole body folded around Top's foot like a deflating balloon and then he dropped to the floor with a strangled squeak.

We swarmed him and had plastic cuffs on his wrists and ankles before he could manage to drag in a full breath of air. His dark skin had gone purple. Top went to the door through which the man had passed and looked in, then turned to me and gave a negative shake of the head. Bunny grabbed a handful of the man's shirtfront and screwed the barrel of his pistol into the furrow between the man's eyes. "Be quiet and stay alive," he whispered.

The guy was still bug-eyed from the kick and his eyes bulged even more when he realized that there were three big and well-armed men clustered around him. We had the power of life and death over him and he knew it. Total and unexpected helplessness can be an event that purifies the soul. It sharpens one's mental focus.

I leaned close and said in Farsi, "Do you speak English?"

He shook his head—as much as Bunny's pistol barrel would allow—and then rattled off something in what I think was Myanmar, what they used to call "Burmese." Not one of my languages. "Do you speak English?" I said in my own language.

"Yes . . . yes, English. I speak very good."

"Lucky for you. I'm going to ask you a few questions and if you answer me truthfully and completely my friend here will not shoot you. You understand?"

"Yes, yes, I understand!"

"What's your name?"

"Nujoma."

"Indian? Burmese?"

"Yes, yes, I come from Rangoon. In Burma."

"How many people are in this building?"

"I am only a—" His voice cracked and he tried it again. "I am only a technician."

"That's not what I asked. How many—?"

"I . . . I cannot. They will kill me . . ."

I grabbed him by the throat. "What do you think *I'll* do if you don't answer me?"

"They have my wife. My children. My sister. I cannot."

"Who has them? Where? Are they here in this building?"

"No. They took them from my home. They have them."

"Who took them?" I demanded again. He shook his head.

Bunny tapped him on the forehead with the barrel. "Answer the man's questions or the day's going to end in a way you won't like." But Bunny's threat was of no use. The man's eyes filled with tears and he clamped his mouth shut, giving tiny shakes of his head. I looked into his eyes and felt like I could see all the way down into the man's soul. He wasn't a terrorist; this guy was just another victim.

I shifted back a few inches to try and decrease the sense of threat, and when I spoke I softened my voice. "If you talk to us I promise that we'll see what we can do to help your family." But he shook his head, resolute in his terror.

"Tick-tock," Top muttered.

"Okay," I said. "Juice me." Top fished a hypodermic from his chest pocket, removed the plastic cap and passed it to me. The technician's eyes flared wider and tears spilled down his face. As I positioned the needle over his throat he began murmuring something in his native language; I bent forward, hoping to catch a word or phrase but then realized from the rhythm of his words that he was mumbling prayers. I plunged the needle. The tranquilizer knocked him cold in three seconds and he slumped to the floor.

"Bunny, take him back to the door. Tell Skip to alert Church that we have his prisoner. If he's been infected with the same control disease as the others then we'll need to question him before he kicks. Drop him and get back here asap."

"You got it, Boss . . . but man, I'd hate to be in this guy's shoes. I wouldn't want Church questioning me." He hoisted Nujoma over his shoulders in a fireman's carry and ran down the hall, his pace showing no indication that he was carrying at least a hundred and fifty extra pounds.

Now that we were alone I touched his arm. "Top . . . you seem to have a bug about Ollie. Why him?"

He kept looking down the hall. "Bunny was with us in Room Twelve. Says a lot. Ollie came in with everyone else. I don't like it that he was slow to respond."

"So was Skip."

"Skip's a kid. Whoever this mole is he's got field experience. He's slick enough to have pulled a fast one on Church and the whole DMS. Besides, Ollie's done a lot of work for the Company."

"The CIA? How do you know that?"

"He told us when we were trying to sort out who should be team leader. He said that he'd done extensive covert ops work. He's a spook and I don't trust spooks."

"It could be anyone," I said. "The DMS is ass deep in spooks and spies."

"Yeah," Top agreed slowly, "it sure could be anyone. For all you know it could be me. If I'd opened that door, then going back to Room Twelve with you and Bunny would have been perfect cover. Go in and pop a few caps. Who'd suspect me?"

"Yet you cleared Bunny because he was there. Double standard, Top?"

"Maybe I'm trying to confuse you, Cap'n."

"You're not. So, where's that leave us?"

A smile blossomed on his dark face. It changed him, knocking years off, but even so it never reached his eyes. "I guess it leaves us both up shit creek, Cap'n. Personally, I don't plan to trust nobody."

"Trust is a hard thing to come by in this world."

"It surely is."

We let it drop and turned our attention to the room the Burmese lab tech had come out of. I snapped on the lights and we looked around at banks of computers. Big ones that whirred constantly. The temperature of the room was even lower than the rest of the building; a wall-mounted thermometer read thirty-five degrees. I examined the nearest computer, which was about the size of a Coca-Cola machine. The make and model were on brass plates screwed to the casing. I tapped the mike.

"Cowboy to Deacon, over."

"Deacon."

"Does the name IBM Blue Gene/L mean anything to you?"

"It does. Why?"

"I'm standing in a room full of them. Advise."

"Cowboy, be advised you are holding winning lottery ticket."

"Nice to know. Infil starting to get noisy. One guest catching Z's. Green Giant taking him to back door; Joker is minding that location. Advise."

There was a slight pause and I could imagine Church nibbling the edge of a vanilla wafer as he considered his answer. "Team status?"

"Scarface is MIA. Conducting search. My call is this: radio silence ten minutes plus one second then kick the doors. Cowboy out."

The second I switched back to the team channel Bunny's voice filled my ear. "Cowboy, Cowboy, this is Green Giant. Be advised Joker is MIA."

I looked at Top who was frowning. "Repeat and verify, Green Giant."

"Verified, Joker is MIA. No time for code, boss. Our long guns are gone and the back door is sealed. Some kind of security shutter rolled down over it. We're in a box."

"Drop your cargo and get back here on the double!" I snapped. Top and I rushed out into the hall, guns ready.

"That's two down," Top said.

We turned to see Bunny running up the hall like an offensive tackle after a slow quarterback. He skidded to a stop. "I left the prisoner at the door and called it in. No sign of Skip."

I hit the button for the DMS channel. "Cowboy to Deacon, Cowboy to Deacon, request immediate hard infil. Kick the doors, repeat, kick the doors."

But all I heard over my headset was the hiss of static. The signal was gone.

A sudden noise made us all jump and we formed a fast circle, guns pointing out. Somewhere deep inside the building there was a sound like the dying sigh of a giant as big turbine engines shut down, slowing their whine as they decelerated.

"What the hell was that?" Top growled.

"I think the refrigeration units just shut off," Bunny whispered.

Then there was a loud blast as wall-mounted vents snapped from open and hot air shot into the corridor.

"Uh-oh," Top said softly. The air coming out of the vents was intensely hot and within seconds the temperature in the hall had gone up ten degrees, then fifteen. It continued to climb.

"Something tells me this is not good news," Bunny said, looking over his shoulder at me.

I tried calling Church again but still got only silence. It was the same on all channels. "Signal's being jammed."

"Yeah," Bunny confirmed, "not good news."

"Told you this was a goddamn trap," Top said.

And at that moment the locks on all of the doors along the hallway clicked open. That's when we heard the first moans as dozens of pale-faced people staggered out into the hall in front of us and behind.

This wasn't a trap . . . it was a slaughterhouse.

Chapter Sixty-Three
Crisfield, Maryland / Wednesday, July 1; 3:31 A.M.

WE WERE TRAPPED, front and back.

The closest of the people was twenty feet down the hall. It was a middle-aged woman with lank blond hair and a stained housedress. Her eyes were wide and she staggered and nearly fell as the crowd of them jostled her. I brought my pistol up and put the laser sight on her forehead. Bunny and Top were aiming at opposite ends of the hall, but none of us fired yet. My finger was still outside the trigger guard and I could feel cold slush churning in my stomach. These were civilians. Behind the woman was a young boy of no more than ten; and next to him a pretty teenage girl in a short denim skirt. There were people in business suits and bathing suits, and I caught the flash of a uniform and saw a mailman.

"Orders, sir?" hissed Top.

My finger stayed outside of the trigger guard. "We have to make sure."

"Boss . . . this is getting tight," Bunny whispered.

I wondered if this was what Baker and Charlie teams had felt at St. Michael's. Was it the absolute inhumanity of the necessary response that kept them from shooting? The meatpacking plant had been different; that had been a straight good guys/bad guys shootout, but these people were not enemy combatants. At least, not yet. The crowd choked the hallway in both directions but they milled there, not moving forward, staring at us as we stared back. It was completely surreal.

"Hold your positions," I said, staring at the crowd. The moment felt like it was stretching but in reality I knew that only a second or two had ticked off the clock.

"Maybe they ain't walkers," Bunny said.

"Say, farmboy," Top said, "why don't you go check 'em for a pulse."

"Screw that."

The middle-aged woman took an uncertain step toward us.

I slipped my finger inside the trigger guard.

She opened her mouth and for a moment I thought I saw her smile as if she was showing relief that someone had come to rescue her. But that smile stretched and stretched and stretched until it became a rapacious leer. With a scream like some jungle animal she ran straight at me.

Once she had probably been somebody's mother, somebody's wife. Maybe a grandmother with grandkids in diapers that she spoiled. I didn't know who she was or how she came to be here in this terrible place; all I knew is that she was here and whatever loving personality she might once have had, and whatever memories and secrets she once knew, were gone now, torn away by a prion-driven parasite in her blood that left behind only a shell. A predatory thing in human disguise. This surely was what Baker and Charlie teams had felt: the dreadful certainty that no action could be right in a situation so thoroughly wrong. They must have felt the horror that I now felt as this woman lunged at me, running on pale legs marked with varicose veins, closing the distance in bedroom slippers that had a lilac print; her stomach bouncing, her breasts swaying, her mouth open in a feral grin of unnatural appetite. It was enough to take the heart and soul out of anyone. It had taken the soul out of all those men and women in those other two DMS teams.

But I shot her through the face without hesitation.

Dear God, what does that say about who and what I am?

Behind me Bunny and Top opened up. We all still had the sound suppressors on our guns so the fight became a ballet of muted carnage. The walkers in the back of the crowd moaned—and that sounded low and distant; the ones in the front screeched like cats, and our handguns made high, soft sounds like someone saying, "Psst!" to get everyone's attention. Even as we fired the moment continued to be unreal.

There were at least twenty of them on my side of the corridor, and probably that many charging at my men. The narrow width of the hallway gave us no way out, but it also pushed them together into a line two abreast. They couldn't surround us, couldn't overwhelm us with their numbers. The magazine in my Beretta nine-millimeter carried fifteen rounds and I used them to kill eight of the walkers. I used one round to the chest to slow them and then a second to the brain. I shot the mailman next, and then I killed the teenage girl. I shot two men in business suits and a homeless man in rags. My fifteenth round dropped the little boy.

I dropped the magazine and slapped in another one as fast as I could, the action smooth from years of practice, but even with all my speed they nearly had me. A twenty-something who looked like she could have been a grad student had climbed over the bodies and was crouching to leap when I brought the gun back up. My shot caught her in the throat and flung her back against the others who were crowding forward. It bought me enough time to aim the next shot. And the next.

Behind me Bunny was saying: "Fuck me fuck me fuck me . . ." over and over again as he fired his gun dry and fished for a new magazine. Top fought in silence, but I believed I could feel waves of heartsick terror rolling off him as he fired.

I dropped two more and then my end of the corridor was choked with the dead. The walkers on the other side of the mountain of corpses clawed and tore at the bodies in their way, which was nearly blocked. I dropped my second magazine and fished for a third but now my hands were shaking and I almost dropped the clip. I caught it and fumbled it into place, released the slide, brought the weapon up, ready, ready . . .

"Clear!" Top yelled, and I turned to see that their combined gunfire had brought down all of the walkers on their side.

I didn't hesitate.

"Go, go, go!" I pushed them both ahead of me and we began climbing over the heaped corpses. Top watched forward, I checked behind, as we scrambled awkwardly through the gun smoke and over the tangled limbs. A hand darted out of the tangle of limbs and closed around Top's ankle; I kicked it loose and Top fired down into the mound of bodies. Maybe he hit the target, or maybe not—we didn't linger long enough to find out.

"This is fucked up," Bunny muttered as he pushed aside a fat man in a bowling shirt. Our Hammer suits were streaked with blood and I could feel droplets of it burning on my face. I heard a sound behind me and whirled, a snake of terror coiling in the pit of my stomach.

"They're coming," I snapped as the first of the walkers clambered over the piled dead at the far end. I dropped to one knee and fired two shots. His collapsing body plugged the hole, buying us seconds.

We ran. Ahead of us a door opened and a man stepped out and leveled an AK-47 at us. It was the same man who had argued with the cop. Top put two into him before he could get off a shot.

The hallway ended at another T-junction. The left-hand corridor ended in a brick wall; to our right a set of heavy steel doors stood ajar. A man was trying to pull it shut when Bunny leaped forward and grabbed him by the hair and shoulder and slammed him face forward into the wall. Bunny pounded three vicious uppercuts into his kidneys. The man groaned and sagged to his knees. If he lived through all this he'd be pissing blood for a month.

"Drag him inside," I ordered. Top guarded the hallway while Bunny then threw the dazed man like a sack of cornmeal into the next room. We flanked the doorway to provide cross-fire protection. There were four people in the room, which was a large laboratory cluttered with dozens of worktables and metal shelves of chemicals and materials. Set against one wall were two familiar-looking big blue cases. Both doors were still shut. Three of the men were Middle Eastern, two in lab coats and one dressed in jeans and a tank top. The guy with the tank top had a .45 and was swinging the barrel up when I gave him a triple-tap: two in the chest, one in the head. The men in lab coats were unarmed, but the one closest to me held a small black plastic device in one hand. The other one was already raising his hands in surrender.

The fourth man was Ollie Brown. He was strapped to a chair and his face was covered with blood.

I pointed my gun at the man with the plastic device. "Don't do it!" I yelled in Farsi and then in several other languages.

He cried, *"Seif al Din!"* in a high, hysterical voice and made his move. I shot him in the shoulder to try and stop him from pressing the button on what had to be a detonator, but it was no good: it was rigged with a dead-man's switch. Even as my bullets tore his shoulder to rags his hand flexed open. The signal was sent.

Suddenly there was a rumbling explosion on the far side of the building, the whole place shook all the way down to its foundations. The floor tiles rippled beneath our feet. Lab equipment vibrated to the edge of the tables and fell with a crash to the ground.

The man I'd shot writhed in pain, but he was laughing in triumph, still chanting, *"Seif al Din!"*

The Sword of the Faithful. The holy weapon of God.

The deep-throated roar of the explosions slowly subsided.

"Mother of God!" gasped Bunny.

"That oughta tell the cavalry to come running," said Top. There was a sound in the hall and he leaned out. "Shit. We got company."

"Walkers?" I demanded.

A barrage of bullets pinged and whined as Top ducked out of the doorway and back-kicked the door closed. Bullets pelted the heavy steel. "Not as such," Top said dryly.

"Those are AKs," Bunny said, listening to the gunfire. "Not our boys."

"Cavalry's always late," Top muttered as he threw the locks.

Bunny grabbed the remaining scientist and punched him in the stomach then snapped plastic cuffs on him. "Deal with you later, shit-bag." He crossed to Ollie and slashed at his bonds with a folding knife. "How you doing, hoss?"

Ollie spat blood onto the floor. "I've had better days."

Chapter Sixty-Four

"MA'AM, I'VE LOST the signal," reported the tech who was hunched over the communications board inside one of the ambulances. He tried another line, then another. "Cell lines are out, too. We haven't yet set up the landline to ops. We're blind and deaf. Everything's being jammed by a very powerful transmitter. Has to be military grade, nothing else could cut us off this bad."

Grace bent forward to look at his display and then tapped her earpiece, heard only a hiss.

"Ma'am," called the tech again, "right before we lost our feeds audio picked up a change in ambient sound. I think the refrigeration units have all shut down. I got ten seconds of thermals before we went blind and it looks like the temperature inside the building is spiking."

Allenson, Grace's second in command, gave her a sharp look. "Mr. Church said that Captain Ledger requested backup in silence plus ten minutes."

She turned to the tech. "Do we have that landline yet?"

"Negative. ETA five minutes."

"Bugger that." To Allenson she said, "This whole thing is wrong, I think Echo Team is in trouble."

Allenson grinned. "Alpha Team is locked and loaded, ma'am."

Grace pointed to a technician sitting in front of a screen that showed nothing but white noise. "You! You're a runner. Find Mr. Church, tell him we have a total communications blackout. Apprise him of the temperature change. We need a full-team hit and we need it five minutes ago. Tell him the next sound he hears will be Alpha Team kicking in the door. Move!"

The runner leaped out of the van and tore across the parking lot to the fake cable news van parked outside the gates.

Grace Courtland snatched up her helmet. "Let's go."

By the time the team was assembled at the door one of her men had a fast-pack charge beside the knob. "Fire in the hole!" he yelled and everyone fanned back as the doorknob blew apart. The door swung violently open but beyond it was a flat gray wall. The agent pounded his fist on it. "Steel plates. Going to take a hell of a big bang to get through that."

Then a moment later there was a second and much heavier explosion, but this one was deep inside the building. It shattered the glass in the windows and sent a shiver through the walls, then subsided into a threatening silence.

"That was inside," Allenson said.

Another sound rent the air as heavy steel shutters slammed into place over every window in the building. Grace let out a string of vile curses and hoped that Church had the backup coming fast.

"Make me a hole, Corporal," she snarled, but the man was already sliding the pencil detonators into place.

God, she prayed as they backed away from the explosives, *don't let this be another St. Michael's.* For one brief moment she closed her eyes and imagined Joe Ledger being dragged down by a sea of hungry white-faced ghouls. *Please, God!*

The side of the building exploded.

Chapter Sixty-Five

Crisfield, Maryland / Wednesday, July 1; 3:33 A.M.

"WHAT HAPPENED?" I asked Ollie.

He shook his head like a dog shaking off fleas. "I don't know. I was blindsided. Maybe Tasered. I remember a whole lot of pain and then it all went black. Next thing I know I'm duct-taped to a chair and some asshole is smacking me in the face and yelling in Arabic."

Top gave him a quick once-over and found a wet burn mark on his neck just above the collar and the back of his shirt was soaked. "Looks like you got hit with a liquid Taser, boy."

"Damn. I didn't think those things worked that well."

"Little dab'll do ya," Top said from where he knelt by the scientist I'd shot, applying compresses to the wounds.

Bullets were still whanging off the door, but so far they didn't seem to be able to get in, and eventually they stopped firing. I don't know if Bunny, Ollie, or Top thought that was strange, but I sure as hell did. There was a keycard station outside. How come nobody was trying to use a keycard? I almost said something to the others, but decided to keep it to myself for the moment. As the saying goes, "just because you're paranoid, doesn't mean you aren't being followed." There were too many things in this place that didn't add up.

"The troops should be arriving any second," I said. I looked up at the shuttered windows set high in the wall. "Bet you a dime they'll come through those, so be smart when they enter. If they ask you to lay down your arms you do it. Remember, the first thing they're going to be thinking is that we've been killed or infected. Let's not give anyone a reason to get trigger happy."

"I'm with you on that, boss," said Bunny.

"Hey," Ollie said as he got groggily to his feet, "where's Skip?"

Bunny glanced at me. "Unknown," I said. "He went missing around the same time you did." Ollie looked like he was about to ask a question, but I turned away and looked down at the dying scientist. "How's he doing, Top?"

"This guy's circling the drain. You want to ask him a question now would be the time."

I squatted on my heels. "You're dying," I said in Farsi. "You have a chance to do some good, turn things around before you die. Tell me, what is *Seif al Din*?"

He sneered at me. "The infidels will all drown in rivers of blood."

"Yeah, yeah, whatever. I want you to tell me about the Sword of the Faithful."

He laughed. "You've already seen its power. It will consume your entire country," he said, nodding with fierce joy, delighted at the thought.

"If this thing is a plague, friend, then it's going to consume your people, too."

He barked a laugh and blood flecked his lips. "Allah will protect His people." He mumbled something else but all I caught were the words "generation twelve," and I had no idea what it meant.

I leaned close. "Right now about two hundred Special Forces soldiers are descending on this place. None of your infected subjects are going to get out of here. Not one. Everything you've worked for is going to stop right here, right now."

He tried to spit at me, but he lacked the power. He was fading fast. I glanced at Top who shook his head.

"You have stopped nothing," whispered the dying man, then repeated the word, savoring it. *"Nothing."*

"Is there another lab, another cell?"

"It is . . . past that time," he said with a bloody smile. "El Mujahid is coming. He wields the Sword of the Faithful. You are all too late. Soon all of Islam will be . . . free . . . of you."

Then he threw his head back and screamed out the name of God with such force that it tore the last bits of life out of him. He sank back against Top and his head lolled to one side.

Chapter Sixty-Six
Crisfield, Maryland / Wednesday, July 1; 3:34 A.M.

"ALPHA TEAM! ON me!"

Grace sprinted toward the hole that had been blown in the side of the building. The agents of Alpha Team followed her into what looked like an industrial shower, but the grime-streaked walls were cracked from the blast and one row of metal lockers was torn off the walls. There was no sign of life.

"Redman," she snapped, and the explosives tech was at her side in a second. "This hallway looks like the only exit. Rig it with C4. If backup hasn't arrived and anything comes this way that doesn't look friendly, blow this whole side of the building down. Repeat my orders."

He did so.

"Major!" called Allenson from a few yards up the hall. He knelt over the body of a man wearing a white lab coat and plastic cuffs. "Got a prisoner down. Neck's broken. Blast must have smashed him against the wall."

"Worry about it later." She shone her flashlight down the hall. Every door along the long corridor stood ajar. "Two-by-two cover formation," she ordered. The agents moved past her, covering each other as they pulled the doors wide and shone lights and pointed guns into each of the rooms. Four of them were empty, but they stank of human waste, sweat, and misery. In the corners there were indefinable lumps that might have been bodies. Or parts of bodies.

Forty yards up the hallway was evidence of another explosion—probably the one they'd heard from outside. The walls had been torn outward and the hall was heaped with debris. A cursory glance inside revealed the high-end mainframe sequencing computers Joe had reported. Most of them were melted or torn to pieces, but a few appeared to have withstood the blast.

"Major!" cried Allenson. "My God!"

Grace stepped out of the computer room and her heart froze in her chest. What she had taken for mounds of debris from the blast was something else entirely. The team's unflinching flashlight beams revealed a mound of corpses. Debris and brick dust covered most of it but as Grace played her own flash over the mound she saw that there were dozens of corpses.

"Bloody hell," Grace breathed. "This isn't from the blast." The floor was littered with shell casings and the air was a cordite pall.

There was one more room to check before they would have to climb over the dead to continue down the corridor. Two agents flanked the door and then one went inside.

"Major! In here."

Grace stepped through the doorway. There were seven corpses sprawled on the floor, all of them dropped by multiple head shots. And in the corner, huddled down, shivering with shock and cold despite the terrible heat, was a man. His clothes were torn, his face streaked with blood, his eyes wild. The floor around him was littered with shell casings and he held a pistol in his trembling hands.

"Gun!" Allenson yelled and instantly the man's chest was flickering with red laser sights.

"Don't shoot!" he cried and quickly lowered his pistol. "Please . . . don't shoot!"

Grace Courtland shone her light in his face.

It was Skip. Grace moved forward and took his gun away from him, passing it back to Allenson. "Chief Tyler . . . are you injured? Tyler, have you been bitten?" she snapped.

"No," he gasped, then shook his head. He looked at the blood on his clothes. "No . . . this isn't mine. It's . . . it's . . ."

"Steady on, sailor," she soothed. "Where's Echo Team? Where are your men?" And though she didn't mean to say it, she asked, "Where is Captain Ledger?"

Skip shook his head. "I don't know. Something happened . . . I blacked out and woke up here . . . and those *things* were everywhere!" He rubbed at his neck and Grace shone her light on it.

"Looks like a burn," Allenson said, then speculated, "Liquid Taser?"

Grace signaled to one of her agents. "Beth, go back to the exit and apprise backup of the situation. Tell them to come find us and be bloody quick about it. We'll proceed and try and locate Echo Team."

Beth looked from her to the mound of the dead that blocked the hall. "My God . . . you really want to crawl over that?"

"As the saying goes, life's a bitch." It was a bad joke and as soon as she said it Grace was sorry she'd opened her mouth. The second part of that catchphrase was: "And then you die." The unspoken words hung in the air like a jinx.

The climb over the corpses was horrific.

Don't think about it, don't think about it, she told herself as she crawled to the top of the heaped dead. *Don't think about it.* She scrambled down the far side and jumped onto the concrete as soon as she could, happy to feel hard reality under her boots rather than the yielding madness of the flesh and bone over which she'd come. As her team followed her she saw that each of them were shock-faced and white, their mouths tight, eyes glistening. Some of them looked furious, some hurt. In silence they hurried down the rest of the hall, checking the last few doors but finding nothing alive.

At the T-junction she stopped. With Beth, Redman, and the shooter back at the entrance she was down to nine, with her making ten. She sent Allenson with four agents down the left corridor and she took the right.

MASTER SERGEANT MARK Allenson was thirty years old and had been Marine Force Recon for four years and a DMS agent for fourteen months. He was sharp, intelligent, and had been Major Courtland's first choice as her second in command. She trusted his judgment and relied on the skills and abilities he'd demonstrated in seven separate DMS-related firefights. The team liked him, and Grace was aware that he was more popular with the troops than she was, which was as it should be. It was always better to have a more human number two; it allowed the commander to maintain the necessary aloofness.

Allenson ran along the corridor, his rifle following his line of sight. They reached another junction and Allenson held up his hand to stop the team. The floor was littered with strange debris. Clothes, personal belongings, toys. He measured the amount of it against the number of corpses they'd seen in the hall and the math came out fuzzy. There were a lot of bodies there, but the debris here looked like it belonged to twice that many people. Maybe three times that many.

He crept forward through rusty water to the junction and peered around. There was a steel door fixed in place by a heavy chain. A chill passed through him. He saw the chocolaty-brown smears on the walls and put it all together into a picture that didn't fit comfortably in his head.

"Oh Christ," he whispered as he backed away from it.

To his left an emergency light mounted on the wall suddenly flared and burst, shooting sparks out into the hall that fell onto a large heap of old newspapers and torn clothes overflowing from a trash can. The paper caught instantly and fire leaped up bright and hot. Allenson backed another step away, but a piece of burning paper fell from the can and landed on another heap of rags. Allenson caught a faint chemical whiff just as the rags ignited.

"Sarge," called one of his men, "there's a fire extinguisher right here." He reached to grab the unit.

Allenson spun around, his mouth opening to shout, "No!"

But the world exploded before the word was out of his mouth. He and his team were vaporized in a heartbeat.

GRACE FELT THE blast before she heard it and even as she turned toward the sound the shock wave picked her up and flung her against the wall. She rebounded and fell to her knees. The impact knocked the breath out of her and as she fought for breath a cloud of smoke rolled over her, filling her lungs and twisting her into a paroxysm of painful coughing. Concrete dust stung her eyes. Nearby she could hear her remaining team members gagging and groaning, but the sound was strangely muted and it took her a moment before she realized that she was half-deafened by the blast.

The blast.

"Allenson . . ." she gasped. "My God . . ."

Grace felt blindly for her gun, found it half buried in debris and pulled it to her, using the stock like a crutch to get to her feet. The smoke was thinning, but only enough to see a gray and blurred world. Grace pulled the collar of her T-shirt up through the opening of her Kevlar vest and used it as a filter. Her lungs protested, wanting to cough, but

Grace fought the reflexes, struggling for physical calm. When she could trust her voice, she croaked, "Alpha Team—count off!"

A few voices responded. Only a few, and as she called them together she saw that all she had left of her original team were four agents, all of them bloody and bruised. She staggered back to the T-junction, clutching to the smallest of hopes that one or two others had survived. But there was no one. The corridor walls had been obliterated and there was a huge crater in the floor. She saw some debris. Part of a gun. A hand. Not much else.

In front of her, past the smoking crater torn into the hallway where the heavy steel doors had been, there was movement. Figures, pale as the smoke in which they stood, began moving toward her. Grace raised her flashlight and shone it into the cavernous room. She could see at least a dozen corpses, their bodies torn by the blast; but beyond them, filling the room nearly wall to wall, were walkers. Hundreds of them. Some of them, the ones nearest to the door, were torn apart, missing arms and chunks of flesh; the others farther back were still whole. All of them were staring at the gaping hole in the wall. They saw the light and followed the beam to its source, and their eyes locked on Grace. A mass of shambling dead things, all with black eyes and red mouths that gaped and worked as if practicing for a grisly feast; and as one they set up a dreadful howl of unnatural need and began moving toward her.

"No . . . God, no . . ." someone breathed beside her. Jackson, her only remaining sergeant. Grace knew that to stand and fight was suicide. "Fall back!" she cried, but as she moved backward the walkers shuffled forward over the bodies of their own dead.

Then, around the bend in the corridor, she heard the distant staccato rattle of automatic weapons fire. Even half-deafened, Grace recognized the chatter of AK-47s.

"Joe . . ." she said to herself, then louder, "Joe!" She whirled and pelted down the hallway in the direction of the gunfire. Jackson, Skip, and the remaining Alphas followed. This, at least, was something they could fight; this was something they could understand.

Chapter Sixty-Seven

A SECOND BLAST rocked the whole building, this one ten times louder. Plaster and metal fittings fell from the ceilings and several lights flared white and then exploded in showers of smoky sparks. We all crouched, staring around, waiting for the next shoe to drop, but after a moment the rumblings stopped and the building settled in to an eerie silence.

"The hell was that?" Bunny grumbled.

Top spat out some plaster dust. "Still ain't the cavalry, farmboy. Wrong blast signature."

Outside the door the gunfire started up again, but there was no way they were going to shoot their way in. I wondered why they bothered. Then it hit me . . . gunfire doesn't always have to be an attack: it could also be a lure.

"Grace!" I said aloud, and that fast there was a fresh burst of gunfire—definitely MP5s this time. I paused and looked at Bunny, who was grinning.

"Now that," he said, "is the cavalry."

He took a single step toward the door when the wall blew up. I dove left and pushed Ollie out of the way as the whole door careened inward. Top did a neat little sidestep to avoid a big chunk of twisted metal, but a piece of cinderblock the size of a softball caught Bunny on the helmet and knocked him flat.

Figures began moving through the smoke; Top and I darted to either side, hunkering down behind lab tables, guns held straight and level. Two figures leaped into the room brandishing guns and yelling for us to freeze, to lay down our arms. They yelled in English. The loudest voice belonged to a woman.

Grace.

I started to smile and then I saw the blood on her face and the wild, almost inhuman expression in her eyes and my trigger finger twitched at the same moment my heart slammed against the walls of my chest. *God! Is she infected?*

"Hold your fire!" I yelled and everybody froze. "Grace! Stand down, stand down!"

She wheeled in my direction, bringing the barrel of her weapon up. Her hair was gray with dust and blood flowed freely from cuts on her forehead and cheek. She was panting—whether from effort, stress, or infection I couldn't tell. Though it hurt my soul to do it I put the deathly red finger of my laser sight on her chest, right over her heart.

"Grace . . . stand down!" I shouted.

"J . . . Joe?" A few other Alpha Team agents clustered around her, all of them bleeding, all of them in torn and dusty uniforms. Their barrels aimed past her toward me. They hadn't seen Top from his place of concealment. Ollie was with me, down behind the table, unarmed. Bunny hadn't moved from where he'd fallen.

"Stand down," I repeated, keeping the edge in my voice. "I won't tell you again."

"Joe . . . are you hurt? The walkers . . ."

"No one in here is infected, Grace. What about you?"

She took a breath, and then shook her head as she lowered her gun. To her team she said, "Stand down."

Everyone slowly lowered their weapons except Top and me. He remained where he was, quiet and ready, while I got to my feet and walked toward her, my gun out, the red dot steady on her chest.

"Joe," she said with evident relief, "I'm glad you're all right."

"I'm not looking to take a chance here, Grace. Tell me what happened."

"There was a team of hostiles holding this end of the hallway, trying to get in."

I caught that she said "was." Another figure moved through the dust and as he stepped into the lab I was surprised to see who it was. I lowered my gun and held it down at my side.

"Skip? Where the hell have you been?"

"Sorry, Captain . . . I got blindsided."

The young man looked worse than Grace. His eyes were jumpy and darted back and forth and his smile was both brief and tremulous. I gave him a nod and he stayed where he was, looking around uncertainly as if unsure to which team he belonged.

I moved closer to Grace. "Tell me what happened."

She told me everything in a few terse sentences. The hurt in her face and voice was bottomless. "We saw a group of hostiles trying to shoot their way in," she concluded. "We took them out. All communications are jammed, so we couldn't download a keycard code, so I had Jackson blow the door."

Behind me Bunny swore. I turned to see that Top had helped the big young man to a sitting position. Bunny was groggily shaking his head, blood trickling down the left side of his face. Top removed Bunny's helmet and examined the bruise, then he turned and gave me a quick nod. "Farmboy here took a blunt-force hit to the head. He'll be okay."

"I ain't a farmboy, you shit-kicker," Bunny complained. "I'm from Orange County."

Top patted his shoulder. "Now that the cavalry's here maybe we should saddle up and ride."

"The cavalry's still not here," Grace said softly. "My team is . . . Gus Dietrich and the others should be breaching the wall any minute."

I suddenly felt old and used up. "Well, then we'll have to make our stand here and wait. No back doors, and I don't particularly want to go back down that corridor."

"Sod that," murmured Grace.

Ollie stood by the table looking as much like an uninvited guest as did Skip. I avoided looking at either of them at the moment. Both of them had gone missing in ways as yet unexplained, both miraculously alive despite the terrorists and the walkers. I was going to have to sit down and have long talks with each of them. It would be better for everyone if they both had nice, clear, and believable stories.

Over by the door Jackson called out sharply. "Major . . . Captain Ledger . . . we're about to have company."

"What have you got?" I called.

Jackson looked stricken. "Walkers! Hundreds of them."

"Terrific," Top said sourly. "I'm down to one magazine, Cap'n."

"They're here!"

We all turned to see the shambling mass of walkers round the bend in the hall outside and fill the doorway. Rank upon rank of them.

There was no time to think, just to act.

"Make a barricade!" I grabbed the nearest table to me and heaved. Grace caught the other end and we shoved it forward, the legs screeching on the concrete floor, the vibration sending delicate instruments crashing to the ground, and I hoped we weren't breaking anything that contained a virus or parasite. The Hammer suits would protect us from skin contact but none of us were wearing masks.

Bunny was sick and dazed from his head injury but he bulled his way through it; he grabbed the corner of one big table and with a grunt of effort heaved it over onto its side then rammed it with a shoulder to drive it into the doorway. Top began tossing chairs over the table to create an obstacle course to slow the walkers down. Ollie rushed to help him. Skip looked around and grabbed another table and hauled on it without much effect; I took the other end and we pushed that against the others.

Then the mass of walkers hit the barrier like a tidal surge. They were only as strong as ordinary humans but there was so *many* of them that their sheer weight of numbers acted like a battering ram that drove the barricade backward nearly three feet. Jackson reached over the edge of the barricade and opened up into the massed bodies. A few went down, but most of his bullets tore through chests and limbs without doing much to stop them.

"Pick your bleeding targets, Jackson!" Grace snarled. "Shoot for the head."

The barricade shuddered again and slid farther into the room as hundreds of the living dead surged forward again and again. At the front of the mass a few of the walkers collapsed, crushed by those behind them, and I could hear bones breaking. But it was weird, without screams or grunts, just low moans, even from those who were being trampled.

"It's not going to hold," warned Ollie as he shoved another table against the barricade.

"Nothing gets over that wall!" yelled Grace as she leveled her gun and opened fire, dropping two walkers with headshots and tearing away the jaw of a third. I drew my gun and stepped up next to her and fired; Top and Bunny flanked us and then Skip and Jackson. Ollie and Skip took handguns from Alpha Team members who had MP5s. Eventually all of us had formed a shooting line a few yards on our side of the barrier, shooting point-blank at the walkers as they climbed up the sides of the tables and overturned chairs. The thunder of our combined gunfire was deafening as we fired, fired, fired. The walkers fell but the surge never faltered. As the creatures in front died, the others climbed over them to try and get to us.

The slide of my pistol locked back and I fumbled for my last magazine and slapped it in. Fifteen rounds. "Last mag!" I yelled.

"I'm out!" Top said a moment later. He spun out of the line to look for one of the AK-47s, found it and came back firing, the selector switch set to semiauto.

Grace was shooting slower than the rest of us but she was making more kills. She aimed and fired, aimed and fired, and with each shot a zombie toppled backward, its infernal life force snuffed out. I followed her lead and slowed my rate of fire.

The walkers fell by the dozen. By the score.

The dead were heaped so high that for a moment they blocked the door, but then the surge hit the other side of it and the mountain of corpses toppled into the room. We had to jump backward to keep from being buried by them, and that broke our line. The barricade was gone and now the walkers were climbing into the room over the heaped dead.

"Remember the Spartans," Bunny mumbled as he backed up.

"We ain't dead yet, farmboy," Top said.

"I told you already that I'm not . . . aw, fuck it." He shot two walkers who tried to rush him from his blind side. His gun clicked empty as the slide locked. "Shit! Who's got a mag?"

Nobody answered him. Those of us with bullets kept firing.

"Shit!" he swore again, and threw his pistol so hard at a rushing ghoul that it knocked the creature onto its back. Bunny rushed over to a far wall and tore a fire axe out its metal clips. "C'mon, you undead sonsabitches!"

They came. They swarmed at him and he laid into them with the axe, swinging it with such incredible force that arms and heads flew through the air. His backhand slash dropped two walkers with broken necks. One walker lunged at him and sank its teeth into the fabric of his Hammer suit and though Bunny broke its back with a chop of the axe the creature's bite tore the whole front of the suit open.

I fired my last shot and tossed the gun aside. Grace and her team still had ammunition and they re-formed into a tighter line, firing constantly but now their shots were killing only one in two, and then one in three as their hands went numb from the recoil and their hearts froze in their chests. Even Grace was missing the kill nearly half the time.

"Out!" Top called and fell back. He caught my eye and gave me a wicked grin. "Be nice if this was like the movies. Nobody ever runs out of ammo in the goddamn movies."

Ollie fired his last shot and dropped out of the line, too. "Now what?" he asked.

I cast around for something to use as a weapon and spotted a set of shelves made from wire racks and chrome-plated pipes. I snatched it up and swung it with all my strength against a wall where it exploded into its component parts. I picked out a six-foot-long upright and swung the bar with all the force I could muster from need and terror, and laid into the front rank of the walkers, crushing the head of one and breaking the neck of another. I heard a roaring sound and realized that it was my own voice, raised into an animal howl of rage as I swung and smashed and thrust at the living dead.

I swung low to knock the legs out from under two of the creatures and suddenly Top and Ollie were there, both of them with shorter pieces of chromed pipe in their hands. They crushed the heads of the walkers I'd knocked down and that fast we had a rhythm. I knocked them down and they finished them off. I could hear Bunny's bull roar behind me, as loud as my own. Top's arm was red to the shoulder; then Ollie slipped in a pool of blood and went down with three of the creatures on top of him. In a flash Skip was there, his gun empty but a KA-BAR in his hand, and the blade flashed out, cutting tendons and slashing throats. Top pulled Ollie up and the three of them fanned out behind me as we met the next wave. And the next. And the next.

Five walkers rushed me and I chopped the outermost one in the temple so that he crashed into the others and knocked the whole line off balance. Top leaped at them, hammering away with the pipe, but I could see that his blows were coming slower and with less force. He was tiring. So was I. It had been an insanely long day and this was past human endurance.

I caught movement out of the corner of my eye and wheeled to see three walkers coming at Grace from her blind side.

"Grace! Left flank!" I yelled, and went for a long reach with my pole.

She saw my swing and ducked under it, allowing the bar to smash into the face of one of her attackers. She shot the other two and then she was empty.

I pulled her away and pushed her behind me. "Fall back!" I shouted to the others. There were six tables at the back of the room. If nothing else we could try a second barricade. "Bunny, plow the road!"

Bunny leaped forward and cut down two ghouls with a swing that was so powerful that it cut one of them nearly in half. He hacked his way to us. I realized that both sides of the lab were lined with tall metal cabinets. They were freestanding, not bolted to the wall, and it gave me a spark of hope. "Skip . . . Ollie!" As they turned toward me I grabbed the corner of one of the cabinets and pulled it as hard as I could. It toppled easily and fell with a deafening crash, crushing one of the walkers under its ponderous bulk. The others got the idea at once and immediately began overturning the cabinets so that within seconds we had created a steel corridor that limited how many of them could approach at once.

Grace herded her team back, and Jackson had enough presence of mind to drag our prisoner with them. That showed optimism, I thought. Then something caught my attention and I turned to look at a steel cabinet mounted against one wall. It was chained shut and across it was stenciled ARMS in Farsi.

"Top! Arms locker on your nine o'clock!"

He spun around and saw the cabinet and a big grin broke out on his face. He couldn't read Farsi but he got the picture and with a heave of his whole body he brought his bar down on the lock, shattering it. He pulled open the door and we saw six police-style .38 revolvers hung on pegs and a shelf of boxed cartridges. Top's smile faltered. Automatics and preloaded mags would have been a lot more comforting.

"Buy me some time, farmboy," he called to Bunny as he and Grace began pulling down guns and tearing open boxes.

I stepped into the corridor to meet the rush of walkers who had succeeded in climbing over the piles of their own dead; Bunny flanked me and together we attacked. The pipe felt like it weighed a ton and each time the shock of impact sent painful shudders through my wrists and shoulders. I could barely drag in enough breath, and sweat stung my eyes. Bunny had to feel the same, and we stood there, fighting to hold the line. But every few seconds we were forced back a step and then another.

"Joe!" I heard Grace scream. "Fall back." And suddenly the air around me exploded as six pistols fired at once. The front rank of the walkers was hurled back; then a second volley dropped more of them. I felt one round sing past me so close it burned the air next to my ear. I turned and saw Ollie staring at me with a shocked expression, and the gun in his hand trembled. Was it fatigue? Or fear of the walkers? Or had he missed the target he was aiming at? He opened his mouth to say something but I shot him a hard look as I rushed to get behind the line of guns.

Grace and her team had pushed tables together to create a redoubt. Skip was at the far end, boxed in behind the edge of a table and the last remaining cabinet; the rest were shoulder to shoulder behind the makeshift battlements. It was flimsy, but it was all we had. On the floor at Skip's feet was the lab tech, wide-eyed with fear.

As Top passed me a pistol he murmured, "Getting to be a real nice time for that cavalry, Cap'n."

"Prayer might help," I said. "You a churchgoing man, Top?"

"Not lately, but if things work out right I might start up again."

Grace and I stood behind one table, sharing half a box of bullets, timing our shots so that one fired while the other reloaded. "Some rescue, huh?" she said, trying to make a joke of it even as tears glittered in the corners of her eyes.

"I'm sorry about your team."

She sniffed and cleared her throat. "We're at war. People die."

I looked at her for a long moment but she turned her face toward the door and I could see her features harden up like concrete drying in a hot sun. On top of everything else the loss of her team was a terrible blow, and I hoped it wouldn't be a fatal one. Not only for us in the moment, but for her if she lived through this. Maybe Rudy could help. Or, maybe I could. I hoped the schism didn't run too deep for anyone to reach.

I drew a breath as two more walkers shuffled into the corridor, then three more, then nine. They moaned like lost souls, though I wondered if they were truly without souls or if in some dreadful way the person that these creatures had once been was somehow trapped in those undead bodies; caught there with no way to control the killing machine that their bodies had become, watching with awful impotence as they shambled toward murder or death.

It was bad, bad thinking and I wondered if I was going into shock. *Shit,* I snarled inwardly. *Got to stay solid. Got to stay sharp.*

I squeezed the trigger and the leading walker was flung backward against the others, the whole front of his face disintegrating in a cloud of pink mist. I fired again and Grace shot at the same moment. Then everyone was firing and once more the room became a hell of earsplitting gunfire, the moans of the dead, and the screams of the living. The living dead kept coming, wave after wave of them. We shot well, a head shot nearly every time, but they kept coming.

The hammer of Grace's pistol clicked on an empty cylinder. "Bugger all," she hissed, "I'm out."

One by one we emptied our guns and they kept on coming, moaning, reaching for us. Out of the corner of my eye I could see Grace's profile. Even dirty and marked by strain she was beautiful. So brave and noble. As I fired my last bullet I could feel my heart sink to a lower spot in my chest. The dead were going to get to us. There were still forty or more of them in the room and more of them kept shambling through the door. I knew what I was going to have to do. It would be simple . . . stand up and take her chin in one hand and gather up her hair in the other. It was easy, nothing more than a quick turn of her head and then she'd be free of all of this, beyond the reach of the walkers and their plague. I could do it. I'd done it twice with walkers—with Javad and with the walker in Room 12. I could do it now for Grace to keep her from slipping into that ungodly hell. The last gun clicked empty. Around us the air was filled with the hungry cries of the dead.

I felt myself getting to my feet, felt my hands flexing open, felt myself starting to move toward Grace, the movement necessary but the motion stalled by doubt. What if I'm wrong? What if she stops me and they get us both while we're struggling? What if I . . . and then above us, all at once, six of the steel-shuttered windows blew inward.

We all looked up, and even some of the walkers turned their dead faces upward as the steel panels—buckled and in fragments—tumbled murderously into the room.

"Heads up!" I screamed and my reaching hands closed on her shoulders and pulled Grace back as a huge chunk of steel drove like a logger's maul right down onto the spot where Grace had been leaning, cleaving the table in half. We both screamed as my pull carried us back and down, and then we were rolling over and over each other until we collided with the wall. I wrapped my arms around her and buried my face in the crook of her neck as debris pelted down on my back. The others dove beneath the heavy lab tables or crowded into the corners as hundreds of pounds of jagged steel slammed into the ground. The front three ranks of the walkers were crushed and torn to rags, but the others, unable to feel shock or surprise, tottered forward with no change in their singleness of purpose. We had no cover except the shattered debris of our redoubt, but even as we raised our heads the air was rent by the heavy chatter of automatic gunfire. We scrambled farther back against the walls and covered our ears and eyes as a hail of bullets tore the crowd of walkers to pieces. Ricochets slapped the walls over our heads and dusted us with plaster.

I caught Top's eye and he looked at me, looked up, rolled his eyes and shook his head. Despite the absolute insanity of the moment, he mouthed the words "Hooray for the cavalry." Then he cracked up.

With bullets whipping past us and death all around, I felt a hitch in my chest and thought with horror that I was about to cry, but I burst out laughing instead. Grace looked at us like we'd lost our minds. Bunny joined us and we howled like madmen.

"Bloody Yanks," Grace said, and then was laughing, too, though tears coursed down her cheeks. I pulled her to me and held her as her laughter melted into sobs.

I was still holding her when Gus Dietrich came down through a window on a fast-rope, firing an automatic weapon as he dropped into the room.

Chapter Sixty-Eight

MEN IN BANDAGES walked the decks, or slumped onto chaise longues, or sat in wheelchairs with the brakes locked against the slow pitch and yaw of the freighter. The SS *Albert Schweitzer* had been on semipermanent loan to the International Red Cross for over sixteen years now, and for more than half a decade it had assisted the British and American navies with the transport of wounded and convalescing service personnel from theaters of war to their homelands, or to nations where the right kind of medical treatment was available. Experimental surgery in Switzerland and Holland, reconstructive surgery in Brazil, microsurgery in Canada, thoracic and neurosurgery in the United States. Funding for the ship's staff and enormous operating costs were underwritten by five governments, but in real dollars and cents the government donations barely kept coal in the furnaces. The crew and staff salaries, the medical equipment, the drugs and surgical supplies, and even the food and drink were provided via generous grants from three different multinational corporations: Hamish Dunwoody of Scotland, Ingersol-Spüngen Pharmaceuticals of Holland, and an America-based vaccine company called Synthetic Solutions. The companies shared no known connection, but all three were owned in part, and by several clever removes, by Gen2000. And Gen2000 was Sebastian Gault.

The big man standing by the railing only knew that Gault was involved, though the level and scope of that involvement was unknown to him. Not that it mattered. To El Mujahid the only crucial information was that while aboard this ship he was believed to be Sonny Bertucci, a second-generation Italian American from the tough streets around Coney Island in Brooklyn. In his wallet was a snapshot of Sonny and his wife, Gina, and their two young sons Vincent and Danny. A search of his fingerprints would show that he had worked as a civilian security guard at a Coast Guard base and that he had served for three years with Global Security, a private company licensed to operate in Iraq and

Afghanistan. Even the most scrupulous computer search would only come up with information verifying this identify because all documents, from the New York State driver's license to the frequent blood donor's card he carried in his wallet to the credentials locked in the ship's safe, were issued by the actual organizations. Gault was wired in everywhere.

The fighter rested his muscular forearms on the cool metal rail and looked out over the waters to the far horizon. The swollen summer sun was setting in the west and its dying light was a fierce red that seemed to set each wave top ablaze. Everything was painted with the hellish glow, and the skyline far across the waters was as black as charred stumps against the fiery sky. Closer to the ship, standing all alone in the burning waters, the Statue of Liberty seemed to melt in the inferno of the sun's immolation and in El Mujahid's fierce stare.

Part Four
Killers

*Wild, dark times are rumbling toward us, and the prophet who wishes to
write a new apocalypse will have to invent entirely new beasts,
and beasts so terrible that the ancient animal symbols of St. John
will seem like cooing doves and cupids in comparison.*

—HEINRICH HEINE,
"LUTETIA; OR, PARIS," *AUGSBURG GAZETTE*, 1842

Chapter **Sixty-Nine**

CHURCH DIDN'T ASK me if I was okay. He leaned against the fender of a DMS Humvee and listened as I described everything that had happened in the plant. Around us the DMS operatives and their colleagues from half the civil and federal agencies in the phone book were in full swing. Stadium floodlights had been erected and it was bright as day even though dawn was an hour off. Except for military choppers the airspace above us was designated a no-fly zone; all business and residential properties had been emptied and the whole population of the area moved to a safe distance. The press was not invited in and the scene was officially designated as the target of a "possible" terrorist attack. According to Homeland's complicated playbook this meant that it was considered a war zone and that in turn meant the military could call all the shots.

When I was finished he stared at me, lips pursed judiciously, and then nodded. "Has everyone been thoroughly checked and cleared by the doctors?"

"Yes. Lots of scratches and cuts, but no bites. My guys are suffering from exhaustion and everyone's in some level of shock."

"You as well?" His gaze was penetrating.

"Absolutely. Physically and mentally. Who wouldn't be? I got the shakes and every muscle I own feels like it's been run through a Cuisinart. Hu shot me up with some kind of vitamin cocktail, and I've had hot coffee, food, and a protein shake that tasted like a horse pissed in it. I feel like crap, but I'll live."

He gave a small nod. Mr. Warmth.

"What's your assessment of what happened in there this morning?" he asked.

A dozen smartass replies came to mind but I kept a leash on my tongue. I said, "It was a trap and we walked into it."

"You got out of it."

"We were getting our asses handed to us in there. I got lucky."

"Not counting your two encounters with Javad, this is your third combat situation with the walkers with zero casualties from your own team. In this kind of fight, 'lucky' can be enough."

"Not for Grace's people. Alpha Team got chopped. That's hard, man."

"It's very hard," he agreed.

"They had the whole place booby-trapped and as soon as we broke into the lab they remote-detonated the computer room. The holding pens for the walkers were rigged to open all at once, which means we tripped some kind of alarm, something we didn't see. None of that was an accident. Those bastards knew we were coming."

"Knew that it was today, or knew that it was inevitable?"

It was a crucial question and one that I'd been mulling for the last few hours. Our entire assessment of the enemy and his potential hung on that answer. "I don't know. They were ready, but not completely. Only two of their bombs went off. The walkers didn't come after us fast enough or in the right place. It should have been an all-you-can-eat affair, but we survived. And none of the walkers got out. None of that adds up."

"No," he said, and I think he was as troubled by these facts as I was.

"Y'know, I don't know if we're looking at this thing the right way."

"I'm pretty certain we're not."

"We were expecting to find . . . what, a bunch of guys sitting around a table plotting the downfall of Western civilization? Instead we find what looks to me like a testing facility. These guys were studying the walkers. More so and more thoroughly than down in Delaware."

"What about your team? Did they perform to your expectations?" When I didn't answer, he said, "I expect a frank and open report, Captain. Now's not a good time to be coy."

"I'm not being coy, Church. I've known these guys for less than a full day and all of it's been action. Yesterday they performed superbly. This morning we hit some potholes. Skip Tyler and Ollie Brown both went missing under questionable circumstances and I haven't had time to fully debrief them. There are some . . . twitchy points about that. Skip claims he was jumped and Tasered from his blind side, but that doesn't square with the facts because there were only two ways out of that shower room: the door my team came through and the corridor Skip was watching. He says he got zapped and then woke up in a storeroom, managed to cut his bonds and retrieve his weapon, and was then set upon by walkers. Ollie's story is about the same. Says someone must have opened a door and Tasered him. Both of them have burns on their necks, and most of the guards in the plant carried Tasers." I didn't mention the fact that Ollie had nearly blown my head off during the fight. It was something Ollie and I would discuss at some later time.

"So, for a considerable amount of time you can't account for either of those men?"

"Guess not."

"By your own statement there was a period where you were alone, which means that Sims and Rabbit were not with you throughout the mission. And you told me that Sergeant Rabbit carried a prisoner back to the entrance and it was he who reported that Tyler was missing. How do you know that he didn't disable Tyler and then break the prisoner's neck? We have no immediate proof that the prisoner died as a result of Alpha Team blowing open the door."

"Are you targeting Echo Team? You think that's where the mole is?"

"I have no idea where the mole is and I'm questioning everyone," he said with some edge in his voice. "I'm not a big fan of making assumptions, Captain. Until proven otherwise everyone is under the microscope."

We glared at each other for a minute, but then I nodded. "Yeah, damn it."

Church looked away to watch a truck drive by and when he turned back to me he was completely composed.

"Maybe you should broaden your search," I said. "Instead of just going all Inquisition on everyone in the DMS, you might want to take a close look at whoever sent these people to you. Everyone you have was handpicked, right? Well, then, how sure are you about the people who picked them?"

Church gazed at me for a space and I thought I could hear relays clicking in his head. "Thank you for that suggestion, Captain. It wouldn't surprise me if the mole was planted simply to bring the DMS down. It might not even be connected with the terrorists. After all, everyone in the intelligence community constantly jockeys for funding and there's probably some hard feelings from some quarters that we're getting their funding."

"And are we?"

"Sure, but there's a war on and we're a little more 'frontline' than most. Mind you, there is always some political espionage and backstabbing going on in the intelligence services. Always has been, and it's factored into daily life. The release of the walkers from Room Twelve may have been a terrorist act or it may have been meant to disrupt the DMS and discredit me."

"Mass murder is a pretty extreme thing to do just to discredit someone. Are you that important?"

He shrugged.

"Well then, let me put it another way: are you that vulnerable?"

I didn't expect an answer to that but he surprised me. "Not as much as some people might think." He wouldn't elaborate on that rather enigmatic remark, however, nor did he return to the topic. His cell beeped and he opened it and listened for a moment and then hung up without comment. "Dr. Hu has finished prepping the prisoner for interrogation."

As he turned to go I blocked his way. "Slow your roll one minute more. I failed in there, Church. The quiet infil turned into a full-out assault and people died. You hired me on to lead Echo Team and I led them right into a trap."

He looked at me steadily through the nearly opaque lenses of his glasses. "What do you want to hear? That I'm disappointed? That this was a badly led mission? That I want you to resign?"

I wasn't going to feed him the script to my own dismissal so I waited.

"Sorry," he said, "but you're still Echo Team leader. I don't have much interest in Monday-morning quarterbacking. So far you're still four and oh with walkers. Baker and Charlie teams were totally destroyed; Alpha Team has been cut down by half . . . while Echo Team, small as it is, remains intact."

"Doesn't mean I'm the man for this job—"

He sighed through his nose. "If you need absolution go see a priest. If you want to decompress, talk to Dr. Sanchez. However, if you feel that you have some need to put things right and balance the scales, then help me stop this thing. Besides . . . last night you told me that you wanted to wait until your team was fully rested. We didn't, and we can both take blame for that if blame needs to be assigned."

I said, "What about reinforcements? I thought you had more Echo Team candidates on their way."

"Some of them have already arrived. They're being processed at the warehouse as we speak. They'll be shown the tapes, given the speeches, and when you get back you can start training them."

"Maybe we should send Top Sims back there now. Him and Bunny. They can start training the new guys."

"Not Brown and Tyler?"

"I need to have a chat with each of them first."

His phone rang again and he looked at the display and his mouth twitched with impatience. He flipped his phone open. "Yes, Mr. President," he said. I raised my eyebrows but Church kept his usual composure. He listened for a few moments, then said, "Mr. President, I have neither the time nor the facts to give you a full briefing. What I can tell you now is that the crab plant appears to have been rigged as a trap. Yes, sir, we sustained heavy casualties." He gave a bare-bones account of the hit. The President interrupted him at least six times. "We have one prisoner, Mr. President. Yes, that's correct, just the one. I am on my way to conduct an interview with him right now so time is pressing," Church listened some more and I could actually see the point at which his patience evaporated. He did something that I had never even heard of anyone doing before, and something I would have thought that not even Church would dare. "Mr. President, with all due respect this conversation is wasting my time. The clock is ticking for my interview and if you keep trying to micromanage this we're going to lose the best opportunity we have. Now, please, sir, let's stick to our original agreement. You will be properly informed when I am ready to make my report. Good day, sir."

He didn't wait for a reply but simply closed his phone and put it back in his pocket. He saw me goggling at him and said, "What?"

"Church . . . you just bitch-slapped the President of the United States."

He said nothing,

"Nobody does that. Nobody *can* do that. How the hell did you—?"

Church made a dismissive gesture. "We have an understanding. The DMS was built upon and continues to operate based on that understanding."

"Care to share what that understanding is?"

"No," he said.

Chapter Seventy

Crisfield, Maryland / Wednesday, July 1; 5:22 A.M.

DOCTOR HU HAD the prisoner ready in a big white van that was kitted out with diagnostic equipment. The prisoner sat in what looked like a dentist's chair with his wrists and ankles secured by nylon bands. An IV dripped clear liquid into his veins. Hu didn't meet my eyes. He hadn't forgotten our little dustup after the Room 12 incident. Neither had I.

Church pulled over a stool and sat down. I stood by the door. The prisoner's eyes darted back and forth between Church and me, probably sorting out who was good cop and who was bad cop.

"What is your name?" Church asked.

The man hesitated then shook his head.

Church leaned forward, his forearms on his knees. "You understand English. That's a statement, not a question, so please don't hide behind a pretense of ignorance. I am a representative of the United States government. The other men in this room work for me. I know that you've been infected with a pathogen that will kill you unless you take regular doses of a control substance. You believe that if you stonewall me you'll die, that the disease in your system will shut you down before you can be made to talk. Under normal circumstances that might be true, especially if someone other than me was interrogating you. Listen closely now," Church said, and his voice was calm, conversational. "You will tell me everything that I want to know. You will not die unless I allow you to. You will not keep silent. You will not be rescued."

The man was sweating badly and his eyes were no longer darting over to me. The entirety of his mental and physical focus was locked on Mr. Church.

"We know about the control disease. We know its nature. The IV contains the control formula. Very clever to hide them inside ordinary aspirin; but not really clever enough as you can see. Death will not save you from this conversation. Death will not save you from me. Tell me that you understand."

Muscles bunched in the man's jaws as he fought to keep his mouth clamped shut.

"One of your comrades told us that his family was being held hostage, that they would be killed if he spoke to us. Is this how they are controlling you?"

Church gave him nearly thirty seconds, not blinking once, and then the man gave us a single spasmodic nod.

"Thank you. I have covert operations teams in every country in the

Middle East and Asia. With one phone call I will send a team to find your family. I can order that team to rescue them. Or I can order that team to torture them to death. I can order them to capture your family—wife, children, parents, cousins, nephews, and nieces to the fourth generation. If I order that then your entire family, perhaps your entire village, will cease to exist. Whether they remain in prison, or are tortured, or are released with false identities and money in a new country, is entirely up to you."

The man spat out a single word. The Iranian word for "dog."

"The word you're looking for," said Mr. Church, "is 'monster.'" He said it in flawless Iranian. The word hit the man like a punch and he recoiled from it. "Let us understand each other. I know that you are a subordinate, a scientist or a laboratory technician. Your loyalty has been obtained through fear for your own life and the lives of those you love. A monster did that. Someone like me. That person was willing to kill innocent people—people you love—in order to create and release a weapon that will kill millions. Imagine what I would be willing to do—to you, and to your family—to protect everyone that I love."

The man started to open his mouth, to say something else, but whether it was a curse or a confession was unclear because he found another splinter of resolve and bit down on it. His eyes and mouth tightened again.

Church leaned back and considered the prisoner for two minutes. That's a long time to endure a stare from anyone, let alone from a man with the personal intensity of Mr. Church. The man squirmed and sweated.

"I do not believe that you are a military man," Church said. "Military men are trained to be hard, to be tough, to resist torture. I can see from your face, from the softness of your hands, that you are not going to be able to resist torture. We have chemicals. We have appliances. We can be so very crude, and in the end everyone talks. Everyone. Even I could not endure some of the techniques that could be used, and I am not soft. This man here," and for the first time he indicated me with a slight gesture, "is a battle-trained soldier. You saw him in combat to-day, you saw him kill many people. He is a soldier, a leader of men, a hardened killer. Even he could not endure if the torturer were truly committed."

"I . . . I . . . cannot!" the man said in a voice so hoarse it sounded like there were jagged rocks in his throat.

"Yes you can. You will. No one can outlast what we have. Our science is too good. I have studied torture, I understand its magic. The only thing you can do is to talk to us now, to work with us, to help us fight this thing."

"My children . . ."

"Look at me," Church said with soft intensity. "See me. If you give me information right now I will dispatch my teams to find and protect them. If you don't then I will still get the information out of you, but I will make sure that everyone who has ever heard your name will be hunted down and exterminated so no memory of you or your family will be left upon the earth."

I felt a chill dance along my lower spine and I wanted to get the hell away from this man. If Church was only messing with this guy's head he was doing almost too good a job of it. It was messing with my head, too.

The prisoner opened his mouth again, closed it, opened it again . . . and finally said, "You have to promise that my children will be safe. When they are safe and in American hands then I will—"

Church's face was ice and his look stopped the man mid-sentence. "You misunderstand me, my friend. I will send teams once I have information from you. Every second you waste is a second longer that your masters have to realize that you are in captivity and that means that your children are a second closer to death. You are wasting the seconds of their lives. Is that what you want? Do you want to kill your own children?"

"No! In Allah's name, no!"

"Then talk to me. Save them. Be a hero to them and to the world. Save everyone by talking to me now." He paused for a moment, and then reinforced it. "Now."

The man closed his eyes and tears broke from beneath the closed lids. He bowed his head and shook it for several moments. "My name is Aldin," he said, and a sob convulsed in his chest. "I will tell you everything I know. Please do not let my children die."

Chapter Seventy-One

Crisfield, Maryland / Wednesday, July 1; 6:47 A.M.

WHEN I STEPPED out of the interrogation van I felt dirty. I understood the need for what Church had done, but it still made me feel like a piece of shit. Church had called himself a monster, and I think he meant it.

"Joe!" I heard my name and turned to see Rudy hurrying across the parking lot. He grabbed my hand and shook it, then stepped back to study my face. "*Dios mio!* Major Courtland told me what happened. I . . . I don't have words for it, Joe. How are you?"

"I've been better," I admitted, but before I could explain Gus Dietrich came over at a fast walk.

"Captain Ledger," he said, "I have most of the forensics experts you wanted. The others are all en route and should be here by noon. Jerry Spencer is already on-site."

"Okay, Sergeant, I want everyone cleared out of the building. Tell Jerry that I'll be in there in a few minutes to do the walk-through with him."

Dietrich smiled. "Detective Spencer seems to be pretty mad at you for bringing him into this, especially this early in the morning."

"He'll get over it. Especially once he has a big juicy crime scene to play with."

"Mr. Church requested a medium-sized circus tent to be used as a temporary forensics lab. It's being set up around the corner on the far side of the lot."

"Church was able to get a circus tent on short notice?" Rudy asked.

Dietrich gave him a rueful smile. "Mr. Church has a friend in the industry."

"Jeez," Rudy said, shaking his head.

"Oh, and Gus . . . ?" I said as Dietrich turned away.

"Sir?"

I stuck out my hand. "Thanks for saving our asses in there."

He looked embarrassed as he took my hand. "Sorry it wasn't sooner."

"Believe me when I tell you that it was in the very nick of time."

He nodded and headed off. Rudy and I watched him go.

"He's a good guy," Rudy said. "I had a chance to get to know him yesterday and I saw him in action this morning. If there really is a mole in the DMS, it isn't going to be him."

"Would you bet your life on that?'

Rudy thought about it, nodded. "I surely would."

"Glad to hear it." We started walking over to a card table on which plastic tubs of ice were set. I rummaged inside and pulled out a bottle of green tea for him and a Coke for me.

Rudy tapped my bottle with his. "To life."

"Amen to that. Look, Rude, Church just got finished interrogating the prisoner." I told him about what Church had said to Aldin.

"Will he save the man's family?"

"I think so. I heard him make the call and I don't think he was bluffing."

"That's comforting."

"That's all you have to say? The guy's a self-admitted monster, for Christ's sake!"

"Joe, you're tired and you've got symptoms of postincident stress, so I'm going to cut you a lot of slack. You're all upset because Church threatened the man's family, that he used psychological manipulation, that he—"

"He did more than that, Rude. He tore that guy to pieces."

"Physically?"

"No, but—"

"So, all he did was scare the man into cooperating. No physical torture, no thumbscrews, no sexual or religious humiliation." He shook his head. "I wish I had been there to see it. It sounds brilliant."

I stared at him. "Christ! Don't tell me you approve of this?"

"Approve? Maybe. Admire, certainly. But turn it around, cowboy, and tell me how you would have extracted that same information. Could you have gotten the man to speak without resorting to physical torture? No, what you're upset about is that you don't know whether he was bluffing about the threats to the man's family. You soldiers and cops talk very tough. Over the last twenty-four hours I've heard a lot of 'kill 'em all' and 'let God sort 'em out' stuff; lots of 'we're heartbreakers and widow-makers' trash talk. To a large degree it might even be true, but a fair amount of this stuff is team cheers to get the players ready. Down on the real level you're each human and there's no way you can truly separate yourselves from the realities of war. You might have had to hurt Aldin physically in order to get him to talk; you might even have had to do permanent physical damage to him. Doing that would be hurtful to you, but it's a battlefield thing, ultimately not much different than a sword thrust or a kick to the *cajones*. What you're reacting to here is that Church inflicted damage on a completely different level. He *hurt* the man psychically, emotionally. Tough as you are I'm not sure you can do that, and you are very sure that you can't. And yet . . . Church did not so much as slap this man across the face."

"Okay, okay, I get the relativity of it, O wise Yoda," I griped, "but that still doesn't cover all of it."

"I know," Rudy said, nodding, "you're afraid that Church might have been serious when he threatened that man's children."

I stared into the open mouth of my Coke bottle. "Yeah," I said. "He called himself a monster."

"Yes, but let's both hope that he really isn't *that* kind of monster."

"And if he is?"

Rudy shook his head. "I've said it before, cowboy. It must be terrible to be him."

Chapter Seventy-Two

RUDY WENT BACK into one of the trailers to conduct some postevent sessions with the remnants of Alpha Team. I spotted Grace standing at the aid station and headed over. Her eyes were red-rimmed but for now her tears were done. Maybe she'd cried herself dry, the magazine empty. I hoped Rudy would take some time for her soon.

As I approached she looked up, and in the space of a few seconds several emotions crossed her face. Grief, of course; but also pleasure and a little surprise, maybe as she realized that she was smiling at seeing me. Just as I was smiling to see her, and the sight of her was sending a warm and tingly wave through my stomach. The realization gave me a little jab of surprise, too. I *felt* it down deep. Understand, I've always held office romances in some degree of contempt, regarding the lovers as perpetrators of bad judgment, but as I became aware of feelings for Grace—however new and unformed they were—I couldn't work up the slightest flicker of self-contempt. The angel on my right shoulder was getting his ass handed to him by the devil on my left.

"How are you," I asked. "Or is that the single stupidest question ever asked since Nero asked his friends if they'd like to hear a little music?"

"I'll get by," she answered, handing me a cardboard cup of coffee. "I'm not going to let myself think too much about it . . . about my team." She sniffed and tried to smile. "I plan to have a complete breakdown when this is all over."

"If you want company for that, let me know."

She gave me a penetrating look and nodded. "I may take you up on that." She changed tack. "Your friend Detective Spencer's been asking for you. Or, to be precise, he's been asking where the effing hell you are and what do you think you're playing at having him dragged out by a goon squad while he's on medical leave. Words to that effect. He's not the mildest of men."

"Jerry's okay. Good cop."

"You must know that we interviewed him." She paused. "That's why Mr. Church and I were at the hospital. At St. Michael's. We'd had our eye on Spencer since he first joined the task force, and after he was shot we followed his ambulance to the hospital and 'borrowed' him once he was free of the ER doctors." She shuddered. "I don't like to think what would have happened if Mr. Church hadn't been on site when the infection began spreading through the hospital."

"You think it could have been worse?"

"I know it would have been." She gave me a strange smile. "It's funny, but in all the time I've known him, in all that the DMS has done since I've been seconded here from Barrier, it's the only time I've ever seen Church take direct action."

"I get the feeling that he'd be pretty effective. He has the look. What was he, Special Forces?"

"I truly don't know what his background is, and I've covertly tried to find out. I think he's used his MindReader system to erase his past. No fingerprints, no DNA on file, no voice-print patterns, nothing. He's a ghost and these days no one's a ghost." She shook her head. "When the walkers came flooding down the halls heading toward the lobby Church didn't get angry, didn't even show the shock he had to be feeling. He simply took action. I was outside by then, establishing a perimeter, so I only had glimpses of him through the big glass doors in the lobby. He didn't seem to do much, but as the walkers reached him they fell, one after the other. I've only ever seen one person move with that kind of ruthless efficiency."

"Oh? Who's that? Maybe we should recruit him."

"We did," she said, locking my eyes with hers.

"Ah," I said, feeling enormously uncomfortable. "I guess I need to add 'ruthless efficiency' to my résumé."

"You know what I mean. You don't hesitate. It doesn't seem to affect you."

The image popped into my head of the walkers in the hallway climbing over each other to get to me and how my hands almost slipped as I slapped a magazine into my gun. And then a second and more terrible picture began flashing on the big movie screen in my head: my hands reaching out to Grace in the lab and the moment of hesitation I felt as I worked up the nerve to break her neck to spare her from becoming a zombie.

"Believe me, Grace, it does. Really and truly. I nearly lost it a couple of times over the last day. No joke."

Grace shook her head. " 'Nearly' doesn't count. But even so . . . Church is different, colder. He's less . . ." She tried to put a word to it and couldn't.

"Yeah," I agreed. "I saw a little bit of that today." I told her about the interrogation, but like Rudy Grace seemed unmoved.

"What did you learn?" she asked.

"Not a lot, though Church is still working on him. The code name for the walker plague is *Seif al Din*. Translates as 'the Sword of the Faithful'; but it has a second connection, and that may be the biggest tidbit we got out of Aldin. He confirmed that El Mujahid sometimes takes the name of *Seif al Din*. Kind of like Carlos being the Jackal."

She nodded. "El Mujahid is a clever bastard. There are a lot of blokes in counterterrorism who would love to hang him very slowly from a tall tree."

"I'll buy the rope. But I'm not sure how fast we should label El Mujahid as our supervillain here, Grace. I read the Homeland profile on him when I was with the task force and I don't recall anything that said he has a background in science. Explosives, maybe, but not medicine. He's more of a field general than a lab rat."

"Then he's hired lab rats. Bin Laden isn't an airline pilot but his people still flew planes into the towers."

"Mm," I said noncommittally. "Well, I'd better get inside before Jerry has kittens."

She took my hand and gave it a hard, quick squeeze and started to turn away, then paused, doubt on her face. "Joe . . . ? We have the plant, the army of walkers they were making, the computers. Did Aldin mention anything about any other sites? Any cells we've missed?"

"No. He said he'd overheard the guards talking about possible locations for another site but he didn't think they'd settled on a spot yet. This plant here is the main site. The factory floor, so to speak; and a lot of the stuff that was stored here was intended for use with future cells. He said the Delaware meatpacking plant was relatively new. A tiny lab, no computers, just a bunch of stored walkers. He didn't even know about the captured kids or the experiments planned for them."

"Do you think he was lying?"

I shook my head. "You weren't in the room. Once he started talking he kept on talking. Hu got enough information to begin working on a research protocol."

"Even so, what's your intuition tell you? Have we stopped the immediate threat? Do we have time now to rebuild our teams? Or is the clock still ticking?"

"I . . . don't know, Grace," I told her honestly. She nodded glumly and headed off and I went to find Jerry Spencer.

Chapter Seventy-Three
Crisfield, Maryland / Wednesday, July 1; 7:07 A.M.

JERRY SPENCER WAS pissed.

"Hey," I said. "Thanks for comin—"

"I thought I told you to leave this shit alone, Joe."

"No, you told me that you hadn't heard about the DMS and told me that I hadn't, either."

"Same damn thing. A smarter cop would have backed off, and I don't appreciate being dragged into this. I made that clear to Church and that British broad and I *thought* I'd made it clear to you."

"The British broad's name is *Major* Courtland," I snapped. "And too fucking bad if you don't want to be involved. Look, I know you're short and you've got your whole retirement mapped out, but this is national security. This is a crisis on a par with nine-eleven, and in a lot of ways it's worse. So stop whining about it, grow a set, and help us bag these rat-bastards."

He tried to switch gears. "Why'd you have them drag me into this? FBI's got better crime scene investigators than me."

"Balls. You may be a world-class pain in the ass, Jerry, but you're also the best of the best. I got no time for second team. You got the magic and you were available. You want me to beg? Is that it?"

We glared at each other, but then I could see something shift behind his eyes. Something I'd said had hit the mark. He stepped back and flapped an arm at me. "Ah . . . shit!"

"So what does that mean? Are you in?"

We were inside the shower room of the crab plant and he looked down at the floor as he absently rubbed the spot on his chest where bullets had cracked his sternum. "Thirty years, Joe. Thirty years on the job and I never so much as caught a scratch. Not a splinter, and then that asshole damn near punches my ticket. If I hadn't had the Kevlar I'd be dead."

"Yeah, man, I know. Upside is that you *did* have the Kevlar. Universe threw you a bone."

"Christ, you been reading *The Secret* or some shit?" He scowled at me and then sighed long and deeply, wincing a little as he did so. Then he gave me a crooked little smile. "You're a total pain in my ass you know that? You at least save that Cigarette boat for me?"

"Um, well, no," I said, ". . . we kind of blew it up."

"Crap." He turned and looked around at the ruined shell of the shower room. "All right, dammit, let's get this dog and pony show on the road."

I offered him my hand and we shook. "Thanks, Jer. I owe you on this."

"You owe me a frigging boat."

"I'll see what I can do," I said, wondering if Church had a friend in that industry.

There was an FBI forensics investigator on hand to assist Jerry and I was amused to see that it was Agent Simchek—my old friend Buckethead, who'd braced me at the beach and dragged me into this mess. He didn't return my nod and only gave Jerry a hard and unsympathetic stare. The FBI never likes playing second chair to ordinary cops. Simchek carried a full evidence collection kit and an air of disapproval.

I wasn't fluffing Jerry's ego when I said he was the best. I've worked with him on the task force and on a few other cases that had connections between Washington and Baltimore. I'm good with a crime scene, but Jerry is better than me or anyone I ever heard of. If there was any way I could persuade him to sign on to the DMS as head of forensics I was going to give it a hell of a try. Church said that I could have whatever I wanted.

Jerry looked at the rows of lockers behind which Skip had been hiding. "There was a struggle here." He squatted down, careful of his chest, and looked at the floor and shone a penlight at different angles to evaluate the shadows cast by dust and debris. He asked Simchek for evidence markers, and received a stack of small plastic A-frames. Jerry put four of the numbered orange markers down on the floor and started to get up, then settled back down on his upturned heels and narrowed his eyes for a moment, then grunted and said, "Clever."

Simchek and I looked at each other. Jerry frowned for a moment and then added a fifth marker, right between the first and second set of lockers. That's when I saw it but I can't pretend that I ever would have seen it if Jerry hadn't spotted it first. It's why I asked for him. Simchek, to give him credit, was only a half-step behind me.

"Is that a door?" he asked.

"Uh-huh," Jerry said as he stood. "I understand one of your boys went missing here at the infiltration point. There's no other way out of this room except the corridor and the doorway that they blasted. Scuff marks pretty clearly show that he was using the first set of lockers as a shooting blind. I figured that unless he's a damn fool there had to be another access point, otherwise it would have been impossible to sneak up on an armed sentry. Another door made the most sense, so I looked for one and *voilà!* But we won't open it until the bomb squad checks it out. But I'll bet you a shiny nickel that this puppy opens silently."

I made the call and we moved on but stopped almost immediately as Jerry and Simchek both had their first look at what filled the corridor. The air was thick with blowflies. Corpses were sprawled singly or lay together as if in some grotesque dance; they slumped against the walls or lay in pieces. Beyond the first few bodies was a mountain range of the dead. The air was heavy with the drone of blowflies.

"Holy . . ." Simchek's voice failed him and he closed his eyes. Jerry sagged and almost leaned against the wall for support. After a few moments Jerry took a bottle of Vicks VapoRub from his pocket, dabbed some on his upper lip, and handed it without comment to me; I took some and gave it to Simchek. Even with the menthol goo blocking out the smell the scene was almost too intense to handle. We literally had to crawl over the bodies in order to get to the far end of the corridor. That's an experience I knew was going to stay with me.

When we got to the spur of the hall where the bomb had gone off I saw that a lot of the evidence—the clothes and other items—were gone, blown to atoms along with several members of Alpha Team. All that was left in some places were swatches of cloth and smears of red. Jerry stood for a long time and looked at the clothing that remained, whistling a soundless song.

Simchek leaned close to me and whispered, "He run out of ideas?"

Without turning to us Jerry said, "You want to tell an Italian mother how to make gravy?"

Simchek frowned at me. "What?"

"He means shut the fuck up," I interpreted, and Simchek lapsed into a wounded silence.

Jerry went back to walking the scene but he didn't say a word. His

mood had downshifted and perhaps the scope of this thing had finally
sunk all the way in.

Finally he said, "This is going to take a while, Joe . . . let me work it
alone, okay?"

"Sure, Jer," I said, and left him to it.

Chapter Seventy-Four

Crisfield, Maryland / Wednesday, July 1; 11:54 A.M.

I SAT DOWN across a folding table from Ollie Brown and for two
whole minutes I looked at him and said nothing. He met my stare the
whole time. I was looking for him to sweat, to squirm, to look away. He
didn't.

We were in a small room in the back of a travel trailer belonging to the
DMS. His face was gray with exhaustion and there were dark smudges
under his eyes.

"You're giving me the 'look,' Captain," he said at last.

"What look?"

"The one that says that you have a problem with me."

"Is that what I'm saying?"

"You want me to admit that I screwed up? Okay. I screwed up. There,
I said it."

I waited.

He sighed. "I let myself get blindsided. If you're expecting me to
make excuses or try and worm my way out of it, then forget it. If you
want to bounce me off the team then go right ahead."

"You think that's what this is all about?"

"Isn't it? You called me in here, you make me wait here for an hour
before you come in, and then you sit there giving me the look. What
else could it be about? Or . . . are you going to give me shit about what
happened during the firefight?" I said nothing, so he made a face.
"Shit. Look . . . sir . . . this zombie stuff may not bother you but it's
scaring the living shit out of me. We were losing in there and I started

thinking about what was going to happen. I could see myself being bitten. After seeing those kids yesterday I can't get it out of my head. So, yeah, I get a case of the shakes. My hands are still shaking. I saw one of those walkers coming up fast and I took the shot. You moved right as I fired and the bullet passed close. Things were getting pretty hairy in there and I was scared out of my fricking mind. There, I admit it. You happy now?"

No, I thought; I wasn't. This wasn't where I expected this conversation to go.

"Tell me again how you got taken."

"I told you twice. I told Dr. Sanchez four times, and I told Sergeant Dietrich *five* times. The story isn't going to change because there isn't enough of the story to change. I felt a burn on the back of my neck and next thing I know I wake up strapped to a chair and some towelhead asshole is smacking the crap out of me. Then you, Top, and Bunny come in and you know the rest."

I waited for another few seconds, but Ollie didn't seem like he was about to start sweating anytime soon. If this was all an act then it was a good one.

What I said was, "Room Twelve."

A bad actor would have jumped to his feet, knocked his chair over, and started shouting bloody murder right about then. Ollie cocked his head to one side of me and gave me a look like I'd asked him to explain his involvement in the sack of Rome.

"Ah," he said softly, half smiling. "So that's it."

"That's it."

He sat back and folded his arms across his chest. "No," he said, and he didn't say another word.

SKIP LOOKED JUMPY from what had happened in the plant. He'd been pelted pretty good by the falling debris from Dietrich's rescue and had bruises and butterfly stitches on his face. While he waited for me to speak his fingers kept lacing and unlacing on the tabletop.

"That was some shit, wasn't it?" he asked, giving me a nervous laugh.

"It was memorable," I agreed, and then I gave him another dose of the long silent treatment. His reaction was the exact opposite of Ollie's; Skip was younger and more high-strung. His hands and eyes never stopped moving. He was so jittery that it was hard to get any read at all on him. So far he'd been the least "warriorlike" of the team, though admittedly during both battles with the walkers he'd been quick and efficient. Grace said that he'd been half-crazed when Alpha Team found him, and maybe that's what I was seeing here: the aftereffects of fighting solo against those monsters. I remembered my own reactions after I fought Javad. I freaked, I threw up, and I had the shakes.

On the other hand, he—like Ollie—had told us that he'd been taken off guard at the crab plant. I studied his face. There was no way to know if the mole was even on my team, let alone whether it was Ollie Brown or Skip Tyler. But of the two choices I found it hardest to believe it of Skip. Maybe that was his shtick or maybe he was as innocent as he seemed. I was too exhausted to trust my own judgment.

"Our forensics guy figured out how you got taken," I said after a moment.

He came to point like a bird dog. "What the hell *did* happen? Secret door?"

"Secret door," I agreed.

"Son of a bitch."

I nodded. Skip looked at the tabletop for a long time and when he raised his head his eyes were wet.

"I'm sorry, sir."

I waited.

"I should have checked."

"You're lucky you weren't killed."

He looked away for a moment while he took a steadying breath. "Sir . . . after what I saw in there yesterday and today, after what I *did* . . ."

"What you did?"

"I . . . shot women. And kids. Old ladies. People. I killed a lot of people," he said in a whisper. His mouth trembled and he put his face in his hands and he began to weep.

I sat back in my chair and watched him. His grief was everywhere. It filled the room.

I wondered what Rudy was thinking about all of this. The DMS had cameras that no one could spot, and Rudy was in the adjoining room watching it all.

Chapter **Seventy-Six**
Crisfield, Maryland / Wednesday, July 1; 1:18 P.M.

AFTER I DISMISSED Skip my phone buzzed. It was Grace.

"Joe!" she said urgently. "It's Aldin . . . hurry!"

I ran out of the room and sprinted across the parking lot and into the interrogation van where I saw Aldin lying on the floor. Dr. Hu and two nurses were working frantically over him and the little prisoner was shuddering with convulsions. Everyone was wearing surgical masks and latex gloves. I snatched a set off the table and pulled them on.

"We're losing him," Hu hissed desperately.

"What's happening?" I asked, dropping down beside Grace, who was holding Aldin's feet.

"It's the control disease. It's activated . . . he's dying."

I shot a look at Church. "I thought you said that you gave him the antidote."

"We did," Church said. "It's not working."

"I think it's a different disease," Hu said as he worked. "This one's much more aggressive. Maybe a different strain, I don't know."

I placed my hands on Aldin's chest to try and keep his body from thrashing, but I was pissed. "Oh, come *on*, Doc . . . two different control viruses? That's bullshit."

As if to contradict me Aldin went into full-blown convulsions, every muscle in his body seeming to seize and clutch at once. It was so sudden and so powerful that it nearly threw us off him.

"My—my—" Aldin tried to talk past clenched teeth.

"Clear his mouth," I snapped.

Hu hesitated, looking to Church, who nodded. "The captain gave you an order, Doctor."

With great reluctance Hu removed the air tube. Aldin coughed and gagged. "My—children?" he gasped. "Are they—safe?"

"Yes," I said, not knowing if it was true or not. "We got to them in time. They're safe."

He closed his eyes and the violence of the tremors seemed to diminish as relief flooded his face. "Thank you. Thank . . . Allah."

I put my hand on his shoulder and gave him a little squeeze. He settled back against the floor, the convulsions fading for the moment. "Tell us how to help you?"

Aldin shook his head. "I don't know. The pills always . . . worked before."

Hu looked at me. "We don't have your pills. We're using what we found at the first two sites."

Aldin suddenly went into another fit and when it passed he looked considerably weaker, more dead than alive. He tried to say something but his voice was barely a whisper. I leaned close, strained to hear. "Save—them—"

"Your children are safe," I assured him, but he shook his head.

"No. Save *them*. Save . . . all of them. There—is still—time. Save them!"

"Who? Who do you want us to save?"

"L—L—" He couldn't form the word. Blood seeped from his nose. He closed his eyes and a tear of watery blood fell from his left eye. When he opened his eyes one pupil was massive, a clear sign of a cerebral hemorrhage. He was fighting to hold on with everything he had, and I felt myself admiring him for the ferocity of his struggle—and, truth be told, for the lengths he had been willing to go to protect his children; but this was a fight he couldn't win. He knew it, too. We all did. He forced his mouth to shape the word slowly. "L—Lester—"

"Lester?" I said. He nodded. "Lester who?"

Aldin tried to answer, failed, shook his head. He turned and spat blood onto the floor.

"Aldin . . . who is this Lester? Give me a last name? Who is he? What does he do? Tell me something?"

"Find L-Lester—" he whispered, and struggled as the next wave of spasms tore through him. Blood was welling through his skin, erupting from his pores. It was like his whole body was disintegrating. With the last fragment of his will he shaped another word and I bent close to him to catch it. His voice was faint, a fading whisper. "B-Bell—Bellmaker . . ."

And then he was gone. He sagged down and lay utterly still.

Grace let out the breath she was holding and sat back, pushing a damp strand of hair out of her eyes. She looked at Aldin and then at me. "Lester Bellmaker," she said. "Have you ever heard of him?"

I reached out and closed Aldin's eyes. "No," I said tiredly. "It doesn't mean a thing to me."

"Doesn't ring a 'bell,' huh?" Hu said in an offhand tone, and I wheeled on him.

"You're a half-step away from life on a ventilator, asshole."

Hu recoiled. "Jeez, sorry. I was just trying to make a joke. It's not like he was one of the good guys."

"Shut up," Church said, ever so softly. Hu flinched as if Church had slapped him and he got up and walked to the far end of the van and threw himself into a chair.

I stood as well and looked down at Aldin. "Did I lie to him, Church? Or did we really rescue his kids?"

Church got to his feet and peeled off his mask and gloves. "We were too late by about three days. The whole village was already gone. Someone let some walkers loose. All of the bodies were laid out for us to find. There was another tape. El Mujahid. It's on my laptop."

I punched a nearby cabinet and left a dent in it. "I can't tell you how much I want to find this guy. You can keep my paycheck, Church; just promise me that when we find El Mujahid I get to be locked in a room with him. Him and me."

"You'll have to get in line," snarled Grace.

"First things first," advised Church. "We need to identify this Lester Bellmaker. If he's a link to El Mujahid then we need to jump on it."

"I'll run it through MindReader," offered Grace. "If his name is in anyone's database we'll find him." She hurried out.

Church and I stood there, still looking down at Aldin.

"Did you get anything else out of him?" I asked.

"Bits and pieces. It looks like the crab plant was the hub of this whole operation. People were abducted, infected, and studied. Aldin said that there was no plan that he knew of to release them at the present time. Once a subject was completely transitioned—his word—they were simply stored. He said that his team was studying the varying rates of infection based on age, race, body weight, ethnic background, and so on. The children in Delaware were part of a new phase of the experiment, but he had few details. Sergeant Dietrich tells me that the blast did not destroy all of those computers you found, which means that we should be able to harvest some or all of fourteen months of their findings. Dr. Hu"—and here he cut a brief, hard look at his pet mad scientist—"thinks that it'll shortcut the search for a cure."

"Cure? I thought prion diseases couldn't be cured."

"Doctor?" Church beckoned to him. "If you please."

Hu approached me the way a limping caribou approaches a cheetah. "Okay, true, you can't cure a prion disease. The key is to stop the parasite that triggers the aggression and accelerates the rate of infection. We might be able to get a handle on that based on some things Aldin told us. Stop the parasite and you slow the rate of infection from minutes to months. If we can get ahead of the timetable we might be able to immunize against the parasite. It won't save anyone who gets infected with the prion disease, of course, but it will give us time to isolate the carriers and they probably won't become aggressive and try to bite people. They'll just be sick people."

"You're saying you could inoculate 'everyone'? There are over three hundred million Americans, plus travelers, tourists, illegal aliens . . . how could you produce and distribute enough antidote?"

"Well," he said awkwardly, "we couldn't. We'd have to bring in major pharmaceutical companies to help us. Maybe a lot of them, and it'll be expensive. We're talking billions of dollars in research and more than that in practical distribution. To inoculate everyone who lives in or might ever visit the U.S. . . . that'll cost trillions."

"Which might be the point of all of this," Church said. "A crisis of this magnitude could easily shift the economic focus of the United States away from war and into preventive medicine. We couldn't continue to fund our big-ticket war efforts overseas if we had to throw those kinds of resources into combating diseases. The Jihadists know that they can't put a big enough army into the field to oppose the U.S., so it seems that they've picked a different kind of battlefield, one where our greater numbers work against us."

I whistled. It was a horrible plan, but a damn smart one.

"And it's not like we can choose whether to do it or not," Hu said. "We *have* to because we know they still have the disease."

I nodded. "And just because we know about it doesn't mean they won't try to release the virus anyway."

"I think we should start considering which pharmaceutical companies to approach," Hu said. "I mean . . . after you've talked to the President."

"Mr. Church," I said, "I sure as hell hope you have a few friends in *this* industry."

He almost smiled. "One or two."

Chapter Seventy-Seven

Crisfield, Maryland / Wednesday, July 1; 5:37 P.M.

AFTER I LEFT the interrogation van I went over to the communications center and asked for a secure line to Top Sims who had taken Echo Team back to the warehouse. He gave me a quick rundown and we talked staffing strategies for a few minutes. Then I spent a few hours with Jerry Spencer and gave him my step-by-step account of Echo Team's actions.

With that out of the way I commandeered a DMS Crown Vic, chased the driver off with a grumpy mumble, and climbed in the back to try and grab a few hours of sleep. I felt more than spent; I felt like I'd been opened up, reamed out, and then beaten with hammers. I was no good to any part of this investigation the way I felt.

As I waited for sleep to take me I tried to organize the things that had happened and weigh them against what we'd learned. Now that the combat part of the day was over the cop part of my mind was in charge. I mentally laid out the evidence and let it speak to me the way a crime scene speaks to Jerry.

I drifted off to sleep, but the cop stood his watch.

I DIDN'T WAKE until after midnight, though the sounds outside were the same—shouts, portable generators, the *whup-whup* of helicopters, the buzz of indecipherable conversation.

I lay there and realized that I knew what was going on. With the plant, with the walkers . . . maybe all of it.

Sometimes it happens that way: you go to sleep with puzzle pieces scattered everywhere and somehow in the depths of sleep the puzzle pieces fall into place. When you wake up you can sometimes see with startling clarity.

I opened my eyes and stared at the shadow-darkened ceiling of the car. "Oh man . . ." I said aloud.

Five seconds later I was hurrying to find Jerry Spencer.

Chapter **Seventy-Eight**
Sebastian Gault / The Hotel Ishtar, Baghdad / Thursday, July 2

"LINE?"

"Clear as a bell, my sweet."

"Sebastian . . ." The way Amirah said it made Gault feel warm everywhere. "I've missed you so."

"Me, too." His voice was husky and it nearly cracked. He covered the mouthpiece and cleared his throat. "I want you," he murmured.

"I *need* you," she replied, and Gault could feel the sweat popping out on his forehead.

Gault opened his eyes and looked around the hotel room. It seemed so drab, so overtly empty. Toys had gone shopping in the bazaar with a female rock star who was in town to entertain the troops. Gault wished he were back in Afghanistan. With her. He shook his head and made himself change the subject.

"A lot's happened," he said, his voice suddenly brisk and businesslike. He told her about the raid on the crab plant.

"You let them have the computers?" Her voice sounded shocked, almost frightened.

"I let them have *some* of the computers. All of it was old data, nothing past Generation Three, though they won't be able to tell that from the time-coding. They'll think this is all recent research data."

"You're sure?"

"Quite sure. They'll have more than they need to understand the earlier generations of the pathogen. Scientists will be queuing up to get federal grant money to study it."

"What are you saying? That we're done? That we should call off the operation?"

"Good Lord, no! Your loving husband and his merry little prank is going to be the icing on this cake. Without him the Yanks might lapse into one of those periods of red tape where everything gets talked about in committees but nothing actually gets done. No, dear heart, we need them frightened, terrified . . . so terrified, in fact, that they are too scared *not* to act. Once El Mujahid has pulled off his stunt then they will be in full gear, no doubt about it."

" 'Stunt'?" Amirah said, and Gault could hear the change in her voice, which had suddenly dropped to one degree above freezing. "I would hardly call a heroic sacrifice a 'stunt' or a 'prank.' "

"I'm sorry," he said with a purr, "I don't mean to disparage his sacrifice. Have I offended you?" He listened very closely to her as she replied, and he noted the hesitation—small though it was—before she spoke.

"Oh, of course not." Her voice sounded light. "But I think we should maintain some respect. After all, he is . . . a freedom fighter. He believes in his cause, even if we do not."

And there it was again. The slightest fragment of hesitation before she said "we." It came close to breaking his heart.

"How is the shutdown process going?" he asked, changing tack again.

"It's going . . . well." There it was again. *Damn it.* "We should be completely shut down by the end of the week."

"And the staff?"

"I'll take care of them."

It had always been their intention to gather all nonessential personnel together once El Mujahid's "heroic sacrifice" was under way, and to terminate them. The largest staff room was rigged to lockdown and flood with gas. Only certain key people would be spared and those few would form the nucleus of a new team that would start an entirely new line of research. All records of the *Seif al Din* pathogen and the years of lab work that had gone into its creation would be dumped to coded disks and then stored in one of Gault's most secure locations. Everything else would be deleted or destroyed, all computer memory wiped. That was Amirah's current task and she'd promised to do it, but there was something in her voice that troubled Gault.

"I'm glad you're taking care of things, my love. Do you want me to come and help you clean up the last details?"

"No," she said quickly. "I have everything under control. You have more important things to do."

"Yes, I suppose I have." He paused and said, softly, "I love you, Amirah."

There was a final pause, and then she murmured, "I love you, too."

After the line went dead Gault stood for a long while looking out the window at the plaza below. The erotic elation he'd felt when he had first heard her voice was completely gone. No, that was wrong—there was just enough of it left to make his heart hurt.

"Amirah . . ." he whispered to the night. Grief was like a heavy stone around his neck. Gault was too practiced a deceiver to be deceived; Amirah, though clever, was far less skilled at guile. What was it the Americans were so fond of saying? Never bullshit a bullshitter. Her pauses had been too long and in all the wrong places; some of the inflections were brittle. He wondered if she was aware of it, and doubted it. She was sure of her sexual control over him, Gault was certain of that, just as he was certain she was lying to him. About her lab and her staff. That could be a real problem and he knew that he would need to take a look, that he would need to go back to Afghanistan even though it was a poor security risk with so many things in motion. And she was certainly lying about El Mujahid. Her comment about his "sacrifice" was telling, and the things it implied broke his heart.

He went and built himself a gin and tonic, but as he tumbled ice into the glass he saw that his hands were shaking.

"*God damn her!*" he roared and abruptly hurled the glass across the room with such savage force that it shattered into thousands of silvery fragments that fell glistening to the carpet.

He sagged back against the wet bar. "Damn you," he said again, and now his eyes burned with tears.

What should he infer from this and from the other hints he'd picked up over the last few weeks? Did Amirah really have feelings for her brute of a husband? Was that even possible? After all of the sex, after all of the constant betrayal and the plotting behind the Fighter's back, could she haven fallen back in love with El Mujahid? Gault reached for another glass and mixed another drink, swallowed half of it down a dry throat, and poured more gin into it without adding any extra tonic.

Then something occurred to him that made his heart go still in his chest. He could hear his pulse throbbing in his ears as the new thought blossomed from a seed of suspicion into a fully realized belief. The gin in his stomach turned to sickness as he realized that all of the pieces of this puzzle did actually fit together but that the picture they made was one that he had never expected or foreseen.

What if Amirah had never stopped loving El Mujahid? What if this whole thing, from the very beginning before their clandestine meeting in Tikrit, what if everything she had done for him and with him and *to* him had been part of an older scheme, one that was not of his design? What if this had been something Amirah and El Mujahid had cooked up themselves, something they'd twisted so subtly that he thought he had recruited them? What if they'd suckered him into financing *their* scheme instead of the other way around? Toys had once suggested this as a possibility but Gault had dismissed it with a laugh.

But now . . . what if it was all true?

"Good Christ," he said aloud, and now his hands were shaking so badly that gin sloshed out of his glass onto his shirtfront.

What if Amirah and El Mujahid were not helping him scam the U.S. government out of billions in research and production money? What if money was not even the point? Was that possible? he wondered, but the answer was so obvious. Toys had been right all along. The truth now burned in front of his mind's eye like a flare. There was only one thing more powerful than money, especially in this part of the world.

What if this was *jihad*?

Gault staggered backward and his back crashed against the wet bar. His legs turned to rubber and he sat down hard on the floor, the rest of his drink splashing onto his thighs. He didn't feel the wetness or the cold. All he could feel was a rising sense of terror as the realization that he had given the world's deadliest weapon to a wickedly clever assassin and insured—*insured*—that nothing could stop the release of the *Seif al Din* pathogen. El Mujahid was not carrying the weaker strain of the disease with him, Gault was certain of that now. The Fighter was taking with him Amirah's newest strain, Generation Seven. The unstoppable one. The one that infected too quickly for any kind of response. The Fighter would release it and the plague would sweep the Western Hemisphere. Did Amirah think that its spread could be held back by oceans? Or, in her religious madness did she no longer care?

He crawled across the floor to the table and grabbed his cell phone, hit speed dial and waited through four interminable rings before Toys answered with a musical, "Hello-o-o!"

"Get back here!" Gault said in a hoarse whisper.

"What's wrong?" Toys said sharply, his voice low and urgent.

"It's . . ." Gault began, then a sob broke in his chest. "My God, Toys . . . I think I've killed us all."

The phone fell from his hands as the black reality of apocalypse bloomed like a mushroom cloud.

Chapter **Seventy-Nine**
Crisfield, Maryland / Thursday, July 2; 3:13 P.M.

I SPENT HALF the day with Jerry. Once I'd explained my theories we set about comparing them with what he'd deduced from his forensic walk-throughs. We were both on the same page. I told Jerry to round up all the forensics experts that had arrived while I'd been sleeping and I went off to find Church. Outside I ran into Rudy. He accompanied me to the computer van, where Church and Grace were using MindReader to search for Lester Bellmaker.

"Jerry Spencer's ready to give a preliminary forensics report," I said. "I think we should set that up sooner than later."

"You have something?" Grace asked, searching my face.

"Maybe, but I want you both to hear the forensics first and then we can play 'what-if.' "

Church made a call to set up the meeting.

Grace told us that MindReader had come up with two Lester Bellmakers in North America and six more in the U.K., but so far none of them appeared to have even the slightest connection to terrorists, diseases, or Baltimore. The closest hit had been a Richard Lester Bellmaker who served a tour in the Air Force from 1984 to 1987 and was discharged honorably. That was it. The guy managed a Chuck E. Cheese outside of Akron, Ohio, and no matter how deep Grace searched into his background the guy didn't ring a single damn bell.

"We're getting nowhere," she said.

"And slowly," Church agreed.

"Could Aldin have been lying to us?" Grace asked, cutting a look at Rudy. "You watched the interrogation videos, and you read the telemetry feeds. What's your assessment?"

Rudy shrugged. "From what I could see that man was desperate to tell the truth. That much was in his voice. He was trying to make a dying declaration, and he wanted to go out with as clear a conscience as possible."

"So, he was telling the truth?" Grace asked.

Rudy pursed his lips. "It's probably fair to say that he was telling the truth as he knew it, but we can't discount the possibility that he may have been regurgitating disinformation fed to him by the guards."

"Too right," Grace agreed. "Which means we could be wasting time and resources on a wild-goose chase."

"So what do we do now?" Rudy asked.

"Keep looking," Church said.

Chapter **Eighty**

THE DOOR TO Gault's hotel room banged open and Toys came rushing in with a pistol in his hand. All affect was gone and in its place was a reptilian coldness as he swept the gun across the room. Seeing Gault on the floor, Toys kicked the door shut behind him and rushed to his employer's side.

"Are you hurt?" he asked quickly, searching for signs of blood or damage.

"No," Gault gasped. "No . . . it's . . ." He disintegrated into tears.

Toys studied him with narrowed eyes. He lowered the hammer on his gun and slid it into the shoulder holster he wore under his jacket. Then he caught Gault under the armpits and with surprising strength hauled him to his feet and walked him to a chair. Gault sat there, face in hands, sobbing.

Toys locked the door and verified that the electronic bug detectors were still operating, then he dragged an ottoman over and sat down in front of Gault.

"Sebastian," Toys said softly. "Tell me what happened."

Gault slowly raised a tear-streaked face to him. His eyes had a look of hopeless panic.

"Whatever it is we can deal with it," Toys assured him.

Uncertainly and with stuttering words, Gault told him about the call to Amirah and of the dreadful realization that had bloomed in his mind. Toys's face underwent a process of change from deep concern to disbelief and then to fury.

"That fucking *bitch*!"

"Amirah . . ." Gault's voice disintegrated into tears again.

Without word or warning Toys slapped Gault across the face with vicious speed and force. Gault was flung half out of the chair. Gault stared at him, his tears stilled by the impossibility of what had just happened.

Toys leaned close and in a deadly quiet voice said, "Stop your blubbering, Sebastian. Stop it right fucking now."

Gault was too stunned to speak.

"Try for once to think with your brain instead of your cock; if you had you'd have seen this coming. I bloody well saw it coming, and I've been warning you about that bitch and her husband for years. Christ, Sebastian, I ought to kick the shit out of you."

Gault climbed back into the chair, eyes still unblinking.

Toys sat back and waited until the immediacy of his rage passed. "How sure are you about this? Is this a guess or do you know?"

"I . . . I don't know for sure," Gault managed. "But it all just came to me. In a flash."

"Came to you in a flash." Toys sneered. "Mother Mary, save me."

"I . . . if they . . ."

"Shut up," Toys said as he fished out his phone. He dialed a number. A voice answered on the third ring.

"Line?" Toys asked.

"Clear," said the American.

"I'm calling on behalf of our patron. There's a problem. Listen to me very closely and take all appropriate action. The Princess and the Boxer have gone off the reservation."

"What? *Why?*"

Toys's mouth made an ugly shape as he said, "They think they're still in church."

That wasn't an agreed code word, but Toys was sure the American would grasp the meaning, and he did. "I never trusted those two from the beginning. Jesus H. Christ."

"Yes, well, that's a comfort to all of us, isn't it?"

Toys disconnected and stared at Gault. "Listen to me, Sebastian . . . if El Musclehead is going to launch the latest generation of the plague in America then we have to assume that Amirah has taken some precautions."

Gault's eyes came back into focus. "Precautions?"

"She's a wacko, I agree, but I can't believe that she'd want to destroy the entire world. A lot them are true believers, don't forget."

Gault sat up straight. "What are you saying?"

"I'm saying that she probably has a bloody cure for this thing. Or a treatment. Something that will keep it from wiping out her own people. El Mujahid might already have been inoculated, but that's beside the point. What we have to do is get our ruddy asses to the Bunker, beat some information out of your girlfriend, and then make sure Gen2000 starts cranking out the cure just in case our American friend doesn't stop the Fighter in time."

"The Bunker . . . yes." Gault nodded and his jaw lost some its softness, his eyes grew several degrees colder. "Yes, Amirah will have thought it through."

Toys cut him off. "Understand me, Sebastian," he said in an icy voice, "I work for you and I love you like a brother, but you've endangered me by letting this thing get out of hand. I warned you about Amirah a hundred times and now she's stabbed you in the back. If she has a cure then we are going to bloody well get it." His green eyes glittered. "And then we are going to put a bullet right through that brilliant little brain of hers."

Gault closed his eyes for a moment as if to block out that image, but when he opened them Toys saw that some kind of change had occurred. The eyes that looked out at him from Gault's puffy and tear-streaked face were vicious, almost feral in their hateful intensity.

"Yes," he snarled.

Chapter **Eighty-One**

Crisfield, Maryland / Thursday, July 2; 6:00 P.M.

THE FORENSICS TENT was set up in one corner of the parking lot. As Dietrich had promised it was an actual circus tent. The silk sides and scalloped dome were painted with brightly colored animals— elephants, zebras, giraffes, and monkeys—and around the base was a life-sized line of capering clowns. Inside, Jerry Spencer was the ring-master.

Teams of experts had spent the whole day collecting evidence and transporting it out of the building in protective bags. The tent had several hermetically sealed plastic clean rooms that were marked with the logo of the Centers for Disease Control. Men and women wearing white hazmat suits worked in one of these and they had a production line going with one autopsy after another. A refrigeration truck was backed up to that end of the tent and the bodies of autopsied walkers were double-sealed in body bags and stacked like cordwood inside.

There were a dozen experts at the meeting along with Jerry, Grace, Dietrich, Rudy, and Hu. Somehow Church had managed to change into a clean suit. I was still in the soiled fatigue pants and T-shirt I'd worn under the Hammer suit. I must have smelled pretty ripe.

"Let's start with the bodies," Jerry said as soon as everyone was seated. He nodded to a tall black woman with golden skin and pale brown eyes.

Dr. Clarita McWilliams was a professor of forensic pathology at Thomas Jefferson University Hospital in Philadelphia. "We have a total body count of two hundred seventy-four. That breaks down as follows: eleven terrorist soldiers, five scientists and technicians, two unspecified support staff, five DMS personnel, and two hundred fifty-one of the . . . um . . . 'walkers.'" She briefly looked around the room through her half-moon glasses, then cleared her throat and plowed ahead. "There were ninety-one adult male walkers; one hundred and twenty-two adult female walkers; twenty-one male children under the apparent age of eighteen and seventeen female children of the same approximate age. The ethnic breakdown of the walkers stands at one hundred twenty-four Caucasians, seventy-three black, twenty-eight Asian, and twenty-six Hispanic. If you want a more precise racial breakdown it'll take some time."

"So what does that tell us?" I asked.

"It's close enough to a general population cross section," McWilliams said. "Maybe a little heavy on the male-to-female mix. If there's a pattern it isn't yet apparent."

"What do we know about where these people were from?" I asked.

Dietrich held up his hand. "I've been working on that using recovered wallets, cell phones, and so on. Most of these people seem to be concentrated in Maryland, New Jersey, and Pennsylvania. None from anywhere else."

"Just like the kids in Delaware," I said. "Random but all East Coast."

"Any IDs with the name Lester Bellmaker?" Grace asked. "Or any variation on Bellmaker? Maybe Belmacher or something like that?"

Dietrich scanned a sheet of paper on a clipboard. "Nah. Closest we have there is a Jennifer Bellamy. No Lesters."

"It's a dead end," Church said quietly. "We have to consider that the name is an alias."

"Aldin seemed to think it was important to give it to us," I said. "He used his last breath."

"Time will tell," Church said. "Anything else, Dr. McWilliams?"

She shook her head. "Medically speaking we haven't yet found anything that goes outside of what Dr. Hu has already shared regarding these walkers. One item of interest is that less than half of the victims I've seen displayed any visible bite marks. Most have injection marks and presumably that's how the pathogen was introduced."

Grace asked, "Of the ones with the bite marks have you determined if any of them were bitten postmortem?"

"No. There's no evidence that these walkers preyed on each other. That suggests that they are attracted only to living flesh." She looked ill as she said it.

"Like in the movies," Hu said, but she ignored him.

I turned to Jerry. "What's next?"

"Frank?" he asked, turning to Frank Sessa, a sturdy man of about sixty with a shaved head, wire-framed glasses, and the callused knuckles of a long-time karate practitioner. Frank and I went way back; both in martial arts circles and through chemical analysis work he did for law enforcement.

Sessa laced his fingers and leaned forward on his forearms. "Your terrorists have some odd choices when it comes to explosives. They used explosive organic peroxide. It's a colorless liquid with a pretty strong smell. It's generally stored as a twenty-five-percent solution in dimethyl phthalate to prevent detonation, so whoever rigged the booby traps knew something about temperature control as applied to explosives. This is difficult stuff to work with and way above the level of what I'd expect from a Unabomber wannabe."

He gave us a technical rundown on how this stuff is made, handled, and used. It was pretty damned disturbing news. "Now, I understand that these walker-things are also dormant at low temperatures," Sessa said, "and on the surface there might be a tendency to say, well, the place is already cold so that's why they chose an explosive that is safest at low temps, but I'd hesitate going there. There are plenty of explosives that are not nearly as temperature-sensitive as this stuff. I don't know who your bad guys are, but to me it kinda looks like someone was showing off. It's too much bomb for the purpose to which it was put, and they used the wrong amounts in at least two places."

"What do you mean?" Dietrich asked. I said nothing; I thought I already knew the answer. So did Jerry.

"Well, the amount they had at the door where they were storing the infected people . . . that was too big or too small depending on how you look at it. If the intent was to blow open the door or kill whoever tried to open it, then it was too much; on the other hand if it was intended to destroy the contents of the room it was way too small. If they'd been using dynamite I'd have dismissed it as some fool who doesn't understand how explosives work, but then we have the computer room. There was a good amount of the explosive, but it was all at one end of the room. If their intent had been to destroy all of the computers they could have used less of the material but put a portion inside each of the units. Less blast but much more effect in terms of security." He shook his head.

"No, this is a combination of high-tech knowledge, lots of money, and strange choices."

Jerry gave me a knowing smile, but I kept my face straight.

For the next two hours we heard from one expert after another. Ballistics told us what we expected: the terrorists were using standard AK-47s and a variety of bought-on-the-street handguns. The AKs were converted to take M-16 magazines and standard NATO 7.62-millimeter rounds. That's nothing new; gun collectors have been doing it for years. The fingerprint guys lifted plenty of sets and so far three of the terrorists had popped up in the computers, each with known ties to Al Qaeda or El Mujahid. Of the scientists, none of them were in the computers; but that wasn't particularly surprising.

Church's chief computer wizard, Utada, spoke next. "As Mr. Sessa pointed out we aren't seeing a total loss with the computers. In fact we got pretty lucky because two mainframes are completely intact, and we're salvaging stuff from three more."

"What have we found so far?" Grace asked.

Hu answered that. "Tons. If the data is supported by the lab work my guys are doing right now then we might have a name for some or all of the component parasites. That's going to save us a lot of time in putting together a protocol."

I thanked the forensics experts and let them get back to work, though Jerry stayed behind.

Church said, "We haven't actually heard from you yet, Detective Spencer. What are your thoughts on this?"

Jerry smiled and gave me a sly look. "Captain Hotshot here already knows what I'm thinking, but let me give it to those of you who aren't cops." It was a nice dig at the feds in the room. I did my best not to smirk. "Point one," he said, ticking the items off on his fingers, "this place is built to be a rat maze. The only viable entry point was the door Joe's team used. From an approach point of view nothing else was moderately safe. I believe that these suckers planned it that way. Point two: once Joe and his boys were inside they were offered a single route to follow. Anyone who's in this business would know that they'd leave a man behind to guard the door. There was only one possible position a shooter would take to defend that position and right behind him there was a hidden door on well-oiled hinges. Absolutely silent when it opened, allowing an ambush man to sneak up and Taser young whatshisname."

"Skip Tyler," I supplied.

"Yeah. Tyler. They take him out with a liquid Taser, cart him off and dump him in a room, but they leave his weapons where he can easily find them? Why not just cut his throat or feed him directly to the walkers? There's only one way that makes sense." He didn't elaborate on that point quite yet. "Point three: they take out the second guy." He snapped his fingers at me.

"Ollie Brown."

"Right, they Taser Brown and drag him down to their lab. Now, the bad guys know full well that they've been infiltrated. So why the drama? Why capture Joe's guys instead of killing them? There were only three armed DMS agents left, and between the armed guards in the building and a couple hundred walkers they could easily have simply wiped the team out, or taken them hostage to use as bargaining chips. They didn't try; they didn't even try to use Brown as a hostage when Joe broke in. They didn't try to flee. No, it doesn't add up. This whole thing should have been a massacre or a standoff . . . and it was neither."

"It came pretty bloody close," muttered Grace.

"Don't get me wrong, Major," Jerry said. "I'm not saying they were interested in the well-being of your teams. It probably would have worked out equally well for these guys if you'd all died in there."

"Charming," Grace said.

"My point is that this was not a matter of them fighting back. Nothing that I've seen supports that. Tell me I'm wrong, Joe."

"You know you're right, Jerry," I told him. The others around the table were staring at us and there was a mixture of expressions. Church's face, as usual, told me nothing; but Grace was nodding, putting the pieces together herself. Rudy had one eyebrow raised the way he did when he was looking in at his own thoughts. Dietrich looked a little puzzled and kept looking to Church as if for instructions. Hu looked skeptical.

"Why would they do that?" Hu asked.

"Because they wanted us to find what we found," I said.

Hu shook his head. "No . . . no way. That doesn't make sense."

"Yes it does," murmured Church. We all looked at him, but he nodded to me. "You have the floor."

"All of this is a setup," I said. "Jerry's absolutely right: they could have taken us out and should have. We had a small team and no intelligence at all about the inside of the building. Once we were inside they shut down the refrigeration units and turned up the heat to activate all of the walkers that had been lying dormant before we got there. So, between the booby trap in the big warehouse room, the walkers released into the halls, and the appearance of the guards who suddenly decided to open up with their AKs, we were herded into the lab. They set explosives in the computer room, but not enough to destroy all of their research, and none of the armed guards in the hall tried to use a keycard to enter the lab. Jerry checked . . . their keycards had the right code, but they didn't use them. We were played."

"To what end?" Rudy asked. "I mean, I can see the shape of it when you lay it out like that, but what's the point? You've managed to kill all of the walkers, all of their scientists and personnel are dead, we have the computers, and we have whatever else can be salvaged from the lab. The way you're describing it the terrorists have *handed* us the solution to the threat."

When I didn't answer, he added, "Why would they do something like that?"

THE FREIGHTER *ALBERT Schweitzer* docked at Pier 12 in the shadow of the *Queen Elizabeth 2* and was met by a parking lot filled with ambulances, paratransit vehicles, limousines, and cabs. The ambulatory wounded were escorted down the boarding ramp by nurses and orderlies; the more serious cases wheeled in chairs or on gurneys. Sonny Bertucci walked down under his own steam, though he used a cane and looked frail. He was met by two agents from Global Security. They led him to a white van with the name of a private ambulance company stenciled on the doors. The agents got into the back with Bertucci and the driver shut the door, climbed into the cab, and drove out of the parking lot and within half an hour they were on the New Jersey Turnpike heading south.

At the Thomas Edison Rest Stop the van pulled around behind a row of parked semis and stopped next to a black Ford Explorer with Pennsylvania plates. Both drivers got out and shook hands and together they walked around to the back of the white van. The van driver knocked three times, waited, and knocked once more before opening the door.

"Your ride is—"

That was as far as he got. The driver of the Explorer pressed a silenced .22 against the back of his head and fired two quick shots. The van driver collapsed just as the doors opened; Sonny Bertucci reached out and caught him and together he and the Explorer's driver hauled the corpse into the van, laying it next to the two bodies of the Global Security agents. Both of them had their throats cut, and the big man held the hook of his cane in his left hand. The hook ended in a six-inch wickedly sharp stiletto that had fit into the shaft of the cane, the seam hidden by a decorative metal band.

Bertucci tossed the weapon into the back and together he and the driver of the Explorer closed and locked the van's doors. When they were done they embraced warmly, slapping each other on the back.

"It is so good to see you!" beamed the driver.

El Mujahid grinned despite the pain of his healing wounds. "Ahmed, it is very good to see a friend in this place." He paused and jerked his chin toward the van. "Gault knows?"

"So it seems," said Ahmed. "I received a call about fifteen minutes ago saying that you were to be terminated. I assume one of them," the driver said, jerking his head toward the closed van, "got a similar call."

"Yes. It came in while we were driving. I couldn't hear what was said but I could tell from his eyes that he'd gotten a kill order. Thank you for taking care of things."

"My pleasure. Come, let us go . . . we cannot risk being here if Gault has other agents coming."

Once they were both seated inside the Explorer and pulling back into the flow of traffic, Ahmed asked, "What is the news from home? How is my sister?"

El Mujahid smiled. "Amirah sends her love."

"I miss her."

The Fighter patted the man on the shoulder. "Soon we will all be together, in this world or in paradise."

"Praise Allah," said Ahmed as he accelerated to seventy and headed south.

Chapter **Eighty-Three**
Sebastian Gault / Over Afghani Airspace / Thursday, July 2

"IT'S A REAL honor to have Mr. Gault make this visit," said Nan Yadreen, the Red Cross liaison for Afghanistan. "And a bit of a surprise. If we'd had more notice we would have prepared a better reception."

Toys forced a smile. "Not necessary, Doctor. This is just a visit, not an inspection."

The helicopter's roar made conversation difficult, for which he was grateful. The preening doctor had to shout to be heard. Gault sat across from him, pretending to be asleep but Toys knew better.

The doctor nodded. "I understand. And I suppose advertising it in advance is bad for security."

"Indeed."

"Good thinking, sir," said the doctor.

Too bloody right it's good thinking, Toys mused darkly. Last thing they needed was Amirah knowing that they were on the way. The only people expecting their arrival in Afghanistan was a crack team of mercenaries from Global Security led by one of Toys's favorite people, the ruthless South African, Captain Zeller. Toys had called to make arrangements, explaining what they intended. Zeller didn't bat an eye when Toys told him that this was going to be a wet operation. Wet works were their specialty and they loved the bonuses he'd promised for their pay packets.

The chopper flew on toward the Red Cross field hospital. Gault had pulled himself together on the drive to the heliport, but Toys was cautious. Nothing was ever certain in matters of the heart. He was glad that he didn't have one.

Chapter Eighty-Four

Crisfield, Maryland / Thursday, July 2; 8:30 P.M.

"HERE'S THE PROBLEM," I said. "In one way or another over the last couple of days I've said that I've found it hard to buy the scenario that we've been fed: that this is a group of terrorists who have the smarts, the funding, and the technology to create several new diseases, to pioneer new fields of science in order to manipulate and weaponize those diseases, to locate and hold hostage the families of key scientists, and to manage those scientists through the use of not one but *two* control diseases. And all of it off the radar of all of the world's top intelligence networks?"

"When you put it that way," Dietrich said, shifting uncomfortably.

"From the beginning I was bothered by the control disease because it's way too sophisticated. Who here thinks that a bunch of terrorists really thought that up? Show of hands."

When no one raised a hand, Dietrich said, "But we know that this is the case."

Instead of answering I said, "The next thing to consider is the crab plant itself. As Jerry pointed out it was a trap from the beginning, no doubt about it. The staff inside, to all intents and purposes, were suicide fighters. Either they knew they weren't getting out of there alive, or they were duped into thinking that they were playing a stronger hand than they were."

"I doubt the scientists were in on it," Grace said.

"At least one was," I said, and reminded them about the one with the detonator. "He said that it was already too late. I'm not sure what he meant by that, though it's pretty clear that we'd know if the *Seif al Din* pathogen had been released into the public."

"We're still looking for additional cells," Church said. "This is clearly not over, and directly after this meeting I'll make a conference call to the CDC and the White House."

"Good. Now getting back to my theory. I'm no science geek but from what Rudy and Hu have said, everything we've seen is absolutely cutting edge; stuff that would be science fiction if we hadn't actually experienced it firsthand."

"What's your point?" asked Dietrich. "We know these assholes are smart."

I shook my head. "Yeah, well, 'smart' is a relative term. You can have real geniuses act like idiots sometimes." I tried hard not to look at Hu when I said this, but out of the corner of my eye I saw him shift in his seat. "You see, these guys have done stuff that's needlessly sophisticated. The control diseases, the fancy explosives. Whoever's behind this seems to think that expensive toys work better, but all they really do is send up red flags. He's drawing attention to his own attempts at being slick. Doc," I said to Hu, "correct me if I'm wrong but the compound from the treatment recovered from the warehouse, once removed from the aspirin coating, was able to dissolve in ordinary saline, correct?"

"Yes," he agreed. "It's a very small amount of material, a few chemicals that are all soluble in water or saline. Barely clouded the fluid."

"How easily could it be detected?"

"In food, you mean? Probably not at all. They're mostly vegetable based; organic stuff. None of the compounds would significantly affect the taste or smell of most foods."

"So it could have been dissolved into something strong tasting, say orange juice, without anyone being the wiser?"

"I suppose so."

"Then why wasn't it?"

The others stared, and I could see them catch on, one by one. "Son of a bitch," growled Dietrich.

Grace said, "You're right. The process of hiding it in the aspirin is too clever a step. Impressive, but unnecessary." She was with me on this now, step by step.

"That's one point," I said. "Now the second is their intent. We can presume that they did know they were under surveillance the whole time, which means they could have released the walkers, taken suicide pills, blown the place up. Why wait until we infiltrate?"

Rudy snapped his fingers. "They wanted you to find a functional lab and have a heroic fight. They wanted you to believe that you fought for and obtained the evidence, damaged and partial though it is."

"Right," I said. "Our bad guy wanted to stage a big, scary event that would scare the hell out of us."

"Which it effing well did," Grace said bitterly.

"After Aldin died, it seemed pretty clear that the terrorists were trying to make us afraid of the possibility of an epidemic. That it might be the new threat, a new kind of warfare that would force the U.S. to divert funding away from tanks and missiles and into preventive medicine. That's probably going to happen, at least in part, because we know that this disease actually exists and that terrorists have it. But . . . before we decide that we know the shape of things, let me ask this: if we do start scrambling for new treatments and cures, who stands to benefit?"

"*Dios mio!* A lot of people will get rich," Rudy said. "Pharmaceutical companies, drugstores, health organizations, hospitals . . . pretty much the entire medical profession."

I sat back and stared at him, and then at each person at the table.

"So . . . why are we so damn sure that terrorists are the only ones behind this thing?"

Chapter **Eighty-Five**
Amirah / The Bunker / Thursday, July 2

"SEBASTIAN GAULT HAS been spotted by our man in the Red Cross outpost."

Amirah looked up from her computer screen at the young Yemen woman who stood in front of her desk. "When will he get here?"

"Day after tomorrow at the latest."

Amirah chewed her lip thoughtfully.

"Do you want Abdul to . . . ?" Anah left it unsaid.

But Amirah shook her head. "No, let him come. It should be an enlightening experience for him." She smiled at Anah who flinched before returning the smile. Anah turned and left the room, silently reciting a prayer. For just a moment Amirah's face had looked like that of a desert demon, a *djinn*. Anah was glad to be away from that evil and totally mirthless grin.

Chapter **Eighty-Six**
Crisfield, Maryland / Thursday, July 2; 8:44 P.M.

"YOU LOST ME," Dietrich admitted. "I thought you were saying this was all about shifting the U.S. budget away from war and into research. So . . . what, are we talking about an axis of evil formed by Walgreens and CVS?"

"Think bigger," Rudy said.

"Doctors, hospitals? Drug companies?"

"Bingo," I said. "That's who would stand to make more money if word of this thing got out."

"Then this whole thing is some kind of goddamn advertising campaign?" Dietrich asked.

"In a way," I said. "Show the big scary bug to us, prove to us that terrorists are capable of releasing it, then let us stop the first wave so that we feel like we've caught a break. But at the same time make us so afraid that the bug might still be out there, still in the hands of terrorists, that we have to scramble to get treatments. Everything that happened at the plant supports that. They handed us the first steps in developing the treatment, sure, but even Hu said that it would take billions to fully research it and maybe trillions to distribute the cure."

"So who's the bad guy?" asked Dietrich.

"That's the real question, isn't it?" Grace said. "I'm sure whoever is behind this will make sure they're one among many companies making fortunes. They won't be so rash as to stand out or try to come to market with the only treatment."

"Absolutely," I agreed.

Church pursed his lips and we waited. Finally he nodded. "I think you've hit it, Captain. Excellent work."

"Do I get a cookie?"

"And you are still a world-class smartass."

I bowed in acknowledgment.

"So where does that leave us?" Rudy asked. "Do you know how many pharmaceutical companies are out there?"

"Too many," Church said. "But not all of them could have funded something like this."

"We need to find one company with pockets deep enough to hide the kind of expenditure required for the research and development of this kind of disease. Or *diseases*," I corrected. "Or a group of them who have pooled their resources."

"Surely there must be some way to narrow that list even further,"

Rudy argued. "Not all pharmaceutical companies deal with disease pathogens. Not all of them deal with preventive medicine."

"Will that matter?" Dietrich asked.

"Sure," Rudy replied. "If they aren't prepared to do the research or mass-produce the treatments then they wouldn't be in on the first wave of cash. The big-money wave. Their factories wouldn't be configured for it. But even discounting those, we're still looking at a lot of companies."

"It's likely to be a great deal more complicated than that," Grace said, "because a lot of the big companies are multinational, with divisions peppered liberally all around the world. I doubt any of them would be so daft as to orchestrate this inside the borders of any of the superpowers. The governmental regulations on materials and money would be too risky. I'll bet these bloody bastards have an R and D facility in some third world country. How would we know where to start looking?"

"MindReader," said Church. "Though we're going to have to make a lot of guesses as to what the search arguments are going to be; and this whole thing is still speculation, so we are likely to trip over some of our own assumptions. This presents its own complication, however. No matter who we ultimately discover as the culprit behind this, we still have to bring this to the President and then ask for help from the pharmaceutical companies to prepare in case the disease is ever released, whether that happens deliberately or, more likely, by accident."

"Oh man," Dietrich said, "that means that we're probably going to be making our bad guy pretty damned rich."

"Right up to the moment we put a bullet in his brain," Grace said. She wasn't joking and no one took it as such.

"In the meantime," I said, "we still have to bear in mind the possibility that actual terrorists are involved in this. My guess is that our phantom pharmaceutical company has been funding terrorists to encourage their cooperation."

"It makes sense," Church said. "The terrorists get to benefit from the shift of resources in the superpowers, which gives them a real victory in the eyes of the world. They know that taking hostages didn't work. Hijacking planes and crashing them into buildings didn't work. Blowing up subways didn't work. They may have done a lot of damage, but in the global scheme of things their batting average is low. Now with this they get to rack one up in the 'win' category."

Dietrich chewed on that. "So, they're something like hired guns for the drug company behind all this."

"Something like that," I said, "but one thing we know about terrorists is that they don't give up easily, and they are seldom satisfied with a subtle victory. They're not great team players, they resent being someone else's flunkies, and they suck at sticking to the rules."

"Meaning . . . ?" Rudy asked.

"Meaning," I said, "that just because our bad guy has paid them to arrange some demonstrations of this disease, it doesn't mean that they're going to pack up shop and go home now that the scheme worked. A lot of their people have been killed in the process. If El Mujahid is involved, then hurting the U.S. economy might not be enough to satisfy his needs."

"What needs?" Rudy asked.

"Religious needs," I said.

"Oh crap," Dietrich said softly.

Chapter Eighty-Seven
Sebastian Gault / Afghanistan / Thursday, July 2

"LINE?" ASKED THE American.

"Clear," said Gault. Toys was right there with him, listening in on the call.

"I have some bad news for you. The Boxer slipped the punch."

Gault heard Toys hiss quietly. "How?" Gault asked.

"He KO'd the other players. I think he had a corner man. Police found the vehicle at a rest stop on the Jersey Turnpike. No trace of the Boxer.

Seems like they already had another play running, and the knock-down order reached them too late."

Gault stood up and walked across the tent and stared out into the Afghani darkness. The Red Cross camp was quiet and the sky above was littered with stars.

"What about the chocolate box?" Gault asked, then abruptly swore in frustration. "For Christ's sake, let's skip the sodding code. Tell me what happened?"

After a long pause the American said, "The trigger device has already been picked up. Someone identifying herself as the wife of Sonny Bertucci picked it up an hour ago. The woman fit the description of the woman that's been sleeping with Ahmed Mahoud, El Mujahid's brother-in-law."

"Then they're already two steps ahead of us," Gault said. "That means that you're going to have to find some way to stop him when he makes his run,"

The American swore and the line went dead.

"Bloody hell," Gault said. "It's all coming apart."

"Don't start," Toys snapped. Since the moment when he'd slapped Gault the dynamic of their relationship had undergone a change. He'd stepped up into a position of greater power even though Amirah's betrayal had only made Gault stumble rather than collapse. They had not drifted back into their old pattern, and maybe never would. Both of them were aware of it though neither put the topic on the table. "Now we have to be very careful, Sebastian. If the Yank has to spill his guts to the authorities in order to stop El Mujahid then your name is going to be mud on five continents."

Gault snorted. "Oh, you think?"

"Well, just be glad we planned well in advance. You have enough false identities and bolt-holes to stay hidden for years, probably forever." He sniffed and brushed a strand of blond hair from his eyes. "Which means I'll also have to go into hiding. We'll need new faces, new fingerprints . . ." He sighed. "Bugger all."

Gault saw the misery in Toys's face. "I'm sorry. It was all working so well."

"That's a consolation."

Gault stared up into the limitless nothing of the sky. "We'll be at the Bunker day after tomorrow. If there's any luck left in the bottle then Amirah will have a cure and then maybe we can find a way to bring it to market while there's still an intact world economy."

Or an intact world, Gault thought, but he didn't say it.

Chapter Eighty-Eight

Crisfield, Maryland / Friday, July 3; 10:01 A.M.

I STAYED AT the plant again that night and spent Friday alternately working with Jerry and working with Church to concoct a news story that would calm the public. The new story, which was released to the press via the Maryland governor's office, said that a major meth lab had been raided by a task force under the direction of the ATF, but during the raid part of the lab blew up. Church's computer techs cobbled together bits of video footage of other raids—enhanced with some nifty computer graphics—that showed tactical teams raiding the plant. It was pretty convincing, and it did what we wanted it to do: it knocked the phrase "terrorist attack" right off the headlines and out of the CNN news crawls.

BY LATE FRIDAY night I was totally fried. So was everyone else so we bagged it and decided to head back to the Warehouse. In DMS parlance the temporary headquarters on the Baltimore docks was now being called the Warehouse, capital *W*; just as the Brooklyn facility at Floyd Bennett Field was called the Hanger. Grace said that the Warehouse would probably become one of the organization's permanent sites, it being conveniently close to D.C.

Church wasn't going with us. He said that he needed to brief the President personally and he took a Bell Jet Ranger to Washington; Hu went with him, but before they boarded I took Church aside.

"Every time I close my eyes I see the face of that lab tech with the detonator saying that it's all too late. It's nagging at me."

"You're not alone in that," he admitted. "Do you have a suggestion?"

"I do. You already said that if this thing was launched on some big event that it would get out of control. Tomorrow's the Fourth of July and there's no bigger event that I know of than the rededication of the Liberty Bell."

He nodded. "I've already alerted their security teams to be on ultra-high alert."

"I was supposed to be on that detail," I said, "and I think I want to follow through on that. But I want to make it a field trip. I want to take Echo Team to Philly and let them put their eyes to work. Give them some fieldwork that doesn't involve zombies. Maybe take Grace and Gus, too."

When I said Grace's name there was the faintest flicker of amusement in his face, but it was gone in an instant. Maybe I imagined it.

"Is this a hunch?" he asked.

"Not really. Maybe half a hunch. It's just that if I were going to launch this thing, that's where I'd do it."

Church leaned a shoulder against the chopper and considered the point. "The First Lady will be there. Perhaps I should request that she be removed from the event."

"That's your call. I could be wrong about this. There are a lot of big celebrations tomorrow, all over the country; and maybe these guys are too smart to pick the one where about every third person in the crowd is carrying a federal badge. No, I can't see disrupting the event on a half a hunch, but I think you should reinforce your warning to all commands to stay extra frosty."

He nodded. "I'll do that; and I'll be with the President in a couple of hours and he can punctuate the request. But I'll have some National Guard units on standby just in case."

"Fair enough."

We shook hands and he climbed into the chopper.

The rest of us climbed into the Seahawks and we rose into the night sky, flying across Maryland with two Apaches giving close air support. For some strange reason going back to the Warehouse felt like going home.

Chapter Eighty-Nine

Baltimore, Maryland / Saturday, July 4; 1:12 A.M.

BACK AT THE Warehouse we each went our separate ways. Echo Team was already sacked out for the night but Top had left me reams of notes on the new recruits. I put that aside for later and headed off to get clean. In the shower I let the hot water blast me for a long time. I do some of my best thinking in the shower and as I washed, rinsed, and repeated I wondered about who Lester Bellmaker might be and despite furious lathering I came up with nothing.

It was already into the early hours of July 4. I figured we'd head out early and get to Philadelphia in time to add a little security muscle to the event. And if nothing happened . . . at least they have great hot dogs, soft pretzels, and beer in that town.

Back in my room I was bemused to notice that Cobbler had been fed and even his cat litter changed.

When I climbed between the sheets Cobbler crouched at the foot of the bed and stared at me like I was a stranger. I told myself that he was only spooked by having been handled by someone he didn't know, but I knew that wasn't really it. It was me. Rudy was right—I'd been changed, too. Cobbler could see it in my eyes and he kept his distance. After five minutes of trying to coax him nearer I gave up and turned out the light.

I could feel him watching me with his wise cat eyes.

I finally fell asleep around one or so but within minutes a tap at the door woke me. It was tentative. I lay in the dark and listened, uncertain whether it was real or part of some complicated dream. Then it came again. Firmer this time.

I switched on the bedside light and padded to the door in sleeping shorts and a T-shirt. There was no peephole or intercom so I unlatched it and peered cautiously through the crack. I guess I expected Rudy, or Church. Maybe Top Sims or Sergeant Dietrich.

I never expected Grace Courtland.

Chapter Ninety

Baltimore, Maryland / Saturday, July 4; 1:17 A.M.

SHE WORE MAKESHIFT pajamas—blue hospital scrubs and a black tank top. Her hair was untidy, there were fatigue smudges under her eyes. She held a six-pack of Sam Adams Summer Ale beer by the handle of the cardboard carrier.

"Did I wake you?"

"Yes."

"Good, because I can't sleep. Let me in." She let the sixer of beer swing from her finger.

"Okay," I said, and stepped back to pull the door open. Grace nodded and walked past me into the room. She gave it a quick, flat appraising look and grunted.

"They brought a lot of your things."

"They brought my cat," I said as I closed the door. Cobbler jumped off the bed and came over to her, sniffing tentatively. "Cobbler, be nice to the major."

Cobbler still looked cautious but when Grace squatted down to pet him he allowed it. Her fingers flexed luxuriantly in his fur.

"Have a seat," I said, indicating the recliner. I got the bottle opener that was attached to my key chain, opened two bottles and handed her one. I took mine and sat on the edge of the bed.

She rose and stood looking down at the cat for a moment, sipping thoughtfully.

"I like your friend Dr. Sanchez."

"Rudy."

"Rudy. We met outside the showers, had a bit of a heart-to-heart. He's a good man."

"You any judge?"

"I've known a few shrinks in my time." She looked away, but I saw that her eyes were wet. Cobbler was still close so she busied herself by scratching between his ears, then she tilted the bottle back and drank nearly all of it.

"These last few days have been unreal," she said softly. "Ungodly . . ."

She shook her head, sniffing back tears. She finished her beer, got another. I handed her the opener and as she took it her fingers brushed mine. She wanted it to look casual, but she wasn't that good an actress. My skin was hot where she'd touched me.

"It must have been pretty bad at the hospital," I said. "I still haven't seen the tapes, but Rudy told me. Worse even than the crab plant, from what he said."

Back in her chair she looked at the beer bottle as if interested in something on the label. When she spoke her voice was almost a whisper. "When we realized something about . . . about what was going on, when we saw that we were losing control of the situation at St. Michael's . . . I . . ." She stopped, shook her head, tried again. "When we realized what we had to do . . . it was the worst thing in my life. It was worse than . . ." A tear gathered in the corner of her eye.

"Have some beer," I suggested softly.

She drank and then raised her head and looked at me with her red-rimmed eyes. "Joe . . . when I was eighteen I got pregnant by a boy during my first year at university. We were just kids, you know? He freaked and buggered off, but then he came back when I was in my third trimester. We got married. A civil ceremony. We weren't ever really in love, but he stayed with me until the baby was born. Brian Michael. But . . . he was born with a hole in his heart."

The room was utterly silent.

"They tried everything. They did four surgeries, but the heart hadn't formed correctly. Brian lived for three months. There was never really a chance he'd make it, they told me. After the last surgery I sat with my baby day and night. I lost so much weight I was like a ghost. Eighty-seven pounds. They wanted to admit me."

I started to say something, but she shook me off.

"Then one afternoon the doctor told me that there was no brain activity, that for all intents and purposes my baby was dead. They . . . wanted me to . . . they asked me if I would consent to having the respirator disconnected. What could I say? I screamed, I yelled at them, I argued with them. I prayed. For days." The tears broke and cut silvery lines down her face. They looked like scars. "When I finally agreed it was so horrible. I kissed my baby and held his little hand while they stopped the machines. I put my face down to listen to his heartbeat, hoping that it would go on beating, but all I heard was one heartbeat. Just one, he died that quickly. One beat and then a dreadful silence. I *felt* him die, Joe. It was so awful, so terrible that I knew that I would never—*could* never feel anything worse." She drank most of the second bottle. "It ruined me. My husband had left again after the second surgery. I guess to him Brian was already gone. My parents were long gone. I had no one else in my life. I continued to get sicker and I wound up in a psychiatric medical center for nearly three months. Are you shocked?"

She looked at me defiantly, but something in my expression must have reassured her. She nodded.

"In the hospital I had a counselor and she suggested that I look for something that would give me structure. I had no family left and she knew a recruiter. She wrote me a letter of recommendation and two weeks after discharge from hospital I was in the army. It became my life. From there I went to the SAS. I saw combat in a dozen places. I saw death. I *caused* death. None of it touched me. I believed that whatever had made me a person, a human being, was gone, buried in a little coffin with a tiny body. Both of us dead, killed by imperfect hearts."

She wiped at the tears then stared with subdued surprise at the wetness on her fingers. "I hardly ever cry anymore. Except sometimes at
night when I wake up from a dream of holding Brian's hand and hearing his last heartbeat. I haven't cried in years, Joe. Not in years."

My mouth was dry and I drank some beer to be able to breathe.

Grace said, "When Al Qaeda attacked the World Trade Center I
didn't cry. I just got angry. When the bombs went off in the London
subways, I tightened up my resolve. Grace Courtland, Major SAS,
combat veteran, professional hard-ass." She took a big breath, blew out
her cheeks. "And then St. Michael's. God! We went in there hard and
fast, so tough and practiced. You never got a chance to see the DMS at
its best, but everyone in Baker and Charlie teams were absolutely first-
rate. Top-of-the-line combat veterans, not a virgin among them. What
is it you Yanks say? Heartbreakers and life-takers? State-of-the-art
equipment, cutting-edge tactics, nothing left to chance. And you know
what happened? We were *slaughtered*! Grown men and women torn
apart. Civilians killing armed military with their fingers and teeth.
Children taking shot after shot to the chest, falling down and then getting right up again, their bodies torn open, and still they kept running
at our men, tearing and biting them. Eating them."

"God," I whispered.

"God wasn't there that day," she hissed in as bitter a voice as I've
ever heard. "I'm not a religious person, Joe. Faith isn't something I'm
good at, not since I buried Brian; but if there was ever a splinter of belief or hope left in me it ended that day. It was consumed by what happened."

"Grace . . . you do know that you and Church had no other choice?"

"Is that supposed to make me feel better? Do you really think that
makes any difference to me? I *know* we didn't have another choice,
that's why we made the choice we did. We were losing, Joe. Losing.
Suddenly, all the training, all the power that we thought we had was
gone. It failed us. Just as medicine and prayer failed Brian. All we could
do was disconnect another switch, turn off more lives because there

was nothing else left for us." Tears fell steadily but she didn't bother to wipe them away.

She gave me a twisted smile. "The thing is . . . that was even worse than turning off my baby's life support. Worse, do you understand? And afterward do you know what I felt the most? Guilt. Not for having to kill all of those people. No, I felt—I *feel*—guilty because that was the worst moment of my life. It probably always will be. So I feel like I've somehow betrayed or maybe abandoned my baby because now this event is bigger and worse even than that. I feel like I've lost Brian again. Forever this time. It hurts so damn—"

Her voice suddenly disintegrated into terrible sobs and she dropped the bottle and covered her face with both hands. I was up and across the room before her bottle rolled to a stop. I took her by the arms and gathered her to me, pulling her off the chair, wrapping her up against my chest. The sound of her sobs cut through my flesh and into my heart. I held her close—this angry woman, this bitter soldier—and I kissed her hair and held her as close and as tight and as safe as I could.

SHE WEPT FOR a long time.

I walked her to the bed and we lay down together, her face buried against me, her tears soaking through my T-shirt, her body fever-hot. Maybe I said something, some nonsense words, but I don't remember. Her body bucked and spasmed with the tears until slowly, slowly, the immediacy of the storm began to pass. Her arms were wrapped around me, her fingers knotted in my shirt. The knots of tension eased by very slow degrees.

We lay like that for a long time, and then I could feel the change in her as her tension changed from the totality of grief to the awkwardness of awareness. We were as physically close as lovers, but there had been nothing even remotely sexual about her tears or my holding her, not even in our lying down together. Not at first. But now there was a new tension as we both became enormously aware of all the points of contact—of thighs intertwined, of groins pushed forward, of her breasts against my chest, of hot exhalations, and of animal heat and natural musk.

There was a moment when we should have rolled apart, made a few awkward jokes, and retreated to separate corners of the universe. But that moment passed.

After a minute or two she said, very softly, "I didn't come here for this."

"I know."

"It's . . . well, there was no one else. I can't talk to Mr. Church. Not about this. Not like this."

"No."

"And I don't know Dr. Sanchez yet. Not well enough."

"You don't know me, either."

"Yes," she said quietly, her forehead tucked under my chin. "I do. I know about Helen. I know about your mum. You've lost so much. As much as I have."

I nodded, she could feel it.

"Will you make love to me?" she asked.

I leaned back and looked down at her. "Not now," I said. When I saw the hurt on her face I smiled and shook my head. "You've chugged two beers, you're grieving, exhausted, and in shock. I'd have to be the world's biggest jackass to try and take advantage of that kind of vulnerability."

Grace looked at me for a long time. "You're a strange man, Joe Ledger." She pushed one of her hands up between us and touched my face. "I never thought you'd be kind. Not to me. You're an actual gentleman."

"We're a dying breed . . . they're hunting us down one by one."

She laughed and then laid her head against me. "Thanks for listening, Joe."

After another long time of silence she said, "Back at the plant I asked you a question, about whether we've stopped this. Was that the last cell?

Did we stop the terrorist movement here in the States, or did we just burn up our last lead?"

"Bad questions to ask in the dark," I said, stroking her hair.

"Mr. Church spoke with the President and the head of the FDA. The gears are already turning to get the pharmaceutical companies involved. The President will address a closed session of Congress in two days. The full resources of the United States, England, and the other allies will be thrown against this now."

"Yes."

"So why am I still so afraid?" she asked.

The silence swirled around us.

"Same reason I am," I said.

She said nothing more and after a long while her breathing changed to the slow, steady rhythm. I kissed her hair and she wriggled more tightly against me, and after a while, she slept. After a much longer time I, too, drifted off.

Chapter Ninety-One
The DMS Warehouse, Baltimore / Saturday, July 4; 6:01 A.M.

GRACE AND I had a quiet breakfast in the mess hall before first light, then she headed off to muster her team while I made a call. I was hoping I'd wake Church up and get to hear him when he was off balance, but he answered on the first ring. Fricking robot.

Instead of "Hello" he asked, "Is there a problem?"

"No. I wanted to touch base about the Liberty Bell thing. You still cool with me taking Echo Team to Philly?"

"Of course," he said, and it implied that I'd have heard different if he'd changed his mind. The communication flow with him was going to take some getting used to. I'm used to a lot more bureaucracy. "I advised the President of our concerns with safety during the holiday, and he approved all of my recommendations. The gears are already turning to get the pharmaceutical companies involved. The President will address a closed emergency session of Congress tomorrow. The full resources of the United States, England, and the other allies will be thrown against this now."

Church briefly outlined the steps he was taking to bulk up security at the top twenty Fourth of July events scheduled across the country. It meant mobilizing tens of thousands of additional police and military, and though that had to be a red-tape nightmare Church seemed confident that it would all be handled. I guess having a rubber stamp from the Commander in Chief lit a lot of fires under the right asses. Points for Church.

"My question," I said when he'd finished, "is what our actual status is going to be down there in Philly? I mean . . . we can't exactly flash DMS badges, can we?"

"We don't have badges," he said. "I also discussed this with the President and obtained authorization for Echo Team to roll as a special detachment of the Secret Service. How familiar are you with their protocols?"

"I can fake it."

"Last night I called a friend in the garment industry and appropriate clothes should be arriving by six-thirty. IDs were already sent by courier and Sergeant Dietrich has them."

"You don't like wasting time, do you?"

"No," he said, and hung up.

I smiled and shook my head. So this is what it felt like to be in the major league.

I found Dietrich and got the material Church had sent. IDs for everyone plus a detailed set of notes from Church that included the names and numbers of the people we planned to interview.

I found Grace in the computer trailer. I told her about my call to Church. "How is it that he has this much power over the President? I mean . . . who *is* Church?"

Grace shook her head. "I've heard some bits and pieces of things over the last couple of years that add up to his having the goods on a lot of people in Washington."

"The goods? As in . . . blackmail?"

"I think he quite literally knows where all of the bodies are buried, as the saying goes. He has leverage on a lot of power players and he uses it to get what he wants."

"Good thing he's on our side." I paused. "He *is* on our side, isn't he?"

"God, I hope so."

"How'd he get all this dirt?"

"I can make a guess," she said, arching an eyebrow, and then she tilted her head in the direction of the complex array of computer terminals that filled the room.

"MindReader?"

She shrugged. "It makes sense. It's brilliant at digging into everyone else's business without leaving a trace that it was there. That's one of its unique and most dangerous features. With MindReader he can sneak into the Pentagon, read whatever files he wants, and then exit without leaving the usual signature. I've seen him do it."

"Holy smoke." I stared at the computer as if it was Aladdin's lamp. "You ever heard the expression, 'If that were to fall into the wrong hands it'd be curtains for the free world'? Well, that pretty much applies here."

"Too right it does. There are only a handful of people in the world who have access, and Church has to personally grant us access through his mainframe router to allow us to log on each day. It's no joke, and even though MindReader doesn't leave a trace in other computers, all searches and operations are logged on his hard drive."

"So Big Brother really is watching," I mused.

"All the time."

"Does the man ever sleep?"

"God, I've never seen him so much as yawn. I think he's a cyborg."

"At this point, it wouldn't surprise me. Maybe there's something in those vanilla wafers."

She picked up a printout. "These are the names of the agency directors who have sent staff to the DMS. Nearly half of them will be in Philadelphia today for the Liberty Bell event, either as guests or on the job. Because the First Lady, the Vice President's wife, the wives of fifty congressmen, and over a hundred members of Congress are all attending the event, it's a security mishmash. Most of the chiefs will be there to make sure their individual Indians don't let anyone of importance get scalped."

"I know, I was originally assigned to the detail. How's this helping us?"

"The President, at Mr. Church's urging, has contacted each of these directors to put themselves at our disposal. We can set up meetings, and we can interview them personally."

"During a major event?" I goggled.

"Well . . . we'd have to pick our moments," she conceded.

I was skeptical. "All well and good, but how can we interview them with all of the speeches and rallies going on?"

"The rededication only lasts two hours."

"Good point," I said. "Okay, let's mount up and ride."

Chapter Ninety-Two
El Mujahid / The Motorways Motel / July 4

THE FIGHTER SAT on the edge of the motel bed in cotton trousers and a tank top that showed off his huge shoulders, bull neck, and the corded muscles of his arms. He had removed his bandage to let his guests inspect his face and the slash mark was a livid red line surrounded by green and purple bruises.

The two men seated on the couch stared at him. Ahmed, Amirah's brother, was on the left, his face showing concern for his brother-in-law. Next to him was a young black man with wire-framed glasses and a knit *kufi* on his close-cropped hair. His name was Saleem Mohammad but was born as John Norman twenty-six years ago in West Philadelphia. He was a graduate of Temple University's MFA theater program where he specialized in stage makeup and costume design. For two years after graduation he worked on and off Broadway, but eighteen months ago he met an African-American mullah who introduced him first to the teachings of Muhammad and, later, to the more radical teachings of El Mujahid. Saleem had been totally captivated and over the months moved smoothly from a study of the Koran to a more specialized study of fundamentalist politics. Years of repressed anger bubbled up and came to a boil when he saw the tapes of El Mujahid's diatribes on Western interference in Middle East culture and religion. Unlike many of his fellow converts to the faith, Saleem was thoroughly primed to accept the belief that extreme measures were sometimes necessary in order to protect the followers of the one true God. Saleem looked like an artist, which he certainly was, but in his chest beat the heart of a soldier of the Faith.

Sitting there on the couch, he looked very young to El Mujahid, but the Fighter could see familiar fires burning in Saleem's eyes. It pleased him. The Fighter was amused by the young man, but he also felt proud of him, of his depth of conviction. For nearly an hour they had discussed scriptures and had all prayed together. Now, their prayer mats rolled up, they sat and talked. El Mujahid had taken off his shirt and bandages to let Saleem take a close look.

"Can you do it?" the Fighter asked.

"Yes. What you want is . . . easy. I mean, there's nothing to it." Saleem looked at Ahmed. "I thought you said you wanted me to do something difficult?"

Ahmed shook his head. "I said I wanted you to do something important."

"It needs to hide everything," said El Mujahid, "the cut, the bruising."

Saleem smiled earnestly. "Give me an hour and I can guarantee you that no one will recognize you or see that injury. I have everything I need at my apartment."

"That's excellent."

They agreed on a time for Saleem to return and the young man left, looking a little starstruck at having been in the presence of El Mujahid.

One of Ahmed's agents tailed him surreptitiously though both he and El Mujahid were convinced of Saleem's dedication to the cause. When he was gone, the Fighter pulled on a shirt and buttoned it up.

"By now Gault knows that I've eluded his assassins and that we have the trigger device," El Mujahid said. "If he was man enough to grow a beard Gault would be pulling it out by now. He must be very confused over what has happened." He paused. "Where is the shipment from Amirah?"

"Andrea installed it over a week ago, and it is very cleverly hidden. No one will detect it," Ahmed said, referring to his American girlfriend, a woman he'd converted to their brand of Islam a few years ago. He gestured to a suitcase that he'd brought with him.

"Which version did Amirah send? I tried Generation Seven on a village and it was impressive."

"Generation Ten."

"Ten?" gasped the Fighter. "You mean Generation Seven—"

Ahmed grinned and shook his head. "My sister is ambitious and her anger toward the Western Satan is very great. She did not say much in her coded message, but she said that this will sweep America like the breath of God."

El Mujahid murmured a prayer.

Ahmed nodded to the suitcase. "Your clothes, identification, weapons . . . everything is there. Once Saleem performs his magic tricks then you will be able to walk among them and not be suspected. Everything is in place, my brother, and Andrea will be on site to make sure that it all goes smoothly." He paused and gave his lips another nervous lick. "There is one more thing. My sister sent something for us. She shipped it using Gault's own pipeline and it was delivered via international hazardous materials courier to a hospital in Trenton, New Jersey, late yesterday. The accompanying papers and forms were flawless so that no eyebrows were raised. My sister is very clever."

"That she is. What did she send?"

Ahmed smiled. "Well . . . on the package it said that it was samples for bacteriological research. Something to do with plant blight. And in truth that's what most of the contents were, heading from one of Gault's labs in India to a research facility here in the States, but of the twenty-four vials of infectious materials there were two that contained something quite different." He paused and repeated that. "Quite different, Allah be praised."

"Tell me . . ."

"She sent Generation Twelve of the *Seif al Din.*"

"Do we need more? I thought—"

Ahmed shook his head. "This is not a weapon, my brother. If Generation Ten is the Sword, then Generation Twelve is the shield."

The Fighter looked confused, and then as understanding blossomed a great mass of pent-up tension left his body in a long exhale. "Allah be praised, all blessings to His name."

Ahmed reached out and squeezed El Mujahid's arm. "She *did* it!" he said in an excited whisper. "We have an *antidote*. Amirah did what no one else has been able to do . . . she created a cure for the disease. We can release it as planned and then only the godless Americans will die but we—we, my brother—will survive!"

The room swam around him and El Mujahid slid from his chair onto his knees. For weeks now he had been mentally and spiritually preparing himself for what he believed was a suicide mission. He had accepted the will of Allah that he should die from the *Seif al Din* as he released it on the Americans. It was so small a price to pay to deliver a killing stroke unlike anything ever inflicted on an enemy. Total annihilation of the Americans and an ocean between the wasteland that North America would become and the rest of the world. But now . . . *now!*

He lowered his reeling head to the floor and gave praise to Allah, weeping with joy, weeping with the knowledge that the one true God had chosen to spare him and to let him continue to fight for His truth here on Earth. Paradise was a wonderful promise, but El Mujahid was a fighter and had regretted leaving the battle with so much to be done.

Tears sprang into Ahmed's eyes as well and he knelt down next to his brother-in-law, his friend, and together they prayed, both of them knowing that it would all work now, that nothing could stop the *Seif al Din*.

Nothing.

Chapter **Ninety-Three**

WE TOOK TWO cars, a pair of brand-new DMS SUVs—BMW X6s that were equipped like James Bond cars with hidden compartments, armor plating, front and rear video, spy-satellite downlinks, and even fore-and-aft machine guns hidden behind faux foglamps. Church really loved his toys.

"No ejector seats?" I asked Grace as we climbed into the lead vehicle.

"You joke, but we have a Porsche Cayenne with an ejector option for driver or passenger."

"Really?" I grinned and switched to my best Sean Connery. "My name is Ledger. Joe Ledger."

She gave me an icy stare. "So help me God, if you call me Pussy Galore or Holly Goodhead, I'll shoot you and leave you by the side of the road."

"Wouldn't dream of it," I said, and then under my breath added, "Miss Moneypenny."

"I'm serious. Dead in a ditch."

I mimed zipping my mouth shut. We were all dressed in dark suits, red ties, and white shirts, with little American flags on our lapels and wires behind our ears. Pretty damn impressive for twelve hours' work. I mean, I can wear off the rack but Bunny is a moose. I marveled at Church's network of contacts. It must be nice to have so many friends in so many "industries." One of these days I was going to have to find out who the hell Church was.

For hardware I had my old familiar .45 with me, snugged against my ribs, with two extra magazines clipped to my belt. Around my right ankle was a sweet little Smith & Wesson Model 642 Airweight Centennial, a hammerless .38 revolver that is one of the most practical backup guns around. I also had a Rapid Response Folder, a tactical knife that could sit in a pocket clip and with a snap of the wrist would produce a 3.375-inch blade that, although short, was more than enough in the hands of a good knife fighter. I'm a very good knife fighter and I prefer speed over blade length any time. With all that I felt that I was a bit overdressed for the party, considering that we were going to interrogate government officials not storm the Bastille, but I'm one of those guys who believes that the Boy Scout motto is one of the most useful pieces of advice ever given: Be Prepared.

Grace looked very nice in a tailored suit that was a good balance of weapon concealment and curve revealment. No way that this was off the rack. She had on a light touch of makeup and a very enticing pink lipstick. The makeup was within professional guidelines, but the lipstick— I'm pretty damn sure—was a personal choice with a different agenda and I hoped that it wasn't my male ego or wishful thinking at work here.

All I said was, "You clean up pretty good, Major." I gave her my best smile as I said it. The one that puts the crinkles around my eyes. Grace, however, did not pull around to the back of the warehouse and immediately undress. Her fortitude was commendable in the light of that smile.

She said, "Buckle up for safety," and inflected it in such a way as to convey about fifty separate possible meanings.

Just as we were heading toward the main Warehouse doors I saw a figure step into our path: Rudy, and he was also dressed like a Secret Service agent. Grace slowed and when she stopped Rudy opened the back door and climbed in.

I turned around to look at him. "Halloween's not till October."

"You're hilarious," he growled as he thrust an ID wallet into my hands. I opened it.

"Rudolfo Ernesto Sanchez y Martinez, MD. Special Agent, United States Secret Service," I read. "Is this some kind of joke?"

"If it is then Mr. Church is the only one who knows the punch line."

Grace smiled. "Mr. Church is impressed with you, Doctor."

"Rudy," he corrected.

"Sorry. He told me you grilled him pretty thoroughly the other day."

I was surprised. "He admitted that?"

"He didn't go into details, but he gave the impression that you got a good read on him."

"Interesting," said Rudy. "Joe . . . he wants me with you when you do the interviews."

"I'm okay with that, Rude, but if we get into anything today . . ." I let it hang.

"Then I'll run and hide, don't worry, cowboy. I'm a lover not a fighter."

Grace turned and gave him an appraising stare. "I'll bet you could handle yourself." And again there were a lot of ways to interpret that. Rudy gave her an elegant incline of the head and settled back in his seat.

"Are you carrying a gun?" I asked him. At his request I'd taught Rudy to shoot a couple of years ago, shortly after he started working as a police psychiatrist. He thought it would help him with his patients if he more fully understood the power—both real and imagined—of a gun.

"You've seen me shoot, cowboy. Am I qualified to carry a handgun in public?"

"It would not be in the best interests of public safety."

"Then there you go."

Grace put the car in gear and we rolled out of the Warehouse with Echo Team behind us. When we were on I-95 heading north toward Philly, Rudy asked, "Won't the real Secret Service know that we're fakes?"

Grace shrugged. "Only if we tell them, and it will be need-to-know. Our credentials are real, authorized by the President himself."

Rudy said, "Wow." He hadn't voted for the President but the office and what it represented was bigger, and held more meaning, than any single person who had held it. Maybe more than all of them put together. A certain degree of respect was appropriate no matter what your personal political views were. "That's a lot of power."

"Mr. Church knows—" she started to say but Rudy cut her off.

"No, it's a lot of power to give us. Our team." He paused. "The *eight* of us." When I turned to him he went on, "We still have a traitor in the DMS, and that means that one of the men in the car behind us could be a spy or assassin. Or worse, a terrorist sympathizer." He waggled the ID case. "And this is an all-access pass to the President's wife and half of Congress. Is that wise?"

Grace smiled at him in the rearview. "Mr. Church has confidence that we'll stay in control of the situation."

All Rudy said in reply was, "Room Twelve."

Chapter **Ninety-Four**
Sebastian Gault / Helmand Province, Afghanistan / July 4

GAULT'S HELICOPTER TOUCHED down two hundred kilometers from the Bunker, landing near a WHO outpost. The outpost supervisor, a wizened old epidemiologist named Nasheef, was willing to lend Gault a car but cautioned him about the dangers of traveling in the Afghani desert without military escort.

"We'll be fine," Gault assured him. "We have our Red Cross and WHO credentials. Even out here that often gives us safe passage."

But Nasheef insisted on providing a driver, his burley nephew who had fought guerrilla actions against the Soviets. No amount of argument would dissuade Nasheef, and to make too strong a protest would raise suspicions, so they reluctantly agreed.

An hour later they were rolling out of the camp and heading west.

Gault had reclaimed his position as the de facto alpha dog in his relationship with Toys; though every now and then he could feel the ghost of a memory of the slap Toys had given him back in Baghdad.

"Go with God!" Nasheef called after them. It made both of them smile for all the wrong reasons.

Chapter Ninety-Five
Philadelphia, Pennsylvania / July 4; 9:39 A.M.

TRAFFIC WAS HEAVY as we approached Philly. The Phillies were playing a doubleheader, and a bunch of rock stars had put together a Freedom Rocks concert at the Wachovia Center down near the airport. Plus an estimated half million people were descending on Center City and the Liberty Center. Overall it was supposed to be the biggest, loudest, busiest day in Philadelphia history.

"Great day for travel," Rudy grumped from the backseat.

"Almost there," Grace said as she turned off I-95 near Penn's Landing. I'd called ahead and arranged for a pair of motorcycle cops to meet us and help us through the traffic snarls.

Grace filled us in on the people we would try and interview. There were six agencies involved in various aspects of security. The two who interested us most were Robert Howell Lee, the director of special operations for an FBI/Homeland joint command; and Linden Brierly, who was the regional director of the Secret Service and the direct link between the Secret Service and its parent department of Homeland Security. More current and proposed DMS personnel had been recommended by them than all of the other agencies put together. Both of them had extensive military connections and had sent candidates from every branch of the service. It seemed to be the best use of time to start with them first. They were also the men most closely involved with security at the Liberty Center event.

Robert Howell Lee and his FBI team were in charge of the facilities security and had oversight for all interjurisdictional arrangements between local, state, and federal law enforcement. He was an indirect descendant of Richard Henry Lee, the man who had ridden from Virginia to the First Continental Congress with the resolution to declare independence from England. He was an ambitious man of fifty who was almost certainly going to be the next director of the Bureau or maybe ever the top dog in Homeland.

The other man, Linden Brierly, was an equally careercentric man who had been involved in some key phases of the service's transition to Homeland after 9/11. It was Brierly who would be overseeing the personal safety of the First Lady and her party.

They were both powerful men; patriots as well as seasoned field agents and politicians. Move the wrong way with them and we'd not only upset the security applecart but we'd bring down so much heat that maybe even Church's clout would not save the DMS. This was dicey for a couple of big reasons: the careers of everyone involved with the DMS and the belief—which I now shared—that no other organization within the United States government was as equipped as the DMS to counter threats like the one we'd been facing during the last few days. The wrong word to either of these guys could spin everything out of control.

But, no pressure, right?

"We're here," Grace said.

Chapter **Ninety-Six**
Amirah / The Bunker, Afghanistan

"HE'S COMING!"

Amirah turned away from the big glass cage in the central lab as Abdul hurried into the room. Her only reply to his outburst was a slow smile.

"Did you hear me?" he demanded. He had a Kalashnikov hanging by a strap from his right shoulder and his face was dark with anger.

"I heard you, Abdul," she said, her voice soft and dreamy.

"Well . . . what are your orders? Should I have him killed?"

Amirah blinked very slowly, once, twice. "Kill Sebastian?" She abruptly laughed as if it were all a wonderfully funny joke. She covered her laughing mouth like a teenage girl. "Is he alone?"

"He has his assistant with him, and a driver."

"Good. Let them come."

"Come? Come here?" he echoed, incredulous. "Amirah . . . he has to be aware of what we're doing. He's coming to shut us down!"

"Shut us down?" She laughed again.

Abdul stared at her. Amirah's eyes were almost glassy. She looked drugged. Or worse, drunk! But that was unthinkable.

"You certainly don't want him to come in here. Not now. Not when he knows."

She shook her head. "How long until he gets here? Into the bunker?"

"Thirty minutes."

"Assemble the staff in the dining hall, Abdul."

"For what reason?" he demanded, and for a moment the dreamy look on Amirah's face solidified into something else. Something cold and reptilian that glared out at him through her beautiful eyes. Abdul took an involuntary step backward.

Amirah's lip curled and she turned away to stare through the glass at the monsters she had made. Four of them, each one clawing at the inside of the reinforced glass walls, their eyes burning like black stars.

"You have your orders, Abdul," she said without turning.

He backed toward the door, his anger warring with his doubt. He watched Amirah put both her palms on the glass and then lean forward so that her cheek was pressed against the cool surface as the four monsters clustered on the other side, tearing at each other to try and get to her.

Abdul fled.

Chapter Ninety-Seven

WE STOOD IN the Liberty Bell Center, which is located on Market Street between Fifth and Sixth Streets in the Old City part of Philly. Because of the task force's involvement with the event security I'd had a chance to tour the building a few times over the last six months and had a good working knowledge of its layout. The new building had been the centerpiece of a three-hundred-million-dollar makeover of the Independence Mall area, and they'd sunk nearly thirteen million dollars into the center, which opened in October 2003. The place was over thirteen thousand square feet, and was airy, well lighted, and pretty fascinating to any tourist or history buff. The bell itself sits in a glass chamber designed to magnify it so every one of the million-plus yearly visitors has a chance to get a really good look.

I think we all felt somewhat awed by all that it represented. I knew from having taken the tour that this was actually the second bell; the first one was made in the Whitechapel Foundry in England but it cracked shortly after it was cast. A couple of pot-and-pan makers named Pass and Stow recast it from a mixture of copper, tin, and traces of lead, zinc, arsenic, gold, and silver, but the second bell also cracked. That's the one that we were all looking at. The names Pass and Stow were stamped into the front of the bell. Rudy leaned forward and read the rest of the inscription: "Proclaim liberty throughout all the land unto all the inhabitants thereof—Lev. XXV, v. x. By order of the Assembly of the Province of Pensylvania for the State House in Philada."

"They spelled Pennsylvania wrong," Skip remarked.

I shook my head. "It was one of a couple of acceptable spellings at the time."

"Darn thing's broken," Bunny said with a grin.

Behind us was a second large display platform but this one was draped with a Stars and Stripes tent, inside of which was the new Freedom Bell. Because this bell was intended to ring on special events it hadn't been encased in magnifying glass. Time would tell if this one would be crackproof.

These bells symbolized everything for which the DMS had fought, suffered, and died. They were emblematic of the unsullied ideals of freedom, democracy, and fairness. Despite their many flaws the Founding Fathers had been mostly well intentioned. Freedom of speech, freedom of religion. The right to live. Even though those same founders had been unable to unite to abolish slavery and extend equal rights to all people of both sexes, they had at least started the ball rolling. Freedom had rung out across the land, and across the oceans, until its promise, at least, was heard in every country around the world. Without that bravery and optimism we wouldn't be standing together here. Men and women, black and white, foreign and homegrown, united in a single cause: to take a stand against hate and destruction. Despite my years of practiced cynicism I felt a real stirring of good ol' red, white, and blue patriotism.

From beside me Rudy said, "It's a genuine perspective check, isn't it?"

"Hooah," Top said softly.

"Major Courtland . . . ?" We turned to see a big man in a beautifully tailored lightweight charcoal suit come striding across the floor, hand out, a smile on his tanned face. I recognized him at once from Grace's description. Linden Brierly, regional director of the Secret Service. We stepped up to meet him by the podium that had been erected between the display cases. It was a three-step affair heavy with red, white, and blue bunting and bristling with microphones, none of which were currently turned on. I'd checked.

Grace made introductions and offered her hand; Brierly gave it a firm single pump. "Sorry for borrowing the Secret Service as our cover, sir," she said. "The President thought it would be best under the circumstances."

Brierly didn't miss a beat. "Sure, sure, I understand," he said, though he probably didn't like it. I wouldn't if I were in his shoes; but he hadn't gotten this far in his career by letting sour grapes show on his face. He looked around to confirm that there was no one else in the room except Brierly and Echo Team. "I've met your boss. Mr. Deacon." He paused and his smile became a bit rueful. "Or is it Church? There seems to be some disagreement about that."

"He prefers to be called Mr. Church."

"Interesting man," Brierly said. "I tried to run a background check on him and pretty much had my knuckles beaten with a ruler by the Commander in Chief."

Grace returned his smile but said nothing, nor did Rudy. I practiced looking like a cigar-store Indian.

Brierly waited a second, then shrugged. "Okay, I get it. No problem, Major. So, tell me what I can do for you?"

Grace and I had agreed that she'd handle Brierly and I'd take Lee, so she dug right in. "Sir," she said, "we'd like to discuss the candidates you suggested for transfer to the DMS."

That dialed down the wattage of Brierly's smile. "Why is that, Major?"

Instead of answering she asked, "What can you tell me about the men you chose to recommend?" She recited eleven names including Sergeant Michael Sanderson, who was one of Dietrich's security men, and Second Lieutenant Oliver Brown. The others I hadn't yet met.

I saw Brierly flick a glance across the room at Ollie and then return his gaze to Grace. "Can you be a bit more specific?"

"Just dotting the *i*'s and crossing the *t*'s," she said with a smile.

"Uh-huh," he said. "And for that you flash a presidential order?"

Grace said nothing.

Brierly sucked his teeth. "Okay," he said, "you caught me."

I stiffened, but then he upped the wattage on his smile. "A couple of my recommendations were entirely self-serving, I'll admit it. Mike Sanderson is the son of an old friend of mine. Mike's career seemed to stall in place after he left the army and joined the Service. We all thought he'd rise like a meteor but he didn't make the cut to the presidential detail, and when you miss that step you tend to tread water. I promised his dad I'd look out for him and the DMS seemed like a chance for a fresh start."

"And Lieutenant Brown?" Grace asked.

Brierly colored. "Well . . . that's a little more awkward, and I'm not sure if it's something we should even be talking about."

"Sir, we're here on the orders of the President himself."

Brierly sighed and stared at the empty air between Grace and me for a few seconds, the muscles in the sides of his jaw flexing as he thought it through. We let him. Finally he said, "Okay, but it's on your head if this information gets out because I'll damn sure know that it didn't come from me except right here and right now." He nodded to himself, the decision made. "Homeland and the Service have done a number of ultra–top secret operations since nine-eleven. Off-the-books stuff, if you follow me."

"Of course, sir," Grace said. I nodded. A lot of black ops stuff never makes it onto paper. Plausible deniability is easier without a paper trail.

"Ollie was never in Iraq. That, um, was a cover story. He's been Delta Force for four years and has been used in over twenty operations. Extreme stuff. Missions that involved military intelligence, the Service, Homeland, and the CIA . . . but more recently, until he was transferred to the DMS, Lieutenant Brown has officially been a Secret Service agent, but one that we've had out on loan to the Company."

"We know he's with the CIA," I said. "Are you saying he's more than just another one of their spooks?"

He grunted. "Captain, until I transferred him he was one of this government's very best operators. Covert ops, infiltration, and special skills—he has the full package." Brierly looked past me to where the young man was standing foursquare, staring hard in our direction. "And on top of all that, he's the best assassin I've ever seen."

"HOW DO I look?" the Fighter asked.

Ahmed turned in his seat and smiled broadly. "Perfect! Amirah herself would not recognize you!"

El Mujahid leaned over and looked at himself one last time in the Explorer's rearview mirror. With blue contact lenses, an expert hair dye that gave him wavy red hair, skillfully crafted latex appliances, and makeup that gave him pale skin and a scattering of freckles the Fighter looked like a rawboned young Irishman. Saleem had even used special tape to change the shape and angle of El Mujahid's nose, giving it a snubbed and uptilted look. Padding in his gums gave him more prominent cheekbones. Even he could not see the man he was beneath the makeup.

"The boy is a wizard," the Fighter agreed.

"Now . . . there's one last thing to do before we go," said Ahmed as he took a small case from the glove compartment, unzipped it and removed a prefilled syringe. The liquid was a luminous green-gold that sparkled in the sunlight. "Roll up your sleeve."

El Mujahid did so and held out his arm. He didn't even wince when Ahmed plunged the needle into his flesh and injected the entire contents into him.

"Amirah said that the antidote will be at its strongest in forty minutes," Ahmed said, "and advises that you release the plague at that point. She said that you should be completely protected, but also said that once you activate the device you should get away as quickly as possible." He drew a breath. "Besides, things will be getting very violent very quickly."

El Mujahid looked at his wristwatch. "Then we had better move."

Ahmed nodded and removed a second syringe from the case and injected himself. He was wearing a Hawaiian shirt with toucans on it and gave himself the shot high on his shoulder where it wouldn't be seen.

346 | Jonathan Maberry

He put the syringe case back in the glove compartment. He hung a lanyard around his neck to which was clipped a plastic ID holder. It read: PRESS.

"You have only two doses?" the Fighter asked. "What about your woman, Andrea?"

"She's a woman." Ahmed spread his hands in a man-of-the-world gesture. "We all make sacrifices."

El Mujahid nodded. He had made his own sacrifices to the cause where women were concerned.

"There is no God but Allah," Ahmed whispered.

"And Mohammad is His prophet," agreed El Mujahid.

Ahmed put the car in gear and drove off.

Chapter Ninety-Nine

The Liberty Bell Center / Saturday, July 4; 11:26 A.M.

BRIERLY TOLD US that he stood behind his decision to send Ollie to us and that he'd stake his reputation on the fact that Ollie was every inch a "true American." A phrase he used three times. "Look, I have an event to run. The First Lady will be here in a couple of minutes."

"Mind if we loiter about, sir?" asked Grace.

He frowned at her. "Am I going to have some trouble here today?"

I cut in on that. "Wouldn't you agree that since nine-eleven there's been a potential for threat at every major national holiday and political event?"

Brierly studied me for a three-count and then his voice dropped to a less friendly whisper. "Don't fuck with me, Captain. I got a pretty damned cryptic 'keep your eyes open' sort of memo this morning from Washington but it had zero details and I really don't like being kept in the dark. If your team is here because of a specific threat then I need to know about it and right goddamn now."

I opened my mouth to reply in kind, but Grace stepped between us and took Brierly by the elbow and led him out of earshot of everyone in the room. They stood with heads bowed together for three minutes and I could see his body becoming more rigid with each passing second. Then he gave a nod and moved toward the door, walking as if his boxers were filled with jagged glass.

"What'd you tell him?" I asked when she rejoined me.

"The truth," she said. "Or at least as much of it as he needs to know."

"He didn't look happy about it."

"Are you?"

"Point taken."

"He said he'll quietly increase the circle of protection around the First Lady. He has a number of agents in plainclothes who can be seeded into the crowd at the ceremony."

"Good. The more the merrier."

Another agent entered the chamber a minute later and hurried over to us, introducing himself as Colby, Brierly's number two. "I've been asked to brief you on the on-site security." He led us to a STAFF ONLY door hidden behind a screen on which the Declaration of Independence was printed. "If we need to remove the First Lady in the event of a crisis, agents will escort her through here and then lock the door behind them. There are offices and other rooms back there and we have a designated secure spot as well as escape routes."

After he left I dialed the cell number for Robert Howell Lee and, after verifying that the line was secure, identified myself and read the note from the President that ordered everyone to offer complete and immediate assistance to my investigation. He answered that with a long silence and I could imagine him trying to figure out what the hell was going on. I hadn't told him. I broke into the silence and asked him if he could meet us in the bell chamber.

"What . . . you mean *now*?" he demanded. "Are you out of your mind, Captain? Do you have any idea what is going on? We have—"

"We can grab a few minutes after the speeches," I interrupted. "This won't take long."

"Can you at least tell me what the hell this is about?"

Grace had returned and she and Rudy were leaning close to eavesdrop on the call. She mouthed the words: "Play the card, Joe."

So I did. "Yes, sir, we are here representing the Department of Military Sciences." I let him digest that. Whether he was guilty or innocent it was a hell of a bomb to drop and he had to react.

"Jesus Christ," he said. There was another pause. "All right, give me a few minutes. I'm on the other side of Independence Mall in the communications center and I have to get someone to cover for me." He disconnected.

I turned to Rudy. "Well? Did he sound spooked to you?"

He shrugged. "He sounded harried."

Grace nodded. "Let's face it; we picked a bloody stupid time to come up here."

"Can't catch someone off guard if they have time to prepare," Rudy said.

She shrugged and I looked over at my team. Ollie's face was pure hostility and had been ever since he saw that we were there to interview the man who had sent him to the DMS. He eyed me with that cold shooter's squint and I gave it right back to him. Skip saw the look passing between us and frowned; and he took a half-step back from Ollie as if afraid to get in the way of something. I noticed that Top, Bunny, and Gus were casually looking from them to me, but nobody said anything.

The door behind us opened and a big man entered. He was dressed in the standard navy blue and red tie of the Service. He was every bit as big as Bunny, with thick shoulders, flaming red hair, and an Irish snub nose.

"Who are you?" Dietrich asked sharply, moving to intercept him.

"Special Agent Michael O'Brien," the man said in surprise, holding out his ID. He held a metal case in the other hand. "I was detailed to check the room before the First Lady's party moves in here for the speeches."

Gus checked the ID and called it in while he inspected the metal case. It held the standard electronic scanners and nitrate sniffers that would show if anyone had planted bugs or bombs in the room. Dietrich nodded his approval and handed back the ID.

Dietrich closed his phone and sketched a salute to the agent. "Okay, O'Brien . . . the room's yours."

Chapter **One Hundred**
Gault / Outside the Bunker / July 4

THE ROVER SAT in the lee of a stand of palm trees about a hundred yards from the tent that hid the entrance to Amirah's bunker.

"Now what, sir?" asked the driver. "Is your contact meeting you here?"

"In a way," Gault said. "Toys? Would you oblige?"

Without a word Toys drew his pistol and shot the driver in the back of the head. The impact knocked the man against the steering wheel and splashed the window with bright blood.

"Sorry, old chap," Gault said distractedly.

Toys's face was stone as he removed the clip and replaced the round. He didn't want to come up a bullet short at some crucial moment. He looked at his watch. "Zeller's team is still twenty minutes out. Where do you want to wait for him? I don't like being this exposed."

Before Gault could answer the sat phone rang and Toys put it on speaker. For a moment Gault's heart lifted, hoping that it was Amirah, but then the American's voice barked at them.

"Line?"

"Clear, my friend. How are things going?"

The American's voice was shaky. "God . . . they're on to me!"

"What are you talking about?"

"The DMS . . . they've sent agents here to interview me."

"Christ! How did *that* happen?"

"I don't know . . . Sebastian, you have to do something."

Gault almost laughed. "What is it exactly you expect me to do? I'm half a world away."

"I have to get out. We haven't been able to find El Mujahid. He could be anywhere! And these agents are right here . . . *now*."

"You haven't *found* him?" Gault was stunned. "Listen to me, we're paying you too much money for you to let something this important slip through your hands. Fix this!"

"How? The only way I can bring more assets to bear on this would be to go to my own superiors, and that would land me in federal prison for the rest of my life!"

"Well, I daresay that getting arrested is going to be the least of your problems, wouldn't you think?" Gault's voice was cold.

"What should I do?"

"Make whatever calls you have to make to let the proper authorities know about the threat. Call the DMS. Tell them that you received an anonymous tip, something like that. Tell them that there is a biological threat. Just for God's sake don't mention me, and try not to implicate yourself. Maybe they can stop the Fighter before he can open the bloody gates of hell. Then get as far away as you can. An island somewhere. If this thing is released then an island is the only chance you'll have."

"God . . ."

"I'm about to clear up my end of things. I suggest you do the same. Be a hero. Save the day."

The American mumbled something that Gault thought was a Hail Mary, and then the line went dead.

"Bloody hell," he said, staring out through the bloodstained windshield. "The man's a coward and a fool."

"You get what you pay for," Toys said with an irritated sigh. He looked at his watch. "There's still sixteen minutes before Zeller's team reaches the Bunker. We can't just sit here."

"No," agreed Gault. They got out of the vehicle and drew their pistols. Nothing moved, so they moved quickly and quietly toward the line of tents by the mountain wall. The camp appeared to be deserted, but as they darted from the shelter of one tent to another they found four corpses lying in a row, their hands and ankles bound, their throats cut. Their blood had soaked into the desert sand and flies buzzed around them. They were all men on Gault's payroll.

Toys snorted. "So much for the element of surprise."

Chapter **One Hundred One**
The Liberty Bell Center / Saturday July 4; 11:47 A.M.

SPECIAL AGENT O'BRIEN completed his sweep of the center, packed his gear back into the metal case and stowed it under the podium. Linden Brierly entered from another door and with him was a contingent of grim-faced Secret Service agents and at least four members of my old task force, and following them were half the members of Congress, a couple dozen assorted local politicians, and the First Lady and the VP's wife. We faded back against the wall and tried to blend into the woodwork the way the Secret Service are supposed to do. I got some strange looks from my former task force teammates, but no one broke protocol to catch up on old times.

Robert Howell Lee had not yet arrived. I looked at Grace, who shrugged. "Give him time," she said; but there was no time. Brierly, looking stressed and flushed, was trying to guide the ladies to their spots between the two bells, but the women were not cooperating. They were pausing to glad-hand everyone and engage in chitchat while outside the press photographers were snapping pictures through the big glass windows; and beyond the press a veritable sea of people waited for the festivities to commence. Eventually they let about two hundred civilians into the room, which meant that everyone was packed like sardines.

I glanced around. Top and Ollie were directly across from where we stood; Bunny and Skip were on my three o'clock and Gus on our nine.

"This is going to be a bloody circus," Grace said under her breath.

"Brace yourself . . . I think everyone in a suit is about to make a long-winded speech."

"Swell."

The First Lady, looking very stylish in a pretty dress and an absurd hat, mounted the steps to the podium and tapped a microphone, making the usual "Is this on" remark which, strangely, got a laugh. I saw Special Agent O'Brien standing by the far door, slowly scanning the crowd. Our eyes met and he gave me a single, curt nod and then his eyes shifted away. Weird thing was, he was smiling. I don't think I've ever seen a Secret Service agent smile. Not on the job.

As the First Lady launched into her speech I scanned the crowd looking for Robert Howell Lee, but my eyes kept flicking back to O'Brien. That smile bothered me.

Chapter One Hundred Two
Gault / The Bunker

GAULT RADIOED HIS assault team to let them know he and Toys were proceeding inside. "If you don't hear from us in ten minutes come in hard and fast."

"We'll be there," assured Captain Zeller.

Then Gault and Toys entered the shallow cave that led to the Bunker's hatch. They encountered no one but they weren't fooled and both men kept their pistols ready. Toys stood guard while Gault accessed the entry keypad that was hidden in the wall. He didn't use the standard code. Amirah was too clever for that. Instead he entered a number sequence that bypassed the security using a back door he'd written into the security software. The new code disabled all external video scanners, including the ones in the cave and the monitors that watched the back door. Zeller's team would now be able to approach unseen.

Gault punched in a second code and a door swung open. It wasn't the big airlock that swung open; instead, to his left, a tall, slender ridge of rock slid upward on silent hydraulics to reveal a narrow passage. No one, not even Amirah, knew about this entrance.

As the door opened to his command Gault felt another fragment of his confidence return. There were a number of things Amirah didn't know about the Bunker. After all, it wasn't really her facility.

It belonged to Gault.

Chapter One Hundred Three
The Liberty Bell Center / Saturday, July 4; 11:59 A.M.

I LEANED CLOSE to Grace. "Call me paranoid, but I'm getting a weird vibe from that agent over there." I told her where to look and she glanced surreptitiously at O'Brien and then flipped open her phone to call in a request for a physical description of Special Agent Michael O'Brien.

"Description matches," she said, but from the expression on her face she clearly was getting the same bad feeling. Into the phone she said, "Transfer me to Director Brierly's secure channel."

Across the room I saw Brierly's head swivel around to find us. "Sir," said Grace, "this may be nothing but Captain Ledger has some concerns about one of the attending agents. O'Brien. Big red-haired bloke by the press entrance."

We watched Brierly turn. "Michael O'Brien? He's part of the team sent from D.C. Do you want him removed?"

"If you can do it quietly," she said, and I winced. The Secret Service could do just about anything quietly. The word "secret" wasn't there for show, but I understood what Grace was doing. She was putting the onus on Brierly to handle something correctly and we could learn a lot from the way he played it.

"Stand by," he said, and switched channels. Almost immediately two of his agents began making their way around the perimeter of the room toward O'Brien.

My spider sense was going haywire now. I told Grace to get Brierly back on the line.

ON THE PODIUM the First Lady launched into a crushingly dull speech that was apparently going to chronicle the history of the Liberty Bell from the moment someone cooked up the idea, minute by minute, to today. "In 1752," she intoned, "the Pennsylvania Assembly ordered a two-thousand-pound bell to place in the steeple of the new State House—what we now call Independence Hall."

One of the approaching agents reached O'Brien and bent to whisper in the man's ear. It must have been couched as a repositioning order because O'Brien merely nodded and began moving toward the exit which was directly behind him. The ranks of reporters made it necessary for him to thread his way through and the two other agents followed.

"He's not bolting," Grace said. "Maybe you're wrong."

"If I am I'll apologize," but I was still watching O'Brien.

"The order for the bell was sent to the Whitechapel Foundry in England," continued the First Lady, "and noted metalsmith Thomas Lester was contracted to cast the first liberty bell and to inscribe it with these historic words: 'Proclaim Liberty throughout all the Land unto all the Inhabitants thereof.' Sadly that first bell cracked shortly after it was mounted and a replacement bell was—"

The First Lady kept speaking but something she had said jolted me as my brain replayed those words.

. . . *noted metalsmith Thomas Lester was contracted to cast the first liberty bell* . . .

"And today we will be unveiling a new bell, designed and cast by Andrea Lester—who is with us today." She indicated a small, unsmiling woman in a yellow pantsuit. "Ms. Lester is the last descendant of the original bell maker and is a resident of North Carolina. She is here with us today to help dedicate this new—"

My mind was reeling. Rudy must have caught it, too; he turned and was staring wide-eyed at me. He mouthed the word: "Bellmaker."

Thomas Lester. The metalsmith who made the original Liberty Bell. His descendant Andrea Lester, maker of the new bell.

Lester . . . the bell maker!

Holy Christ! Aldin had told us, but he hadn't told us enough.

I saw Andrea Lester glance very quickly from the First Lady, to the doorway where Agent O'Brien had paused, his hand on the glass door. He turned and looked back into the room, straight at Andrea Lester. The agents with him put their hands on his upper arms to try to move him along quietly; not wasting to make a scene.

I grabbed Grace's arm so hard she flinched in pain and nearly dropped her phone.

"Grace! Oh my God . . . it isn't Lester Bellmaker. It's Andrea Lester, the bell *maker*. She made the Freedom Bell!"

Just as I started moving the First Lady's aides pulled the cords that released the drapes over the Freedom Bell; the red, white, and blue fluttered to the floor. In my mind the falling colors became a horrible promise of disaster. On the other side of the room I saw Special Agent Michael O'Brien shrug off the two agents and, his smile broader than ever, pull a small device out of his pocket.

It was a detonator.

Chapter One Hundred Four
Amirah / The Bunker

SHE STOOD ON a metal walkway that circled twenty feet above the main laboratory, watching as her entire staff stood in patient lines, their sleeves rolled up as nurses moved among them to administer injections. Everyone looked so proud. They knew that they were part of something vastly important, that they had contributed something so crucial to the war against the infidel.

Amirah smiled down at them.

One of the nurses flicked a glance up at Amirah and they shared the briefest of smiles. No one noticed that the liquid in the bottle from which she had filled her needles had been the slightest bit different in color. A touch of green, where the others tended more to amber; but the nurse used a nearly opaque white syringe and she moved very quickly, filling her syringe, injecting, wiping the needle point with alcohol-soaked cotton, drawing more, moving on down the line.

Amirah glanced down at her own forearm, and absently rubbed the injection spot. Black lines had begun radiating out from the needle mark. She was perspiring heavily now, her robes far too hot; sweat ran down her back and pooled at her waist. She gripped the metal rail to steady herself as the whole room took a sickening sideways lurch.

"Where are you, Sebastian?" she whispered. On the wall the clock ticked away the seconds.

Chapter One Hundred Five
The Liberty Bell Center / Saturday, July 4; Noon

EVERYTHING FROZE DOWN to a single white-hot fragment of a second that moved in bizarrely slow motion. The First Lady was leading the applause for the unveiling of the Freedom Bell. Beside her on the podium Andrea Lester was reaching in her pocket. Grace's phone was falling from her hand as she pulled back the flap of her coat to reach for her gun. Agent O'Brien was starting to raise the detonator.

My gun was in my hand.

I could hear myself screaming but I had no idea what I was saying.

Every eye in the room was turning toward me. Agents were clawing at their guns.

I had no shot at O'Brien—the First Lady was between me and him. On the podium Andrea Lester was reaching for the President's wife. Something flashed in her hand and I realized that she had a blade. Not steel—the Secret Service would have caught that—but probably one of the many polymer knives that were nearly as hard as steel and would never trip a metal detector.

With a scream of *"Allah akbar!"* she lunged at the First Lady.

I shot Andrea Lester twice in the chest. The bullets spun her away from her intended victim but the polymer knife tore a long gash in the First Lady's sleeve.

Everyone started screaming; panic was immediate and total. I ran forward, grabbing people and hurling them out of my way as I fought to get to the podium where I could get a shot at O'Brien, who had bolted for the podium. The two agents flanking him were already moving, one of them tried to tackle him while the other stepped back and drew his sidearm. Then the crowd surged between us and I lost sight of them.

A shattering volley of gunfire erupted from the far side of the podium, and as I pushed Rudy and the secretary of the interior out of my way I saw that the agent who had drawn his weapon on O'Brien was falling backward, a bullet hole in his temple. The shot hadn't come from O'Brien—it had come to my left. I turned and saw a gun in Ollie Brown's hands and as I watched he swung a pistol around and fired two shots and then the throng hid him from view. Had he shot the agent? It seemed like everyone in the room had a gun and bullets burned past me. There was too much commotion to tell who was who, and I didn't know how many people in this crowd were Brierly's agents or members of some terrorist hit cell. It was total chaos.

I pivoted and started toward O'Brien but as I located him in the screaming crowd I saw the second agent go down, blood jutting from a slashed throat. O'Brien moved back toward the podium, the detonator still clutched in his big hand.

And suddenly I understood.

It was the bell.

"Seal the room!" I bellowed as I raised my gun once more, then I saw out of the corner of my eye that the First Lady was still on the podium. Andrea Lester was down, and one of the First Lady's bodyguards was down; other agents were rushing the podium, guns drawn, racing to protect the President's wife. Gunfire was coming from every point in the room and I saw agents in blue blazers shooting at civilians; I saw a man dressed in carnival pattern shorts standing guard over a pair of congressmen while nearby a Secret Service agent was trying to wrestle a plastic handgun from the hand of what looked like a news reporter. I needed to get to the top of the podium so I could see the room and try to see O'Brien so I could stop him before he pushed that button.

Grace split off to my left and vanished into the press. I saw a swarm of agents pull the First Lady down and hustle her toward the STAFF ONLY door; but in the confusion the wife of the Vice President was still there, nearly lost in the press of congressmen fighting to get away from the gunshots, her agents down and bleeding. Several people were firing now and I couldn't tell if it was a pitched gun battle or panic shooting; then I saw an agent mount the steps to protect the VP's wife, but a split second later he staggered and went down, his white shirtfront blooming with red. A second agent leaped up but he also took two in the chest and pirouetted into the crowd. I saw a hand holding a gun pulling back into the crowd. It was bare—no coat sleeve, just a flash of a Hawaiian shirt. One of the tourists? A reporter? Shit . . . how many of these bastards were in the crowd?

"Top!" I yelled when I saw him fight his way out of a knot of panicking people. "It's O'Brien!"

He nodded and plunged into the crowd again, but there was so much resistance he made no headway. Some of the guests were trying to drop down to the floor to avoid the gunfire, but the storming crowds trampled them. I saw Rudy pushing a group of Girl Scouts into a corner to keep them from getting crushed by the rush of people. There were screams of pain interspersed with the din of the terrified crowd and the constant barrage of gunshots. I heard the distinctive commanding yells of Secret Service agents but no one was heeding their orders to drop and remain down. I had no idea where Grace or the rest of Echo Team was and I continued to fight my way toward the podium. The VP's wife was huddled down, arms wrapped around her head, flanked on both sides by dead agents. There were hundreds of people yelling and screaming and fighting to try and get out of the Liberty Bell Center.

I caught another flash glimpse of O'Brien. He was still smiling as he raised his hand to bring the detonator up above the level of the crowd.

I had no time to think. I launched myself into the air and my shoulder caught the Vice President's wife in the side; I wrapped my arms around her and my momentum carried us off the podium just as Michael O'Brien depressed the button.

The Freedom Bell exploded.

Chapter One Hundred Six
Gault / The Bunker

THEY CROUCHED TOGETHER in the gloom of a narrow corridor that ran inside the walls of the Bunker. LEDs set into the floor cast just enough light so they could pick their way through the darkness.

"Let's split up," Gault suggested. "Go to the rear hatch and make sure Captain Zeller's team can get in. Kill anyone who gets in your way."

"And what are you going to do?"

"I'm going to the lab."

"To do what?" Toys asked, his tone brimming with unspoken accusation. "Remember that we came here to kill her. Not to snog and make up."

Anger flared in Gault's chest. "Don't tell me my business," he snapped. "I'm tired of—"

"Tired of what, Sebastian?" Toys cut him off. "Don't try to assert your authority over me at this late date. The time for that passed when you let your girlfriend develop a doomsday weapon."

Gault's pistol was in his hand, the barrel almost but not quite pointed in Toys's direction. His assistant looked down at it, then with a smile he reached down and pushed the barrel toward him so that it pointed right at Toys's heart. Toys leaned close, forcing contact with the gun.

"Either kill her or kill me," Toys said calmly.

They stared at each other over the gulf that was opening between them.

"Toys . . . I . . ."

Toys pushed the gun aside. He bent forward quickly and kissed Gault on the cheek. "I love you, Sebastian. You and I are family. Remember that."

With that he turned and vanished down the corridor, leaving Gault alone in the dark.

Chapter One Hundred Seven

The Liberty Bell Center / Saturday, July 4; 12:01 P.M.

THE OUTER COVERING of the Freedom Bell must have been a thin veneer of painted foil that covered hundreds of small ports. Deep inside the bell, in the actual metal of its body, the signal from the detonator ignited countless pockets of highly compressed gas. The whole surface of the bell disintegrated as thousands upon thousands of tiny glass darts were propelled outward with a whoosh of compressed air. No gunpowder, no nitrates: the bell itself was a giant air gun. Each dart was pointed at one end and had walls as thin as spun sugar. Half of them burst as they struck the foil layer on the outside of the bell and they discharged their contents harmlessly into the air. But the other half—maybe fifteen hundred darts in all—tore into the flesh of members of Congress and the press, stinging the hands and faces of tourists and local dignitaries and ambassadors from a dozen nations. I could feel the wave of them pass over me as I toppled to the ground with the Vice President's wife under me. I had no idea if I'd been hit or not. Everyone was screaming. The VP's wife shrieked in agony as we crashed onto the concrete floor.

I rolled off her and spun over into a kneeling shooter's position. How the hell I'd held on to my gun is beyond me, but it was in my hand and I brought it up, fanning it around to find O'Brien, but he was nowhere in sight. All I could see were legs and torsos as people scattered and stumbled and fell. People kicked me as they ran and I had to scramble back from being trampled to death.

I could hear Grace's voice, high and shrill, ordering the agents in the room to seal the doors. She knew, she understood what we were facing: all of those glass beads fired from the bell were filled with the plague. From her voice I could tell she was every bit as terrified as me.

The *Seif al Din* had been launched. After all we'd been through, we could lose it all right now if even one of the infected got out.

God . . .

"Echo Team!" I roared, and suddenly Bunny was there, his face white as paste and splashed with blood.

"Are you hit?" he yelled.

"To hell with that—we have to seal the doors!"

"It's already done!" I heard a voice yell with enormous force and then realized it was Brierly shouting through the amplification of my earjack. "The doors are sealed. I have teams converging to reinforce us from outside."

The crowd hit the glass walls like a wave and some of the people closest to the doors had to be crushed by the sheer violent mass. There were screams of rage and terror, and pain.

"I have the VP's wife," I said. "But I can't see the First Lady, Brierly, did she get out?"

"My assistant, Colby, and a team of agents got her to the safe room," he said. "What the hell is going on, Ledger?"

"I'm on the back side of the podium. Find me," I said. "Now!"

As I turned to start looking for him, Bunny said, "Boss, those darts . . ."

"I know. Keep an eye out. If anyone starts acting twitchy you take the shot."

I could see how the weight of what we might have to do hurt the big young man, but he nodded. I looked around and saw Rudy still with the Girl Scouts. One of them was bleeding but from that distance I couldn't tell if it was from the darts or the panic of the crush.

"Bunny, stay with the VP's wife," I ordered. "And keep your eyes open for Agent O'Brien. He's our hostile. If you see him, kill him." I gripped his sleeve. "Bunny . . . did you see who Ollie was shooting at?"

"Negative. Everybody's shooting," he said, and as if to punctuate his comment a couple of rounds whined over his head and he flinched. The wild gunfire erupted again and the screams rose to a higher pitch.

"Just in case, don't stand in front of him if he has a gun."

Bunny turned to me and his eyes searched my face. "Copy that, boss." He dropped down into a crouch over the Vice President's wife, who was curled into a fetal ball, her face knotted with pain. Three Secret Service agents converged on him and together they formed a protective ring.

I got to my feet and saw Top and Ollie racing toward one of the doors. They were working together to prevent the crowds from getting out. Grace was already blocking the other door, her pistol out.

I saw Gus Dietrich bent over the governor of Pennsylvania, who was covered with blood. Dietrich was sheltering him with his own body and he had a smoking pistol in his hand. On the floor beside him was a Secret Service agent who had taken the blast of the glass darts full in the face. I met Dietrich's eyes for a second and we exchanged the briefest of nods. I was conscious of the fact that several of the TV cameramen were still on their feet, their cameras mounted on their shoulders. How the hell they had kept their heads was beyond me, and I could only imagine how half the country was reacting to this. I hoped the networks had blacked it out.

I saw Brierly and grabbed him by the shoulder and pulled him against the podium. There were no more gunshots but the air was still torn by screams and yells. We had to bend close and shout in each other's ear.

"Why the hell did you shoot that woman?" he demanded, and I was conscious of the fact that his pistol was half turned toward me. I batted it aside.

"Andrea Lester was a traitor and a terrorist sympathizer. She rigged her own bell to fire those darts." I pulled him closer. "She's working with El Mujahid, and your agent, O'Brien, is one of them. He set off the device."

That hit him hard. "My . . . *God*! We screened her, she was cleared to be here."

"These guys must have had inside help. Trust no one right now."

"Inside—?"

"No time for that. Listen to me and listen close. The darts from the Bell . . . they contain the infectious agent Grace told you about. You know Ebola? This is a hundred times worse." I pulled his ear to within an inch of my mouth. "If one single person gets out of this room we'll have a worldwide plague on our hands. There is no cure." I said that slowly, punctuating each word. "Believe it."

Brierly's face twisted into a mask of such utter horror that I thought he was going to scream. Then he ducked as bullets struck the plastic walls around the Liberty Bell. I turned and saw someone dressed like a Philly cop pointing his pistol at us. He fired again and I pushed Brierly out of the way and returned fire. The fake cop pitched back.

I said, "Contact your men outside. Nobody leaves this building. Nobody! We're going to need troops and a class-A biohazard team."

He licked his lips, blinking several times as the devastating news sank in, and then I saw the man behind the bureaucrat take over. "Christ, I hope you're wrong about this, Ledger."

"I wish I was," I said. "But I'm not."

Brierly tapped his mike and began rapping out a series of curt commands. He ordered that all teams seal and defend every exit in the building, and he reinforced that to include exits that led off from the offices and rooms beyond the STAFF ONLY. "Hummingbird is to be located and secured." Hummingbird was the code name for the First Lady. Junebug was the VP's wife. When he got confirmations he turned to me.

"Okay, the First Lady is in the safe room. The VP's wife is being guarded by one of your men and three of my agents. We'll move her to the safe room in a bit." He looked marginally relieved.

"Brierly, you need to make sure everyone understands that we can't let *anyone* out of here. Not even the President's wife."

He stared at me, torn by his responsibility to protect his charges and the greater reality of the plague. Finally he nodded and keyed his mike. "This is Director Linden Brierly. This is an all-stations alert. On presidential orders no one is to leave this building. No exceptions. Repeat and confirm." All posts confirmed, but I could imagine a lot of them were either scratching their heads or getting really spooked. "You'd better be right about this."

I left him to his job and went to try and find O'Brien but I couldn't see him anywhere. The gunfire was dwindling now, just sporadic shots interspersed with yells and screams.

Movement to my right made me turn and Grace was there, with Top right behind her, both with guns drawn. Grace had blood on her clothes but when she saw my expression she glanced down at her clothes then met my eyes. She shook her head. "There was a young woman standing right in front of me," she said, and left it there.

The gunfire stopped but the crowd was still surging back and forth like frightened animals in a pen.

"Grace . . . we have to calm these people down!"

"I'm on it," she said and spun off, calling to Top and Dietrich and soon they were moving like bulls through the crowd, shoving people back, yelling orders to everyone, grabbing Secret Service agents and putting them to work. Skip Tyler was near the back wall, reloading his gun.

"Skip," I said as I rushed over, "help me find O'Brien."

"The red-haired guy? He went through there a second ago." He pointed to the STAFF ONLY door that was tucked into a corner. We raced over but the door was locked from the other side.

"You sure he went this way?"

"Yeah, him and Ollie followed a whole bunch of Secret Service agents who were hustling the First Lady into the safe room." He looked confused. "That was the protocol, right?"

"Son of a bitch," I snarled and kicked the door in. "Skip, guard this door. Get Grace or Top to give me some backup, but nobody else gets in. You hear me? Nobody. I'm counting on you to hold this line."

The young sailor gave me a serious nod and took up a defensive stance. "You got it, Captain."

I ran through the doorway.

Chapter **One Hundred Eight**
Gault and Amirah / The Bunker

GAULT OPENED A slit in a wall panel and peered through it and almost gasped. Amirah was not five feet from him. Below her the nurses had nearly completed the injections.

He steeled himself and aimed his pistol through the gap and put the red dot of his laser, light as a whisper, on Amirah's back, right between her shoulders. One shot from this distance would punch through her spine, tear through her heart, and burst from between her breasts to leave a gaping red hole the size of a golf ball. One flex of his finger and the traitorous bitch would be dead. He could do it. He knew he could.

Damn you, Amirah, he said, and without meaning to he mentally added, *my love*.

Tears jeweled his vision, warping her with prismatic distortion. The barrel of the pistol wavered. His assault team would be entering the cave any moment and Toys would lead them here. Gault shivered, partly at the thought of the firestorm Captain Zeller would be unleashing here in the Bunker, and partly at the thought of Toys's transformation. Had his assistant actually changed that much or had Gault been blind all these years to the scorpion he kept by his side?

The seconds ticked away. Soon the whole Bunker would be a hell of bullets and blood. Soon everyone would be dead. Amirah, too, whether he killed her himself or not. His orders to Zeller had been specific. Kill everyone, no exceptions.

Amirah.

God.

Tears broke and rolled down his cheeks and before he could stop it a single, heartbroken sob escaped his throat. He saw Amirah stiffen, but she did not turn, and Gault forced his hands to steady, to hold the red pinprick of the laser sight on her back. *Be a fucking man,* he snarled inwardly.

Amirah.

And then she spoke.

"Sebastian," she said.

Amirah turned without haste to face him. Her head was bowed, looking down to see the red laser dot on her chest, wavering right over her heart. She raised her head slowly.

Gault felt a cold hand reach into his own chest and squeeze his heart to a tiny block of ice. Amirah's eyes were wide and glassy, bright with fever. She reached a hand up to the front of her *chadri*, gathered the black cloth in her fingers, and slowly pulled the scarf down to reveal her smiling mouth. Her lovely olive skin had paled to a sickly sand color, almost gray, and her full lips were stained with fresh blood.

"Sebastian," she said softly as her lips peeled back from her teeth in a snarl of vicious animal hunger.

"My God." Gault recoiled in horror. "What have you *done?*"

Amirah advanced toward the wall and even through the narrow opening of the observation slit he could smell her. A fetid, rotting-meat stink that rolled off her like the perfume of hell.

"Seif al Din," she whispered, leaning to peer in through the slit.

"You're infected!" His gun hand was shaking so bad that he almost dropped the weapon. Sweat burst from his pores and his pulse snapped like firecrackers. "What have you done?" he asked again in a terrified whisper.

She shook her head, still smiling. "No, Sebastian, I'm not infected. I'm *reborn*. I'm more alive now than I ever imagined."

"This will kill you!"

She shook her head again. "The pathogen is no longer fatal . . . I've perfected it. You only saw Generation Seven." She giggled. "That one scared you, Sebastian. You almost screamed like a woman." Amirah wiped drool from her lips. "By now my lovely El Mujahid should have launched Generation Ten on the American people. They will be dying soon, Sebastian. All of them. *Seif al Din* is so quick." She snapped her fingers in front of the slot and Gault jumped.

"Generation Ten? You're insane!"

"I'm immortal," she countered. "You see . . . we had a breakthrough, Sebastian. We've been working so hard for so long, and you thought we were plodding along with Generation Three. But, oh . . . Generation Ten is immediate. The body reanimates immediately. No lag time, no time to quarantine the infected. Generation Ten is the perfect plague."

"Perfect?" The word was like bile in his mouth.

She ignored him, totally rapt by her discoveries. "But we went further still. Generation Eleven was a disappointment, but, oh . . . Generation *Twelve!*" She drew the word out, filling it with wonder and with threat. "We broke through into an entirely new area of science. It's what I've been laboring on for the last year while you left me here in this bunker. The killer pathogen was developed to Generation Ten before you even knew of the second generation." She laughed at the look of shocked hurt on his face. "We had the plague but we couldn't use it until we had the cure. And now . . . Oh, Sebastian, it's a fire in my blood! I can feel it moving through me."

"You . . . used it on yourself! You've turned yourself into one of those damned monsters . . ."

"Do I look like a monster?" she said. She stepped back from the slot and cupped her breasts through her robes. "Do you think I'm a monster, Sebastian?"

"God . . ."

Amirah's face instantly changed and she whipped her hands away from her breasts and slapped them against the wall on either side of the slot. It was like an entirely different personality had shoved itself into place behind her dark eyes. "God? How dare you even mention Him! Your god is money, you worthless piece of shit."

Gault recoiled and raised the pistol.

"You don't even understand what it means to *worship* God. You couldn't know, Sebastian, what it feels like to feel Him in every thought, every breath, to hear His words flowing over the desert sands. You pretended to read the writings of the Prophet to fool El Mujahid, but you lacked even the depth of understanding to let those words enter your soul! You think you made me into your whore? Do you think that I would truly betray my husband, my people, my *faith*, for you?" She spat at him and he dodged away, terrified of what might be in that sputum. He swung the pistol up and put the dot of the laser sight on her forehead where it glowed like an Indian *bindhi*.

"I loved you," he said weakly. And then his mind replayed those words and he realized that he had said "loved," not "love." It nearly broke him. In his mind's eye he saw himself turning away from her and bringing the barrel of his pistol up to his own temple. Better to snuff out that loss than endure its absence.

But although his hands trembled the gun did not move.

Amirah ignored it. "Have you figured it out yet? You must have or why else would you be here, Sebastian?" She was using his name like a whip and each time it stung him. "You think you found us, but we had been looking for you for years. Not specifically you—you're just not that important—no, we were looking for any faithless greedy dog who had the resources you have. It was so easy!" She laughed and shook her head, delighting in the pain she caused him. "It was so easy to lure you with covert hints through your network of spies, to draw you to us step by step, to stage things so that you always felt that you were in control when all the time this was a plan my husband and I had made. Yes . . . my *husband*. El Mujahid, the greatest of God's warriors on Earth. A true soldier of the Faith, a man who lives the words of the Prophet every minute of every day."

"But . . . you . . . we . . ."

She spat again, but this time on the floor. "What? We *made love*? Is that what you were going to say?" Her voice made the words intensely ugly. "I'm not a man, Sebastian. I can't go into battle with guns and knives like my husband and his soldiers. I'm a woman and I am forced to use other weapons . . . no matter how utterly disgusting and humiliating it has been to open my body to you."

"No," Gault snapped back, anger flaring. "I know you loved me. I *know*."

He saw the mad look in her eyes flicker and for a second that other personality, the dreamy one, seemed to drift back. And Gault knew—knew for sure—that he saw the fires of love still there. Or maybe it was only the embers, for in the next moment the hard and murderous personality reemerged.

"Each day I get down on my knees to beg forgiveness from Allah for what I have done, even though it is His will and serves His ends. You made me a whore in the eyes of God, Sebastian. How many deaths does that earn you?"

Behind Amirah there was a strange sound. The gathered scientists and technicians were all jabbering loudly, some in shocked protest, others in fury. Amirah stepped back to allow Gault to see what was happening.

"They think we have an antidote," she said softly as below more than two thirds of the crowd were sinking down to their knees or collapsing onto tables. "They think we are all safe from *Seif al Din*."

"What have you done?"

She turned to him. "I gave my best people—a few fighters, a few scientists—Generation Twelve. Like me." She raised her arm and pulled back her sleeve to show the needle mark on her arm. From the dark pinprick black lines of infection radiated out like a dark spider-web.

"You've killed your own people."

"Oh no . . . not all. The rest of them were given Generation Ten, and soon I'll open the Bunker doors and they'll spread out across Arabia like the plague they are. The Great Satan does not have enough bullets to stop the waves of them that will come."

"You're insane! You've doomed us all."

But Amirah shook her head. "No . . . Generation Twelve is different. We don't die like they do. We . . . *ascend*. I've already ascended. I died without dying, Sebastian, but I suffered no brain death, no loss of brain or motor function, no loss of intellect. I am me, Amirah, scientist, wife of El Mujahid, loyal handmaiden to Allah, a servant of the word of the Prophet . . . but now I cannot ever die. I've been reborn, you see. *Seif al Din* has cut through me like a purifying scythe. My sins, my earthly attachments have been carved away by the Sword of the Faithful. What remains is pure. What remains is the instrument of God on Earth."

"Oh . . . Amirah . . . my princess," Gault murmured, tears cascading down his cheeks. "What have you done? What have you done . . . ?"

"Beginning today thousands of doses of Generation Twelve will be sent from here to those fighters who have proven their faith. Once they have ascended they will share the gift with their families and their most trusted friends, and then we will sit back and watch the rest of the godless world devour itself!"

"I won't let you!"

Amirah reached out to grasp the lip of the observation slit. She pulled herself close and whispered like a child conveying a great secret. "I know everything about the Bunker, Sebastian. *Everything*. I know all your secrets."

Gault stared at her, puzzled, and then he heard the slow scuff of shambling feet in the darkness of the corridor behind him.

Chapter One Hundred Nine

AS SOON AS I was inside the sound of chaos diminished and I crept into a long, darkened corridor that led, I knew, into a maze of offices and workrooms. The center wasn't that big but there were still a hundred places someone could hide. I moved forward through several rooms, encountering one locked door after another. It would be suicide to kick each door, but these were interior locks and I could trip most of them with a stiff piece of plastic. I used my Barnes & Noble member card. It was slow going, searching and clearing every room without backup. I wondered what was taking Skip so damn long to send someone after me.

I was hoping that O'Brien and Ollie had tried to make a run at the First Lady and had been cut down by Colby and his team. Agents on the Presidential Detail are incredibly tough and resourceful. But with every step my hopes diminished. I didn't know who or what O'Brien was, but if Brierly was right and Ollie was a top CIA killer, then this was exactly his sort of operation: a hunt-and-kill.

What confused me was the fact that Brierly did not seem to be our man. Having spoken with him and seen him in action I could not believe that he was any part of the chaos back in the hall; and yet Ollie had been with O'Brien. And someone had fired those shots that saved O'Brien. Very accurate shooting in a hysterical situation, which showed professional calm.

I stopped when I saw a splash of blood on the floor. Very fresh. Creeping forward I found more, and then a place where feet had scuffed in the blood. Two sets of shoes. A scuffle? Had someone else come in following O'Brien and Ollie and been ambushed by them, or had the two traitors had a falling-out?

Then it occurred to me that one of them might have become infected. What if the walker plague had turned one of them into a monster? Was I chasing two armed men or one man and a zombie? Or two zombies? The thought chilled me.

"Joe?"

Grace's voice in my earjack made me jump and I faded to one side and crouched down behind the open door of a mop closet, pistol aimed into the darkness.

"Joe . . . where are you?"

"I'm inside the center," I whispered. "O'Brien came in here with Ollie Brown. I'm following a blood trail but no sign of them yet. I could use some backup."

"Top Sims is on his way in with Skip. I have two other agents on the door."

"Good. What's the situation outside?"

"It's bad. We're getting the crowd quieted down, but I think some of them are already infected. Several people are showing signs of sickness. I have our people going through the crowd and separating out anyone who was hit by those darts."

"Grace . . . if they start to turn . . ."

"I know, Joe," she said in a voice that was hard but scared. We were both thinking about St. Michael's, but this was much worse. Members of Congress were here, and the VP's wife; and on both sides of the glass were TV cameras. "I called Church and he had the President order an immediate media blackout. Church said that the President has declared a state of emergency for the Philadelphia metropolitan area. Oh God!"

Through the mike I could hear a fresh wave of screams.

And then gunfire.

Then nothing as Grace's link went dead.

"Grace . . ." I said into the silent link. I wanted to run back. I needed to go forward. I was totally torn.

I heard a muffled sound behind me and whirled, but it was one of the Secret Service agents standing in the shadow of an open doorway. I recognized him. Agent Colby, Brierly's second in command. I could see a couple of other agents behind him.

"God, am I glad to see you. Is that the safe room? Is the First Lady okay?"

Colby took a step into the hallway and smiled.

But it wasn't a smile.

His lips peeled back from his teeth and bloody drool dripped from his mouth. With a feral growl like a hunting cat Colby and the other agents rushed me.

Chapter One Hundred Ten
The Bunker

ABDUL STEPPED INTO the hall, his automatic rifle ready. He was happy to be away from the hall where all sense and reason seemed to have fled. Though he understood the plan El Mujahid and Amirah had devised he still thought it was insane. It did not fit with his understanding of the Koran; but there was nothing he could do about it. He knew enough about the *Seif al Din* to realize that Amirah was distributing two different versions of it, one to the general staff and another to the more valuable team members. Anah, Amirah's assistant, had tried to give him a shot but he'd fended her off, not wanting any part of this.

He was almost happy when the alarms rang, warning of an intrusion at the rear hatch.

The monitors were offline but Abdul had a good idea what was happening. Gault was not fool enough to have come here alone. So Abdul sent a team of soldiers to the hatch to intercept whatever backup the infidel had brought with him. Now he was hurrying that way himself to take charge of the situation.

He switched off the safety and took a more comfortable grip on his weapon as he stepped through a portal from the side corridor to the one that led to the hatch.

Toys stepped out from behind a stack of crates and put the barrel of his pistol against the back of Abdul's head.

"Shhhhh," Toys said with a smile.

COLBY CAME AT me with incredible speed, reaching with hooked fingers, teeth snapping at me while he was still two yards away. Even with everything that had happened—everything that was still happening— it took me totally off guard. I brought my gun up but not in time as he leaped in and drove me back against the wall. The other agents were three steps behind him.

My back slammed into the wall and for a fragment of a second the thought *I'm dead* flashed through my mind; but even as I was thinking that my body was moving. Years of conditioning make the limbs move at the reflexive level, and it was all of those years of drills, of repetitive movements, that saved me. But it was so close.

As I hit the wall my hips turned to the left and I slammed the butt of my pistol into Colby's temple. It made his mass turn with mine and we rolled down the wall together, turn after vertical turn, putting distance between us and the other walkers. When we hit the doorway we jolted to a stop and I rammed the barrel of the .45 into Colby's mouth, and even as he bit down on it I pulled the trigger. The big hollow-point blew out the back of his head and punched a hole the size of a nickel through the forehead of the agent right behind him. Both of them were instantly dead, but the sudden drop of Colby's body coupled with the locked teeth around the pistol jerked the weapon out of my hand.

I pushed myself away and dodged instantly to my left as a third walker lunged over the corpses of his fellows. His arms closed around empty space.

There were three more of them—four in all. The one who had jumped at me had fallen forward. He made a grab for my ankle but I rushed forward to meet the attack of the next closest walker.

Even as I closed the short six-foot distance I whipped the folding RRF knife from its pocket holster and with a flick snapped the blade into place. The motion took a fraction of a second and as the lead walker hit me I spun away like a ballet dancer but at the end of the pirouette I ducked low and slashed him across the back of the knee. The RRF was wickedly sharp and the creature's tendons parted like old string. As he staggered and went down I shoved him toward the second walker and lunged past their colliding bodies and slammed into the third, using a hard palm at the end of a stiffened arm to drive him back; then I ducked under his outstretched arms, avoiding his snapping teeth, and came up behind him. I grabbed his hair with my left hand and slammed the point of the knife up into the sweet spot—the arched opening at the base of the skull. The blade pierced the spinal cord and the walker shuddered to a stop and instantly fell forward.

The walker who'd tried to grab me after I'd killed Colby was scuttling forward now, running at me low and fast. I used my knife arm to parry his reaching arms and sidestepped like a bullfighter, then brought the RRF up and over and down and buried the entire blade in the windgate, the soft spot at the top of the skull. I gave the blade a brutal half turn and yanked it up, sidestepping to avoid the arching spray of blood and brain tissue.

That left two.

The one I'd crippled was crawling along the floor toward me but the other was up and running at me. When he was two paces out I stepped in and to the side so that his mass missed me by half an inch. Again I changed my step into a pivot and came up behind him and tried for the sweet spot again, but the hair was greasy with gel and he slipped away with my blade stuck into the solid bone of his skull. His twist wrenched the handle out of my hand and it wasn't worth fighting for, so I let it go and wrapped my arm around his throat and gave him a reverse hip throw. When you're facing forward it's a hard fall but not fatal; when the thrower is back to back with the person he's trying to throw then all of the hundreds of pounds of force are trapped in the weakest body point. His neck snapped like a bundle of wet sticks.

The last walker was crawling forward, but I jumped over his arms and came down on the small of his back. The vertebrae cracked audibly. He flopped down, dead from the waist down. I couldn't leave him like that so I recovered the RRF. This time there was no way for the walker to twist away as my blade found its target and shut him off.

Chapter One Hundred Twelve
Grace / The Bell Chamber / Saturday, July 4; 12:05 P.M.

ONE MOMENT GRACE was speaking to Joe via commlink and then next the air around her was whining with bullets. A reporter was blasted backward as a bullet punched through his chest and he knocked Grace back and down. As she fell she saw three men separate themselves from the crowd. Each of them had guns and she recognized the weapons as the high-density plastic handguns that terrorists used to sneak through airport metal detectors. Probably firing ceramic rounds. No metal at all, she thought as she pushed the dead reporter off her and drew her weapon.

The foremost of the three gunmen saw her and raised his weapon but Grace gave him a double tap—chest and head—and flung him back against the wall. She swung her gun to the second killer just as two figures came suddenly in from the killers' blind side. Gus Dietrich took the left-hand gunman out with three quick shots: two to the middle of his back and one to the back of his head. Next to him, Bunny appeared, no weapon in his hand, but he didn't need one for the other killer: he chopped down on the man's wrist with a balled fist, knocking the gun to the floor, then grabbed him by throat and crotch and slammed him into a corner of the Liberty Bell display case. He stepped back to let the broken body drop.

Then a fourth man stepped out of the crowd of tourists and pointed a polymer pistol at the back of Bunny's head. Grace didn't bother to call a warning; she put two rounds in the man and he spun away trailing blood. Bunny threw her a grim nod and scooped up the man's plastic pistol.

Then the rest of the Secret Service agents were there.

"There are still hostiles in the crowd," Grace yelled. "Search everyone."

The agents moved very fast, and they plowed into the crowd, gruffly shoving congressmen and tourists alike. They found one final hostile, a trembling young man dressed like a Japanese tourist. He managed to get his pistol into his mouth before the agents could tackle him. The blast took off the top of his head.

Rudy pushed his way through the crowd toward Grace.

"Are you all right—?" she began, but he interrupted.

"Grace . . . some of these people are getting sick. It's happening already . . . faster than before. We have to do something. We have to separate them before this becomes another St. Michael's."

As he spoke one of the reporters staggered forward and dropped to his knees and vomited. He looked up at them with a fevered face and eyes that were already becoming glassy. The man reached out a desperate claw of a hand toward them. "Help . . . me . . ."

Chapter One Hundred Thirteen

The Liberty Bell Center / Saturday, July 4; 12:07 P.M.

I WIPED MY knife and slid it back into its pocket clip then retrieved my gun and cleaned it quickly on Colby's tie. I had no idea how many agents had gone with the First Lady. Was there a chance she was safe somewhere? Would we get that much of a break?

I tapped my ear mike but there was nothing, not even static. It must have been damaged when I'd hit the wall. I was alone.

I was also furious with myself for not having brought a stronger force here to Philly; or maybe for not pressuring Church into canceling the event. We'd both looked at this as a likely scenario and we'd still allowed it go forward. I realized as I thought these things that this was one of the aftershocks of 9/11. For a while after that everything that could draw a crowd was canceled, but then our culture moved on and there were no more attacks. We became complacent. Maybe we even thought that, against all evidence, we really had Al Qaeda on the run and that we'd taken the fight so effectively to them that we could settle back into normal life here in the States.

Today we were paying the price for complacence. Did the blame belong to me? Church? Or was this a cultural failing? If I lived through the day I'd have to take a closer look at those questions; but social philosophy doesn't help you in the heat of a firefight, so I pressed on.

There was still no sign of backup coming for me, but I couldn't wait. I crept forward, going room by darkened room. I tried light switches in the hallway and in several rooms but got nothing. Someone must have thrown the circuit breakers. The only light was the dim red glow of emergency lamps. I had to check every locked room, every closet to see if I could locate the First Lady, or Agent O'Brien, and throughout I could feel a hot spot between my eyes as if Ollie Brown was laying his laser sight on me and waiting for the right moment to punch my ticket.

Five rooms in I heard wet sounds coming from the far side of a row of desks. I knew what those sounds would be and I really didn't want to look; but I had no choice. Taking a fresh grip on my .45 I rounded the desks on the balls of my feet.

There were three of them on their knees, heads bent forward, like lions around a zebra carcass. Only the carcass was that of a Secret Service agent and the lions were office workers—two women and a man wearing business casual and sporting Liberty Bell Center IDs around their necks. Their hands and mouths were black with blood.

Bile rose in my throat and I gagged. Just a tiny sound, just enough so that their heads snapped up like the wary predators they were. The closest of them, a woman, hissed at me.

I shot her in the head. The impact flung her back and she toppled over the dead agent in a perverse imitation of intimacy.

The other two rose up and lunged but I was ready.

Two shots, two kills.

I stared at the bodies, and then at the dead agent. His throat had been savaged. Would he reanimate, or was this beyond the pathogen's wound-repair mechanism? I pointed my gun at his head and just as my finger was tightening around the trigger I heard three separate sounds at the same moment.

From far behind me I heard Top Sims calling my name. At my feet I heard the first feeble twitch as some new and monstrous force fired the engines that would raise this fallen hero up as an undead killer. And up ahead I heard the First Lady scream.

Chapter One Hundred Fourteen
Gault and Amirah / The Bunker

GAULT WHIRLED AND pointed his pistol into the shadows. Five fig-ures crowded the narrow corridor, their bare feet scuffing the floor. In the pale glow of the LED panels their faces were a ghostly white, but their eyes and mouths were as black as sin.

He recognized one of the monsters: Khalid, the soldier who had been the first of El Mujahid's men to take Gault's money for personal services. Gault had liked him. The man had always been tough and crafty, but now he merely looked dead. His skin hung slack on his skull and his mouth sagged open to utter a moan of mindless need.

"I'm sorry," Gault whispered. His first shot took Khalid in the shoulder and spun him around so that his outstretched hands slapped the second zombie across the face. If Gault had watched the scene in a movie it would have been comical, a dark slapstick; but this was no zombie comedy, no BBC pantomime. This was death. This was horror.

The creatures behind Khalid pushed him forward so that he kept moving toward Gault even though he was facing the wrong direction, like flotsam on a current that flowed from the bowels of hell. Gault gagged and fired again. Khalid's face disintegrated and he collapsed. Two others stumbled over him, falling down to crack bones on the hard concrete. Gault shot them each in the head; but the final two were already climbing over them, their mouths working as the scent of blood filled the air.

He fired and fired and fired. Behind him, through the narrow observation slit in the wall, he heard Amirah's mad laughter.

Chapter One Hundred Fifteen
Grace / The Bell Chamber / Saturday, July 4; 12:11 P.M.

"FOR GOD'S SAKE . . . help me!" The junior senator from the state of Alabama raised his head and stared pleadingly at Grace Courtland. His skin had already turned from a healthy tan to the color of old parchment. There were two puncture marks on his cheek from where a pair of the glass darts had struck him.

Grace raised her pistol and pointed it at him. "Get against the wall, sir," she said tightly.

"I . . . don't feel . . ." He shook his head as if trying to clear muddy thoughts. "I'm . . . sick . . ."

"Sir . . . for the love of God, please get against the wall with the others."

Behind her a woman's voice slashed the air. "Agent . . . what the hell do you think you're doing? Lower your weapon immediately." It was not the first time the Vice President's wife had yelled at her in the last few minutes. Grace stood her ground.

The room was silent except for sobs from the wounded. Grace, Bunny, Dietrich, and Brierly had worked through the crowd, separating out anyone who had been stung by the darts. Over sixty people, all of them sick and shivering with fever, were huddled together in a cluster by the wall farthest from the STAFF ONLY door. Rudy moved among them making quick and purely visual assessments of them. His face was rigid with shock. A line of Secret Service agents, fifteen of them, stood with their pistols pointed at the sick and wounded, but even the toughest agents among them looked confused and frightened. Outside, on the other side of the thick glass walls, the National Guard were setting up machine gun emplacements, and the sky above Independence Mall was filled with army gunships.

Things had started brewing to a panic and so Grace had climbed to the top of the podium and fired a shot into the ceiling to get them to listen. "Listen to me!" she shouted.

Bunny and Dietrich took up positions around the base of the podium, their guns at the ready. The fifteen remaining Secret Service agents stood in a line between the infected and the rest, their faces showing the terrible doubt and conflict they each felt.

In a few short sentences Grace told everyone that the Freedom Bell had been rigged by terrorists and that anyone who had been struck by the darts was likely to become infected with a highly contagious disease. That helped with the separation as the uninjured moved quickly away from them. The disease, she told them, would cause erratic and violent behavior. As she spoke she looked for signs of infection in anyone who had not admitted to having been stung.

That's when Audrey Collins, the VP's wife, had suddenly spoken up to champion the cause of the infected. Collins was a thin woman with a hatchet face and fierce blue eyes, and despite the agony from three cracked ribs, she managed to muster enough personal power to take a commanding position in the conflict. "You will lower your weapon, Agent, or so help me God, I will make sure that you are punished to the fullest extent of the law."

Grace stepped down from the podium, and Dietrich turned and brought his gun up to cover the infected junior senator. Grace said, "Ma'am, you have to be quiet and let us do our jobs—"

Collins cut her off. "Do you know who I am?"

"Yes, ma'am, I know who you are and I know full well that your husband can have me jailed, deported, and probably stood against a wall and shot . . . but right now I am trying to save the lives of most of the people in this room and probably all of the people in this country. If you interfere with me or prevent me from doing what I have to do I will knock you on your ass."

"You wouldn't dare."

Grace took a step closer and the savage look in her eyes was so ferocious that the people who had gathered behind the VP's wife faded back, leaving the woman alone with Grace.

"Ma'am, if you do anything—*anything*—to try and stop me I'll put you against the wall with them. Believe me, you don't want me to do that."

"Ma'am," said Rudy, stepping up beside Grace. "I implore you to listen."

"Slow down here, Major," Brierly said, coming up on Grace's other side. "Everyone's scared here."

The remaining Presidential Detail agents milled uncertainly near Mrs. Collins. Brierly had briefed them and had even channeled the President himself on to the team's command link. The President's voice had been trembling with fear and rage but he had been clear: Grace Courtland was in charge. Even so, threats to their principal went against all of their training.

"No one more than me, sir," Grace said, but her eyes locked on the VP's wife. "But this is not something I can back down on. You *know* that."

Bunny moved to Grace's right with a good shooter's angle to the presidential agents.

"Mrs. Collins . . . ?" implored the junior senator.

Audrey Collins, apart from being married to the Vice President, was a career politician in her own right and she was used to giving orders rather than taking them. But for all her bluster she was no fool. She shifted her furious stare from Grace and looked at the young senator; and changed her expression from anger to wretched concern.

"Do what the major says, Tom," she said to the frightened congressman. "Everything will be okay."

She turned to Grace and the look they shared insisted that nothing was going to be okay. Not now, and maybe not ever. "If you're wrong about this," said Mrs. Collins, "I'll—"

"I'm not," Grace interrupted. Then she softened her own expression. "Thank you."

"Fuck you," said the Vice President's wife.

Grace almost smiled, but then someone screamed.

"My God! She's biting him!"

Everyone turned toward the wall, to where the anchorwoman for the local ABC affiliate was hunched over the unconscious body of a tourist in a Hawaiian shirt. The anchorwoman, a petite blonde with sculpted nails and Prada shoes, was chewing on the tourist's arm.

"No," Bunny said. "Come on . . . *no!*"

"God help us all," Grace said and raised her gun.

What happened next was unspeakable.

Chapter One Hundred Sixteen
The Liberty Bell Center / Saturday, July 4; 12:12 P.M.

THERE WAS NO time to think. I put a shot into the head of the agent and spun on my heel before he flopped back against the ground, sprinting in the direction of the scream. That wasn't the hunting-cat screech of a walker—it was filled with very human terror. I just hoped it wasn't her last scream.

Screw caution—I ran. I tore through room after room. Twice white-faced figures lunged at me out of the shadows and each time I put them down with single shots without breaking stride. I could still hear voices behind. Top and Skip calling my name. They were smart enough to follow the trail of bodies.

The First Lady screamed again, just ahead, on the other side of a closed door.

I hit the door with a jumping kick that tore it off its hinges. The door crashed onto a walker and crushed him underneath. I leaped into the room, taking in the scene as I landed in a combat crouch.

The First Lady was huddled in the corner of an office cubicle. Her Secret Service detail had been slaughtered. Only one agent remained and there was a crowd of seven walkers trying to bring him down. The agent was bleeding from half a dozen bites and his face was white with pain and panic. Two of the walkers were the last remaining agents; the rest were employees of the Liberty Bell Center. No sign of Ollie or O'Brien.

I opened fire and took one of the walkers in the back of the neck. He crashed forward and dragged down two others as he fell.

"Help!" the First Lady screamed. "Oh God, please help us!"

The nearest walkers had turned toward me at the sound of my shot and they rushed me. I shot one but then there was a blast from behind me and the walker to my right pitched back with a gaping hole in his temple.

"On your six!" I heard Top growl and then he and Skip were rushing the group of walkers from either flank. Top used double taps each time, stalling them with a chest shot and then putting one through the brain. Skip's shots were more random and he hit walkers over and over again in the body, wasting shots.

"Head shots, goddamn it!" Top yelled at him and blew away a walker that was rushing at Skip from his left.

The remaining Secret Service agent fired his last shot, a wild blast that nearly hit Top, and then the last walker tackled him so that they fell into the cubicle, crashing down at the First Lady's feet. She screamed but then she snatched a laptop off the desk and used it to beat in the back of the walker's head. None of us could take a shot because she was so close, and she laid into the monster with a will, her fear becoming fury. The walker shivered and collapsed into a terminal stillness. Beneath him the agent groaned and reached out an imploring hand to her.

"Roger!" she said and reached for him.

"No!" I yelled and darted forward to slap her hand away. "Don't! He's infected."

Around us the room became unnaturally still as the gunshot echoes faded. The only sound was a painful wheeze from Roger, the wounded agent.

"I'm . . . sorry, ma'am," he said, struggling to get the words out.

The First Lady looked at me. "Help him, for God's sake!"

I stepped between her and Roger, then squatted down and offered him my left hand. He closed his hand around it with ferocious desperation as if it was a lifeline that could pull him up from hell. "Listen to me," I said gently. "Your name's Roger?"

"Agent . . . Roger Jefferson."

"I'm Joe Ledger. Listen, Roger . . . there's been an outbreak. A plague. You understand? From the Freedom Bell."

He nodded. His breathing was getting worse.

"That's what happened to your men. One or more of them must have been exposed. It . . . changes people."

He nodded again. "I . . . saw. Barney . . . Linus . . . all of them. God . . ."

"I'm sorry, man."

"Is . . . is she . . . ?" He turned his head, looking for the First Lady, but I don't think he could see her anymore.

The First Lady put a hand on my shoulder and leaned over. "Roger. I'm right here."

"Are . . . are you . . . all . . . ?"

"I'm fine, Roger. You didn't let them get me."

Roger smiled and his eyes drifted shut, but his grip was still strong. He whispered something that I had to bend close to hear.

"Cap'n," warned Top.

Roger said, "I . . . saw how it works." Blood seeped from the corners of his mouth. "You do . . . what you have to do."

"I will," I promised. "Rest easy, Roger. You saved the First Lady."

With his last strength he gave me a trembling smile. "All . . . part of the job." He tried to laugh but there was not enough left of him and he settled back.

"Get her out of here," I said to Top. "Do it now."

"What do you mean?" she protested as Top closed in. "We can't just leave him here."

"Ma'am," Top said, "you saw what happens. Let the captain do what he has to do. It's the best thing . . . it's best for Roger."

"Top . . . get her out now!"

The First Lady straightened her back and though tears flowed down her face she walked away with great dignity. I hadn't voted for her husband, but I sure as hell admired her.

When they were out of the room I disengaged my hand from Roger's slack grip. I reached over and took a cushion off the nearest chair and put it over his face. I was counting seconds. I felt the first twitch in less than forty seconds since his last breath and I put the barrel of my gun against the pad and fired. Maybe it was because the pad would muffle the shot and make it easier for the First Lady, or maybe it was because it would cover his face and grant him a slice of dignity. Or maybe it was that I couldn't bear to see another good man become one of those things. Probably all three.

I stood up and looked at Skip. The young sailor wouldn't meet my eyes. He just turned away and I followed him out of the cubicle and into the next room. The First Lady was sitting on a leather office chair and Top had brought her a cup of water from a nearby cooler. She sipped it and when she saw me she just stared at me, her expression unreadable.

The office was big and looked to be the graphic arts department for the center, with worktables, advertising sketches pinned to the walls, and machines for printing posters. Two offices led off from the main room, both with doors that stood ajar. I had just opened my mouth to order Skip to check them out when two figures stepped out of the shadows of the left-hand office. They came in quick and they had guns in their hands.

Ollie Brown and Special Agent Michael O'Brien.

"MAJOR . . . WATCH!" BUNNY yelled, and Grace whirled just as the anchorwoman for Channels 6 News leaped at her from the podium. The anchor's skin was wax-white and her eyes as round and empty as silver dollars, but she growled with hunger as she lunged for Grace's throat.

"Bloody hell!" Grace shot the woman twice in the face. Blood splattered the faces of the three snarling figures that were mounting the steps behind her.

"What the hell are you *doing*?" screamed Mrs. Collins, and she made a grab for Grace's gun arm and succeeded in pulling it down so that the next round chopped a divot out of the marble floor and ricocheted up to punch a red hole through the thigh of the Canadian ambassador. The ambassador dropped with a shriek of pain and instantly two of the walkers leaped from the podium and pounced on him. Grace wrestled with the Vice President's wife, who had a surprising amount of wiry strength and in the end she had to let go with her left hand and chop Mrs. Collins on the side of the neck. It dropped the woman to her knees and Grace tore her gun arm free just as the third walker dove at her. Grace put two rounds in him and the corpse skidded to a stop inches from Mrs. Collins.

IT WAS COMPLETE pandemonium in the Bell Chamber as the infected who had lapsed into comas instantly snapped awake as walkers and attacked the crowd. Even with the warnings Grace, Brierly, and Rudy had given them about the nature of the infection the fifteen remaining Secret Service agents faltered, hesitating, unable to open fire on citizens, congressmen, and dignitaries.

Bunny muscled one dazed agent out of the way just as a journalist from the *Daily News* was about to grab him. The hulking sergeant snaked out a hand and caught the walker by the throat, buried his borrowed polymer pistol against the creature's head and fired. He flung the corpse into the path of a second walker and killed that one, but then six of them came at him in a bunch and he fell back, dragging the startled agent with him.

"Fire, goddamn it!" Bunny yelled, and the agent seemed to snap out of his stupor. They found a clear patch of floor and the pair of them made their stand, opening up with both guns. Bunny had four shots left and used them all; the agent wasted an entire clip to bring down just one walker.

That left two from the pack still on their feet. Bunny stepped in and kicked the lead one in the stomach and when it doubled over he arched up and then brought his balled fist down as hard as he could on the back of the exposed skull. The walker immediately went into a boneless sprawl; but his companion just kept coming. He was three steps out when a shot snapped his head back. Bunny turned to see the agent, reloaded now, holding his smoking pistol in a two-hand grip.

BEHIND THEM RUDY, holding a flagpole, stood his ground between a huddled group of Girl Scouts and a walker in a Hawaiian shirt with toucans on it. The walker took a step forward but then ducked back away from the swing of the pole. Rudy frowned. He'd seen all of the tapes of the DMS encounters with the walkers, and he'd noted that they never flinched, never dodged. They lacked the cognitive powers to do it, and even their unnatural reflexes did not include any defensive reactions. And yet this one dodged once, twice.

And he smiled.

He pointed a crooked finger at the little girls behind Rudy and then he did something else walkers can't do. He spoke.

"Mine!"

"Dios mio!" breathed Rudy, and the idea of a walker still capable of thought and deliberate action nearly took the heart out of him. But the

whimpers of the girls behind him put strength in his hands. He held his ground.

AHMED, BROTHER OF Amirah, lover of Andrea Lester and El Mujahid's chief agent in the United States, leered at Rudy and the girls. He felt amazing, immensely powerful and more completely alive than ever. The Generation Twelve pathogen burned like wildfire in his veins and when he had come awake moments ago he was overwhelmed by the clarity of focus it bestowed. Even after a life lived in dedication to the teachings of the Prophet he had never before *understood* so completely. The will of Allah was a white-hot light in his brain.

Consumed by his purpose and bursting with immortal power, he rushed forward to do the will of God. As the flagpole swung at him he caught it with one palm and with the other he grabbed Rudy Sanchez by the throat.

Chapter One Hundred Eighteen

The Liberty Bell Center / Saturday, July 4; 12:14 P.M.

I RAISED MY pistol and put the laser sight on Ollie Brown who had a Glock in his hand though the barrel was pointed down at the floor.

"You fucking bastard," I said, and slipped my finger inside the trigger guard, but before I could fire a gunshot shattered the air. Ollie gave me a crooked smile and when he opened his mouth blood gushed over his chin. Ollie dropped his pistol and staggered forward and I realized that O'Brien had shot him. The CIA assassin stumbled, dropped to hands and knees, fighting to keep his head raised. He looked up at me, his eyes glazing.

"S . . . sorry . . ." he said, though his voice was a gurgle. "I . . . I . . ."

And then he collapsed onto the floor.

O'Brien began to raise his gun toward me.

"Drop the weapon!" I snarled. "Do it now!"

"Or what?" he asked, and suddenly his voice was different, no longer the bland American accent he had used before. Now he sounded British. "What will you do? Shoot me?" He laughed. "What do I care?"

"Say the word," Top murmured from behind me, "and we'll waste this shitbag."

"Drop it," I warned. "Last chance."

O'Brien closed his eyes for a moment. He was bathed in sweat and his color was bad. He lowered his pistol and then took a sagging sideways step; but his hand snaked out fast as a cobra and caught the doorframe to keep him from falling.

I took a cautious forward step, my pistol rock-steady, the laser sight tattooed on the front of his muscular chest. The agent shook his head as if trying to clear his thoughts, the pistol hung from his hand but he had not dropped it. On the floor I could see Ollie's fingers open and close slowly. There was a bullet hole in the back of his sports coat from which blood still bubbled sluggishly. I couldn't have cared less, though. If he was dying, then let him die. Saying that he was sorry didn't hold much weight for me.

"Drop the gun," I commanded.

Behind me I could hear Top and Skip moving closer. O'Brien was outnumbered and outgunned.

And still the son of a bitch made a try for it. He raised his head and smiled at me, and I could see that there was something odd about his face. The heavy sweat that soaked his face seemed to be washing the color out of him. His freckles looked like they were melting, and I could see a faint jagged line beneath his skin as if he had a thick scar running diagonally across his face. Was he wearing . . . makeup?

O'Brien looked at me, his eyes going in and out of focus. Then I saw the muscles around his eyes tighten as he suddenly whipped his gun up and screamed: *"Allah akbar!"*

I shot him twice in the chest.

The impact slammed him back through the doorway and he collapsed into the darkness of the office beyond. He went down hard and I could hear the crunch of elbows, skull, and heels as he struck the linoleum floor.

The moment stretched as a haze of gun smoke washed the air with a faint gray.

All I could see was the soles of his shoes, but after a single twitch he stopped moving. I didn't trust it, though, and I kept my pistol on him as I moved into the room, crouched and pressed fingers to his throat.

Nothing. Absolutely nothing.

I felt some of the tension leave me and I rose and went back into the main room, but I was frowning. The tips of the fingers I'd used to check his pulse were smeared with color and I sniffed it. I was right: stage makeup.

"Nice shot, boss," Top said. He lowered his piece but didn't put it away. He knelt down to check on Ollie, but his face showed his distaste for the effort wasted. "He's alive. Maybe he'll live long enough to hang. Traitorous prick."

Skip was standing behind him, staring past me. He bent and picked up Ollie's pistol and then retreated to stand beside the First Lady, who was staring in renewed horror.

"Jesus," Skip breathed, his eyes fixed on O'Brien. "You actually killed him."

"Yeah," I said, "that sometimes happens when you shoot someone."

"Shame you can't collect the reward," Skip said.

"What reward?"

He gave me a quirky grin. "For bagging El Mujahid, boss. Last I heard there was a million-dollar reward for him."

I frowned, puzzled. "The hell are you talking about?"

Skip nodded past me. "O'Brien. He's El Mujahid. You didn't figure that out?"

I turned and glanced down at the big corpse, then looked back at Skip. "How the hell do you know that?"

Skip raised both guns. He put the barrel of one against the First Lady's temple and pointed the other at my face.

"A little bird told me," he said with a twinkle in his eye.

Son of a bitch.

Chapter One Hundred Nineteen
Gault and Amirah / The Bunker

GAULT TURNED BACK to face Amirah. Her hunger and hate were so strong that the metal wall between them felt paper-thin. He glanced down at his watch and felt his heart skip a beat. The team from Global Security should have been here by now.

"Are you expecting someone, Sebastian?" Amirah purred.

"You can't win this," he retorted. "I won't let you destroy everything."

Her face darkened. "Won't let me? What does it matter what you want? It is the will of Allah that matters. That is the only thing that matters."

Fury was beginning to burn away his grief. "You know, I'm getting so bloody tired of religious tirades, my dear. Why don't I shoot you and then you can go and see your god."

She ignored the threat. "There's someone out here who wants to talk to you, Sebastian."

He took a cautious half step forward as she moved back to allow him a better view. Down below the moans and screams had intensified. There was blood splashed on the walls as the infected who had transitioned first had now turned on those who had not yet succumbed. What he saw was a picture out of a nightmare, a Hieronymus Bosch painting come to terrible life; but that wasn't what Amirah wanted to show him. Instead a second figure stepped into view.

It was Anah, a young woman Gault knew to be a cousin of El Mujahid. She had the same dreamy half-mad look as Amirah, and the same gray skin, but the young woman's mouth was smeared with red and in her hands she held something so grotesque that Gault had to clamp a hand to his mouth to keep from vomiting.

Anah carried the head of Captain Zeller. The leader of the Global Security rescue team.

Gagging, Gault thrust the barrel of the pistol through the observation slot and fired shot after shot into Anah, punching holes through her chest and face, staggering her back to the metal rail and then blasting her over. Anah fell without a scream and crashed down into the mass of creatures fighting below.

"You mad bitch!" he screamed at Amirah and shot her. His first bullet hit her in the stomach. Amirah staggered back and her face twisted into a grimace of agony.

No . . .

Not pain. Amirah was laughing. She whirled and ran along the corridor as Gault fired after her, trying to hit her, needing to kill her, wanting her death. He hit her at least three more times until she was so far down the corridor that he could no longer get an angle for a useful shot. He knew that he'd hit her, he'd seen her robes fluff out with the impacts, had seen blood splash the walls. But Amirah hadn't even slowed down . . . and as she ran she called his name in a mocking laugh.

The slide on Gault's pistol locked back and he reeled away from the slot, gasping, blood roaring in his ears. With trembling fingers he fumbled for a new magazine and slapped it into place. Sweat coursed down his face and chest.

He had a flash of panic and pulled out his sat phone, but Toys did not answer. No help was coming. He was alone. Panic howled in his head.

Amirah knew about the secret passages he'd built into the place. If she and El Mujahid had been playing him then there was a good chance she'd somehow hacked into his computer. The network of hidden passages was on there. And, dammit, so were the detonation codes he had created to blow this place to atoms. Okay, that option was gone. Just as the rescue was gone.

He had two full magazines plus the one in the gun, which gave him about a third as many bullets as he would need even if every shot was a kill, and that was unlikely.

"Head shots, you bloody fool." He cursed himself for wasting a chance to kill that witch.

Witch. He'd called her that so many times that now it came back to haunt him. It was more accurate a label than he had ever known. What she had done was the blackest kind of sorcery. A true deal with the devil, and it occurred to Gault that it hadn't been cuckold's horns that El Mujahid had worn. They were the king and queen of Hell. Damn them both.

He paused at a T-juncture in the corridor. To his left he could hear the hiss of hydraulics as someone—Amirah or one of her monsters—opened a doorway to his right. *Okay,* he thought, *that simplifies things;* and he took the other fork of the juncture.

There was only one more thing that he could do. One final chance left to stop Amirah's doomsday scheme. At least the part of it that she wanted to launch here in the Middle East. He only hoped the American had been able to somehow warn the authorities before things got out of control over there. He rushed down the hallway, knowing that his one chance was slim, and even then he had almost no hope of surviving. Somehow it amused him to think that he might actually sacrifice himself to save the world.

"God . . . they really will think I'm a saint now," he mused. He almost laughed as he raced along through the shadows.

Chapter One Hundred Twenty

The Liberty Bell Center / Saturday, July 4; 12:16 P.M.

I STARED AT Skip. "You?"

"Yeah," he said. "What . . . you thought it was Dudley Do-Right over there?" He jerked his head at Ollie.

"You piece of shit," growled Top, but Skip jabbed the First Lady with the pistol. She sat rigid and terrified, her eyes locked on mine, pleading silently for me to do something. But Skip held all the best cards.

"Put your piece down, boss," Skip ordered. "Two fingers, nice and slow. Now kick it away. Good. The knife, too. You, too, Top. You even think about doing anything funny and I pop the lady first."

"Why?" I demanded. "What's your stake in all this?"

"Well," he said with a grin, "if you're wondering if I've embraced the teachings of the prophet Mohammad, then no. I've pretty much embraced ten million dollars in an offshore account."

"You're doing this for money?"

"Of *course* I'm doing it for money."

"That doesn't make sense . . . you fought side by side with us against these things."

"Yeah, and it's the best cover story in the world. And that whole 'Taser' thing was a setup. Cute, huh? Once you and the others went to explore the crab plant I slipped into the hidden passage. Oh, don't look surprised. They downloaded the whole floor plan to me before we ever set out. We planned the whole thing via text messages—it went off like clockwork. I told them to take out one of the other guys with a liquid Taser and then I faked my own abduction. I had to fake my own burn with a lighter, but we all make sacrifices. The rest was window dressing to confuse things. I pop caps in a bunch of walkers, rub dust in my eyes to get the tears flowing, and then wait to be rescued. I should get a frickin' Academy Award. That Courtland bitch bought it hook, line, and sinker. And if you're wondering about the fight in the laboratory, I'd have made it out of there, too. There was an exit door behind the last meds chest, right near where I was standing. I'm sure Jerry Spencer will probably find it eventually, not that it'll matter now. If that asswipe Dietrich had been another ten seconds slower I'd have ducked out as soon as you guys started getting chomped."

"You're a real piece of work."

"Just doing my job. Funny thing is, I wasn't even supposed to be the point man for this gig. Lieutenant Colonel Hanley was supposed to step up and lead Echo Team, with me as his backup, but then you come along and go all Jackie Chan on him. Ah well. More cash for me."

"And Room Twelve . . . ?"

He shrugged. "Couldn't let you interrogate the tech from the Delaware lab. That hit hadn't been part of the plan and they weren't ready for you. I never even got a chance to send a warning 'cause we were wheels up so fast. So I opened Room Twelve, popped a cap in the prisoner, and let the walkers out to play. If you guys hadn't cleaned it up so fast I would have gotten there and played hero . . . but it worked out okay."

"Don't you realize the people you're working with are trying to start a plague that will wipe out—"

He cut me off with a laugh. "Oh come on, Captain . . . you don't buy any of that shit, do you. We *fed* you the clues. This was even timed to happen right before the Fourth so that there would be some concerns about this event. I was tickled pink when I heard that we were coming down here 'cause it meant that absolutely everything was falling into place. We gave you everything you need to stop the plague before it goes anywhere. All you have to do is spend a shitload of money on re- search and inoculation. That Chink doctor from the DMS is already working on a treatment. There are enough agents and cops here in Philly to keep the infection contained. None of this was ever going to get out of the center. You'll be happy to know that was the last planned release of the plague. Nah . . . this isn't about the end of the world, it's just about the moolah. Always has been, always will be."

"Ten million dollars sounds like a cheap price tag for your soul, Skip."

"It'll do. Especially where I'm going. I can live well and stay off the radar for the rest of my life."

"What about all the people who've died? All the DMS agents, the people they turned into walkers at the crab plant . . ."

I looked for a flicker of conscience in his eyes but there was nothing. He was as dead inside as one of the walkers. "The fuck do I care? I'm only a player. You want to lay a guilt trip on someone, boss, blame the asshole you just shot. Yeah, that really is El Mujahid. Made up to look like a Secret Service agent. I worked on getting his papers and ID ready before my boss transferred me to the DMS. Everything worked fine, too."

"Your boss. You mean Robert Howell Lee?"

Skip blinked but recovered quickly. "Good call. Maybe you're better than I thought, not that it matters. You can have Lee. I don't give a shit. He's a weasel. Me . . . I'm outta here."

"At least tell me something, Skip," I said. "Who started all of this? I'm betting on some pharmaceutical company, with the terrorists as hired help."

He blinked again. "Okay, points for that. Yeah, this is all big-business shit."

"Care to share which companies?"

"As if," he said, then half shrugged. He kept one gun on me but lowered the other and moved forward a couple of paces and put the barrel of his second piece against the back of Top's head. "Actually, I don't know much more than you do. All I was told is that some big pharmacy company is footing the bill." Again he nodded past me to where El Mujahid lay in a pool of blood. "Somebody's going to make a lot of money."

"Maybe, but they won't be able to spend much of it. We'll catch them."

He snorted. "The DMS might, Captain, but you won't. And even if they do, what's it to me? I'm a contract player here. I got no personal stake in this no matter how it turns out, and when the shit really hits the fan I'll be far, far away in Happily Ever After Land. I'll bet it won't even make the papers where I'll be."

"I get out of this, kid," said Top softly, "you'd better keep looking over your shoulder 'cause one of these days I'll be right there."

"Wow. I'm really scared." He jabbed Top again with the gun. "You take a run at me, old man, and I'll cut off your balls and make you eat them."

There was a renewed rattle of gunfire from down the hall. Out in the Bell Chamber.

Grace.

Skip smiled. "I'll bet we can all guess what's happening out there. Zombie madness, and on national TV. That's gonna be some real shit. But that's also my cue to get the hell out of Dodge. A little hysteria is very useful, don't you think, Captain?"

"For someone who's supposed to be a cold-blooded killer you're doing a lot of talking. What's the problem, Skip? You getting cold feet about capping your teammates?"

He laughed. "Man, that's precious. You're right out of Psychology 101. Try to manipulate the emotions of the hostage taker by establishing a bond between him and his captives. Please. No, Captain, I wanted to make sure that I got the chance to get a little payback for you kicking my ass the other day. I'm not huge on the whole forgive-and-forget thing."

"You want to go another round? Sure. You want to do it hand to hand or are you looking for a knife fight? According to your file you're quite a hotshot with a blade . . ."

"Get real. You think I'm an idiot? I know you can take me in a fair fight. Why do you think I'm not fighting fair, asshole?"

"Okay . . . then you have me confused here, kid. What do you have in mind?"

"I want to see you get your ass kicked by someone you *can't* take."

"Oh? And who would that be?"

"Me . . ." hissed a guttural voice behind me.

I whirled.

El Mujahid stood hulking in the doorway. And, yes, he was dead. Not that it much mattered at the moment. He smiled at me and bared his teeth.

From behind me, in a mocking voice, Skip said, "Now ain't that a bitch."

GAULT HAD TO crawl through two access tunnels and climb down four cold metal ladders to reach the very heart of the facility, far below the Bunker. He was making for a set of controls that he'd had built into the Bunker from the beginning, just in case all other options failed. He was careful not to make a sound in case Amirah or some of her creatures—alive or dead—had followed him. It was nearly black down here, with security lights spaced out only every hundred feet, so he had to pick his way. It was also terribly hot down here.

Below the Bunker was a deep drill hole that had punched into a lava stream buried far beneath the desert. The geothermal energy that powered the Bunker was virtually limitless, and a series of six vents—each a half-mile-long segment of reinforced piping—kept the heat converters from building up too much of a charge. If even half of them collapsed the venting would still keep the station safe from a critical overload. But there was a single point where they all joined: a huge vertical shaft that was bored straight down into the cathedral roof of the lava chamber. Superheated gasses rose up into the shaft and then dispersed through the six upward-slanting vents. Heat always rises, and that kept the engines turning and at the same time created a vulnerability because heat could only vent if nothing prevented it. Block the vents—all of them—and the heat would be trapped below the generators. With lava funneling that much heat it would be a matter of minutes before the generators either melted to slag or blew up. In either case it would trip all of the Bunker's fail-safe devices—protocols that were hardwired into the station's structure with so many redundancies that even a deliberate attempt to disable them would trigger them. Once triggered the fail-safe would send electrical signals to explosive bolts that would slam every door shut and then burst-weld them into place. The fail-safe system would then start a series of asbestos-coated alloy fans that would take the superheated gasses and blow them into every room and chamber in the Bunker. Gault had designed the Bunker that way to keep his pathogens from escaping. He really did not want to destroy the world. All he wanted was to become the richest man in it.

He crawled along the tunnel, pouring sweat, inching toward a spot that could only be found by touch: markings like Braille that Gault himself had etched into the plate steel. Behind that plate were six hydraulic levers. Each one would cause about a ton of rock to crash down onto a separate vent pipe. Easy as pie.

Forty feet to go.

Thirty. Twenty. Then he heard it. A voice whispering in the darkness somewhere behind him.

"Sebastian," she called. Low and sweet and dreadful.

Chapter One Hundred Twenty-Two
The Liberty Bell Center / Saturday July 4; 12:19 P.M.

I STAGGERED BACK from El Mujahid as he lumbered forward out of the darkened office.

"Mother of God," I heard Top whisper.

The makeup on El Mujahid's face had run, giving him a weirdly melted look. It revealed a wicked cut, like a knife slash, that bisected his face. It was the first time I'd been this close to him. He had to be six five and two-fifty if he was an ounce. He pulled off the jacket he'd worn as part of his Secret Service disguise, then jerked the tie loose and tore that off, dropping it on the floor. His white shirt was soaked with blood, and he touched the bullet holes. They were in the right place, they had to have clipped his heart. He smiled.

"It worked," he said in wonder. "My princess has found the way . . ."

Skip said, "Here's an incentive for you, boss. My employers may not have been trying to bring about the end of the world . . . but this asshole? Shit, he's one of the horsemen of the apocalypse. He gets out of this place and it really will be game over."

El Mujahid snarled at Skip, and out of the corner of my eye I could see Skip staring at the big terrorist with a mixture of admiration and disgust. Then I noticed that Top was looking straight at me, his dark eyes intense and unblinking. My hands were at my side and as I turned my face toward El Mujahid I curled the thumb and pinky of my left hand so that I showed three fingers. Then I curled the ring finger up, then the forefinger. Then the index, hoping that Top had read me the right way.

Abruptly I lunged at El Mujahid and chopped him across the throat with as hard a knife-hand blow as I'd ever used on a human being. At the same instant Top pivoted, his speed powered by adrenaline and fear and a hell of a lot of indignation. He grabbed Skip's wrist with one hand and drove his opposite elbow back into the young man's stomach. Skip's finger clutched in a spasm of pain and the bullet burned across the side of Top's temple. Top bellowed in pain but he came up off the floor and tackled Skip, driving him halfway across the room so that they both crashed onto a desk. The pistol flew into a corner.

Skip shoved Top back with a curse and with a shake of his wrist a knife dropped from a sleeve holster into the palm of his hand. He opened his mouth to taunt Top, but First Sergeant Sims moved forward in a blur and slammed into Skip. They hit the desk and then rolled off on the far side and out of sight.

I couldn't go help. I had my own problems.

The blow that I'd used on El Mujahid should have killed him. At very least it should have crippled him. It would have done that to any man.

But El Mujahid was no longer a man. He coughed but then he expanded his chest and I could actually hear the fragments of his shattered hyoid bone click together. It was the creepiest sound I'd ever heard.

In a hoarse rasp of a voice he growled, "My princess has made me immortal. Praise Allah!" His eyes had looked dazed and dull when he'd first come out of the room, but I could see them becoming more focused. I didn't understand it. If he was a walker, then why was he able to talk? Or think?

He took a step toward me. The first step was wobbly, as if he was uncertain how to use his body. But the second step was firmer. The third step showed no instability at all.

Crap.

His face took on an expression that was half triumphant leer and half naked hunger, and a fanatical light burned like a solar flare in his eyes. "Allah is the only God and I am his wrath on Earth!"

"Whatever," I said as I dodged to one side and kicked him on the meat of the thigh with the steel toe of my shoe, a blow that would cripple anyone. But again it did nothing to him.

"It's funny," he said in Farsi, "but it doesn't even hurt. Oh, Amirah . . . how I love you."

I made a lunge for my fallen pistol but El Mujahid leaped at me. Any awkwardness he might have experienced upon returning to life was gone. For all his size he moved with cat quickness and he body-blocked me away from the piece and kicked the gun under a desk. I slewed around and came up into a fighting crouch. *Okay,* I thought, *c'mon, Joe, you've done this before. Break the neck and you stop these buggers.*

So I jumped in and tried to grab his chin and hair. Most people have only seen this move in movies. They won't recognize it when someone tries it on them, and it's such a fast move that by the time they figure it out they're on the cold side of being dead.

Unfortunately for me El Mujahid wasn't a novice. He parried my lunge and hit me in the ribs with a short chopping punch that lifted me completely off the ground; then he combined off that and planted an overhand right that nearly took my head off. I managed to get a shoulder up in time to save my head, but El Mujahid was a tank and his punch dropped me. I landed hard and immediately tucked into a sideways roll and barely managed to avoid a stamp that would have crushed my skull.

The First Lady was screaming over and over again and I wondered if her mind had snapped.

I came out of my roll on fingertips and toes and tried to reach for the

.38 on my ankle, but he rushed me with a flying tackle that sent us both rolling over and over across the floor. At the end of the roll I managed to get a knee up between us and braced it against his chest as he tried to pull me into a bear hug. With his arms he'd have splintered my back. I drove my shoulders back and used the greater power of my legs to break his grab. He skidded back and I again went for my pistol, this time getting it out; but El Mujahid threw himself forward like a dolphin jumping out of the water onto the side of a pool. It was a sloppy move, all momentum, but it worked and he made a big reach and swatted the pistol out of my hand.

So I kicked him in the face and back-rolled to my feet.

I had my back to the wall and he was between me and any guns. He rose slowly, head down, shoulders hunched, hands forward and out. This was a son of a bitch who really knew how to fight. Without rules, just react and destroy. Like me.

Past him I could see parts of the tussle that was going on behind the desk. Legs and arms, and a lot of cursing. I had no idea who was winning that fight.

El Mujahid stalked me, cutting left and right to try and box me into the corner. Against most opponents a corner is a pretty good place to make a stand, it allows for a lot of options when flight is no longer in the mix; but with a fighter like this bruiser it would be a death trap.

He leered at me and bit the air with a clack of teeth. "I think I'll take a bite out of you," he said, pitching it to sound like a joke. I wasn't laughing.

I could still hear gunfire and screams coming from the Bell Chamber. It must be one hell of a battle in there. Would Grace survive it, or had she already fallen? Would she rise as one of the mindless walkers or as a new and improved thinking monster like the one I faced?

What would Church and the President do? Let everyone in the Liberty Bell Center kill each other and then torch the whole place? Could the President risk any other response, even with his wife here?

Then I realized that the First Lady was no longer screaming. El Mujahid noticed, too, and we both turned to see that she had picked up my

.45 and was pointing it at the big terrorist. She fired, but in her panic she jerked the trigger instead of squeezing it and the gun bucked upward and the shot punched a hole in the ceiling.

I rushed in her direction, wanting that damn gun, but El Mujahid lunged in to cut me off, pawing at me with a fast grab. I parried it, but it was a fake and he snaked the other hand in and caught me by the sleeve of my suit jacket.

The First Lady got off another shot but it just tore a chunk out of El Mujahid's hip.

He jerked me forward with such force that I flew off the ground, and he hit me with an elbow shot that broke a black bomb in my head. I sagged in his grip and as he bent toward me I could feel his hot breath on my exposed throat.

Chapter One Hundred Twenty-Three
Gault and Amirah / The Bunker

GAULT SCRAMBLED FORWARD in a panic, feeling for the etched markings as Amirah's eerie voice floated through the darkness toward him, louder each time she called his name.

"Sebastian!" She drew it out, making it a perverse song.

His fingers scrabbled across an uneven spot on the wall and he stopped, fumbling at it. Yes! He felt for the upper-right corner of the panel and then punched it with the side of his fist. The corner folded inward and he gripped the edges and tore the whole panel away. A small red light flicked on inside the compartment, illuminating the rubber-coated handles of six big levers.

"Sebastian!"

"Witch," he breathed and grabbed the first handle and pulled. It was much harder than he thought it would be, and the angle was bad. He had to stand hunched over and throw his entire weight backward to move the handle. On the first pull it only moved five inches.

"Bastard!" he growled and tried again, screaming with effort. This time the handle tilted toward him and locked into place. There was an anticlimactic silence for a few seconds and then far away there was a heavy rumbling that he felt more than heard.

He grabbed the second handle and again it took him two pulls to lock it down.

"*Sebastian!*"

Her voice was close. God, he thought . . . God!

Even as the rumbling started for the second collapsing vent pipe he threw himself back with the third, and this one locked down on the first try. The rumbling started at once.

"*Sebastian!*" Now there was a different tone in her voice. Perhaps a faint flicker of doubt. He grabbed the fourth lever and pulled. It was so hard, so stiff that it took him five tries to lock it down, but finally it clicked and the rumbling started.

"*Sebastian!*" He could hear the hurried scuff of her feet and her voice definitely had a note of alarm in it. It gave him strength to hear the fear and he tackled the fifth lever with a will and in two grunting pulls it locked down. Already the ambient temperature was rising as the super-heated gasses began recoiling from blocked vents. A deep red glow was reflected through the steel passages and it bathed him in a bloody light.

"Sebastian!"

He turned and she was there, not twenty feet away. Her robes were torn and she was covered in blood. God knows whose blood it was. In the fiery glow of the lava she looked like a monster from hell itself. The blood on her lips and hands was black and her eyes were so shadowed that she looked more like a skull than a woman whose beauty had once made him gasp with but a single slanting glance.

"Listen to me, Sebastian," she said, her voice thick and heavy. "Stop this . . . I can share Generation Twelve with you. If you truly embrace the Koran and the teachings of the Prophet I can make you one of us; I can make you one of God's immortals."

"You're insane, Amirah. You've turned yourself into a monster." He put his hand on the sixth lever.

"I am *Seif al Din*," she retorted, her dark eyes flashing. "Don't you understand? I am the plague, I am the Sword of the Faithful. We don't need laboratories or test subjects anymore. I am the breath of God that will blow across the entire world. The faithless will die and the faithful will become immortals. Like me. Like El Mujahid." She reached a hand toward him. "Like you, Sebastian . . . if you only *accept*."

He shook his head and tears spilled down his cheeks. "I'm a greedy heartless bastard, Amirah . . . but I'm not a monster."

Amirah spread her hands and smiled at him. "Am I a monster, my love?" she said in that old familiar voice that turned a knife in his heart. It was so bizarrely at odds with the bloodstained *thing* she had become.

"Yes, you effing well are!" The answering voice came from the shadow behind her. *Toys*.

Amirah turned to look behind her and there was Toys, his clothes torn, his face streaked with blood, his eyes swimming with pain. He leaned one bloody hand against the wall and with the other he held his pistol aimed at her. The barrel trembled.

Amirah hissed at him; and Toys managed a mean little smile and hissed back. He looked past her at Gault and at the lever he held in his hands. Toys took a ragged breath.

"Do it," he said.

Amirah swung back toward Gault.

"No!"

"God," he said softly as the mountains rumbled around him and the heat scorched the air between them. "I loved you, Amirah."

"Sebastian . . ." They both said it, Amirah and Toys.

Gault tightened his grip around the handle and tensed his muscles.

"God help me," he murmured, "but I will always love you."

She lunged at him as Toys fired the gun and Gault threw his weight back and pulled the lever. Their screams were lost in the rumble as tons of rock collapsed onto the last pipe. In the bowels of the earth, in the furnace of hell, the hand of Satan clutched its fiery fingers into a fist and punched upward toward the Bunker.

HIS BREATH WAS as hot as the wind from hell and I recoiled from it, twisting in his grip, turning my hips as hard and fast as I could. I drove my knee up into his crotch and at the same time drove the stiffened tips of my fingers up under his jaw, crushing tissue and cartilage above the Adam's apple. Another killing blow that I knew couldn't kill him; but it jolted him so that his head jerked back just enough for me to hit him right over his left ear. Once, twice, three times, rocking his whole body with each shot. I could hear his neck bones grind with the third shot and then El Mujahid suddenly flung me away from him. Maybe when he felt his vertebre start to shift he realized his one vulnerability.

I landed hard and tried a back roll but I didn't have the room and crashed into a filing cabinet so I ended up nearly standing on my head. My own neck sent a lance of pain through my shoulder and back, but I bit down on it, planted my palms on the floor, and hopped backward onto my feet. It wasn't gold medal gymnastics but it got me right side up and I pivoted fast as El Mujahid rushed at me again.

The First Lady shot again and missed and then the slide locked back on the gun.

I knew I couldn't keep this up. I was getting tired and I was getting hurt and this son of a bitch was immortal. He was a monster who couldn't feel pain. Sooner or later he was going to wear me down and then he'd go to work on me with his teeth.

Across the room I heard someone howl in pain and couldn't tell if it was Skip or Top, and I couldn't spare the second it would take to look.

I crabbed sideways to circle him, but he lunged forward to cut the line. That was fine because as he dodged in I jumped sideways to pass him on his left. His sweeping grab clipped my ear and though it rang my chimes it didn't stop me. I used the impact to spin into a sloppy pirouette that sent me halfway across the office toward one of the artist's tables. At the far end of the table I'd seen what I wanted, but El

Mujahid was already coming at me, his face almost black with rage and his teeth snapping as he rushed forward.

Rage, in an opponent, is a very useful thing. It makes smart people do stupid things. If you backpedal from the enraged attacker you simply get smashed against a wall and then he proceeds to beat you to a pulp—or, in this case, tear you apart with his teeth. So I didn't backpedal; instead I went forward to meet him. Not chest to chest like a pair of bulls. I lunged in and down and tucked myself into a cannonball and rolled hard at his lower legs, hitting him full onto his left shin and clipping his right. With his greater upper-body weight and my two hundred pounds of rolling mass he went flying forward and smashed facefirst into a row of metal cabinets.

I came out of my roll, pivoted, and leaped back toward the artist's table, grabbing at the item I'd seen: a big paper cutter that was bolted to the metal tabletop. I yanked the cutter arm up, grabbed the handle with both hands, and surged my weight to my right. The bolt that hinged the big blade to the cutter board was not designed for sideways resistance and the whole cutter arm tore off with a loud snap of broken fittings. I whirled and El Mujahid was already in motion, coming hard and fast, deadly and fearless, completely unhurt by the collision with the cabinets.

Again I rushed to meet him in the middle of his lunge, but this time I swung the big cutter like a sword, the curved blade whistling through the air. I caught him square, right on the left side of his neck, and the edge of the blade bit deep. The impact jerked El Mujahid to an abrupt stop and he goggled at me, his eyes and mouth gaping in shock. His fingers reached up to feel the heavy blade buried into muscle and tendon. It hadn't cut all the way through his neck, but the very edge of the blade must have buried itself in the big man's spinal cord.

Half an inch was enough.

His immense strength immediately began to melt away as his muscles lost all order and control. He dropped to his knees like a supplicant preparing to abase himself. Gasping for breath, I braced one foot against his body and then ripped the handle free in a spray of blood.

"You can't stop the will of God . . ." he said with a throat that was filled with blood.

"This was never about God's will, you stupid bastard!" I growled as I raised it above my shoulder and then with a scream of pure rage I swung the blade again.

The blade sheared all the way through what was left of his neck and the force of the swing tore the cutter from my hands. It buried itself point first in the linoleum floor and stood there, quivering.

El Mujahid's head bounced and then rolled to a stop, his wild eyes staring with infinite shock up to the heavens.

I staggered back and almost fell.

The First Lady screamed.

Then I heard another cry of pain and turned, my body tingling with nervous tension, my mind reeling from what I'd just done, and I saw Skip Tyler coming toward me, a bloody knife in one hand. He looked at me, and then down at the terrorist. He smiled with bloody teeth.

"Well," he said hoarsely, "aren't you the goddamn hero."

And then his eyes rolled up in their sockets and he fell flat on his face.

There were half a dozen pencils jammed into a tight grouping in his back, buried deep into the right kidney.

A bloody, trembling shape climbed up from behind the desk. Top was covered with cuts and painted with blood.

"Tough little son of a bitch," he said. He coughed and slumped down to his knees, catching himself with one arm on the desk. The First Lady and I both rushed to him. She got there first and she helped him down into a sloppy sitting position. Her face was as flushed as his. I wobbled toward them and then my legs gave out and I almost fell. Top waved me off. "I'll live, Cap'n. But . . . gimme a second to catch my breath." He lowered his head and sat there, dripping blood onto the floor. The First Lady stroked his hair and held on to him, both giving and taking comfort.

"Did . . . you get him?" a voice asked, and I turned to see Ollie Brown peering up at me with one half-opened eye.

I tottered over and sank down beside him. He was in bad shape. I looked at Top and shook my head. Top winced and hung his head.

"Hey, kid," I said, putting my hand on Ollie's shoulder. "You hold on now."

"Bastard blindsided me. O'Brien . . . son of a bitch was the—" he began and then coughed bloody phlegm onto the floor. "I should have . . . figured it out. S-sorry for letting you down."

His voice was almost gone. I took his hand and held it just as I'd held Roger Jefferson's, and like Jefferson, Ollie held on tightly as if through it he could cling to life.

"He fooled us all. It wasn't your fault. If anything, Ollie," I said, "it was mine."

He shook his head. "Was it . . . Skip? Was he the one?"

"Yeah."

"You get him, too?"

"Top did."

"He had that baby face." He smiled weakly. "Guess . . . guess it was easier to think it was me."

"I'm sorry I ever doubted you, Ollie."

He coughed. "Shit happens, Cap." He tried to turn his head. "I can't hear . . . gunshots. Is it over?"

I listened and he was right. There was only silence from the Bell Chamber. I turned to look down at Ollie, wanting to give him some comfort, but for him it was already over. His eyes were open but he was looking into a whole different world.

I bowed my head and held his hand.

Behind me, down the hallway, I could hear new sounds. Running steps. Voices. It took a lot for me to raise my head and look as several figures rushed into the room. Bunny was first, his face streaked with blood and his pistol in a two-hand grip. Gus Dietrich was right behind him. And then she was there.

Grace.

Alive. All of them, alive.

"Joe!" she cried and rushed to me and I pulled her to me, down on the floor.

"We stopped it, boss," growled Bunny, who was bending over Top, his face lined with concern.

Grace wrapped her arms around me and I held Ollie's hand—a man I'd mistrusted and wronged—and I wept for all of us.

Chapter One Hundred Twenty-Five
The Liberty Bell Center / Saturday, July 4; 12:28 P.M.

A FRESH WAVE of Secret Service agents were the first to enter the Liberty Bell Center. Dressed in hazmat suits, they surged through the building until they found the First Lady. They whisked her away through a back door. Paramedics came to get us. Bunny lingered in the doorway to the office where Ollie and the others lay dead. EMTs worked on Top Sims, putting compresses on over a dozen slashes and stab wounds before loading him onto a gurney. Bunny hovered over them like a mother hen, giving them evil looks every time he thought they were a little too rough. He followed them out, offering a string of suggestions on how to do their jobs. They were probably happy their protective suits hid their faces.

I later learned that Skip Tyler had sixteen broken bones and a ruptured liver, apart from all the pencils Top had rammed through his kidney. Must have been one hell of a fight, but I was only marginally sorry I missed it. I'd had enough of violence. Maybe enough for the rest of my life. Even the Warrior who lurked in the back of my soul was glutted for now.

Ollie Brown and the fallen Secret Service agents were zippered into black rubber body bags. Skip and El Mujahid were left to lie where they were. Forensics teams would need to take pictures first. They could rot for all I cared. The EMTs all stopped and stared at the two pieces of El Mujahid. They gave me strange looks and didn't get too close.

Grace sat beside me, her hand on my shoulder, as the EMTs plastered me with bandages and ice packs. When they were done, I said, "How bad was it?"

She was a long time answering that. "Bad," was all she said.

I took her hand and held it. Her fingers were cold as ice.

"Rudy?" I asked, afraid of the answer.

She nodded. "Safe."

When I felt able to walk she and I went back to the Bell Chamber. Brierly saw us and came over. "They tell me you and your man saved the First Lady."

"Men," I corrected. "First Sergeant Bradley Sims and Lieutenant Oliver Brown. They both did their part and Ollie died in action." I paused. "I wanted you to know that Ollie died serving his country."

Brierly nodded. "Thanks, Captain. He was a good man."

"Yes," I said. "He was."

We shook hands and he took Grace aside for a conference call with Church. "I'll be back," she said.

"I still owe you a drink."

"Yes," she said, giving me a sad little smile, "you bloody well do."

There were no more crowds. The victims lay in rows and men in white plastic suits were draping sheets over them and searching for identification. Someone had rigged blue Tyvek tarps over all of the windows, but the crowds were gone; all of Independence Mall had been cleared and the whole city was under martial law. The National Guard occupied Center City and dozens of choppers packed with federal agents, scientists, medical personnel, and a lot of other folks were descending on the town.

Rudy sat on the edge of the podium, jacket off, sleeves rolled up, the ends of his tie hanging limply from either side of his throat. He looked up at me and started to offer his hand, but both of our hands were stained with blood. He withdrew his hand and sighed.

"*Dios mio,* cowboy."

"Yeah."

"Bunny told me that it was Skip after all. Not Ollie. We were wrong."

"Everyone was. Even Church thought that it might be Ollie. Ollie looked best for it. These bastards probably picked Skip as much for his innocent face as for his greedy black heart. They fooled us and it almost cost everyone here their lives."

I sat down next to him and for a long time neither of us said a word. His gaze was fixed on a point across the room and I followed his line of sight to where a man in a Hawaiian shirt lay sprawled. Someone had rammed the broken end of a wooden flagpole through his eye socket.

"I didn't know it could be like this," Rudy said at length. "I mean, I've counseled hundreds of cops, but . . ." He shook his head.

I understood and I could hear the deep hurt in his voice. But what could I say? We'd all had to do our parts; and I knew there would be long summer nights to come where we'd sit out in his backyard and watch the stars wheel overhead and drink beer as we talked it through. But that time wasn't now and we both knew it. Across the room some of the Secret Service agents were standing like ghosts, their faces pale, their eyes haunted, as they tried not to look at the bodies lying under sheets.

"It must have been terrible for them," Rudy said.

"For you, too, man."

He shook his head. "I mostly watched. I . . . I'm not sure I could have done what they did. They had to shoot congressmen, civilians . . ."

"You blame them for gunning down these people?"

"God, no. They're heroes. Every one of them."

I nodded. "They don't think so."

"No," he agreed.

"They're marked," I said. "This is what you were talking about. The look on their faces, in their eyes. It'll never go away. Violence always leaves a mark. You taught me that."

He sighed. "We ask so much of the people who protect us. Firemen, cops, soldiers . . . They sign up to do some good, to make a difference, but we sometimes ask too much."

"They're warriors," I said softly. "Some of them will be stronger because of today. For some people battle is a clarifying experience. It forces all of the senses to come awake, it makes you become totally aware, totally alive."

"And some of them will be broken because of today," he said quietly. "Not everyone has a warrior soul. You taught me that, Joe. Some people have only so much courage, only so much tolerance for violence, even when it's for the right cause. For some of these people this may be a breaking point. Today might kill some of those young folks. Not right away, maybe not for twenty years, but a few of them may never shake the memory of what they had to do today, what they were forced to do. They'll know all the logic about how it *had* to happen, how they had no choice; and for a while that will keep them steady . . . but some of them will never survive this. Not ultimately."

I wanted to argue with him, but I knew that he was right. Being a hero doesn't mean that a person can become comfortable with being a killer, too.

"They're going to need you, Rudy."

"I can't help them all."

"They couldn't save all the people here," I said. Rudy closed his eyes for a moment, then he stood up and looked down at me.

"And what about you, cowboy? Have you reached your limit?"

When I didn't answer, he sighed and nodded. He patted my shoulder then turned and walked over to the group of agents. I watched him go, saw the process of change that happens when he goes from being my friend Rudy to Dr. Sanchez. He always seems bigger, taller. A rock for those who need something to cling to. But I knew the truth: he, too, was marked, and like the rest of us he would carry this with him forever.

So . . . what about me? I wondered. I could already feel the shock ebbing within me. As the adrenaline washed its way out of my bloodstream my deep grief and horror was dipping lower and lower. In the reeds there in the back of my mind the Warrior was already beginning to sharpen his knife again. I knew it, I could feel it.

I looked at the agents, and all of them looked so young and so hurt.

Only one looked back at me and held my gaze. He was in his late twenties, not all that much younger than me, but his eyes were older than his face. His expression reflected less shock than the others. He read my face and I read his, and we exchanged a brief nod that none of the others saw, or if they did then they didn't understand it. They weren't of the same species as we were. The young agent turned back and listened to Rudy, but I was sure that he was already working through the experience in his own head. The way I was. The way warriors do. He and I did not need to be marked by our experiences. We were born with that mark.

Epilogue

1.

IN ALL NINETY-ONE people died at the Liberty Bell Center. Fourteen members of Congress were among them. Terrorists were blamed, of course, but in the official version of the story there was no apocalyptic plague. It was a "nerve gas" that caused violent behavior. The news footage that had gone out live was a public relations nightmare, but although there were eyewitness accounts of Secret Service agents gunning down unarmed civilians, the President was able to trot out a couple dozen top-flight scientists who babbled on and on about the psychotic effects of the nerve gas. No one who had been in the fight at the center was held responsible for their actions. Blame was focused instead on El Mujahid and his terrorist network, and that worked well as a way of channeling the massive national outrage. In death he became an even more hated figure than Osama bin Laden. The credit for bagging him was given to the Secret Service. Medals were eventually handed out, though the DMS was kept out of it. A national day of mourning was scheduled for the last day of July.

No attempt was made to create a new version of the Freedom Bell. When DMS agents investigated Andrea Lester's apartment they found correspondence and other evidence linking her to Ahmed Mahoud, a terrorist operative whose body was recovered at the Liberty Bell Center; he'd been one of the infected and Rudy had taken him down with the broken shaft of a pole for the American flag. If that had gotten into the press it would have become an iconic moment, but it was never mentioned.

Mahoud was later identified as the brother-in-law of El Mujahid, and the investigation clearly established that Lester and Mahoud were lovers. She had secretly converted to Islam more than three years ago, long before she was hired to cast the Freedom Bell, and Church speculated that it might have been her connection with the rededication project that inspired the whole terrorist plan. It seemed likely, but we'd probably never know for sure.

Director Brierly initiated a hunt to find Robert Howell Lee. They found him in his bedroom at home. He'd driven home after speaking to me on the phone at the Liberty Bell Center, taken his wife's bottle of sleeping pills from the medicine cabinet, written a suicide note that asked for forgiveness, and swallowed the whole bottle. Brierly's people got there with maybe ten minutes to spare. The EMTs pumped him out and Mr. Church flexed his muscles and made sure that the ambulance was redirected to a secure location. Church was on the first thing smoking, and by the time Lee had shaken off the effects of the sleeping pills he woke up to find Mr. Church sitting by the side of his bed. It would have been better if the pills had worked faster. He later admitted to having known about El Mujahid's more deadly strain of the plague but it was clear he had done nothing to warn the authorities. He said he'd ordered Skip Tyler to prevent El Mujahid from escaping, but even that didn't square with the facts. Lee was a traitor, a coward, and a goddamn fool.

Grace and I found Church sitting alone in a deserted anteroom at the FBI field office in Philadelphia, quietly munching vanilla wafers.

"Did you learn anything?" I asked, but he was a long time in responding.

"Mr. Church . . . ?" Grace prompted softly.

Church drank some water. "He gave us a name." He leaned back in his chair and considered the half-eaten cookie he held between thumb and forefinger. "Sebastian Gault."

Grace blanched. "No . . ."

She told me who Gault was, but even I'd heard of him. Who hadn't? "If this is true . . ."

Church didn't look at her. "It's true. Lee was ultimately . . ." He paused and thought about the right word. "Forthcoming."

"God. This will hurt a lot of people."

Church nodded. "I called Aunt Sallie. She's initiated a worldwide search for him. Very quiet, but very thorough."

Grace shook her head. "So . . . this was all for money?"

"No," he said. "For Gault it clearly was; but not for El Mujahid. He was doing this for his God. He said as much to Captain Ledger and Lee verified it. He said that Gault had been funding the terrorists with the agenda of scaring the U.S. into backing out of the Middle East. It's what you thought, Captain, and it probably would have worked. But El Mujahid apparently had a separate agenda and he really was trying to release the plague, and it was worse even than that: he wasn't just willing to die for his cause, he was willing to become a monster. He had no use for Gault's money. What good would it be to him? To what he became?"

"What was he?" I asked. "He clearly wasn't a walker."

"Yes he was. We found Ahmed Mahoud's car. There were two spent vials of a different strain of the pathogen. Hu's labeled it a 'transformative mutation.' It kept the oxygen flowing to El Mujahid's brain so there was no loss of higher function. Hu surmises that El Mujahid planned to share that version with other fundamentalists so that even if the plague got out of hand and they were infected they would still retain awareness, and with awareness, faith." He sighed. "Hu tells me that the version of the pathogen fired from the Freedom Bell was yet another strain. Far more virulent." He looked at me. "If you hadn't ordered Brierly to seal the doors at the Liberty Center . . ."

"God," Grace breathed. I couldn't think of anything to add to that.

Church pushed the plate of cookies over to me without any further comment. Grace and I both had one.

2.

A pillar of smoke rose three hundred feet above the smoking pit that still burned deep in the Helmand Province of Afghanistan. British Army helicopters circled the vicinity and satellites were retasked to probe the region. Something had happened deep beneath the sands that no seismograph had predicted. There were known spots of deeply buried geothermal activity, but nothing like this had happened in over a hundred years. It would take years to uncover the cause.

3.

About ten days later I found Church in his office at the Warehouse. I'd heard that he was moving back to the Hangar at Floyd Bennett Field.

"Are you closing the Warehouse?"

"No . . . you and Grace can run it. We need a base here."

I liked the sound of that, but I kept the smile off my face. Grace and I had been too busy to share that drink since the Liberty Bell Center catastrophe, but we had a rendezvous planned for tonight. From the secret smiles she'd been giving me I thought we might go beyond the platonic sleepover. I pulled up a chair and sat down. "So, where are we?" I asked him.

Church set down the papers he had been sorting and spread his hands. "We saved the world, Captain Ledger. More or less. And we certainly saved the economy of the United States. We also took down a major terrorist network. We're heroes and we have the thanks of a grateful nation, though no one will ever say so. But along the way we embarrassed a lot of people and made a few enemies. The Vice President's wife would like to see Major Courtland's head on a pike. On the other hand the First Lady wants you and First Sergeant Sims canonized."

"What will all that mean for us?"

"Us?"

"For the DMS," I said.

Church shrugged. "We're still open for business."

I looked him straight in the eyes. "Who *are* you, Church?"

"Just a government paper pusher."

"Bullshit."

"Who do you think I am?"

"Grace thinks you can keep all of the Washington power players at bay because you know where the bodies are buried."

He gave me the bleakest, saddest smile I'd ever seen.

"I should," he said softly. "I buried a lot of them."

4.

That night, as Grace lay in my arms, we talked about things. We were both naked. The beer, untouched, sat on the floor amid a tangle of clothes. Some of the clothes were ripped. Mine and hers.

"So, you're staying with us?" she asked. I knew she meant the DMS, but as usual she'd implied a bunch of other meanings.

"Sure. Rudy signed on. Jerry, too." I paused and flexed my fingers, which were intertwined with hers. "I think I've found a home here."

Grace was silent for a long, long time.

"Me, too," she said.

I closed my eyes and pulled her closer to me.

5.

The medical ship HMS *Agatha* pitched and yawed slowly in the sluggish rollers that wandered across the Arabian Sea. It was a blistering night in mid-July and the staff had brought some of the more ambulatory soldiers on deck to allow them to get some relief from the sluggish breeze that moved across the wave tops. Some of the men and women were so badly injured that even the breeze gave no trace of relief, and of these the burn victims suffered most. Hot winds, poor air-conditioning belowdecks, and salt spray were each separate tortures.

But the man who sat alone in a wheelchair by the stern rail never voiced a single word of complaint. His face and hands were swathed heavily in gauze and one eye was clouded to a milky whiteness. The doctors had said that it had been virtually boiled in his skull. How the man had made it through the desert was a total mystery. He had no fingerprints left, but a DNA test revealed that his name was Steven Garrett, a medic assigned to a British unit that had been virtually wiped out during a series of suicide raids by insurgents. The burned man was incoherent with pain and once he'd been medivacked to the air station and then shuttled to the *Agatha* he had lapsed into a total silence. His experiences had broken him, the doctors agreed. Poor man.

The ship steered west toward the Gulf of Aden and then turned northwest into the Red Sea. The burned man watched the sun set over the rocky hills. He closed his eyes and bowed his head.

Next to him sat a slim young man with cat-green eyes and dark hair. He, too, was burned, but not badly. He wore a bandage on his face and one on his neck; and even though his hands were wrapped in gauze he held the other man's hand, like a father would. Or a brother.

The badly burned man looked at him for a while and then stared back at the setting sun.

"Amirah . . ." he whispered.

His companion patted his hand again and smiled. "Shhh," Toys whispered as the ship plowed on out of troubled waters.